BOLAN SCOOPED UP THE GRENADE AND HURLED IT THROUGH THE WINDOW

The warrior dived behind the bed, protected from the flying glass and wood that blew back into the room. Rolling to his feet, he drew the Desert Eagle and sprinted to the window. He targeted a gunner near the house but held his fire as the door to the hall opened behind him.

The Executioner whirled, the .50 Magnum held in a two-handed combat grip. His finger relaxed on the trigger as Lieutenant De Groot appeared in the doorway. Two small discrepancies in the man's usual demeanor registered in the warrior's brain—the lieutenant held one of his hands behind his back, and he looked as guilty as hell.

The commando brought around his gun, and the men fired simultaneously. De Groot's bullet flew high, striking the frame above the window. Bolan shot true, the big Magnum round cutting through the traitorous Recce's chin and into his brain.

Bolan rose to his feet and headed for the door, stopping for a moment to check the hall before crossing to Dingaan's room. He found the black leader sitting peacefully on his bed.

"Let's go, sir," he said. "We don't know who to trust anymore."

"Welcome to South Africa. Have you any idea where we can go?"

Yes, the warrior had a destination in mind. But getting there alive would take some doing.

Other titles available in this series:

DON PENDLETON'S
MACK BOLAN.
STONY MAN VIII

A GOLD EAGLE BOOK FROM
WORLDWIDE.

TORONTO • NEW YORK • LONDON
AMSTERDAM • PARIS • SYDNEY • HAMBURG
STOCKHOLM • ATHENS • TOKYO • MILAN
MADRID • WARSAW • BUDAPEST • AUCKLAND

First edition October 1993

ISBN 0-373-61892-1

Special thanks and acknowledgment to Jerry VanCook
for his contribution to this work.

STONY MAN VIII

STONY MAN VIII

PROLOGUE

Stark white walls gave the Van Valkenburg Room on the third floor of the presidential palace a ghostly atmosphere. The room was devoid of adornment, the stained teak conference table and chairs its only furniture.

The room where South Africa's fate was to be decided was as somber as the mood that hung in the air.

But that was all right with Lindall Dingaan. The leader of the African Civil Assembly knew that he and the representatives of the other groups seated around the table weren't there to socialize. They had come to change a nation.

Dingaan watched Robert De Arnhem rise from his seat at the head of the table. The South African president's eyes skipped from face to face, and Dingaan's own eyes followed. The members of the Conference for a Democratic South Africa—the men in attendance today—represented most of the moderate organizations within the country. Dingaan himself, a Zulu chief who now led the ACA, sat just to De Arnhem's right. Hans Willingham who directed the progressive white Nationalist Party, was seated across from him. Willingham's eyes were closed, his hands folded on the tabletop as if in prayer.

Dingaan smiled. After centuries of white rule and persecution, things were finally beginning to change in South Africa. The Zulu didn't delude himself—little of the change came from the goodness in the souls of men. Most of the progress he had witnessed over the past few years was the direct result of economic sanctions from the rest of the world. The message from the United States and other countries had been simple: end apartheid or perish.

De Arnhem cleared his throat. "Gentlemen," he said, "I thank you for coming today. I also invited representatives of several other groups, most notably the Conservative Party and Black Charge. Unfortunately Mr. LeBeir and Mr. Mbengu declined to attend."

Hans Willingham grunted. "It isn't so unfortunate, Mr. President," he said. "We're better off without radicals interrupting the process, be they white or black." Murmurs of agreement came from around the table.

Dingaan let the smile broaden. While Willingham's remark hadn't been the most tasteful or diplomatic, there had been no dissension. It had even confirmed the bond the Zulu suspected had already been established among the various leaders. Regardless of their personal reasons, all present wanted an end to apartheid and the oppression of the black man in South Africa.

That was all that could be expected, or even hoped for, at this point. The meeting was off to a good start.

De Arnhem cleared his throat again. He pulled a handkerchief from his pocket and mopped his forehead, as if reluctant to get a meeting of such magnitude under way, lest it fail. Dingaan felt the dryness in the back of his own throat. The room was stifling—

some problem with the air-conditioning, De Arnhem had said.

The president started to speak once more. "It goes without saying that we're all delighted by the passing of the referendum," he said. "For the first time in the history of our country, we'll have a one-voter–one-vote system. It's the first step to opening the doors of opportunity to—" Arnhem stopped suddenly as the door opened.

A man wearing black tails and a waiter's apron stepped into the room carrying a tray of silver goblets. De Arnhem nodded, then paused to allow the waiter to circle the table, setting a goblet in front of each man. Dingaan waited, as well, anxious to cool his burning throat and dry mouth.

His heart sank when he saw what the goblets contained. Iced tea. Because of his delicate heart condition, his doctor had prohibited him from drinking either tea or coffee.

The waiter left, and Dingaan watched the president stir several spoonfuls of white sugar into his goblet. De Arnhem was known for his indulgences in food and drink. He was at least forty pounds overweight, worked long, hard hours and never exercised.

Silently the leader of the African Civil Assembly prayed that De Arnhem's health would hold up. The president of South Africa had been the catalyst of change for the black man, and Dingaan feared what might happen if he were no longer in office.

De Arnhem drained his goblet and poured more from the silver pitcher next to him.

Dingaan watched him spoon the sugar again. The black leader's simple upbringing among the Zulus had instilled in him a tradition of a healthy diet, and even though he was now exposed to more excessive lifestyles, his heart prevented him from indulging.

De Arnhem set down his goblet and smiled nervously, then spoke once more. "This is only the beginning. We have much work to do, gentlemen, if we are to achieve true equality. Perhaps we can learn best from both the victories and mistakes that the United States has experienced in its own crusade, although our racial problem is antithetical to theirs in one basic way."

Willingham's eyebrows lowered as he raised his goblet to his lips. "And what way would that be, Mr. President?"

Dingaan stared at his untouched goblet. He knew what De Arnhem was about to say. However wellmeaning the president might be, he was still a white man. He could never fully understand the feelings of dark-skinned people whose homes and land—whose *lives*—had been stolen.

"In the U.S.," De Arnhem said, "the black man is the newcomer. In South Africa it is we who have invaded the black man's home." He glanced toward Dingaan, anxious to see if he'd scored a point.

It was Dingaan's turn to clear his throat, and all eyes turned his way when he did. "With all due respect, Mr. President," the black leader said, "there are red men in the United States of America who might argue the point that the white man was the first occupant. And the white man came to South Africa of his own free will. Few of the blacks whose descendants are now in the U.S. offered themselves willingly to the chains of the slave traders." He paused, glanced down at his goblet, then went on. "I am sorry, but I am of the opinion that while the U.S. might be doing its best to solve its own problems, we must find a better example. I would like to avoid patterning ourselves after a country that had to fight a civil war to establish equality, then spent one hundred and thirty years finding ways to get around that 'equality.'"

De Arnhem's face reddened in embarrassment. But he smiled, and Dingaan could see that the smile was genuine.

Yes, this man meant well. He was the right man to have as president during these times of strife.

De Arnhem mopped more sweat from his fleshy cheeks, then said, "Your point is well-taken, Mr. Dingaan." He swallowed several gulps from his goblet.

"But is that not the reason we are here?" Willingham asked. "We all agree that the black man must achieve equal status with the white. We are simply having trouble agreeing on a feasible time frame." He took another drink of his own tea. "I represent white men and women throughout our great nation—whites who were born in South Africa as surely as Mr. Dingaan himself. They aren't bigots. But this is their home, as well. And they don't care to lose what they have worked so hard to obtain."

De Arnhem stared at Willingham. Slowly his eyes began to bulge in their sockets, and for a moment Dingaan wondered if the president was angry. De Arnhem opened his mouth to speak, then clamped it shut as blood rushed to his face.

Around him, Dingaan heard uncomfortable coughs. What was happening? he wondered. Had he missed something? Surely Willingham had said nothing so controversial as to render the president speechless.

Then, with no further warning, Robert De Arnhem fell face forward onto the table. His forehead struck the wood with a dull thud. He twisted, then rolled off the edge of the table and tumbled to the floor.

"Get a doctor!" Willingham cried. "It's his heart! It must be his—" He stopped in midsentence, grasped his stomach and fell over the table in a parody of the president. The white man opened his mouth, and the contents of his stomach shot over the carefully polished teak.

Two more of the South African leaders fell back into their chairs, grimaces of pain covering their faces. Another flopped to the floor.

The door burst open, and a man wearing a stethoscope surveyed the room in horror, then hurried to De Arnhem. The doctor knelt on the carpet as the men around the room continued to vomit and fall.

The man with the stethoscope pressed the round metal disk against Arnhem's chest. There was a moment's silence, then Dingaan heard him whisper, "He's dead."

Dingaan's stomach suddenly turned as sour as those of the other men as the first of two truths sank into his mind.

Robert De Arnhem hadn't died from a heart attack. He had been poisoned.

Dingaan looked around the room and saw that the rest of the men had stopped moving. He alone still sat in his chair, and it was then that the second truth struck him.

He knew who would be blamed.

CHAPTER ONE

Three hours later, hidden within the Shenandoah Mountains, in the basement of what appeared to be nothing more than the farmhouse of another working farm of the area, another meeting took place. The room in which this meeting was held was as sparsely decorated as the Van Valkenburg Room. The mood was just as somber. This room, too, was meant for business, but here the similarities stopped.

The business that took place in this room was war, and the room had been so named. The War Room of Stony Man Farm.

Hal Brognola, high-ranking official within the U.S. Department of Justice and director of sensitive operations at Stony Man Farm, dropped the manila file in his hand onto the long conference table and bit down on the end of his unlit cigar. Seated around him, notebooks open, pens and pencils in hand, were the members of Stony Man's top two counterterrorist squads, Phoenix Force and Able Team. They were ready for briefing.

Brognola glanced for the tenth time to the heavy metal door that led to the hall. Where was Bolan?

Carl Lyons, the former LAPD detective who now piloted Able Team, seemed to read Brognola's thoughts. "He wouldn't be late unless it was important, Hal," the big ex-cop said.

"You haven't heard from him since you made the first call?" a short, older man asked from the other side of the table.

Brognola looked up into the lined face of Yakov Katzenelenbogen, or Katz, as he was also known. The Phoenix Force leader's gaze met his.

The big Fed shook his head. "He said he had an idea and he'd be in as soon as he'd looked into it."

A lithe black man sitting next to Katz crossed his legs. "He didn't say what that idea was?"

Again Brognola shook his head. He lifted the receiver from the phone on the table next to him and punched three numbers, ringing upstairs to the mission-control room. "Any word, Barbara?" he said into the phone.

Barbara Price, Stony Man Farm's mission controller, knew what he meant without asking. Her answer was simple. "No."

The buzzer sounded as soon as Brognola had replaced the receiver, and he snatched it from the cradle. "Yes?"

"He here yet?" asked Cowboy John Kissinger, the Farm's chief gunsmith and armorer.

Brognola sighed and shook his head. Then, realizing Kissinger could hardly see his gesture through the phone, said, "No, Cowboy. No word yet."

"Okay, chief," Kissinger said. "Holler at me when he does and he's got a free moment. I got something for him."

Brognola heard a click and hung up. He looked up at the anxious faces around the room. It wasn't like Bolan to be late. The man known to the world as the Executioner, and to the staff of Stony Man Farm by his code name "Striker," was a stickler for time-tables.

A wave of trepidation washed over Stony Man's director. Could it be possible that after all these years, after all the wars Bolan had fought, after—

This time it was Gary Manning, Phoenix Force's big Canadian explosives expert, who broke into Brognola's thoughts. "Relax, Hal. Mack's a big boy. He can take care of himself."

"The biggest," Encizo agreed.

"Either one of those could go down as the understatement of the century," David McCarter added. The former Special Air Service officer pursed his lips and shook his head, telling Brognola that whatever had detained Bolan was nothing to worry about.

Brognola knew they were right. Whatever Striker was up to, he was okay. Neither Bolan nor any of the men seated around the table needed him worrying about them like a mother hen. He shuffled the papers one last time and stood. "Okay," he said. "Let's get started without him. Anything he misses, I'll fill him in on later." He pulled the top page off the stack and held it up. "The CIA has a man with connections into the South African medical examiner's office. The autopsy report came out thirty minutes ago. It was nicotine. Pure nicotine. They found it in De Arnhem, the others and the iced tea."

"Damn," Lyons said. "How'd they mask the taste? That stuff's rancid."

Brognola turned to him. "De Arnhem has a reputation as a heavy smoker. He's also known to stir enough sugar into his tea to support the economy of Hawaii."

"So," Rosario "Pol" Blancanales said, "besides him, how many others bit the dust?"

"All but Dingaan. He doesn't drink coffee or tea. Heart condition."

"I guess we all know how that's going to look," Encizo said.

"He's already being blamed," Brognola replied. "Not by the government, but by the more radical Boers." He lifted his cigar from the ashtray next to the phone and stuck the chewed end into his mouth. "There are threats of retaliation from the Boer Resistance Movement."

Calvin James shook his head. "Déjà vu," he whispered. "Remember the L.A. riots?"

Brognola nodded. "It could turn into that...or worse. We're betting on worse. But we're convinced there's more to this than meets the eye." He pulled the withered cigar from his mouth and turned to McCarter. "David," he said, "as your great fictional British detective used to say, there's something afoot. Something far bigger than just the mere assassination of the South African president and the other leaders. Even though a lot of the economic sanctions have been lifted on South Africa since the referendum, the country's going to hell in a handcart, fast. Civil unrest is the biggest contributor, but it's not the only one. They've just seen the worst drought in decades. Corn production is down seventy-five percent."

"That's their main staple crop, isn't it?" Manning asked.

Brognola nodded. "To put it bluntly, gentlemen, the South African economy is in the shit house. Nobody, from the government on down, has money."

"I get the feeling there's an 'except' you're about to hit us with," Gadgets Schwarz said.

"You're right. There's money coming in to certain special-interest groups. *Lots* of money. Two weeks ago, S.A. Customs seized a shipment of AM-180 submachine guns. They were all equipped with Laser Lok sights."

"Whew," Blancanales said. "You're talking funds, all right. That's state-of-the-art stuff."

"Any idea where the shipment was headed?" Katz asked.

"Yeah. Several identical weapons were recovered from a bloody slaughterhouse that used to be a Seshoeshoe village. The Boer Resistance Movement is suspected to have been behind the attack."

"That means the AMs weren't an isolated gun run," James said. "The Boers have gotten their hands on more firepower."

"It's like dope," Lyons spoke up. "If you catch a tenth of what crosses the border, you've got to call yourself lucky."

"There's more," Brognola went on. "The racist Conservative Party has stepped up its propaganda war tenfold. We're talking inflammatory white supremacist leaflets, tracts and other publications that had to have cost hundreds of thousands of dollars. In short there's a massive amount of money being pumped into anything that will cause racial unrest."

"I've got to figure that if you had any idea who was behind the money, you'd have already told us," Manning said.

"That's right."

"So what's the purpose?" Schwarz asked. "It's got to be more complicated than just wanting to stir up trouble."

"It is," Brognola replied. "What's happening is that the tribes—Zulu, Sepedi, Xhosa and others—are starting to get restless. And that just flat scares the hell out of your average white 'fence sitter.' The radical white groups are gaining more support every day. Already there's a bill before parliament calling for a new election, an election that would repeal the referendum and take South Africa back to the days of total apartheid."

A cold silence fell over the room.

All of the men in the room hated racism. Some of them had experienced it firsthand.

"What's the situation at present?" Manning asked.

"A pot ready to boil over. Norman Van Peebles, the vice president, has already been sworn into office. He's trying to keep the lid on things, but it's only a matter of time before—"

The buzzer on the phone sounded again, and Brognola took the call. "Yes?"

Barbara Price's voice came back. "Striker's on his way down. And he's brought a surprise."

THE NINETY-NINE-STORY Ijsselmeer Building rose out of the ground in Amsterdam's business district like a giant redwood in the desert. Direk Brouer sipped at his Geneva gin cocktail and stared down at the intertwined mosaic of concentric canals. From these canals the ships of Holland sailed to all points on the globe. In the seventeenth century ships had brought his country almost to the brink of world power after their victory over Spain in the Eighty Years' War.

Brouer set his glass down on the George I gilt gesso side table next to the window, pausing for a moment to run his hand across the foliate strapwork top. His eyes traveled down to the knees of the legs, which were decorated with the ornately carved heads of Red Indians.

He turned back toward his desk, as beautiful and expensive as the table. On the wall behind the silk-covered office chair hung an unsigned canvas—*Portrait of the Two Sons of Wajid Ali Shah.* The painting featured the two male children of the ancient ruler of the Kingdom of Oudh, resplendent in their red-and-blue jeweled gowns.

Brouer dropped into the chair and ran his hand along the silk. Nice. He closed his eyes. He had always liked nice things, even as a child when his friends taunted him about it. Even then, he had known he was different than the other sons of the fishermen and sailors who used the docks as their playground. He had known he was destined for more than a life at sea. Much more. And when it had come, he had worked hard to wash away not only the smell of the Amsterdam loading docks, but also the crude uncultured manners he had learned from his parents.

He opened his eyes. Yes, he had known there would be more. But until recently he had never dreamed how much more.

Sighing, the chief executive officer of Ijsselmeer, Inc., the largest gold and diamond cartel in Holland and soon the world, let his hand travel toward the intercom on his desk. The three men waiting in the reception area had been there for over an hour. That should be long enough to subtly remind them that they were at his disposal. They worked for *him*.

Brouer pressed the button. "Send them in," he said politely.

The door opened. David Yancy, Barry Lanzerac and Frank Cliff stepped into the office. Brouer motioned toward the three chairs in front of his desk and waited without speaking as Yancy led the way. The Ijsselmeer CEO carefully hid his contempt for the trio's clothing as they settled into the chairs. Yancy, as usual, wore a cheap Western suit that would have looked better on a Dallas used-car salesman. Cliff was worse. He had been picked up by helicopter shortly after serving the iced tea at the presidential palace in South Africa, and still wore the black tails. Now he stared questioningly at Brouer. The man's assignment had been to poison *all* of the delegates to the conference. Yet Lindall Dingaan, the most dangerous of all, still lived. The stare told the Ijsselmeer CEO that Cliff wondered just where he now stood.

Brouer turned to Lanzerac. The South African had dressed in dark khaki slacks and a safari jacket that didn't quite match, and made him look like he read too much Hemingway. Or, Brouer reasoned as the three men took their chairs, perhaps the leader of the Boer Resistance Movement has decided he must look the part during this first face-to-face meeting with his benefactor.

"Good afternoon, sir," Yancy said, smiling. He crossed one leg over the other, and again Brouer was forced to hide his distaste. Along with the cheap suit, Yancy wore his ever-present snakeskin Western boots.

Brouer had never been able to identify the many colors the flaky skin contained; he simply knew they never went with any of the shabby suits Yancy picked out.

The CEO forced a smile. "Good afternoon," he said. "I know Mr. Cliff, of course. But am I to assume that this is Mr. Lanzerac?"

Yancy jumped up. "Hot damn! Where's my manners? Sorry, sir." He stepped back and spoke in short choppy sentences, as if reading from a cue card. "Mr. Brouer. Please meet Mr. Barry Lanzerac. Mr. Lanzerac. This is Mr. Direk Brouer."

Brouer's face smiled harder as the contempt in his heart deepened. He reminded himself that in spite of Yancy's social shortcomings, the American ex-Marine and former rodeo cowboy was the best at what he did: kill. Sometimes one simply had to tolerate unsophisticated behavior in the interest of business.

"So," Brouer said as Yancy sat back down. "It seems we have a mutual interest, Mr. Lanzerac."

"Yes, Mr. Brouer. It appears we do. We both want to keep the kaffirs from taking over my country."

Brouer listened to the heavily accented South African voice, that mixture of English and Dutch accents that made his skin crawl as if a stereo needle had skipped across the tracks of a record. He grit his teeth, continuing to force the smile to stay on his face. "Yes," he said. "But for different reasons. Yours, Mr. Lanzerac, are political. Mine are financial. Ijsselmeer has pumped millions into your mining industry in the last few months. We never expected the referendum to pass."

Lanzerac scratched the side of his face. "Nor did we, mate. Nor did we."

Brouer bristled inwardly at the familiarity. Perhaps now was the time to discipline Cliff. It might also impress Lanzerac that respect for his betters needed to be shown.

The CEO turned to Cliff, who had continued to stare nervously at him during his conversation with Lanzerac. "Before we continue, can you tell me what went wrong with our plan in the Van Valkenburg Room, Frank?"

Cliff shifted uncomfortably in his chair. "I, uh, I didn't realize Dingaan never drank tea. I sabotaged the air-conditioning to make sure they'd all be thirsty. I just didn't realize—"

"Sounds as if you neglected your research," Brouer interrupted. He held up a hand when Cliff started to speak again, then dropped it to a desk drawer. He made a show of rummaging through the drawer as nonchalantly as if seeking a pencil, then his fingers closed around a tiny nickel-plated Beretta Jetfire. He set it on the desk, refusing to look up to catch the men's reactions. He took his time straightening the contents of the drawer, closed it, lifted the gun again and shot Cliff between the eyes.

Frank Cliff sat back in his chair dead, the dull stare in his eyes never changing.

Brouer placed the Beretta on his desk, then turned to Lanzerac, noting the shock in the man's eyes. He continued speaking as if nothing had happened. "And if the kaffirs, as you call them Mr. Lanzerac, are allowed to vote—Lindall Dingaan is certain to become the next South African president?"

Lanzerac swallowed hard. "He is, Mr. Brouer, sir."

Brouer smiled inwardly, then felt the happiness he had experienced at the change in Lanzerac's attitude suddenly turn to hatred. He pictured Lindall Dingaan in the black man's ever-present Zulu robe. Dingaan had already suggested nationalizing the mining industry to help the South African economy. If he did, it would spell death for Ijsselmeer.

Lanzerac glanced at the dead man seated next to him, then broke into Brouer's thoughts. "They'll never get the vote," he said anxiously. "Yancy and I will see to that."

"I hope so. I've sent you enough equipment and financial support to create a fine little hell in your country. And my records reflect that your personal account in Switzerland is beginning to look quite impressive."

"Yes, sir, Mr. Brouer. It is. No complaints there."

"Then I'd like a quick rundown on the status quo, Mr. Lanzerac. As well as a summary of what lies ahead."

The Boer leader cleared his throat and pulled a small spiral notebook from the breast pocket of his safari jacket. Flipping open the cover, he squinted at the first page. "We've got surgical strikes planned against the kaffirs who lead all the major rabble-rousing groups," he began, then looked up. "Dingaan will be difficult, though. Since the poisonings, he's being protected by the government."

Brouer chuckled politely. "Several government officials have their own Swiss bank accounts from Ijsselmeer."

Lanzerac grinned. "How do I contact them?"

"You don't," Brouer said. "I do. *You* just stay prepared. Another chance at Dingaan will come."

The South African shrugged. He looked back down to his notebook. "We've got attacks planned on whites, as well. Hans Willingham of the Nationalist Party went down with the tea party, but there's other kaffir-loving bastards who need to join him."

"Yes," Brouer agreed. "But some of the more conservative whites must go, as well. We want the white voter terrified and outraged, Mr. Lanzerac. It must look as if the blacks are waging their own war against anyone with light skin."

Lanzerac stiffened in his seat. "I can't kill my mates, Mr. Brouer."

Brouer swiveled to the side in his chair, held his hands in the air palms up and shrugged. "Sacrifices are sometimes necessary," he said. He waved a quick hand at Frank Cliff, then said, "Tell me about Mr. LeBeir."

"LeBeir's Conservative Party are all good men," he said, his voice hoarse. "They've got more anti-kaffir literature floating around than I've ever seen. And their newspaper reaches—"

The CEO cut him off with a wave of the hand. "Handing out leaflets and editing a newspaper are simple jobs. Whoever succeeds LeBeir can handle it. Sacrifice him."

"But, Mr. Brouer—"

Brouer didn't let him finish. "I understand it will be difficult for you emotionally," he said. "Do it anyway." He smiled hard. "I will compensate you accordingly. Now, go on."

"We plan to turn the Bants against each other—"

"The Bants?"

"Zulus, Xhosa," Yancy cut in. "All the tribes that speak Bantu." He beamed at Brouer.

"Thank you, David," Brouer said with only a trace of sarcasm. He looked back to Lanzerac. "Continue."

"We'll get the riots started soon," Lanzerac said. "Capetown, for sure. Johannesburg." He glanced at Yancy. "We're going to make what happened in Los Angeles look like a birthday party." Turning back to the desk, he looked Brouer in the eye. "By the time we're finished, the average white man will believe if the kaffirs get the vote, South Africa will become another Rhodesia. We're talking complete anarchy, if necessary, Mr. Brouer." He paused, looking uneasy.

"Yes?" Brouer asked.

"Well, can I ask you a question, sir?"

"Of course."

Lanzerac recrossed his legs. "How can the collapse of the government help your mining industry, Mr. Brouer? You won't be able to get labor or—"

"Just leave that to me," he said. He stood up slowly to indicate the meeting was over. The other two men jumped to their feet. "Speed things up a bit," he said as he walked the men to the door and shook their hands, reminding himself to wash his own as soon as they left.

He nodded to Lanzerac as the man left the room. "Oh, David," he said, looking at Yancy. "Please stay a moment."

Yancy closed the door.

"Is Mr. Lanzerac competent?" Brouer asked.

"Yeah, I mean, yes, sir. I think so anyway."

"Good. But go with him. Watch him closely and keep me informed. He hesitated a little when I mentioned what must happen to Mr. LeBeir."

Yancy grinned. "I'll remind him of Cliff if he gets cold feet, Mr. Brouer." Yancy turned back toward the door.

"Good. By the way, take Frank with you and dispose of him, will you?"

"Certainly, sir." He retraced his steps to the chairs, grabbed Cliff under the armpits and began backing out of the room, dragging the body with him.

"Oh, and one other thing, David," Brouer said as Yancy reached the door.

"Yes, sir?"

Brouer nodded toward Cliff. "In case I forget to tell you later, just as soon as this is all over, I'd like Mr. Lanzerac to meet a similar fate."

Yancy's grin rivaled Brouer's own. He opened the door and manhandled the body through.

Brouer returned to the window, retrieved his glass from the side table and looked down over the city. He chuckled out loud, thinking again about Lanzerac's question concerning the South African officials on his payroll. *How do I contact them?*

The Ijsselmeer CEO shook his head in disbelief. As if he would trust that information to someone like Lanzerac. The double agents were the most valuable part of the operation. So valuable that the list was in code and divided into two parts, with each part in different areas of the world. And even if the two halves came together, only he knew the key to unravel the code.

Well, one other person might know the key. But that person didn't even realize what he had.

Brouer raised his glass to his lips and took a sip, grimacing when he realized that the ice had melted. Lanzerac was different than Yancy. He had a brain. Not a good brain, perhaps, but he had one. He asked too many questions, the one about contacting the government informants being only one. The second about how the collapse of the government could help the mining industry, reflected a curiosity about Ijsselmeer's overall goals that Brouer didn't like.

He put his glass on the table. The truth was that anarchy in South Africa *wouldn't* help his mining industry. At least not at first. But anarchy never lasted forever. People soon tired of fighting for food, shelter and their very lives, and when they did they formed new governments.

Those new governments were always led by whoever had fed and clothed them through the chaos.

Direk Brouer moved to the bar, fixed himself another drink, then turned to the Ijsselmeer logo on the wall. He smiled at the ship making its way along one of the intertwined canals.

"I wonder who might have enough money to help the poor people of South Africa through their hardships?"

THE MEN SEATED around the table in Stony Man Farm's War Room heard the musical tones as the access code was punched into the steel door. A moment later the door swung open, and a big man wearing a navy blue sport coat and khaki slacks led another man into the room.

The second man wore faded blue jeans, black athletic sandals and a multicolored *dashiki*. His wrists had been handcuffed behind his back. A camouflage bandanna covered his eyes, another served as a gag. Above the blindfold the man's ebony skin glistened with sweat.

Mack Bolan loosened the tie around his neck and looked toward the head of the table. "Sorry I'm late, Hal. But I brought you a present to make up for it." He reached up and removed the blindfold from his prisoner's eyes.

The black man blinked.

Hal Brognola grinned. He recognized the face from a recent FBI Wanted poster. A midlevel man within the American cell of South Africa's Black Charge movement, he was wanted for the recent assassination attempt of a South African diplomat in Washington. The G-man turned to the members of Phoenix Force and Able Team. "Gentlemen," he said, "meet Jonathan Shomari."

"Where the hell am I?" Shomari growled.

"We'll keep that our little secret," Brognola told him. Looking at Bolan, he asked, "Where'd you come up with him?"

The Executioner shrugged. "Still here in Washington. His name came up in a drug deal I was busting last night. I convinced the dealer that it would be wise to give him to me."

Brognola grinned. Mack Bolan could be the most "convincing" person he'd ever met.

Bolan stepped behind Shomari, removed the cuffs and pointed to an empty chair. The man glanced quickly at the locked steel door, decided his chances of escape couldn't even be computed and sat down. The Executioner took the seat next to him.

Brognola stared into the cold brown eyes. "Let's cut through the bullshit," he said. "You're facing twenty years minimum on the assassination attempt. Maybe more. You cooperate, and I'll see what I can—"

Shomari spit on the table.

Carl Lyons stood up on the other side of the table and pulled a lead-weighted leather sap from the side pocket of his sport coat. "What do you say we *really* cut through the bullshit, Hal?" he said as he started around the table.

Brognola held up a hand. "Wait." He stared at Shomari.

The South African stared back. Slowly the snarl on his lips disappeared. When he spoke, his voice was a curious blend of South African accent and American "jive" he'd picked up since arriving in the States. "I don't know where this be," he said. "But I still be in the U.S. I got rights, man."

Lyons slapped the sap against his palm, the sound echoing off the bare concrete walls. The ex-cop started around the table. "You sure do," he said. "I'll read them to you. You got the right to turn black-and-blue. You got the right to bleed before, during and for a hell of a long time after questioning. You got—"

Again Brognola raised his hand, his eyes on Shomari. He watched the man try to stare down Lyons, but the brown eyes had already lost some of their earlier confidence.

The big Fed had interrogated hundreds of hard-core criminals and terrorists during his career, and in the dark eyes he thought he saw something else, as well.

Given a chance to save face, Shomari would cooperate. He wanted to flip. Roll over, sing. Whatever you wanted to call it, Jonathan Shomari wanted to do it. The man didn't care to spend the better part of his life in some federal penitentiary.

Brognola glanced at Lyons, who barely nodded.

The former LAPD detective had seen Shomari's eyes, too.

Calvin James had never been a cop, but he picked up on what Brognola and Lyons were up to, and saw his opportunity. "Hey, go easy on the brother, huh?"

Shomari's eyes jerked to James. "What you doin' with the enemy, man?" he demanded.

James's face remained deadpan. "You got it wrong, brother. These guys ain't the enemy. They're on our side. You don't believe it, just listen to the questions. We ain't tryin' to find out nothin' 'bout Black Charge, man. It's the *enemy, our* enemy, we're goin' after."

"Who you talkin' 'bout?" Shomari asked.

"Whoever be providin' the Boers with fireworks, bro," James said.

Shomari spit on the table again. "Well, it sure as hell ain't the black man, fool."

Brognola leaned forward, bracing himself on the table with his arms. "Of course not," he said carefully. "But we've got to figure your group has some counterintelligence on what's happening. That's what we want to know."

Shomari closed his eyes for a moment in thought. Brognola could see he was weakening. Now, if they could just find a way for the African to bow out gracefully...

"I got conditions," Shomari said suddenly, opening his eyes. "First, I don't answer no questions about the brothers here. You got that."

Brognola shrugged.

"Second, you get me off on the attempted-murder gig."

The big Justice man shook his head. "I can't promise that, and you know it. But I'll put in a good word. Tell them you cooperated. The rest is up to the court."

Shomari hesitated. "Last," he finally said, staring across the table to where Lyons still held the sap, "I want that big ugly motherfucker out of here. I ain't sayin' shit with him around."

Lyons leaned forward, and James jumped up, grabbing his wrist. For a moment Lyons's and Shomari's eyes locked in hatred, then the ex-cop let James lower his weapon.

He turned toward Brognola. "Hal?" he asked.

Brognola nodded and indicated the door with his head.

The big ex-cop started to protest, then blew air through his clenched teeth in disgust and marched around the table. As soon as he was out of Shomari's vision, the scowl on his face turned to a smile of victory. He gave Bolan a thumbs-up behind the prisoner's back, then punched the code into the door and stalked into the hall.

Brognola smiled politely. "Okay, Shomari. You've got what you wanted. Now, you agree to help?"

The man nodded.

"Then you can start by telling us everything you know about the money and guns coming into the right-wing racist groups in South Africa."

Shomari shifted uncomfortably in his seat. "Anybody got a smoke?" he asked.

Yakov Katzenelenbogen leaned across the table and shook a Camel from his rumpled pack. He lit it with a gold lighter as Manning and Encizo, both militant nonsmokers, looked at each other in disgust.

Shomari inhaled. As the smoke trickled out his nose and mouth, he said, "It's comin' from Europe, man."

"Europe's a big place," Bolan said. "Where in Europe?"

Shomari shrugged. "Don't know. But one of the Chargers works the loading docks at Capetown. Says the boat they busted flew Spanish colors. It don't make no sense to go too far out of the way to get them in, so we figure it could be anyplace on the continent."

Brognola looked at Bolan. "A business interest in South Africa," he said. "Somebody, or a group of somebodies, who'd be jeopardized by democracy."

The Executioner nodded. "Go on," he told Shomari.

The South African gritted his teeth. "We figure whoever it is has cut some kind of deal with the supremacists. Particularly Boer Resistance. There's too much money—"

"We know that," Brognola interupted. "What else?"

Shomari sucked on the cigarette again. "The Chargers got hold of a white dude who was in the raid at the village. A guy named Miers. He told them there's some timetable of shit about to go down. Bombings. Assassinations. They're goin' to raise hell, man, but nobody knows exactly how."

Brognola frowned. Black Charge was famous for its brutal interrogations, and he could imagine what happened to any white supremacists who fell into their hands. Before it was over, Miers would have told them anything. "Miers didn't tell them anything specific? Where or when the Boers planned to attack?"

Shomari shook his head. "Dude was a bleeder," he said. "Died too soon. But there was one more thing. Whoever it is behind the money has double agents, man. Dudes in the government on his payroll."

"But Miers didn't know who?"

Shomari nodded. "Miers didn't know who."

"Anything else?" Brognola asked.

He shook his head. "No." The South African saw Brognola's face and said, "Hey, you got to believe me. I ain't that high on the totem pole, you know? You're lucky this much trickled down through the ranks to me."

Brognola hesitated. Shomari might or might not be telling the truth. But there was only one way to find out. He lifted the phone. "Ironman up there with you, Barb?" he asked.

"Yes."

"Send him back down."

A moment later Lyons walked back through the door and took his seat. He stared at Brognola, avoiding Shomari's eyes.

"Ironman," Brognola began, "Gadgets and Pol can fill you in later on what little info our new friend was able to provide." He turned to the man in the *da-*

shiki. "I want the four of you in the air for Washington in five minutes. Shomari can introduce you to his superiors. Come up with an undercover story in flight. Find out anything else Black Charge knows about—"

Shomari jumped to his feet. "Wait a minute, goddammit!" he screamed. "I never agreed to—"

Bolan grabbed him by the arm and jerked him into his seat. "You agreed to help," the Executioner said.

"Yeah, but nobody said nothin' about—"

Brognola leaned forward. "Do I take it you're refusing?"

"You're motherfuckin' right I'm refusing! If you think I'm goin' to snitch off my own—"

Brognola lifted the receiver to his ear. "Barb, get the federal marshal's office on the line. Tell them I've got Jonathan Shomari in custody and we'll turn him over to them at..." He glanced at his wrist.

"Ah...fuck," Shomari cursed.

The big Fed covered the mouthpiece with his hand. "Change of heart?" he asked.

Shomari stared at the tabletop. Slowly he nodded.

"Forget it, Barb," Brognola said, and hung up.

Shomari's hands clenched into fists. He glared first at Schwarz, then Blancanales, his eyes finally coming to rest on Lyons. "So you want me to take *these* three to my people?" he asked.

Brognola nodded.

"Fine. I see only one problem. Which one of these white boys sings the best rap?"

Brognola didn't do it often, but for once he'd overlooked the obvious. Black Charge would be far more likely to accept another black man into their confidence than they would a white.

He turned to the only other black man at the table. "Calvin," he said, "how'd you like a temporary reassignment to Able Team?"

James nodded.

"Then get going, the five of you," Brognola said. "Calvin, you handle the undercover end with Shomari. The rest of you run surveillance and stay out of the limelight."

James, Jonathan Shomari and Able Team rose from their chairs.

Gadgets Schwarz looked at James as he opened the steel door. "God help us," he quipped good-naturedly as he held it for the Phoenix Force warrior. "We've had to call in the second string."

James faked a punch to his arm as he passed.

Brognola turned to the remaining members of Phoenix Force. "Katz," he said, "take your men to South Africa. We know the Boer Resistance Movement has more strikes planned, but we don't know what they are. I want you ready for the next threat as soon as it raises its ugly head." He paused, taking a deep breath. "Stay in contact. I'll put Kurtzman and the rest of the computer commandos to work on finding out just exactly who it is behind the money. As soon as we get a name, you'll be on your way to Europe."

Katz, Manning, Encizo and McCarter rose as one and were gone.

Brognola looked down at the big man in the navy blue sport coat. He stared for a moment into the penetrating eyes that had fought injustice the world over for so long, then turned and faced the wall.

Mack Bolan might not officially work for him any-more, but the Executioner was always up to the challenge when Brognola needed him. It was Bolan who had come up with the idea for Stony Man Farm so many years ago, and if the truth was known, it was Bolan who was still the heart and soul of the top-secret installation.

"Striker," Brognola said, using Bolan's code name, "we have no direct Intel, but Lindall Dingaan is bound to be at the top of the Boers' hit list. The South African government's protecting him, but with the double agents Shomari just informed us of, I'd feel safer knowing you were running that show." He paused. "How about it?"

The room was silent.

Brognola turned around, and what he saw brought a smile to his face.

The chair Bolan had occupied was empty.

The Executioner was already on his way.

CHAPTER TWO

Mack Bolan dropped the brown-paper-wrapped package into his carryon as the wheels of the plane hit the tarmac. Though he hadn't opened the box since Cowboy John Kissinger had pressed it into his hands as he left Stony Man Farm, the Executioner knew what it contained. And he never ceased marveling at the speed and skill with which Kissinger could modify and adjust weapons.

Transferring his attention from the package to the runway, Bolan saw several limousines waiting at the end. As Jack Grimaldi slowed the engines and the jet ground to a halt, he recognized the uniforms of the armed men surrounding the cars. South African reconnaissance commandos. The new president had called out his best to serve as bodyguards. The Recces wore traditional OD-green floppy bush hats, heavy web gear and rucksacks over their khaki fatigues. Belgian 7.62 mm FN FAL assault rifles hung from their shoulders, and Lyttleton Z-88 9 mm pistols were holstered on their hips. The Z-88s were almost identical to the Beretta 92, the semiauto version of the full-auto 93-R the warrior carried now in shoulder leather.

Bolan made a mental note. If push came to shove, the Z-88 magazines would work in his own side arm. He turned to Grimaldi, the pilot who had flown him on more missions than he could remember. "Stick around, Jack," he said. "Who knows when we'll be in the air again."

Grimaldi tapped the bill of his suede Alaskan bush pilot's cap. "Affirmative, Sarge. And good luck."

Bolan opened the hatch and dropped onto the runway. Several of the Recces formed a cocoon of protection around a short man with bifocals as he stepped out of one of the limos and onto the tarmac. The procession moved toward Bolan. The man in the glasses stopped three feet away and extended his hand. "Colonel Pollock?" he asked, squinting through the double lenses.

The Executioner nodded and gripped the hand. As always when he worked through Stony Man, he was using the false identity created for him at the farm. Colonel Rance Pollock might be fictional, but over the years he had created almost as big a reputation within military circles as Mack Bolan, a.k.a. the Executioner, had in the private sector.

"Welcome to South Africa," President Van Peebles said. He turned and indicated the limo he had exited. Past the mass of khaki uniforms, through the windshield, Bolan saw a colorful caftan in the back seat. Lindall Dingaan.

"Shall we go?" the new South African president asked, pointing toward the car.

Bolan followed him, taking a seat in the front next to the driver. Van Peebles climbed in next to Dingaan. The Recces waited until their superiors were secure, then climbed into the other vehicles.

"Mr. Dingaan," Van Peebles said as the procession started away from the runway toward the highway, "I have the pleasure of introducing Colonel Rance Pollock of the United States Army."

A bony, wrinkled hand shot from under the caftan over the seat. Bolan turned and gripped it. He looked past the arm into the eyes of the most powerful black man in South Africa. He liked what he saw. Lindall Dingaan's eyes glowed with two things the Executioner respected. Honesty and kindness. And the aging man was a Zulu chief, which meant he had once been a warrior.

"I am pleased to meet you, Colonel Pollock," Dingaan said. His voice was weak and labored, and the Executioner remembered the report he'd read during the flight that emphasized Dingaan's poor health. "Your President assures me you are the best security man in the world. I am afraid that is exactly what we may need."

Bolan didn't answer.

"We plan for you and Mr. Dingaan to switch vehicles in a parking garage on the edge of Pretoria," Van Peebles said. "Then, what I believe people of your profession refer to as a safehouse has been prepared."

"Any particular reason you don't want to continue keeping Mr. Dingaan at the palace?" the Executioner asked. "Under the circumstances, that would seem—"

"I know, I know," Van Peebles said. "I have tortured myself for two days now, trying to decide. But in light of the poisoning, and the Intelligence provided by you Americans concerning paid traitors within our midst..." His voice trailed off.

Bolan turned to face the front of the vehicle as the driver sped down the highway. The limo slowed as they entered Pretoria, then turned onto a side street.

"There will be a contingent of Recce commandos waiting with your car when we reach the garage," Van Peebles said. "They are assigned to you. Please exit quickly. It is our hope that if anyone is watching, it will appear that we simply passed through the garage to spot any...what is the word?" The president looked at the driver.

"Tail," the man replied. "To spot a tail."

"Yes."

Bolan frowned. There was something about the whole thing he didn't like, though he couldn't put his finger on it. He forced himself to relax. As soon as they switched vehicles, he'd take command. And when they reached the safehouse, he'd post the Recces as guards and concentrate on Dingaan himself.

A high rise appeared a block away. The driver slowed. A moment later the limo turned into the parking garage attached to the building and started up a ramp. Halfway there, more Recce guards appeared as if from nowhere. With them was a black man in a caftan identical to Dingaan's.

Bolan grabbed his carryon and hurried out of the front seat. He opened Dingaan's door and helped the man out.

A black Nissan Maxima skidded to a halt next to the limo, and two men dressed in jeans and sweatshirts jumped out. They threw a gray calf-length raincoat over Dingaan's caftan, and Bolan hustled him into the Maxima's back seat while his double jumped into the limousine. One of the men in sweatshirts took the wheel. The other two sandwiched Dingaan between them in the back seat.

Fifteen seconds after the limo had stopped, it was heading through the parking garage as the Maxima exited the door through which they'd entered.

The Executioner's trained eyes scanned the road ahead as the new driver held the wheel with one hand and stuck his right across the seat. "I'm Captain Willem Vanleirburg, Colonel Pollock," he said, "in charge of this security unit." He glanced over his shoulder. "That's Jameson and Smuts in the back. It's a pleasure to—"

The captain's words were suddenly cut off as the windshield shattered, raining shards of glass over the front seat. Vanleirburg turned toward Bolan, his eyes wide in astonishment.

As the Executioner gripped the captain's hand, a second volley of fire tore through Vanleirburg's face, obliterating his features.

AARON KURTZMAN'S FINGERS flew across the computer keyboard. He hit Return, and the monitor screen went blank.

He sat back in his wheelchair, waiting for access into the U.S. Department of Corrections data bank. He glanced at his wristwatch. Charlie Mott, Stony Man Farm's number-two pilot, should be touching down in Washington with Able Team and Calvin James about now, which meant that the man known as "the Bear" had damn sure better hurry.

Stony Man Farm's top computer man swiveled his wheelchair to one side and looked down the ramp to where Akiro Tokaido worked at his own computer.

The young Japanese was dressed in his usual gaudy manner. Wiry bare arms extended to his terminal from the frayed shoulders of a cut-off denim jacket covered with silver studs. The back of the jacket advertised the latest tour of some heavy-metal rock band Kurtzman had never heard of. Tokaido's long black samurai-style topknot jiggled and jumped as the young man pounded his keyboard and stared intently at the screen.

Kurtzman couldn't suppress a smile. Tokaido looked like a punk who would be more at home leading some Oriental street gang in L.A. or New York. But the truth of the matter was, he was smart, educated, loyal and one of the best computer men around.

The Stony Man computer ace heard a click and turned back to the computer. The screen lit up suddenly, and the words "authorization in process—enter code" flashed on and off in bold green letters. He glanced at the yellow legal pad on the console, then punched in the number for the federal penitentiary at Leavenworth, Kansas. He pressed the palms of his hands together, popping the knuckles of his fingers, as the computer digested the information with its own series of clicks.

He turned again, looking past Tokaido to Carmen Delahunt and Huntington Wethers. Both the woman in the bright red skirt-suit and the dignified black man with the graying temples were as busy as Tokaido. He had a good team at Stony Man. No, he had a great team. The best in the world. It was only a matter of time before one of them came across the right file and learned what European firm was pumping money into the racist groups in South Africa.

Kurtzman's own screen flashed again. "Access complete—enter identification code." He pulled a manual from the shelf next to the screen, flipped it open and randomly chose the number for the Atlanta, Georgia, police department.

Well, Kurtzman thought as he typed the number in. He had to choose somebody—Stony Man Farm didn't have its own number. As far as the U.S. Department of Corrections, or the rest of the world for that matter, was concerned, Stony Man Farm didn't exist.

As soon as he'd gained entry to the prison's files, Kurtzman typed in "Edmond Jacob Nxumalo a.k.a. Eddie Nix." He paused a moment frowning, then added another a.k.a.—Arthur Washington a.k.a. Johnny Buxton—for good measure.

Although the last two names hadn't been in the phony undercover identity James had hurriedly worked out just before he left, and wouldn't be used on the mission, Kurtzman had never known an international gunrunner who had used only one alias. This would look better if the enemy happened to have access to police files.

Kurtzman went on, adding details to the file as his eyes flew back and forth from the screen to James's scribbled notes on the legal pad. Eddie Nix became a fourth-generation American whose great-grandfather had immigrated to the U.S. from South Africa during the Boer War. Nix had a lengthy arrest record, mostly for firearms violations, but only one conviction. It had resulted in his three-year stay at Leavenworth. The computer man added suspected connections to radical black groups, both in the U.S. and abroad, to the dossier.

He punched out of the prison linkup and began working on access into the Bureau of Alcohol, Tobacco and Firearms. He looked again at his watch. By now Shomari and "Eddie Nix" would have landed, rented a vehicle and be on their way to the Black Charge safehouse in the Washington ghetto.

The screen flashed again. Kurtzman entered basically the same information, affixing enough minor discrepancies to make it believable. He knew that men weren't computers; no two human beings viewed, or reported, the same incident identically. That included cops. He closed out the file by adding several Intelligence reports concerning Eddie Nix's activities since being released from prison.

Stony Man's computer whiz sighed as he began the entry process for the FBI. Here he would need only a few isolated reports and perhaps several investigations in conjunction with the BATF in which Nix's name had come up. But that would take time, and another check of his wrist told him time was the one commodity he didn't have. He glanced around the room, surveying the millions of dollars of electronic devices it contained, and realized that was always the case at the Farm.

Stony Man had state-of-the-art firepower, computers and people. But they never had much time.

Kurtzman's eyes turned to the glass dividing wall that separated the computer room from the communications section as he waited for the screen to light up again. Through the glass he saw Barbara Price seated behind her console. The slim, pretty honey blonde had the telephone receiver pressed to her ear, her eyebrows knitted in concentration.

The computer buzzed, and Kurtzman entered the Eddie Nix info into the FBI files and exited. Now, he thought, for the main attraction. If anyone Calvin James encountered wanted to check out his story and had the connections to do so, that person would turn first to the National Crime Information Center files. But Kurtzman knew that NCIC had a double-check system that would reject any info not on file at local levels, and the groundwork had to be set up first.

Kurtzman began the long process of accessing NCIC and entering the final fictional background for Eddie Nix. Could he get it done before Calvin James walked headfirst into the lion's den? He glanced for a final time at his watch.

It was going to be damn close.

THE BLACK CHARGE safehouse, an apartment on the third floor of a crumbling tenement, stood less than a mile from the White House in the heart of the Washington, D.C., ghetto. Elderly black men in sweat-soaked white undershirts and women in faded floral-print dresses with babies in their arms sat on the front steps as James and Shomari strolled down the street.

James's U.S. Navy SEAL-trained eyes skirted the neighborhood as they neared the building. The stench of poverty hung in the air in the combined odors of rotting garbage, unwashed bodies and stale urine. Signs of destitution and despair were everywhere.

But so were the signs of sudden wealth.

Here and there James saw teenaged boys and girls in gang colors, wearing hundred-dollar athletic shoes, Major League Baseball jerseys that went for seventy-five dollars a pop and gold on their fingers and necks that had to have cost a small fortune. These status symbols hadn't come from frying Big Macs or shoveling the Colonel's chicken. They had been bought with money made from drugs; the scourge of Calvin James's race.

He shook his head in sadness as he and Shomari mounted the steps of the tenement, then switched his attention to the matter at hand. In a few moments, posing as Eddie Nix, he would meet Shomari's taskmaster—the leader of the Washington cell of Black Charge. The South African went by the name Bernell Freeman, though James felt certain it had to be an alias.

Shomari led the way through the open front door and up a staircase, stopping in front of a door. He rapped his knuckles against the peeling green paint.

A few seconds later the door swung open to the end of a chain. Eyes above a broad nose swept from Shomari to James, then a voice growled, "Who he be?"

"Chill out, Azizi," Shomari said. "He's with me."

The door closed, and James heard the chain slide off. A moment later Azizi opened it again, and Shomari led the way into the dingy apartment.

A half-dozen black men in a combination of *dashiki* and athletic clothes sat on worn couches and chairs in the living room. A tall, lanky man wearing a San Francisco 49ers cap stood up and stretched his arms high over his head. "This the dude you called me about, Jon?" he asked. He had an accent similar to Shomari's.

The South African nodded.

The man in the cap dropped his arms to his sides, then looked at James as one hand scratched his chest. "He don't look like much to me."

James waited. There were times to be tough in this business and times to keep a low profile. And for the time being, he'd try the easy way. He was the unknown quantity in the room, and it was only natural that Freeman would want to feel him out a little before the Black Charge leader agreed to do business.

"You don't hear so good, Jack, or what?" Freeman said. "I said you don't look like so awful much to me. Least not the big-time gat-dude Shomari made you out to be over the phone."

James let a smile creep across his face. "I ain't so awful much, dude," he said. "But I'm enough for you. And that's all you need."

A powerfully built man in a tank top rose from the couch across the room. "He's got a mouth on him, Free," he growled. "Think I ought to close it for him?"

Freeman chuckled. "Might ought to at that."

The man in the tank top crossed the room slowly, the muscles and veins in his arms popping with every step. James waited calmly.

The time for a low profile, he knew, had ended.

The bodybuilder stopped a foot away and flexed his shoulders.

James grinned. "This the free-posing round, or what?" he asked. "You got something to do, blood, do it."

The big man drew back a fist that looked like a small roast. Dipping almost to the ground, he drove it forward toward James's chin.

The Phoenix Force warrior stepped quickly to the side and let the punch whiz past. The muscle man's own inertia threw him forward, off balance. James threw a sweep kick, his instep catching the body-builder on the ankle and sending him facedown to the floor.

James stepped back and drew the American Derringer Model 6 from his pocket. The long six-inch barrel looked out of proportion on the small weapon as it swung back and forth across the room.

Shomari gasped. The other men reached under their shirts, then froze as James settled the derringer on Freeman and said, "I may get only two of you. But you'll be the first, Free. Which barrel you want? The .410 or .45?"

Freeman brought his hands to waist level, palms down. "Chill out, bro," he said calmly. "We were just havin' a little fun."

"Yeah," James growled. "Me too."

Slowly the hands beneath the shirts came back into view. James shoved the derringer into his pocket. "I'd hoped for a little warmer reception, blood." He turned to Shomari as the man in the tank top crawled to his feet and limped to his chair.

Tiny beads of sweat had broken on Shomari's forehead. He blew air from between his clenched lips, then said, "Free, meet Eddie Nix. Nix got a deal for us I think you gonna like."

Freeman sat in his chair. Pointing toward an empty space on the couch across the room, he said, "Let's hear it."

James crossed the room to the couch. Shomari stayed where he was, standing nervously with his back against the wall.

"M-16s," James said as soon as he'd taken his seat. "Ten dozen. That's a hundred and twenty of the best fully automatic rifles made, and the easiest ammo to find. I'll cut you a deal, because I back what you're doing."

"Killin' honkies?"

James forced a smile. "Damn straight."

"Where'd you get the guns, man?"

"It's my business to get guns, man," James replied. "I don't ask nobody about their business, and I don't tell nobody about mine."

Freeman reached for a beer can on the table next to his chair and raised it to his lips. "Why you so interested in helping us?" he asked.

"Like I said, I believe in what you're doing."

"Bullshit." Freeman drained the can, crushed it in his hand and dropped it to the floor. "You don't know shit about us, or what the white man's done to us in South Africa. You ain't no African. You a fuckin' Oreo. Inside, you as white as a fuckin' Dutchman."

James bristled. He was a black man, he'd grown up a poor black kid on the streets of Chicago and he'd been the victim of racism himself on more than one occasion. But rather than turn him against the white man, those experiences had instilled in him a properly directed hatred for racism itself.

Calvin James didn't like bigotry. He didn't like racial slurs against blacks *or* whites.

"Yeah, I'm a fuckin' Dutchman," he forced himself to say. "I got this tan with Coppertone." He stood, started for the door, then stopped. He had hoped he could avoid getting too deep into the Edmond Nxumalo ID. He didn't know that Black Charge had the contacts to check out the alias, but he didn't know that they *didn't*, either. The Phoenix Force warrior did know the computer files would take time to set up, and he wasn't sure Kurtzman had gotten the necessary info in place yet.

Well, he had a choice. He could leave now, blowing the whole deal, or he could chance it.

"Look," James said, turning back to the Black Charge leader. "Let's cut through all the bullshit, okay? My great-grandfather's name was Nxumalo. He was born in Lesotho." He saw Freeman's eyes flicker slightly with interest. "He cut out of the country during the Boer War and came to the States. I don't really give a rat's ass whether you believe me, but it's the truth. I still remember the old man from when I was a kid, and his stories about the Boers and what they'd done to our people. From the time I was old enough to listen, I've wanted to go to South Africa and kill them myself."

"So why didn't you?" one of the men on the couches asked.

"I did, more or less. I've been runnin' guns into the country off and on for years."

"You never been busted?"

"Yeah, I been busted. From here all the way to fuckin' L.A."

"Done any time?"

"Leavenworth. Three years, eight months."

"What's your real name, Eddie Nix?"

"What's *yours*, Bernell Freeman?"

Freeman shrugged. "You want to do business, you tell me. It's that simple."

"Edmond Nxumalo." James paused. "Hey, you don't want to believe it, then fuck you." He started for the door again.

"Sit down, Nxumalo."

James stopped, paused, then slowly returned to his chair.

Freeman nodded at the man in the tank top. The muscle man got up and disappeared into the rear of the apartment.

The Phoenix warrior heard a door close, and a lump began to form in his throat. The man was obviously off to make a phone call to either confirm or disprove his story.

Kurtzman was the best computer man James had ever known. He could circle the electronic codes and traps almost as fast as a normal programmer could enter the system legally. Yeah, the Bear was the best. But had the best been good enough?

Freeman smiled. Then the smile gradually faded, and the Black Charge leader's eyes narrowed as he spoke. "We gonna check you out, Mr. Edmond Nxumalo," he said. "We find out you be who you say you be, we gonna do business."

James nodded. "Fair enough."

"But we find out you some kind a cop or something, I'm gonna personally cut your fuckin' balls off."

CHAPTER THREE

Katz heard the landing gear lock into place as the DC-10 dropped through the sky toward Pretoria. Through the windshield, the leader of Phoenix Force could see the skyline of South Africa's administrative capital. Beneath the tall buildings, thousands of jacaranda trees bloomed in a purple so loud it could almost be heard. The Israeli made out the distinctive lines of the Voortrekker Monument, erected to commemorate the Boers who had trekked north from the Cape of Good Hope to the Transvaal.

The Israeli nodded to himself as the pilot lifted the microphone and gained landing clearance from the tower. It had taken courage almost beyond belief for the Boers to make the trip into uncharted country. Many men, women and children had given their lives in order to settle the rich farming area and break the ground for the school and churches that followed. Which meant that in spite of the wrongs some of these early South Africans might have performed upon the natives, there had been good, brave Boers, as well. In short the average South African was no different than the average Israeli, American or Saudi, or the typical Jew, Christian or Muslim.

Neither all good nor all bad. A mixture of both the best and the worst humanity had to offer. Capable of great kindness, charity and love, as well as prejudice and cruelty almost beyond understanding.

As the wheels hit the runway, Katz opened the briefcase in his lap and produced a cellular telephone. Quickly he tapped in the numbers for Stony Man and waited as the instrument relayed through a satellite and connected to the Farm. The cellular phone had been brought along for two reasons. First, Phoenix Force would be working unofficially in South Africa, and would hardly be able to contact the nearest police headquarters for the latest update on the situation. But equally important, the "computer commandos" under Aaron Kurtzman's supervision were already making headway in their investigation to identify the money behind the trouble in the country.

And as soon as they did, Katz and company would be off to Europe to eliminate the problem at the source.

"Phoenix One here," Katz said as soon as Barbara Price had answered. "Anything new?"

Price took a deep breath. "To put it mildly, Phoenix One. There's a raid going on right now in the Transvaal. Burning and looting of white farms. Pretoria's got the army moving that way."

Katz felt the muscles in his abdomen tighten. "On the ground? They'll never get there in time. Any idea who's behind the attacks?"

"They're blaming the Black African Caucus," Price said.

"You don't buy it?"

"Negative, One. Our satellite photos just came in. There's maybe three dozen fires going on, and they all went up within minutes of one another. The Caucus is radical enough to try something like this, but it isn't that big. Somebody else is either doing it or helping them."

The DC slowed at the end of the runway. Katz turned toward the pilot, one of the blacksuits who regularly did a stint at the Farm. "How long will it take to get clearance to take off again?"

The man shrugged. "Depends on how busy they are, and they look busy. Want me to run the red light? Wouldn't be my first."

"Floor it," Katz replied. He turned back to the phone. "Can you get us coordinates on the nearest farm?" he asked Price.

"Affirmative." She read off the numbers as the pilot suddenly made a wide U-turn off the runway onto the grass. The DC's right wing dipped low into the ground, sending dirt and grass flying through the air.

The radio blasted with excitement as the control tower demanded to know what was going on. With a grin in place the pilot ignored them.

Katz jotted down the coordinates on the cover of the flight book and glanced at the map on the control panel. The nearest farm wasn't far. He held the book up for the pilot to read. The flyer nodded.

Thirty seconds later the big DC-10 was airborne, heading north into the Transvaal area of South Africa.

Katzenelenbogen turned over his seat to the rear of the plane. The rest of Phoenix Force, minus Calvin James, sat waiting his orders. He pulled the parachute from behind his seat and slipped into it. "Grab your umbrellas, gentlemen," he said. "We jump in—'' He glanced at the pilot, who looked at the control panel.

"Six minutes."

The DC-10 continued through the sky as the team checked its chutes, weapons and other gear. The pilot pulled the plane higher with each second. The door slid open, and a rush of wind filled the aircraft. Katz pulled his headset over his ears and climbed into the back. He saw David McCarter standing next to the doorway. Behind him were Rafael Encizo and Gary Manning.

The Israeli took his place at the end of the line. How many times had the five members of Phoenix Force entered battle together? Too many to count. Enough to know one another's every move. As if they all operated off one central brain, like the fingers and thumb of a hand. Often enough to notice any small change in that hand.

Like the fact that one of the fingers was now missing.

"Ten seconds," Katz heard the blacksuit say over the headset. The pilot twisted in his seat, holding one hand up in the okay sign.

Ten seconds later the four men of Phoenix Force were falling through the sky toward the flaming buildings of the Boer farm below.

MORE AUTOMATIC GUNFIRE peppered the Maxima. The car skidded to the left, scraping the side of a small compact car parked on the street.

Bolan leaned down and across the front seat, jerking Vanleirburg's dead foot from the accelerator. At the same time his other hand reached past the corpse and found the door handle.

This was no time for sentimentality. As glass broke and metal trim ripped from the sports car, the Executioner pushed open the door and shoved Vanleirburg's body onto the pavement.

Still in Drive, the car crept forward on idle. A steady stream of gunfire now tore through the side windows. Behind him Bolan heard the other two Recce guards firing their pistols.

Sliding across the seat, the Executioner grabbed the wheel with both hands and hit the accelerator. The Maxima raced down the street, the autofire fading in the distance.

Bolan glanced into the rearview mirror. Jameson and Smuts still held Z-88s in their hands. It had all happened so quickly that the expressions of astonishment had never left their faces. Smuts had pushed Lindall Dingaan down between them. Now he lifted his arm, and Dingaan's head slowly rose in the mirror.

"Is it clear?" the black leader asked calmly.

Bolan nodded.

Dingaan sat back against the seat and took a deep breath. "They knew where we would be."

The Executioner nodded again. Dingaan was right. Well, almost right. Not *they*. There had been only one gun in the attack—an Uzi 9 mm by the sound—and that gun had been on top of the parking garage.

Bolan slowed and cut down a side street. Steam began to hiss from under the hood. The engine coughed. "We're going to need a cleaner car," he said, staring through the shards of glass that clung to the edges of the windshield.

"We have a backup waiting a few miles from here," Jameson said. "Turn left."

The Executioner spun the wheel and sped through a low-income residential district, then turned again at Jameson's direction. Dusk, then night, fell over the city as he drove through the streets. Jameson finally stopped him in a seedy retail section of town.

Bolan jumped out of the sputtering Maxima, his eyes searching the storefronts—a few taverns, a pawnshop. People, mainly men talking to heavily made-up women in short skirts, filled the sidewalk.

The two Recces helped Dingaan from the back seat and led him through a glass door under a sign reading Show And Tell. The Executioner brought up the rear, his hand inside his jacket on the butt of the Beretta 93-R. Smuts shoved past a surprised man behind a counter in what appeared to be a waiting room.

"Hey!" the man said.

Jameson drew the Z-88 from under his sweatshirt and shoved it into the man's face. Without a word the procession continued through a swing door into a dimly lit hallway. A moment later they were in an alley. Jameson slid behind the wheel of a red-and-gray GMC Yukon, and the others piled in through the passenger's door.

"We're not far," Smuts said. "Five minutes, max."

The Executioner watched their tail as Jameson pulled out of the alley and onto the street. If anyone had followed them from the parking garage, they had lost them.

Two miles later they pulled into the driveway of a one-story frame house and parked behind a Jeep Wrangler and Pontiac Grand Prix. A tricycle and assorted trash filled the front yard, helping it blend into the rest of the run-down neighborhood. Bolan and Smuts hustled Dingaan up the front steps to the porch while Jameson knocked softly on the door.

The porch light never came on. The door just swung open, and they hurried inside.

The warrior glanced around the living room and saw several Recces in full combat gear. A tall slender man wearing lieutenant's bars closed the door, looked out the window, then turned around and said, "You brought the Yukon. Problems?"

Jameson nodded. "Sniper as we left the garage." He turned to Bolan. "Colonel Pollock, this is Lieutenant De Groot. He's in charge on-site.

Bolan looked into the face of a short man with arms too long for his body. "How many men have you got here, Lieutenant?"

"Eight," De Groot said.

"Okay. Let's see the layout." The Executioner glanced through an archway and saw a kitchen, then walked across the living room and down a short hallway. The layout of the small safehouse was simple. Three bedrooms—one facing the street, the other two at the rear of the house. The bath was at the end of the hall.

Bolan opened the door to one of the rear bedrooms and walked to the window. Peering around the edge of the closed curtain, he saw a small backyard. A metal shed sat near the alley to the right, and more broken toys and garbage littered the yard.

The Executioner turned back to De Groot and Jameson, who had followed him into the room. "I want Dingaan in here," he said. "Post two men outside the door in the hallway. Three in the backyard, and three in the front. Tell them to keep out of sight. They can use the shed in back, the cars in front."

"Colonel Pollock," De Groot said, his chest puffing out, "*I* am in char—"

Bolan shook his head, and the movement alone ended the lieutenant's sentence. He stared into De Groot's narrowed eyes. He had been in-country less than an hour, and already an attempt had been made on Dingaan's life. That meant he didn't have time to play footsy with some prima donna who'd had his feelings hurt by losing his command.

"No," he said simply. "President Van Peebles didn't bring me all the way from the U.S. to do what any other soldier could do. You'll take orders from me from now on, Lieutenant, and if you've got any problems with that, there's the phone." He pointed toward the instrument on the table.

When De Groot didn't respond, he went on. "Jameson, Smuts and you and I will be inside. I want all weapons primed and ready. The attack at the garage proved that the enemy has connections. They might already be aware of the safehouse."

De Groot's eyes narrowed farther, and in them Bolan saw more than just bruised pride. He saw pure, untainted hatred.

Then the lieutenant pivoted on the balls of his feet and stalked out of the room.

Bolan followed him out and walked to Dingaan as De Groot barked orders to his men. The Executioner noticed for the first time the sudden fatigue that had replaced the sparkle in the black man's eyes.

Dingaan's hand moved slowly beneath the raincoat and caftan to a trouser pocket. He produced a small bottle, unscrewed the lid and popped a tiny white pill into his mouth.

"You need a glass of water, Mr. Dingaan?" Bolan asked.

The black leader shook his head. "It is nitroglycerin," he said. "It dissolves under the tongue. But I have another favor to ask of you."

"Yes?"

"You have saved my life, Colonel Pollock. The least you could do is call me Lindall." The sparkle returned briefly to the weary eyes.

Bolan smiled. "Fair enough." He took Dingaan's arm and led him down the hallway to the bedroom. "Go in and make yourself comfortable. You look like you could use some rest."

"Yes, I could." Looking at the Executioner, he said, "Thank you again," then closed the door behind him.

The warrior returned to the living room. The front and rear guards had already moved outside the house to take up their positions. Jameson, De Groot and Smuts stood near the front door. The Executioner grabbed his carryon from the floor and took the front bedroom across from Dingaan's. The window faced the street, and through it Bolan could see the shadowy forms of the men in and around the cars.

He sat on the bed and pulled from his bag the package Kissinger had given him. He tore the paper away and opened the brown walnut case he found inside, revealing what appeared to be a duplicate of the Desert Eagle .44 Magnum autopistol that presently rode on the Executioner's right hip.

Bolan lifted the heavy weapon and pulled back the slide. Only the most trained of eyes could notice the difference in chamber circumference. He dropped the magazine from the butt of the weapon and held it in front of his face. The mouth was slightly wider— again, almost imperceptibly so. He reached inside his carryon and pulled out another box—.44 Remington Magnum, the cover said.

The Executioner knew better.

Flipping the side tab on the box, he pulled the foam tray from the cardboard and dumped the contents onto the bed. The holes in the foam were mashed and flattened, having been stretched by rounds larger than the holder had been made for. The Executioner lifted one of the bullets to his eyes and glanced at the rim around the primer. Fifty-caliber Magnum had been engraved in the brass.

Bolan smiled. The rounds had been carefully hand loaded by Cowboy John Kissinger. Even more powerful than the mammoth .44s in the other Desert Eagle, they would serve as "guinea pigs" as he field-tested Israeli Military Industries' newest offering in their Desert Eagle line.

The Executioner's mind returned to Lindall Dingaan as he cocked the big .50 and tested the trigger pull. He had known Dingaan barely an hour, but already he could tell he was a good man, intent on helping his people. Dingaan knew that atrocities had been committed on both sides of South Africa's racial barrier over the years, and that the only road toward a peaceful South Africa lay in forgiveness by both black and white.

Satisfied that Kissinger had lightened the trigger pull to his specifications, Bolan flipped the safety from the empty weapon from fire to safe. Cowboy had installed a wider target safety switch that moved easily from one position to the other. Unlike the "out of the box" Desert Eagle, it could be manipulated without shifting the hand out of a proper combat grip.

The Executioner broke the new Desert Eagle down and gave it a quick inspection. He had test fired it on the range at Stony Man Farm a few days earlier, then returned it to Kissinger with his modification list. Cowboy had left the insides of the big .50 as spotlessly clean as the exterior. A light film of oil covered the working parts.

Bolan loaded the magazine, shoved it into the grips and slid a round into the chamber. Two extra mags rested in recesses in the foam rubber of the walnut case, and he filled them with more of Kissinger's hand loads. Digging through the carryon again, he found the left-handed "pancake" holster and slid it through his belt opposite the .44.

The Executioner buckled his belt and sat back down.

As he did, the glass in the window facing the street suddenly shattered.

Bolan heard a thud on the carpet, and what appeared at first to be a rock rolled across the floor and bounced off the wall. The object rolled back, coming to a stop three feet from where his feet rested on the floor.

The Executioner looked down to see the coarse pineapple texture of a primed fragmentation grenade.

BRIGHT YELLOW WORDS and numbers flashed across the monitor. Kurtzman waited, his hands poised over the keyboard like those of a fighter ready to throw a one-two-three combination as soon as his opponent let down his guard. The words "Entry complete" suddenly settled on the screen, then a one-word question.

"Revise?"

Kurtzman entered *N* for no, hit the Enter key, then booted out of the linkup.

The computer hissed, clicked and buzzed as the final insertion of Edmond Nxumalo a.k.a. Eddie Nix flew over the wires to the computer banks of NCIC.

He sat back in the wheelchair and caught his breath. Had he gotten James's undercover ID in place in time? He didn't know.

Kurtzman grasped the wheels on his chair. He rolled back, then twirled toward the ramp, heading for the coffee station. Seconds later he lifted the carafe and poured a half cup into a white ceramic mug.

Kurtzman placed the mug in the holder on his wheelchair and rolled past the ramp to where Tokaido sat working at his keyboard. The young Japanese had the headset of his disk player clamped over his ears. When Kurtzman tapped him on the shoulder, he stopped typing and turned. He smiled widely and removed the headset. "Yes, Aaron?"

"Any luck?"

Tokaido shook his head. "A grain wholesaler in Germany looked promising for a while. Big connections in Capetown and a record of shady deals. But I ran it to the end. It's not likely."

Kurtzman nodded. He turned to Carmen Delahunt, who had stopped work to listen to him and Tokaido. She anticipated his question and shook her head.

Kurtzman got the same response from Huntington Wethers. "Same story. A few possibles, but they all fizzle out when you look close. But we're narrowing down the field, Aaron. Eventually we'll know who it is."

Stony Man's computer chief nodded, then turned and wheeled himself back up the ramp. He took a sip of his coffee and set the mug on the console next to the keyboard. He wondered again about Calvin James, but pushed the worries quickly out of his mind.

He had done what he could, as fast as he could. If he had failed to get the Nix background in place in time and it cost James his life, he would have to live with that failure. But in the meantime, there was more work to do.

Like finding out who was pulling the strings behind the scene in South Africa. Who was it who wanted to keep the black man down so bad?

Kurtzman hit the Escape key and cleared the screen. He typed in "European consortiums with holdings in South Africa," then linked into the "probability" program he had recently invented and installed in all the computers. Tokaido, Delahunt and Wethers were already using it, and it was time he joined the hunt.

The Stony Man computer genius popped his knuckles as the program came up on the screen. He took a deep breath before starting, telling himself to relax. They needed to find whoever was responsible for the problems in South Africa as quickly as possible, but there was no hurried timetable on this one. None of the teams were in jeopardy.

Kurtzman started to type again, then reality sank in. There *was* a timetable at work, all right. Every minute that went by without the Stony Man warriors knowing who their real enemy was, was a minute during which another innocent person might die.

He allowed himself a quick, indulgent sip of his coffee, knowing it would be his last for some time. Then he began to work.

CALVIN JAMES WATCHED the muscle man in the tank top walk back into the living room. Freeman turned to him and arched an inquiring brow.

The bodybuilder nodded. "He's okay, Free. Dude be who he say he be. Kind of wish he weren't. I was hopin' to get another shot at his ass."

James didn't answer. But inside, the Phoenix Force warrior breathed a silent sigh of relief. Kurtzman had come through.

"So," Freeman said. "Tell me more 'bout what you got on your mind."

The ex-SEAL leaned forward. "I got '16s comin' out the ass, bro'. Rounded them up for a buyer in San Juan."

"So what happened?" Freeman wanted to know.

James was playing it off the cuff. "You read the papers?" he asked.

Freeman didn't answer.

"Dude's about to go to trial here in the States. Feds kidnapped his ass right off the streets of Mexico City."

He saw a flicker of recognition in Freeman's eyes. Only the week before, the U.S. Federal Court had ruled that the kidnapping of foreign nationals in their home countries didn't violate constitutional law, and law enforcement had wasted no time taking advantage of the decision. "So I'm sittin' on these guns, man. And no buyer."

Freeman frowned. He turned to the man in the tank top. "Willis, how heavy is he, really?"

"Oh, he got connections, Free. Ought to be able to find another buyer."

James didn't wait for Freeman's reaction. "That's right. I can find another buyer. These are choice weapons. But it'll take a little time, and when I bumped into Shomari last night—"

"That reminds me," Freeman said. "Where *did* you meet this guy, Shomari?"

The midlevel Black Charge man shrugged. "Down at Hattie's Place," he said, sticking to the thin undercover story they'd worked out on the flight from Stony Man Farm. "I known him a week or two."

"You trust him?"

"Yeah. He helped me out of a jam with some rednecks who came in one night."

The Black Charge leader turned back to James. "How many '16s you say you got?"

"Ten dozen."

Freeman reached for a pack of cigarettes on the table next to his chair. He took his time lighting one, then blew smoke through his nose and said, "That's too heavy for Washington. You gonna have to talk to Mingo."

"Who's Mingo?" James asked.

Freeman stood. "You'll find out." He walked across the room and found a pen in the drawer of another table, then fished through the cluttered mess inside until he came up with a used envelope. He wrote something on the back and handed it to James. "If he's not there when you get there, they'll know where to find him. I'll call and tell him you're comin', and that we checked you out."

James nodded. He glanced at the envelope. "Guess I better buy me a tie," he said, then stuffed it into his pocket, stood up and started toward the door.

"Hey, Nix." He stopped and turned back around.

"Don't fuck with Mingo," Freeman said. "You think I'm tough, wait until you get a load of him."

James stared at the man for a moment, then put on his most gracious of smiles. "But I *don't* think you're tough, Freeman. And tell Mingo he'd be wise not to fuck with *me.*"

He was still smiling when he opened the door, walked down the hall and descended the steps, Shomari at his heels.

CHAPTER FOUR

The scene below the falling men of Phoenix Force was one of carnage, pure and simple.

Flames shot skyward from the farmhouse, barn and several sheds and outbuildings. Livestock scurried blindly about, seeking safety from the fires. Punctuated by the pops of rifle fire, the frantic moos of cattle and the clucks of frenzied chickens rose to meet the parachutes like howls from hell.

As his chute dropped him slowly toward the ground, Yakov Katzenelenbogen saw two tiny figures sprint suddenly from the front door of the burning farmhouse. One wore a wide-brimmed straw hat, pinstriped bib overalls, and carried a lever-action rifle in one hand. The farmer's other hand was wrapped around the waist of a woman wearing a light cotton dress. She pressed a handkerchief to her nose with one hand and cradled a small toddler with the other.

As the farmer herded his wife and child away from the house, he fired and cocked, fired and cocked, swinging the rifle forward on the lever one-handed as he ran.

Katz saw the black man in OD fatigues before the farmer did. He peered around the edge of the shed as the farmer ran forward, waiting.

The Israeli clutched the grips of his Uzi in frustration. He was still too high, out of range with his subgun.

As the farmer neared the shed, the green-clad man leaped around the corner. A burst of autofire rang out, and the farmer fell dead in his tracks, his rifle flipping up into the air as his dead muscles contracted in spasm.

A scream drifted up through the bedlam from the woman at the farmer's side. She set the child on the ground and knelt next to her husband.

A second burst from the invader's weapon sent blood spurting from the woman. She fell over her husband as the toddler, a boy of three or four—Katz could see that now—walked around their bodies in confused circles.

The killer walked toward the boy, his weapon upraised.

Katz aimed his Uzi, then dropped it to the end of the sling as a curse blew from his lips. Still too far. He stood as much chance of hitting the child as he did the gunner.

As he continued to fall, he began to make out the forms of roughly two dozen black men around the house and other buildings. Dressed in olive-drab fatigues, matching boonie hats and khaki canvas boots, they fired FN Herstal P-90 machine pistols at everything that moved.

The Israeli frowned. These killers were supposed to be the ragtag members of the Black African Caucus? From this height, their boots and fatigues looked clean and pressed, as if they'd just come out of the box. Katz had spent some time in Africa over the years, and he'd never yet come across even a regular army whose livery was so uniform. The jungles and deserts were rough on fabric. Boots and clothing soon showed the signs of wear.

And the Belgian-made machine pistols? They were uncommon in Africa, and therefore expensive. Where had the BAC gotten the funds?

A quick glance to his sides told Katz that Mc-Carter, Manning and Encizo were falling at approximately the same height and speed as he was. He looked down. So far, the men on the ground had been too occupied to notice Phoenix Force's descent. But that kind of luck couldn't last.

Katz squinted as the man who had killed the farm couple stopped less than ten feet from the crying little boy. The killer hesitated, as if trying to decide whether to murder the child, too.

The Israeli gritted his teeth. He was two hundred yards or so from the ground. Still too far for a good shot. Still too much chance of killing the boy.

A voice sounded through his headset. "Do it, Katz," Manning said. "You're the closest. You've got to." The Phoenix Force leader saw the big Canadian falling through the air a hundred feet away.

"I can't," Katz whispered back. "I'll hit the kid." Below he saw the man in the fatigues raise his gun and aim at the boy.

"You've got to chance it," Manning urged. "The bastard's made up his mind." He paused. "If you don't, I will."

Through the earphones, Katz heard the sound of the bolt on Manning's Uzi slide home. He raised his own subgun, flipped the selector to semiauto and sighted down the barrel. The sight bounced back and forth in the wind, falling first on the child, then the man holding the machine pistol. It wavered back to the little boy, then bounced to the side of both.

The Israeli took a deep breath. His finger pressed slowly back against the trigger, the sight still moving, hopping man to boy, boy to man. Then, as the Uzi barrel returned to the green fatigues, he jerked the trigger.

The machine pistol barked. For a good five seconds, both the boy and man stood in place, and Katz felt his blood run cold as he wondered which one he'd hit. Then the man in the carefully pressed uniform toppled to the ground, his P-90 spraying empty air.

The sound of overhead gunfire sent a dozen heads jerking skyward, as well as steady streams of bullets. Phoenix Force returned fire, matching the invaders' rounds with volleys of 9 mm fire as they neared the ground.

McCarter's feet hit first. The Briton released the chute, and it billowed back into the sky.

As his own boots touched down, Katz saw the former SAS commando wrap the little boy in one arm and sprint for cover behind the nearest outbuilding.

The stench of burning wood filled the Israeli's nostrils as he released his own chute and fired a burst of 9 mm rounds toward a blur of green to his side. He turned with the movement of the subgun and saw one of the killers go down.

More gunfire drew his attention to the barn. Tiny flames rose from the roof. Katz saw Encizo touch down and cut loose with a steady stream of fire at the doorway. Two men in green dropped their weapons as they fell to the dirt. Two more took their place, firing through the door to force Encizo to his belly.

From the corner of his eye, Katz saw Manning cutting swaths through a contingent of armed men who had been caught in the open between the house and barn. The Israeli added two 3-round bursts to Manning's attack, and watched a pair of killers dance in death as he sprinted to help his comrade.

The little Cuban fired from the prone position, his subgun jerking upward as a burst caught a gunner in the chest and blew him back into the barn.

Katz brought his Uzi to chest level as he hustled toward the building. He squeezed gently, and the fourth gunner near the barn flew back out of sight. The Uzi locked open. The former Mossad agent dropped the magazine and pulled a fresh one from his combat harness.

Encizo sprang to his feet and zigzagged toward the barn as the flames crackled louder from the roof. Behind Katz, Manning's voice rose over the pandemonium. "They're withdrawing!"

The Israeli saw several men in green bolt from the cover of the buildings and take off toward the scraggly stalks of corn in the surrounding fields. "Go after them!" he shouted on the run. "I want at least one of them alive!"

Encizo reached the doorway and pressed his back against the wall, his subgun held near his temple. He motioned Katz to the other side of the door, then held his finger to his lips.

Katz leaped over the bodies at the front of the barn and took a position opposite Encizo. Through the opening, he heard a woman scream.

Crude laughter followed.

The Phoenix Force leader peered around the corner. Inside the barn horse stalls ran the length of one wall. The horses whinnied in fear as the flames from the roof danced above their heads.

The laughter and screams came from the rear of the building, to one side of a parked tractor. Through the dim light and shadows, the Israeli saw a blond girl of perhaps sixteen. The teenager lay on her back on a mound of hay, and four men knelt around her. Two held her arms. The other two fought to spread her kicking legs.

The girl's plaid skirt had been torn from her body and hung over the steering wheel of the tractor.

The Israeli looked across the doorway at his comrade and nodded. The two men stepped into the doorway, Uzis chattering. Hot brass casings flew from the chamber, stinging Katz's face and neck, as one of the men holding the girl's arms flew backward into the hay.

The second man tried to stand, his hands groping for the P-90 slung from his shoulder.

Katz dropped to a knee, firing up, away from the girl. His 3-round burst caught the would-be rapist in the face and sent blood and fragments of bone flying from his skull.

A triburst from both Katz and Encizo took out the other two hardmen. The girl rolled to the side, then crawled under the tractor before scampering beneath the doorway of one of the horse stalls.

Footsteps sounded behind the Phoenix warriors, and they whirled, weapons at the ready. They lowered their Uzis as McCarter sprinted toward them, the little boy tucked under his arm. The Briton nodded toward the fields as he entered the barn. "They're getting away."

Katz glanced overhead. The fire on the roof had burned down to the walls, igniting them. It wouldn't be long before the whole building collapsed. "Gary's in pursuit," he said. "Leave the boy with us and go help him. And remember, we need at least one of these bastards who can still talk."

McCarter handed the boy to Katz and ran back out of the barn.

The Phoenix Force leader turned toward the stalls. Encizo had already pulled the girl's skirt from the tractor and was moving toward the door.

Frightened whimpers came from the stall. Encizo stopped at the door. "Miss," he said softly.

"No!" the girl screamed. The prongs of a pitchfork shot under the door. Encizo jumped back, the points missing his boots by inches.

The Cuban walked to the side, then dropped the skirt over the stall. "It's okay," he said. "You're safe now."

The boy in Katz's arms suddenly wiggled free. Still crying, he ran on wobbly legs for the stall. "Greta?" he cried in his tiny voice. "Greta?"

The door to the stall swung open suddenly. The girl, nude from the waist down, stood in the opening, the pitchfork gripped like a spear. Her eyes were narrowed in hatred and anger. "You hurt my brother and I'll—"

Katz held up his hands. "We don't want to hurt anyone," he said quietly. "We came to help you." He glanced overhead again. "But we've got to hurry. This place is about to come down."

Little by little the girl's eyes began to relax. Then, as if just becoming aware of her nakedness, she dropped the pitchfork and snatched her skirt from the wall. Wrapping it around her waist, she stepped out into the barn, then fell to her knees on the hay and wept.

The little boy walked slowly up and placed a hand on her shoulder. "It's okay, Greta."

Katz walked carefully forward as the girl threw her arms around her brother. He turned to Encizo and jerked his head toward the barn door.

The Cuban nodded, then hurried out of the barn.

The Phoenix Force leader knelt on one knee next to the children. "The men who attacked you," he whispered. "Do you know who they were?"

The girl's head shot up defiantly. "The Black African Caucus," she said through clenched teeth. "Who else?"

He shook his head, remembering the accents of some of the men shouting commands. "I don't think so."

"My parents," the girl whispered. "Are they...?"

Katz shook his head.

Greta nodded, then dried her tears with the back of her hand.

He stood and helped her to her feet. The fire crackled overhead, then a charred beam fell, hitting the hay less than ten feet away. "Come on," Katz said. "Hurry!"

Greta clung to the Israeli's hand as she lifted her brother into her arms. Together they fled the burning barn.

Encizo had moved the mother and father out of sight by the time they left the structure. The little Cuban stood behind a shed, his Uzi poised and ready as he covered the fields where McCarter and Manning had gone after the killers.

Manning stepped out of the cornfield as Katz and the children stopped next to Encizo. He shook his head. "They're gone."

A few minutes later McCarter came jogging out of the stalks. "No luck," the Briton said. "They had too much lead time."

As the flames of the house and barn continued to leap into the air, Katz stared down at the children. He made a silent vow to find the rest of the men who had made them orphans. Not just because it was his job, but because of the pain and emotional scars these two would carry for the rest of their lives.

BOLAN FIELDED the grenade off the floor like a first baseman scooping up a bunt this side of the foul line. In one smooth motion he transferred the bomb from his left hand to his right and hurled it through the window.

The Executioner dived behind the bed, protected from the flying glass and wood that blew back into the room.

Rolling to his feet, he drew the Desert Eagle .50 Magnum and sprinted to the window. At least a dozen men in plain clothes were advancing on the house, firing their automatic weapons.

Two of the three Recce commandos assigned to the front of the house lay dead on the lawn. There was no sign of the third.

Bolan dropped to his knees and drove the big .50 through what remained of the glass, centering the front sight on the leader of the pack. The autopistol bucked, and the gunner was blown off his feet, a deep wound ruining his chest.

The warrior fired a double tap into the next charging gunman, who spun a full circle before hitting the grass. The Executioner swung the Desert Eagle to a bald man pumping a 12-gauge riot gun, but as he did, he heard the door to the hall open behind him.

Bolan spun, the Magnum gripped in a two-handed combat grip. His finger relaxed on the trigger as Lieutenant De Groot appeared in the opening.

Then two tiny discrepancies in the Recce's demeanor registered in the Executioner's battle-seasoned mind.

First, one of the lieutenant's hands was hidden behind his back. And second, De Groot looked as guilty as hell.

A split second later the man brought around his arm and pointed his Z-88 9 mm at the Executioner.

The men fired simultaneously.

De Groot's bullet flew high, striking the frame around the top of the window. Bolan shot true, the big .50 Magnum round cutting up through the traitorous Recce's chin and into his brain.

The warrior glanced over his shoulder, seeing that several more of the attackers had fallen to the defenders' fire.

Bolan rose to his feet and leaped over De Groot's body. He stopped at the open door, looking up and down the hallway before he crossed the hall and drove a shoulder through the door to Dingaan's room. He found the black leader sitting peacefully on his bed, the nitroglycerin bottle opened and in his hands.

Covering the distance between them in two long strides, the Executioner took the man by the arm and helped him to his feet. "Let's go, sir. We don't know who we can trust anymore."

Dingaan nodded. "Welcome to South Africa, have a nice day."

Gunfire exploded from the rear of the house, shattering the window behind them as Bolan dragged Dingaan toward the hall. The warrior cracked the door and looked toward the living room. He saw a boonie hat above a snarling face, then a volley of fire from an Armscor BXP submachine gun drove him back into the bedroom.

Bolan took a deep breath, let go of Dingaan's wrist and dropped to his knees. Okay. That answered his question about other Recce traitors. But who, and how many? And how was he supposed to get Lindall Dingaan out of the house not knowing? A split-second hesitation at the wrong moment would kill them both.

But shooting indiscriminately could mean the killing of innocent and dedicated South African troops, men as intent on protecting Dingaan as he was.

The Executioner knew the answer even as he swung the Desert Eagle back into the hallway and drove a .50-caliber Magnum round into the chest of the second traitor. He'd have to use himself as bait. The

Recces who'd sold out knew they'd have to kill him to get to Dingaan, so they'd go after the harder kill first.

And he'd have to let them, relying on his training and instincts, and hoping he could be a nanosecond faster in each case.

Bolan rose to his feet and said, "Stay behind me, Mr. Dingaan. *Right* behind me." He took the man's frail hand, turned sideways and forced Dingaan to grab a handful of the back of his jacket. Then, with another quick glance down the hall, he hurried through the door.

The Executioner made his way toward the living room. He heard movement behind him and turned toward the bathroom, Dingaan right with him. A Recce guard stepped into the hallway, saw the two men and raised his Armscor.

The warrior pumped two rounds into the traitor, the blasts of the big Magnum shaking the walls of the hallway. He'd fired seven rounds so far and figured he'd better drop the magazine to reload while he had the chance. But as his thumb hit the release, another khaki uniform stepped into the hallway from the living room.

The Executioner drew the .44 Desert Eagle with his left hand, cocking the hammer as the weapon rose. Jameson came into view, and Bolan's finger moved off the trigger.

Both Jameson and Smuts had had better opportunities than this to take out Dingaan. If they'd wanted to kill the black leader, or the Executioner for that matter, chances were they'd have already tried.

"This way!" Jameson yelled as the Armscor in his hands lowered.

Bolan started down the hall, Dingaan still clutching the back of his jacket. He stopped in the living room. The bodies of two Recces who'd been hit by the enemy lay facedown on the carpet. Other than that, the room was empty.

Gunfire still pounded both the front and rear of the house as Jameson led them through the kitchen toward a door. "Got any idea who we can trust?" the Executioner shouted over the noise.

The Recce shook his head as he gripped the doorknob. "I'd trust Smuts with my life. Other than him, your guess is as good as mine."

"Where *is* Smuts?" Bolan asked, turning to give Dingaan a gentle push ahead of him.

"On the living room floor," Jameson replied. He swung the door open. A Saturn sedan stood in the center of the garage, facing the overhead door.

Bolan opened the Saturn's back door and told Dingaan to get onto the floorboards. Jameson climbed into the back seat over him, his BXP in his lap. As the Executioner slid behind the wheel, he saw the Recce push a button.

Two gun ports slid open between the rear windshield and rear windows, one on each side.

"It's armored," Jameson said as he extended the barrel of his weapon through the one to his left.

Bolan nodded. He found the automatic garage-door opener on the seat next to him. "Ready?" he asked.

"Ready."

The Executioner hit the button, and the door began to rise with maddening slowness.

It was halfway up when a man in a blue suit ducked under, into the garage. A burst of 5.57 mm fire struck the bulletproof windshield and ricocheted off. Bolan threw the Saturn into Drive and floored the accelerator.

The bumper struck the gunner across the thighs, knocking him up over the hood and onto the roof. The vehicle raced under the still-rising door, and the man was scooped off and thrown back into the garage.

Gunfire blasted all four sides of the car as Bolan raced down the driveway to the street. Jameson returned fire through the gun ports. Empty casings from the Recce's spent rounds rained through the Saturn like a brass hailstorm. The Executioner cranked the wheel, and the tires screamed painfully as the heavy armored car fishtailed out of the driveway and down the street.

More automatic fire peppered the back of the vehicle as it raced away. Then suddenly the shooting faded, sounding like distant firecrackers.

Bolan let up on the accelerator as the danger passed. He heard Jameson sigh, then the man leaned over the front seat. "Where to?" he asked. "I'm afraid we've used up both of our contingency plans already."

The warrior didn't answer. With the exception of Jameson, he no longer knew whom he could or couldn't trust among the Recce guards. He had to get Dingaan to temporary safety, then contact President Van Peebles.

"Any ideas?" Jameson pressed. "Know *anybody* we can trust?"

Again Bolan remained silent. Then a hard smile tugged at the corners of his mouth. "Yeah," he finally said. "I might just know a few guys we can count on."

A MIDDLE-AGED MAN with a tall glass in his hand staggered past Calvin James and looped his arm around a street post for support. The Phoenix Force warrior shook his head as the man caught his balance, took a deep breath and downed the rest of liquid in his glass.

The Phoenix Force warrior straightened his tie, smoothed the collar of his new charcoal gray Hart, Shaftner and Marx suit, and walked on. Jonathan Shomari at his side, he dodged more inebriated zombies stumbling into the T-shirt stores, oyster bars and porn theaters along Bourbon Street in New Orleans. Dixieland jazz blasted from the open doors of the clubs, and barkers lined the sidewalks in front of the strip joints urging every man and woman who passed to step inside, if only for a "peek."

As they passed a hole-in-the-wall diner, James glanced at the sign overhead. Muff's, it read simply. The odor of greasy hamburgers frying on the grill wafted into the street. He tucked his chin slightly, whispering into the microphone concealed beneath his collar. "Hey, guys, you might want to try out Muff's while we're in the Creole. It's close by, and the food looks great." Glancing over his shoulder, he saw Lyons, Schwarz and Blancanales across the street a block behind him. He grinned at them, thankful he couldn't hear what they had to say in return.

A half block later, they came to the Creole Café. Shomari led the way up the steps and opened the door. James stepped inside, then stopped in front of the empty maître d's station. The enticing smells of foods spiced with garlic, heavy oils and red and black cayenne drifted into the foyer. James and Shomari waited as a man in a black tuxedo approached.

With the exception of world-famous Antoine's, the Creole Café was the oldest family-owned restaurant in America. Like Antoine's, and a few other of the "Big Easy's" older institutions, it clung stubbornly to the old style of Creole cooking, and cholesterol counts be damned.

The man in the tux stepped behind the podium at his station and stood at attention. "Good evening, sir," he said with a French-Cajun accent.

"Good evening," James replied. "Nix. Mr. Edmond Nix. Reservation for two."

The maître d' glanced at the open reservation book on the podium. "Ah, yes," he said. "There is a gentlemen who asked if he might join you. One of our regular patrons. Do you mind?"

James nodded. "We were expecting him," he said as his hand moved casually into the side pocket of his jacket. He produced a diamond-studded money clip, surreptitiously removed a hundred-dollar bill from the top and pressed it into the maître d's hand.

The man smiled. The bill disappeared into his tux, and he said, "This way, please."

They made their way through several large rooms filled with diners. Although dress was semiformal, the atmosphere in the restaurant was relaxed, even noisy from a few of the tables. They came to a hall, and the man in the tux led them to a closed door at the end. A tall black man sporting a shaved head and goatee stood in front of the door, his arms crossed. He stepped forward as they approached and raised his hands.

Shomari glanced nervously at James as the bald man patted him down for weapons. James knew why. Finding a gun would be no big deal. All Mingo's bodyguard would do was take it until the meeting was over.

But if his hands came across the receiver wires or Nagra recorder beneath James's shirt...

The tall man finished frisking Shomari and turned to James.

"Let me save you some time," the Phoenix Force warrior said. He unbuttoned his jacket, jerked the Beretta 92 out of his belt and handed it to the tall man.

The man with the goatee shoved it into his own belt but still stepped forward. "I'm sorry for the inconvenience," he said. "But I'll still have to—"

James held his coat wide open and spun a full circle. He stopped, facing the doorman again, and in a deep, menacing voice said, "I'm clean. And in case you're planning a strip search, forget it. You're not my type."

The bald man hesitated, a look of indecision on his face. Then he shrugged, stepped back and opened the door.

The room inside was small but elaborately decorated. Ornately carved French Colonial love seats and chairs lined the walls beneath oil paintings and framed clippings. A long dining table sat in the center of the room.

A lone man occupied one of the two chairs at the table, facing the door. As the maître d' ushered James and Shomari into the room, he began to stand up.

The maître d' led the way to the table as James fought to keep his lower lip from dropping open.

Mingo was at least seven and a half feet tall, and almost half as wide. He wore a red silk tie and light cotton off-white suit that must have been cut for him at New Orleans Tent & Awning. Beneath the suit, James knew, was layer upon layer of fat. But Mingo didn't look like anybody's wimp. His head was the size of a basketball, and a long unruly beard covered his face.

The Black Charge man didn't smile. He just extended a hand. James took it, and his own hand vanished to the wrist.

"I am Mingo," the man said. His voice was hardcore black South Africa. "And you are known as Eddie Nix."

James nodded.

Mingo indicated the chair across from him. "Won't you please be seated?" He turned toward Shomari, acknowledging the man's presence for the first time. "And you must be Jonathan Shomari."

A heavy film of sweat covered Shomari's forehead. He nodded.

"The maître d' will show you to a table in the Red Oak Room. I do not wish to be rude, but I would prefer to speak with Mr. Nix privately."

"Yes, sir," Shomari said. Relief flooded over his face as he turned and disappeared into the hallway.

James took a seat, noting the difference in demeanor between Mingo and the Black Charge men he'd met in Washington. There was none of the mixture of American black "jive" in the giant's speech. His comportment was dignified, cultured. Formal.

The Phoenix Force warrior started to speak, but another man wearing a tux and carrying a wine list entered. He extended the list to Mingo, but the man shook his enormous head. "You know my tastes, André."

The wine steward nodded and exited.

James sat quietly. Mingo was making it obvious who would be in charge during the dinner meeting—he hadn't even consulted him about the wine. The South African was setting things so as to have the psychological advantage.

That was okay. It served James's purposes as well as Mingo's.

Mingo leaned back in his chair and folded his hands across his immense belly, lacing the fingers. "So, Mr. Nix...or would you prefer Nxumalo?" he began.

"Either's fine. You're one of the few who pronounces Nxumalo correctly. But Nix is shorter. Take your pick."

For the first time Mingo smiled. "I will call you Edmond, then," he said. "Perhaps we can then begin our relationship on a friendly basis."

"That'd be nice," James said. "But having your watch dog shake me down in the hall didn't do much to get the ball rolling."

Mingo glanced down at the table. "You have my apologies. But we have had trouble recently with your American Nazi Party. Four of our men have been assassinated."

"They're not *my* American Nazi Party." James raised a hand to his face, inspecting it. "Not a lot of Aryan in me. Last time I looked, my skin was as dark as yours." He lowered his hand back to his lap. "You know a lot of black Nazis, do know?"

"I meant simply that you are American. No, the Nazis do not accept members of African descent. But they have been known to buy the services of black men when it served their purposes." He paused, took a sip of water from his glass, then said, "Money sometimes overrides racial loyalty." Then, changing the subject, he said, "Tell me, Edmond. Why do you wish to help us?"

James frowned. "Your people in Washington didn't tell you?"

"They did. But I wish to hear the words from your own lips."

The Phoenix warrior shrugged. "My roots go back to the same place yours do. I grew up on stories of South Africa, and what the Boers had done to my people."

Mingo's eyes drilled holes through his. It was obvious that the black giant was skeptical.

"That's the ideological side of my motives," James said. "From a purely business standpoint, I can always use new customers. I can even afford to take a small loss on the M-16s, and I intend to let that be my introduction to your organization. I'll make a profit on future deals."

The huge brown orbs in Mingo's face softened. James could see this made more sense to him. Slowly the Black Charge leader nodded.

The door opened again, and the wine steward set a stemmed crystal wineglass in front of each man. He uncorked a bottle of burgundy. Mingo sniffed the cork, tasted it and waved the steward to pour.

James felt a mild anger wash through his veins. He wanted equality for the black South African as much as anybody, but he didn't believe in killing innocent people of other races to achieve that equality. And here was a man who was not only doing that, but he was also drinking the finest wines, eating in the best restaurants and growing fat off the money that was supposed to go to his cause.

Two reasons why Calvin James didn't intend to let Mingo and Black Charge stay in business.

The Phoenix Force warrior took a sip of his wine. He had started to speak when a waiter appeared and circled the table, handing out menus. The man stopped next to James. "The menu is in French," he said. "Rather than translate, may I suggest—"

James looked up. "No, you may not," he said in perfect French. "I will manage just fine." He turned back to Mingo in time to see a flicker of amusement in the black giant's eyes. Mingo nodded the waiter out of the room.

"You have one hundred and twenty M-16s, I am given to understand," Mingo said as soon as the man had gone. "It is enough to arm a small village. I have two questions—can you get ammunition, and can you get more weapons in the future?"

"Of course. More guns will take a little time. But the ammo—close to a hundred thousand rounds—is on hand and I'll throw it in gratis with the price of the rifles."

Mingo leaned forward. "And what is that price, Edmond?"

"Hundred and fifty apiece. That's eighteen grand."

The big man stared at him. "I will give you fifteen thousand dollars."

James returned the stare. The bottom line was, it didn't matter what price they agreed on. Mingo wasn't ever going to take possession of the guns. But that didn't mean the bargaining process wasn't important. If he appeared too eager, the Black Charge leader would become suspicious. He shook his head. "No. I'm already giving you a price that's less than I paid for the weapons myself. And I've got overhead expenses. I'm willing to take a loss, Mingo, but I'm not running a going-out-of-business sale, either."

Mingo didn't answer. A moment later James felt a presence in the room behind him, and then the waiter walked timidly into his vision. Mingo nodded, and the man approached the table. The black giant's eyes softened again, and he said, "I know you are fluent in French, Edmond, but might I suggest the *tournedos marchant de vin* with soufflé? It is excellent."

James opened his menu. "How is the same in bernaise?"

"Good, but not as good," Mingo said.

"Then I'll take your suggestion." James closed the menu and handed it to the waiter.

"Excellent. I'll have the same, Pieter. Let's begin with an order of crawfish. You do like crawfish, don't you, Edmond?"

"Of course."

The waiter left, and Mingo clasped his hands over his stomach again. "I will agree to your price of eighteen thousand," he said slowly, "if you will deliver the weapons to Miami."

James raised a hand to his face and scratched his cheek. Stony Man had been set up to do the deal in Washington, then it had been transferred to New Orleans. Now, unless he could get Mingo to change his mind, they'd have to scratch that plan and return to the drawing board once more. It could be done in Miami, but it wouldn't be easy. "That's more expense on my part. Not to mention additional transportation risks...." He let the words trail off and paused.

"It is necessary."

The ex-Navy SEAL continued to stall. "You don't have people who can get the guns to Miami themselves?"

"I do," Mingo said. "I want to see if *you* do."

James scratched his face again and stared at the ceiling. He could tell the man wasn't about to change his mind. Finally he said, "Okay. This time. But I've got to tell you, Mingo, I'm losing money. How soon you want them?

"Tomorrow."

James paused again. Stony Man already had the weapons in stock and waiting. But Cowboy John Kissinger had decided to render each one inoperable just in case the unexpected happened and they ended up in the wrong hands on a permanent basis. Doing that to over a hundred M-16s without making it obvious would take time.

"Can't do it," James said. "The guns are a long way from here. I can't—"

"Then the deal is off," Mingo said simply.

James sighed. "You drive a hard bargain, big man," he said, and could see that the reference to his size pleased the South African. "Okay. I'll see what I can do. But we'll have to negotiate differently next time around."

"Prove that you can be relied on, Edmond, and we will." Mingo glanced around the elaborate decor of the room, then indicated the table with a sweep of his mammoth hand. "As you can see, we are not without funds."

"I can see that," James said. He let a smile creep onto his face, took a sip of his wine and set the glass down. "You and I have much in common, Mingo," he forced himself to say. The words tasted bad in his mouth, and he lifted his wineglass again. "We both realize that we can help the plight of our brothers and still live well at the same time."

Mingo chuckled. He raised his own glass and downed the contents. Then, looking at the empty crystal and smacking his lips, he said, "That we do, Edmond, that we do."

CARL LYONS LIFTED the hamburger toward his mouth. Drops of brown grease dripped from between the buns to splash the counter. The ex-LAPD detective dropped the oily mess back on his plastic plate and pulled several napkins from the metal container in front of him.

When they were on stakeout, bad food was usually better that no food at all. But Muff's was proving to be the exception. The french fries had been so dry they crumbled when he picked them up, but the grease in the hamburger made up for them.

Lyons stared at the mess soaking through the bun as his stomach growled with hunger. He wasn't a gourmet, by any means. But he wasn't an alley cat or a goat, either.

Dropping the burgerlike substance back to his plate, Lyons turned toward the window and watched a jazz band march down the street. He swiveled to his side and looked at Blancanales. The man had ordered a salad, and now picked through it with his fork, removing black objects too large to be pepper, before taking cautious bites.

On the other side of Blancanales, Schwarz, oblivious to the same grease that had caused Lyons to abort dinner, worked his way through his third cheeseburger.

Blancanales reached up and adjusted the headset over his ears. Each of the Able Team warriors wore what appeared to be a personal cassette player. But the radio receivers to James's "bug" that the small boxes clipped to their belts really contained were far more sophisticated than the components of a tape player.

It was a little unusual for three grown men to all be wearing headsets, Lyons had thought when they'd first opted to use them. Then he had gotten a look at Bourbon Street after dark, and realized they could have probably all worn clown costumes and still gone unnoticed.

Nothing seemed out of place in New Orleans's French Quarter.

Blancanales gave up on his salad and lifted his glass to the light. He squinted at something floating inside, then set it back down untasted. Swiveling his stool to face Lyons, he said, "What do you suppose *they're* having?"

As if he'd heard the question in the Creole a block away, Lyons heard Mingo speak in his ear. *"Tournedos marchant de vin,"* the Black Charge man said.

"Got any idea what that is?" Lyons asked.

"Steak, I think," Blancanales answered. "In wine sauce, maybe? Sounds good."

"Yuck," Schwarz said. He poured half a bottle of ketchup over his double order of fries and went to work on them with a fork.

"Maybe we can find a McDonald's or something after—" Blancanales stopped abruptly when talk of the M-16s resumed.

"I will agree to your price of eighteen thousand," Mingo said, then threw James a curve, demanding that the weapons be delivered to Miami.

"Shit," Schwarz said. "There goes Plan B." He dropped his fork and looked past Blancanales to Lyons.

The Able Team leader read his mind. "Get on it, fast. There's one in the corner, by the men's room."

Schwarz stood up, rummaging in a pocket for a quarter as he hurried toward the pay phone.

Lyons felt his eyebrows lower in concentration as James was forced to agree to the delivery to Miami. Then he stood, dropped a twenty-dollar bill on top of the oil-stained food bill on the counter and joined Schwarz at the phone.

"Just a second," Schwarz said into the receiver. He turned to Lyons. "Cowboy's been working straight through. He's half-finished. He thinks he can have them ready. But it's going to be close."

A tiny voice inside the receiver spoke loudly. "I'll have a hell of a lot better chance if you'll hang up and let me get back to work."

Lyons took the phone. "Get on it, then." The line clicked, then Barbara Price came on.

"Ironman?"

"Yeah."

"Everything else is a go. It doesn't make any difference where it goes down, except for the guns."

"Okay, Barb," the Able Team leader said. "We'll get back to you later." He hung up and returned to his stool.

Blancanales stood. "Want to move on down the street closer?"

Lyons nodded.

"But I'm not finished yet," Schwarz complained, picking up what remained of his cheeseburger. "Besides, they're just eating and talking about the food right now. There's no need to—"

Blancanales grabbed his arm, pulled him from the stool and pointed him toward the door. Nodding toward the cheeseburger, he said, "Come on, Gadgets. This won't be the first time I've saved your life."

CHAPTER FIVE

It didn't seem to matter how much they enlarged the armory at Stony Man Farm, Cowboy John Kissinger never had enough space, especially in the small-arms room. Tools, spare parts, five-gallon cans of gun oils and cleaning solvents and miscellaneous other equipment and supplies filled the shelves that lined the room, spilling over into stacked piles on the floor and tables.

Kissinger hung up the phone and looked at the mess. He didn't demand spotless working conditions, but he liked things orderly. A little organization, knowing where things were when he needed them, saved time when he had a rush job.

Like now.

Kissinger's brown lizard-skin boots tapped across the tile as he returned to the M-16A2 on the workbench. With the skill of a brain surgeon performing surgery, the master armorer broke the weapon down, removed the firing pin and dropped it into an empty can on the floor. Reaching over another row of cans, he grabbed what appeared to be an identical firing pin from a stack in the center of the workbench. Shoving the new part into the M-16, he reassembled the weapon, then turned and leaned it against the wall next to the sixty-three other assault rifles he had already altered.

He pulled another M-16 from the open crate on the floor, his mind drifting as he broke it down. Calvin James and Able Team's gun deal with Black Charge had presented him with a unique problem, a problem that had been more fun to solve mentally than the "assembly-line" work it now took to complete the solution. While James and the men of Able Team had no intention of letting Black Charge get away with the weapons, everyone at the Farm—from Brognola on down—was a seasoned veteran of both combat and clandestine operations. As such, they knew that ops never turned out quite the way they'd been planned.

Things sometimes went wrong. And if this turned out to be one of those times, no one wanted to see the militant South African group end up with ten dozen full-auto M-16s, courtesy of Stony Man Farm.

Kissinger dropped another firing pin into the can and reached across the table. So the answer had been to render the M-16s inoperable, just in case.

Easy? Well, yes and no.

The gunsmith inserted the new pin, reassembled the rifle, stacked it next to the others and began the process anew. John Kissinger hadn't fallen off the turnip truck yesterday, and he knew it was a rare exchange of illegal firearms in which the buyer didn't demand demonstrative proof that the weapons were operable. This Mingo fellow, whoever he was, would want to see at least a few of the rifles work. And there was no way to tell which ones he'd choose to test.

So the problem had become more complex.

He finished seven more rifles, then walked to the phone on the wall. He lifted the receiver, tapped Barbara Price's button and waited until she'd answered.

"Barb, I'm well over halfway home in here," he said. "If you want to round up some of the boys and get them to loading, now's the time."

Price okayed the idea, and Kissinger went back to his bench to break down another M-16. He pulled the pin and held it in one hand while his other reached for an identical part. The phone rang suddenly, and he set them down side by side.

"Got the troops on their way down, Cowboy," Price said. "They'll be there in a few minutes."

"I'll buzz them in."

Kissinger went back to work, wishing briefly that he could go along with the troops to Miami. He knew the special-alloy firing pins he had constructed would do what he had intended them to do—hold up under fire for one magazine of rounds, two max. They'd work; he had no doubt about it.

But damn, just once he'd like to actually *see* one of his inventions in action.

DIREK BROUER SPREAD his fingers around the small black ball and stared down the waxed wooden alley. Ten squatty pins, resembling the forms of chubby white ducks swimming on a lake, stood at the end. The Ijsselmeer CEO took a deep breath and let it out as his eyes focused on the one-three pocket. He drew back his arm, then stepped forward and arched the smooth black sphere forward.

The ball hit the alley with a light thump, rolled straight into the pocket and sent the pins flying to the back and sides.

Brouer smiled. He had tried tranquilizers. They made him woozy. He had tried jogging. It hurt his back. He had tried bicycling, lifting weights, karate, transcendental meditation and massage. None of them had relaxed him.

But duckpins did. Regardless of how stressed out he got, the sight of the round black ball demolishing the stumpy little pins somehow soothed the nerves that seemed to be part of his job description. It was for that reason he had had the alley built in the basement of the Ijsselmeer Building. The pins never failed him. Even now, in the middle of a "corporate takeover" that erased the line between business and politics. Even now, after the phone call from one of his South African government moles that told of the big American sent to protect Lindall Dingaan and the failed attempts on the black man's life, he could feel his blood pressure going down as if someone had tapped a bleed-off valve.

Brouer stepped away from the foul line and walked back to the table behind him. He lifted a tubular cardboard container and shook powder over his bowling hand. He was wiping the hand with a rag when a feminine voice sounded from the speaker over his head.

"Mr. Brouer?"

"Yes, Gwendolyn."

"Mr. Yancy and Mr. Lanzerac have arrived." There was a pause. "Should I send them down?"

Brouer glanced toward the alley as the automatic pin machine reset the pins. He had a perfect game going. Six frames, all strikes. The best he'd bowled in months. Should he...?

No. Definitely not. He had an image to maintain, and that image didn't include having two proletariat gunmen witness him at his leisure. Yancy and Lanzerac needed to see him as they always did, behind his desk. In charge. Ruling.

Ruling Ijsselmeer, Inc., as he would soon be ruling South Africa.

"Send them to my office," Brouer replied. "I'll be there in a few moments. He heard the intercom click off and walked hurriedly to the sink against the wall. Turning the tap, he ran warm water over his hands, washed away the powder, then hurried back to the table. The coat to his stern navy blue business suit was draped over the chair and he threw it over his arm as he strode to the elevator. Pushing the button, he slipped into the jacket and straightened his tie in the bronze reflection of the door as the car began to rise.

A minute later the elevator stopped in the hall behind Ijsselmeer's penthouse suite. Brouer stuck his key in the door and slipped into his office in time to catch the intercom. "Mr. Brouer," his secretary said over the speaker phone. "Misters Yancy and—"

"Send them in."

David Yancy led the way into the office. Brouer noted that the man wore another of his cheap Western suits, this one a royal blue that looked as if it belonged on the manager of some second-rate nightclub. The ever-present snakeskin boots extended from the short cuffs.

Brouer tapped the intercom. "Three cups of coffee," he said bluntly, then looked up. "Cream? Sugar?"

"Both," Lanzerac replied.

Yancy shook his head.

Brouer cut the intercom off again. He studied the men's faces. Lanzerac's could have held any hand in a poker game, but the strain of Yancy's showed the dread he felt about reporting the semifailures.

"Gentlemen," the CEO began, "I don't wish to appear rude, but I have other pressing matters. Shall we get down to business?"

The two nodded.

Though he knew most of what had happened from several phone calls from moles within the South African government and military, Brouer decided to make the American merc tell him the whole story. "Have things proceeded as we hoped?"

Yancy glanced to the floor. "Fairly well."

Brouer felt his fists clench lightly. "Perhaps you should explain."

"You've been reading the papers?"

The CEO nodded. The mercenary was stalling, buying time, hoping he would come up with a last-minute way of softening the failures to kill Dingaan. "Yes, I have read the papers. But I would prefer your version of the story. Tell me about the raids on the Boer farms in the Transvaal."

Yancy coughed. "The raids went perfectly. All except one, that is, and it wasn't bad."

"Oh?"

Lanzerac broke in, his lips curling in a nervous smile. "Some kind of commando team turned up and drove the men off. But the farm got torched first." The BRM man glanced toward the empty third chair next to him, where Frank Cliff had sat during his previous visit.

"Tell me about these fleeing men," Brouer ordered.

Yancy coughed. "Well, they were the mercs we hired. You know who they were and where they came from. Amateurs. No balls. No loyalty. They ran as soon as the commandos arrived. But the farm was a wreck, and as far as we know, there weren't any survivors." He shifted uncomfortably in his chair.

"These commandos you keep referring to," Brouer said. "Tell me about them."

"I don't know much," Yancy replied. "But Lanzerac doesn't think they were South Africans." He turned toward the man, kicking the ball into his court.

Lanzerac crossed a boot over his leg. "There were close to a hundred of them, according to the mercs. Our men had to retreat or get killed. But I doubt it. Yancy and I checked the scene later, and there weren't enough tracks or empty 9 mm casings to have been that many men."

Brouer swiveled to face the Ijsselmeer crest on the wall. "I see. And why do you doubt they were South African troops?"

"The casings had come out of Uzis," Lanzerac said. "You can tell by the marks the ejector leaves on them. S.A. doesn't use Uzis."

Brouer turned back to Yancy, forming a steeple with his fingertips beneath his chin. "Is there anything else I should know?"

"No, sir, Mr. Brouer," Yancy said. "Just, well, maybe you should know that Dingaan's got some new bodyguard, a big son of a bitch. Tougher then nails. He got Dingaan away from the parking garage, then saved him again at the safehouse. By all rights, the bastard should be dead twice over right now.''

Brouer continued to look at the crest. He had reached his present position by refusing to accept even partial failure in himself. He didn't like it in others. But occasionally he had to accept the imperfections of others.

The CEO closed his eyes. What he'd like to do right now, was to have both Yancy and Lanzerac killed. He had other men on his payroll more than capable of the task.

But that would create more problems. At least for the time being, there was no one else he could turn to to replace the cowboy or South African.

''I'm sorry, Mr. Brouer.'' Yancy's voice was almost a whimper.

Brouer didn't answer. Let the bastard sweat a few more minutes, at least. The bottom line was that *most* of what they had attempted had succeeded. From a political standpoint, many of the organizations that made up the Conference for a Democratic South Africa were threatening to withdraw. At the very least the plans to write a new constitution would be delayed. And sympathy for the return to total rule by the whites was gaining momentum with the Boers.

The trick now would be keeping the flames fanned like this until the election.

The Ijsselmeer CEO swiveled back to face the men. ''Let us summarize what still needs to be done,'' he said. ''For the time being you may forget Lindall Dingaan. I have another idea that should take care of him and his American bodyguard at the same time. Move on to the Zulu and Xhosa. You know the plan.

Get them ready for war with each other, and the whites. The shipment of automatic rifles and ammunition should have arrived in Capetown by the time the two of you return. See to it that the tribes receive the guns immediately after you attack." He stood suddenly behind his desk.

Yancy and Lanzerac followed suit.

"Good day, gentlemen." Brouer stood at attention until the men had left the room. As soon as the door had closed behind them, he exited the rear door and crossed the hallway to the elevator.

Two minutes later, a light film of powder covering his bowling hand, Brouer lifted the ball. He glanced down at the score sheet clipped to the table, again noting the long row of Xs that marked his perfect game. As he moved to the foul line, the tight band around his chest began to relax.

The problems in South Africa could be worse. For the most part things were going well. And from here on out, things would go perfectly.

Like the game of duckpins in which he was presently engaged.

Brouer drew back his arm and sent the ball rolling down the alley with more force than usual. It zipped into the one-three pocket like a bullet.

The pins flew harder and faster than they ever had before, one of them flipping out of the alley altogether.

The CEO smiled. Then his eyes focused on the lone duckpin still wobbling at the end of the alley. It teetered left, then right, then settled back into place.

Brouer cursed.

And for some reason, as he moved back to the table and lifted the scoring pencil, his thoughts fell on the big American who was guarding Lindall Dingaan.

AKIRO TOKAIDO'S HEAD bobbed and dipped in time to the music flooding into his ears. In spite of the music, the young Japanese remained focused on the screen in front of him. He had entered a state void of conscious thought known as *mushin;* a mental condition in which cognizant reasoning gave way to the more productive power of the subconscious mind.

At the moment Tokaido knew nothing. Yet he was aware of, and alert to, all.

As if programmed by remote control, Tokaido's fingers tapped the keyboard of his computer, calling up a file for Harlingen Wholesale out of Harlingen, Holland. He ran the information through Kurtzman's probability program, learning that the company exported processed foods such as condensed milk, beet sugar, chocolate and cheese. Tokaido typed in "Net profit, previous six years," and the word "improbable" suddenly lit up in the bottom right-hand corner of the screen.

He glanced at the numbers, then exited the file almost as quickly as he had entered. Harlingen averaged less than a million dollars a year, with less than ten percent of that coming from South Africa.

Far too little to make it worth their while to subsidize a revolution.

He called up the next file on his list, a Czechoslovakian firm, Hradcany Mining. The red "improbable" became "impossible." The computer went on to explain that only a month before, the Czechoslovakian mining company, formed hurriedly after the fall of communism, had fallen victim to the scourge of capitalism. Bankruptcy.

Tokaido typed on, checking and discarding more of the European interests on his list. Hudiskvall Leather Goods in Sweden flashed "improbable" due to limited trade interests south of the equator, and a textile manufacturer and exporter in Hull, England, drew a "possible," which quickly changed to "improbable" when Tokaido checked its overall holdings. And like the Czechoslovakian mining corporation, Hunadoara Grain and Seed in Romania had recently gone out of business.

The young Japanese brought himself out of *mushin.* He pulled the headset from his ears, set it on the console and turned toward the kitchenette area along the wall. He had brewed a pot of herbal tea over an hour ago, then forgotten about it. He glanced down at the list in front of him. He had worked his way through all of the companies up to those beginning with *I.* And there were only two under that listing, Iddo Island Transport and Ijsselmeer, Inc. The tea would be cold by now, and he might as well get those two out of the way before he took a break and popped it into the microwave.

Tokaido typed "Iddo Island Transport" onto the screen and hit Enter. Iddo had originated in Paris as LeForce Transport twenty years earlier, then changed its name when it moved its offices to Nigeria for tax reasons. Iddo Island rated a "possible," having diversified some of its profits into African real estate.

He tagged the file and decided to return to it later if nothing better came up. True, Jonathan Shomari had said that the company pumping money and arms into South Africa was based in Europe. But the Black Charge middleman had gotten the rumor as it came down the pipes of his organization. Rumors were often distorted, and the fact that Iddo had originated in Paris could have easily been the cause of a discrepancy.

Tokaido looked back to the list. Ijsselmeer, Inc. Amsterdam, Netherlands. He yawned as he entered the words.

The young man's jaws clamped shut as the word "likely" immediately appeared on the screen. He had checked more than two hundred businesses so far, and none had drawn anything more promising than "possible." Tapping further into the file, he saw that Ijsselmeer was a multimillion dollar conglomerate with vast mining interests in South Africa. Headed by Chief Executive Officer Direk Brouer, Ijsselmeer had invested close to a hundred million dollars in the country during the past ten years.

And unlike many of the other foreign investors he'd come across, the company hadn't eased off when the recent trouble had flared.

Tokaido typed in "Brouer, Direk—personal history," and hit Enter. The computer clicked and hummed, then the passport picture of a gray-haired man entering the tail end of middle age appeared. He studied the picture, then moved the cursor down the screen to the words below. Brouer had been born in Amsterdam, the son of a poor fisherman. He had worked his way through school and risen the ladder of corporate success to the top of Ijsselmeer, the largest gold-and-diamond mining cartel in Europe.

On a hunch Tokaido exited the file and entered the network for Interpol. Quickly passing through a series of codes, he reentered Brouer's name. "No file" came flashing on the screen.

Tokaido felt his heart jump. Rather than the yellow letters Interpol usually used for the message, these words were of a slightly orange hue. The Japanese knew what that meant.

There was a file on Brouer, all right, a secret file that technically violated the CEO's right of privacy. A computer ace who knew the right codes could get to it.

Tokaido sat back in his chair. He had no idea what code to use to keep from alerting Interpol that their files were being tapped into by an unauthorized source.

But he knew someone who would. And if he didn't, he'd figure out a way around the problem.

The young man turned and looked up the ramp. "Oh, Aaron."

Kurtzman looked down like Zeus from Olympus and stopped typing. "What?"

"We need to talk."

LISTED AS JOHANNESBURG'S contribution to *The Three Hundred Best Hotels in The World,* the Hotel President on the corner of Eloff and Pleinn streets boasted 239 rooms, twenty-one suites, three restaurants and ten shops. As flashy as the South African gold-rush times during which it was built, the President was the favorite resting place and watering hole of wealthy, world-traveling hunters, both before and after safari.

People in every type of dress, from tuxedos to sweat suits, crowded the halls. But khaki trousers, bush jackets, and safari hats sporting leopard- and tiger-skin bands were the preferred fashion.

Which was why the Executioner had chosen the Hotel President.

Bolan looked over his shoulder at Lindall Dingaan as Jameson pulled the Saturn to a stop on a dark side street. The overcoat that had hidden the black leader's bright tribal robe had been abandoned during the rush from the safehouse. But Dingaan had been the top television news story for two days running, and the Executioner knew that even if he could have found a change of clothing, the famous face would be recognized.

The Executioner watched Jameson exit the vehicle. It had taken little alteration of Jameson's Recce uniform—tearing the stripes off the sleeves and losing the beret, to be exact—to make him look as if he'd just stepped out of a hunting tent instead of a military base. That would enable him to blend in with the crowd, registering at the President while Bolan stayed in the car with Dingaan.

Jameson returned ten minutes later. "We're logged in under the name you gave me," he said. "Room 233. There's a servants' entrance down the alley." He pointed into the darkness. "You ready?"

Bolan nodded. He slipped the .50 Desert Eagle out of its holster and held it under his jacket as he stepped out of the vehicle. Jameson opened the door for Dingaan, and they ducked into the alleyway.

The Executioner scanned the dark passage as they neared the lone light bulb over the steel door. The assassination attempt on the black African Civil Assembly leader at the safehouse, and the subsequent traitorous behavior of De Groot and some of the other Recce guards, had shown Bolan that he could trust no one but Jameson.

The sergeant had proved himself several times over, and for that Bolan was grateful. But he knew he'd need more help than the lone commando could provide if he was to keep Dingaan alive.

He needed Phoenix Force. But at the moment Katz and company were out of pocket. Last word from Stony Man Farm had been that they were north in the Transvaal, fighting what appeared to be an attack on Boer farmhouses by black militants. Bolan had left word that he'd be hiding out at the President under the name Pat Harkin, and that Phoenix Force should contact him there as soon as they surfaced.

Jameson opened the door, and Bolan stuck his head inside. A short hallway forked out in front of him, one prong leading to a swing door with a large window in the upper half. Through the window, the Executioner could see a man wearing a white apron chopping meat with a cleaver. One of the restaurants.

The other hallway led to a closed door. The sign above it read Rooms 132-147.

Bolan led the way, followed by Dingaan, then Jameson. The Executioner opened the door, glanced up and down the deserted hallway and saw the stairs. "Let's go," he said over his shoulder. "Be quick."

The three men hurried down the hall and started up the stairs. Footsteps suddenly sounded above them, and Bolan looked up to see a middle-aged man and a woman descending. The man wore a light pink golf shirt that stretched over his portly abdomen. The woman had on a light cotton dress and matching beige straw bush hat with a bright red scarf serving as the band.

The two stopped in their tracks, halfway down the steps.

"Hey, Peggy!" the man shouted in a Southern American accent. "Look! It's—"

Bolan whipped the huge .50 Desert Eagle from under his coat and pointed it at the man's face. "Shh."

The American man's mouth dropped open. The woman pressed her hand to her heart.

The Executioner motioned up the stairs with his weapon. "Keep quiet," he growled.

"Look, please..." the man whispered. "If it's money you want..."

Footsteps heading their way pounded on the floor below. Bolan grabbed the man by the arm and began dragging him up the stairs. Jameson and Dingaan followed, the Recce cupping a hand over the woman's mouth as she started to scream.

"You can't—" the man said.

The warrior pushed the Desert Eagle into the man's ribs, and he fell silent.

Reaching the second floor, the Executioner dropped the fat man's arm long enough to take the key from Jameson. The Recce kept his hand over the woman's mouth as Bolan opened the door to Room 233 and hurried them all inside.

A king-size bed stood in the middle of the spacious room. French Provincial furniture lined the walls.

Bolan sprinted across the room to the window as Jameson settled the man and woman into a pair of overstuffed chairs. Below, he saw several swimmers in the pool. Beyond that, a half-filled parking lot. He turned back to the room. "Okay," he told the frightened couple. "Relax. We've got no intention of hurting you—you just happened to be in the wrong place at the wrong time." He paused, then said, "What are your names?"

The man looked up, his face a mask of fear. The Executioner holstered the Desert Eagle, and the worried face relaxed slightly. "I'm Herb, uh, Pendergrast?" he stuttered, as if not sure. "This, uh, this is my wife, Peggy." He clasped his hands in front of him. "What...what are you going to do to us?"

"I told you, I'm not going to do anything *to* you," Bolan replied. "The question is, what do I do *with* you?" He moved back and took a seat on the bed facing them.

Jameson stood next to the door, his eye pressed to the peephole. Lindall Dingaan had fallen onto the bed in exhaustion the minute he'd entered the room. Now he dragged himself to his feet and crossed the room to the Pendergrasts.

"Mr. and Mrs. Pendergrast," he said calmly. "Do you know who I am?"

"Of course," Herb Pendergrast replied. "And it appears that's what got us into this mess."

"For that, I will be eternally sorry," he said. "But as Colonel Pollock said, we will not harm you."

Pendergrast turned to Bolan. "What are you, with the army or something?"

Dingaan answered. "Colonel Pollock is an American, like yourselves."

The knowledge seemed to comfort the Pendergrasts. Herb's face brightened with excitement. "You're American? We hail from Fort Smith, Arkansas, the missus and me. Came here for a photo safari and—"

"Someone coming down the hall," Jameson whispered to the room.

Bolan drew the big .50 again and stood.

Peggy Pendergrast gasped.

"Please, do not worry," Dingaan said, placing a hand over hers as the Executioner moved toward the door. "We are in good hands."

Bolan heard voices as he neared the door. Jameson stepped to the side, and the Executioner pressed an eye to the hole. Two men wearing light slacks and open-collared shirts passed by. A second later a key scratched into the lock of the door next to them.

The warrior moved across the room to the phone by the bed as Lindall Dingaan continued to chat politely with the Pendergrasts. The whole incident had frightened the unlucky couple, and the Executioner felt sorry for them.

Lifting the receiver, Bolan punched President Van Peebles's direct number into the instrument and waited. He knew what he wanted out of the South African leader—a plane and a pilot. No more, no less. He knew only one place in the entire country where Dingaan could remain in safety for any length of time. They needed to get there fast, and that meant a plane.

A woman's voice answered the phone. "President Van Peebles's office."

"Mr. Van Peebles, please."

"I'm sorry, the president is out of the office. If you'd care to—"

Bolan hung up. He didn't want to leave word of where he was, or what he wanted, with anyone else. The way things had gone down so far, it was too risky. He rejoined Jameson at the door.

The Recce sergeant knew the score. He nodded toward the man and woman seated in front of Dingaan and put it into words. "What do we do with them, Colonel?"

The Executioner didn't have an answer. At least not yet. It might be feasible to just leave them in the room when Phoenix Force arrived. Right now he could hear Lindall Dingaan skillfully explaining the situation in a voice that could rock a baby to sleep. The Pendergrasts had both leaned toward the charismatic leader, and nodded after everything he said. Peggy was even smiling.

But what would happen after the couple from Fort Smith were no longer under the influence of Dingaan's almost narcotic powers of persuasion? They'd begin to wonder. They'd remember some of the distorted news stories they'd seen on TV, and then one of them would realize that they'd seen no proof that Bolan was an American.

In fact, they'd realize, they had no proof to substantiate a shred of the three men's story. So Herb would say to Peggy, "Maybe we'd better call the police just to be safe."

And word would be out.

The ringing phone suddenly broke into the Executioner's thoughts. Herb and Peggy jumped as if the sound had been a bullet. Bolan strode back across the room and lifted the receiver.

"Mr. Harkin?" a deep voice said.

"Yes."

"Uh, Mr. Harkin, this is the manager. I'm sorry, sir... this is very embarrassing... but we have a new desk clerk on this evening. Please understand that what happened is certainly not the policy of the Hotel President...."

The Executioner felt a surge of adrenaline shoot through his veins. "What *did* happen?" he asked.

"Well, sir, several men came to the desk looking for you. Said you'd been on a hunt and would be... Well, the bottom line, sir, is that the new clerk gave them your room number. I believe they're on their way up."

"Thank you," Bolan said, and hung up the phone. He hurried to the window. Below, facing the hotel, he saw a car in the parking lot that hadn't been there earlier. The shadowy heads of two men were visible in the front seat, and two more were in the back.

The dark silhouette of a rifle barrel poked up next to the driver.

Bolan turned to Dingaan and the Pendergrasts. "I want all three of you under the bed, now!"

Dingaan rose, took a hand from both of the Pendergrasts and then knelt with them on the floor. They began squirming under the bed.

Jameson had moved away from the door to join Bolan. "We have guests coming?"

The Executioner nodded. "Take position behind the bed. I'll take the bathroom." Jameson jerked his Z-88 from under his shirt and dropped to his knees behind the bed, the pistol gripped in both hands and braced over the edge of the bed.

Bolan heard the footsteps as he hurried toward the door, then cut into the bathroom next to it. He would be out of the direct line of vision as the men kicked through the door, and should be able to take out at least the first couple of gunners. Maybe more, if he could cause a pileup in the doorway. And anyone who got through would be in Jameson's sights.

How many men were there? The manager had said several, which might mean three. Or a dozen.

The Executioner drew the big .50 caliber Magnum with his right hand, the familiar .44 with his left. He aimed both massive weapons toward the hall door.

Bolan took a deep breath, then let half of it out. Slowly his index fingers moved inside the trigger guards of both guns.

A soft knock sounded on the door.

The Executioner waited. The knock came again.

Silently the warrior moved out of the bathroom and pressed an eye to the peephole.

Several men wearing long black overcoats stood just outside. Their hands were hidden under their coats or in pockets. Below the tails of the long garments, Bolan saw that they all wore scuffed combat boots.

The Executioner holstered the .50-caliber, keeping the .44 in his left hand. Then, with one swift movement, he grabbed the knob, twisted it and threw open the door.

"*Lachaim,*" Yakov Katzenelenbogen said as he stepped into the room. "Just happened to be in the neighborhood and thought we'd drop in."

CHAPTER SIX

Gateway Marina on Biscayne Bay was a small operation compared to the dozen or other privately owned docks south of Miami. But it was big enough.

Calvin James and Able Team stood on the dock, looking out past the sloops, ketches and power launches lashed to the rails. Anchored beyond the small boats, larger craft swayed in the gentle waves.

Carl Lyons glanced at his wristwatch. "They're late," he said matter-of-factly.

"Fifteen minutes is all." Blancanales shrugged. "I never did an undercover deal yet that went like clockwork. Still too early to get nervous."

James shifted his feet nervously as the conversation died again. His sweaty finger slipped inside his shirt, reassuring him that the Berretta 92 still rode snugly in his belt. Damn, he hated the waiting. He'd take direct combat over undercover work any day. At least when somebody shot at you, you knew where you stood. Wiping his palm across the front of his shirt, he watched a set of lights appear suddenly two hundred yards out in the bay.

"Bingo," Blancanales said.

"You with us, Gadgets?" James said into the microphone beneath his collar.

"That's affirmative," Schwarz's voice came back from the panel truck in the parking lot.

"Be ready," Lyons said into his own mike. "We don't know how Mingo and his buddies will take to new faces being thrown at them."

"Especially a couple of white faces he's never seen," Blancanales added.

"Hell," Schwarz said into each of their ears, "I've seen your faces, and even I don't like them. You know what Mingo told James about the Nazis, Ironman? Do your best not to act like a storm trooper for once."

Lyons ignored the good-natured ribbing as the lights drew nearer. Finally he said, "Okay, girls, cut the chatter. We don't want them to know we're wired."

A click sounded beneath James's shirt as Schwarz cut his transmitter off.

As the powerboat entered the docking area, James squinted into the darkness. It was a medium-size craft. Probably not one they'd sail all the way to Africa, which meant they planned to transfer the M-16s to a larger ship somewhere at sea.

James stepped forward as a dozen figures rose to stand on the deck. Arms extended the barrels of a variety of assault rifles and submachine guns over the rail of what looked to be a Sabreline 36 Motoryacht. The stillness of the night was broken by the metallic sounds of rifle bolts being drawn back to chamber rounds.

Mingo's giant head appeared amid the men. Then the leader of Black Charge crossed the deck, threw a foot over the side and dropped onto the dock. James and Able Team fought to keep their balance as the big man's weight rocked the dock.

The big man walked forward, a MAC-10 machine pistol all but lost in his massive hand. He stopped three feet from James and dropped the sights to the Phoenix Force warrior's belly. Then, glancing at Lyons and Blancanales, he said, "I don't remember sending out party invitations to any white boys."

James chuckled. "You didn't expect me to come unescorted, did you, Mingo?" He indicated the deck of the Sabreline with a nod of his head. "Looks like you had several dates tonight yourself."

Mingo didn't answer. He continued to stare back and forth between Lyons and Blancanales, his eyes finally narrowing and coming to rest on the former LAPD detective. "You look like a cop to me."

"That's 'cause I am one," Lyons replied.

Mingo swung the MAC-10 his way.

"How the hell you think it is that Mr. Nix here stays in business?" Lyons asked.

Slowly Mingo's lips parted. He threw back his head and laughed. "Ten-four, constable," he said. Then his eyes narrowed again, and he jabbed the machine pistol toward Blancanales. "How about him?"

James took a tentative step forward, and the MAC swung back his way. "Mingo, let's go over here." He nodded down the dock, then started walking slowly away from Lyons and Blancanales. "Let me talk to you privately."

Mingo hesitated, then followed.

As soon as they were out of earshot, James turned to face the Black Charge leader. "His name's Cabeio, man," the Phoenix Force warrior whispered. "He's what you might call a rich over-the-hill hippie. Real pansy-ass liberal. Always wanting to save us poor downtrodden blacks, know what I mean?"

Mingo's face didn't change.

"He comes up with the front money when I get caught short. Thinks he's helping the black man on everything I do. Don't worry. He's harmless. And the cop's okay, too. He gets paid well."

Mingo's black eyes drilled through James's for a moment, then he turned on his heel and marched back to the other two men. James followed, coming to a stop at the Black Charge leader's side.

The South African thrust the barrel of the machine pistol into Lyons's abdomen. "Show me a badge," he demanded.

Lyons hand moved under his jacket, and the black giant jammed the barrel in harder. *"Slow."* Lyons produced a ballistic nylon badge case and let one end fall open. The overhead light reflected off the gold metal that appeared.

Mingo turned toward the boat. A nod of his behemoth head brought a dozen armed men clambering over the side. They formed a ring around the men from Stony Man Farm, their subguns, assault rifles and riot guns aiming toward the center like the spokes of a wheel.

Another nod from their leader, and the weapons lowered.

Mingo turned back to James. "Let's do it," he said simply.

James turned and led the way up the concrete steps to the parking lot overlooking the marina. The panel truck sat parked against the curb. Although the marina had been deserted during the wee morning hours, three cars were parked casually around the lot.

Schwarz's head appeared just above the panel truck's steering wheel. The electronics expert jumped out of the vehicle, circled the side and opened the rear door.

Mingo let the MAC-10 fall to the end of its sling and pulled a knife from his pocket. The bulky five-inch blade looked like a penknife in his meaty palm as he pried the lid off the nearest wooden case. He lifted an M-16 out of the box, tore the oily packing paper away and turned to James. "Where is the ammunition?"

James opened a smaller crate, reached in and handed him a box.

"Do not take this as mistrust," the Black Charge leader said. "But I want to make sure the weapons are functional." He yanked the 20-round magazine from the rifle and began filling it with bullets.

"What's wrong, Mingo? You don't trust me?"

Mingo stopped loading the mag only long enough to look up and say "Can you honestly tell me the thought of ripping me off never crossed your mind?"

James nodded. "You don't get repeat business from guys you rip off."

This time Mingo didn't bother to look up. He continued to push bullets beyond the lip of the magazine as he calmly said, "I considered killing you and taking your cargo. It would have been simple, and much less expensive."

James knew that could still happen. His hand inched slowly toward the gun in his belt. "So why didn't you?"

Mingo finished loading the magazine and slammed it into the M-16. His head finally tilted back, and the cold black eyes proved to James what he had just suggested would have been the Black Charge leader's preferred course of action. "Because as you said, one

does not do repeat business by killing the supplier."
He drew back the assault rifle's bolt, turned and
squeezed the trigger.

A full-auto stream of 5.56 mm bullets sprayed the
water on one side of the Sabreline.

Mingo dropped the weapon on top of the others,
then reached down and lifted the wooden crate as if it
were a shoe box and set in on the ground behind him.
He used the knife on another lid, then dug down to the
fourth weapon in the stack. He repeated the process of
loading and firing nine more times, selecting a rifle at
random from each of the remaining cases.

James held his breath. John Kissinger was the best
gunsmith around. But even the best could fall prey to
faulty material. And the Cowboy was walking a fine
line, trying to use firing pins that broke almost on
command.

As soon as the last magazine had emptied into the
water, Mingo turned toward the boat, stuck his fingers in his mouth and whistled.

A man wearing a black Chicago Bulls T-shirt and
carrying a briefcase jumped to the dock as the men
next to Mingo began carting the M-16s to the Sabreline.

Mingo took the briefcase and handed it to James.
"Check it."

"I trust you."

"No. I insist."

James flipped the lid and saw eighteen neatly
wrapped stacks of hundred-dollar bills. He thumbed
through a packet, counting to ten.

"You are satisfied?" Mingo asked.

"I am."

"So am I."

Mingo whistled again, and ten more men dropped over the side of the boat.

James shook his head. The craft was only thirty-six feet long. Mingo must have packed them in the hold like sardines.

The new men joined their leader as the others finished loading the Sabreline. James hand inched again toward his belt. It was now or never. If Mingo decided he wanted the guns and the money, this was the time to make his move.

Mingo turned toward him. "You have secured a quiet meeting place where we can arrange for future shipments?"

James nodded. "Got a room just up the road. Holiday Inn."

"Then let's go." The big man turned and marched toward a Lincoln Town Car parked a few steps away. He got into the back with one of his men while two others slipped into the front. The rest of the Black Charge gunmen got into the other cars in the lot.

James, Lyons and Blancanales jumped into the back of the panel truck while Schwarz resumed his place behind the wheel. The electronics man pulled out of the lot and started down the road toward the hotel.

"That could have gone bad," James said. "But there was no way around it."

"A calculated risk," Blancanales agreed. "They come up."

Lyons nodded.

James crawled toward the front of the truck and braced a hand on the seat behind Schwarz. "Tell me,

Gadgets. What did you have planned in case they opened fire?''

Schwarz chuckled. He looked down at the dashboard, then pointed toward the fuel gauge. "Look for yourself."

James followed his finger to the green lights on the gauge.

The tank was full.

"And I kept the transmission in gear for a quick start," Schwarz said.

James leaned back against the wall of the truck, shook his head and laughed. He missed the men of Phoenix Force, and there hadn't been a minute go by that he hadn't wondered what they were up to or if they might need him.

But if worse came to worst, Able Team wasn't a bad bunch to work with, either.

SPECIAL AGENT Charlie Johnston of the Drug Enforcement Administration wasn't sure where he'd been the past three weeks. Or where he was going now.

Johnston climbed the ladder of the big Carver Californian and glanced down at the blacksuit stretched across his thighs. A SIG-Sauer 9 mm pistol hung under his arm in a ballistic nylon shoulder rig, with extra magazines countering the weight on the opposite side. Smoke and concussion grenades dangled from his combat harness, and a full-auto Colt 9 mm carbine was slung over his shoulder.

No, he thought as his feet hit the deck, none of the men on board the forty-eight-foot yacht knew exactly what they were doing. But whatever it turned out to be, he knew they'd undergone training to do it.

Waves lapped against the big Californian as Johnston moved to the rail. He felt the presence of other blacksuited bodies taking up positions on both his sides. Other boots shuffled across the deck behind him.

During the past three weeks he had received the most intensive training he'd ever had, either in the military service as a young Green Beret lieutenant, or later as a career law-enforcement officer. In fact, you could take boot camp, Special Forces school, and the DEA Academy and combine them, and they'd still look like kindergarten by comparison.

The DEA agent stared down at the black water. The ship's lights were off, and they were navigating through the moonless night by sonar. He could barely make out the waves as they broke against the hull.

The training grounds and barracks where he'd spent the past three weeks had been called simply the "Farm," and the man in charge was known only as the "director." The director had come with them on this mission, and had kept all thirty-six men hidden inside the craft until nightfall.

Johnston felt the cold sweat under the stretchy combat suit. Even with the Californian's massive air-conditioning running full tilt, it had been stifling with three dozen men crowded into the cabins below. But at least it had given them all a brief respite from the Farm's grueling training schedule.

He and the others—men who had volunteered to take advanced counterterrorism training at a supersecret government installation—had been awakened in the barracks only hours before. There'd been a quick briefing right there around the bunks, and they'd learned it was time to put their training into action.

They were going after an illegal shipment of M-16s destined for South African radicals. The Farm had an inside man on the deal who had done some work on the guns. The weapons wouldn't function after the first magazine was fired.

But that didn't mean the mission wasn't dangerous. A lot of people could die from the twenty rounds a first mag carried. And there was little doubt that there'd be other weapons on board to escort the shipment.

Down the rail to his left, Johnston heard hushed voices. His eyes strained through the night and made out the form of a man wearing an open sport coat moving in and out among the men at the rail.

At the Farm they had been issued their blacksuits and personal weapons, and then hurried into a transport plane. They had bumped around the seatless floor, finally landing on a runway near a sea. What sea? Johnston didn't know.

All he knew was that they had then boarded three identical yachts and been hustled below.

The DEA man heard the rustling of clothes and sensed a new presence at his side. He turned to see the man in the sport coat—the director. The man grasped the rail. Even in the darkness, he wore black sunglasses over his eyes, and again Johnston wondered who he really was. As always, he wore a neatly pressed gray pin-striped suit that made him look more like a business executive than a cop—or whatever he was. The ever-present stubby end of an unlit cigar extended from a corner of his mouth.

The man's voice was deep and level as he spoke around the cigar. "You ready, Johnston?"

"More than ready, sir."

"Good." He patted him on the shoulder and moved toward the man on the other side of the DEA agent. Johnston heard him make similar small talk, then move on down the line.

Boat lights in the distance were suddenly joined by another set. The Californian's engines hummed suddenly, and Johnston gripped the rail harder to keep his balance as the boat sped forward.

The director's voice came over the loudspeaker. "ETA one minute, gentlemen. Lock and load."

Johnston pulled the bolt back on his carbine, chambering a round as the Californian's pilot hit the spotlight and illuminated a Sabreline 36 and an Oceanis 500 Clipper.

Men armed with Uzis, MAC-10s and other submachine guns covered both decks. Four men on the Sabreline's deck stood near the bow, struggling to lift a heavy wooden crate over the side to the Clipper.

All heads turned toward the light, freezing like deer caught in the high beams of a car.

"United States of America!" Brognola boomed over the loudspeaker. "Throw down your weapons and raise your hands in the air!" At the same time two more spotlights flashed on. Similar orders were barked in Spanish, then a language Johnston didn't recognize as the other two yachts triangulated the gunrunners.

The men on the decks of the Sabreline and Oceanis looked around in shock. Then the shock wore off, and they opened fire.

Charlie Johnston found himself aiming down the barrel of his carbine by rote, squeezing the trigger, firing with far more accuracy and precision than he'd ever had before. Four men fell under his first load of fire, and as the bolt locked open he dropped the magazine and inserted another, timing a breath with the movement in order to function with more speed and smoothness.

Return fire spattered the hull of the Californian as the yacht continued to drift through the waves toward the other two ships. Some of the gunrunners gripped M-16s, and the weapons misfired every few rounds.

The Californian's bow bumped the Sabreline as the DEA agent's second magazine ran dry. He repeated the reloading procedure as he vaulted the rail to the smaller ship, feeling almost like a pirate in an old Errol Flynn movie. At his sides, more of the blacksuits leaped onto the Sabreline while others continued to fire onto the larger Oceanis.

Johnston held the trigger back and sent a steady stream of fire into a large black man wearing an African robe. Another black in a *dashiki* turned his way, an M-16 bouncing in the man's hands as brass rained over the deck. Then, in midburst, the assault rifle misfired. The man looked down at the weapon in horror.

Charlie Johnston's 3-round burst of 9 mm slugs wiped the shock off his face.

More of the enemy fell to the decks of the ships as the men in blacksuits continued their assault. Then, as the last of the enemy fell, the night became quiet again.

BOLAN HOLSTERED the Desert Eagle and stepped back as Gary Manning and Rafael Encizo followed Katz into the room. "Where's David?" he asked.

"Downstairs," Katz answered over his shoulder. "He'll be up in a moment." Phoenix Force took seats around the room.

Katz's graying eyebrows lowered. "Where is Din—" He stopped as the heads of Lindall Dingaan, then the Pendergrasts appeared behind the bed. The Israeli turned in his chair toward Bolan. "You have guests?"

"Herb and Peggy Pendergrast," Herb puffed, struggling to his feet and extending his hand to Katz. "Fort Smith, Arkansas. I've got a Chevy and Toyota dealership there, but we're here to help Mr. Dingaan and you guys any way we can."

The Phoenix Force leader turned toward Bolan as he shook Herb's hand, his face a mask of bewilderment.

"Don't ask," Bolan told Katz. Herb's mood had quickly changed from horror to excitement. He had come to Africa to photograph wild animals and add some excitement to what was probably a pretty dull routine back home. Well, he was getting excitement, all right.

"I'll explain later," the Executioner added. "Right now we've got to get Dingaan out of here. You see the cars in the parking lot when you came in?"

Katz nodded. "And there are men in the lobby who raised my eyebrows," the former Mossad agent said. "And we, theirs, I'm afraid." He paused, then said, "I took the liberty of sending David into one of the shops. A disguise for Mr. Dingaan seemed appropriate.''

Bolan had started to answer when another light knock sounded on the door. He drew the .50 Desert Eagle as he walked to the door and pressed his eye to the hole. David McCarter stood outside, holding a paper bag. Bolan let him in.

McCarter dropped the bag on the bed. "I had to guess at the size," he said, holding up a light cotton dress similar to the one Peggy Pendergrast wore. "It isn't Bond Street by any means, but it ought to pass." Reaching back into the bag, he produced a short gray wig and a shoe box.

Katz turned to the leader of the African Civil Assembly. "I hope it does not offend your manhood, Mr. Dingaan."

"Premature death would offend me far more," he said. "What offends me, sir," he added, "is that you men are all risking your lives to save mine, yet you insist on calling me 'mister.' Please. My name is Lindall." He grabbed the dress and wig from the bed and walked into the bathroom.

Bolan dropped into one of the chairs by the table. He didn't know how the enemy had located them so fast, but it didn't matter. They were here, and sooner or later they'd figure out which room Dingaan was in. The dress would help, but even if the black man could pass as a woman, that presented its own problem.

Five white men walking out of the Hotel President with an elderly black woman? That didn't happen in South Africa, and would draw its own type of attention. And what was he supposed to do with the Pendergrasts?

Herb Pendergrast broke the silence by clearing his throat. "Excuse me?" he said timidly.

Bolan turned to him.

"I'd, uh, like I said, we'd like to help."

"Herb!" Peggy said.

"No, really. You're going to have a time of it getting him out. They'll think something's fishy with a bunch of white men with her... him, I mean."

"What's on your mind, Herb?" Bolan asked.

"Well, I was just thinking. Maybe Peggy and I could walk out with her...him. Make it look like we'd hired her as a guide to take us around the city or something."

Bolan frowned. The idea had merit. Guides for hire were common on the streets and in the hotel lobbies of Johannesburg. But the plan had flaws, as well. It would leave Lindall Dingaan unprotected as he left the hotel, and it would put Herb and Peggy directly in the line of fire.

Well, plans could be altered and refined.

The Executioner stood. His eyes fell on McCarter. Too tall for what he had in mind. He looked to Katz. Maybe. Manning? Right. The Canadian was almost as big as the Executioner.

The door to the bathroom suddenly opened. Lindall Dingaan stepped out in the dress and wig, his wrinkled face glowing impishly. The black leader's hairy calves extended to the floor under the hem of the dress, but unshaven female legs were not an uncommon sight in South Africa. "How do I look?"

"I wouldn't ask you for a date," Manning commented.

"Katz," Bolan said, "I want you and Encizo to go back downstairs. Keep a low profile, but each of you get a dress and wig. Rafael, you'll need to lose the mustache. Get a razor. Then double-time it back here."

Katz frowned, then his thin lips curled up into a smile as what the Executioner had in mind sank in. He turned toward the door.

Dingaan nodded in recognition. He grabbed the Israeli's arm as he passed. "I hope it doesn't offend *your* manhood," he said.

THE PANEL TRUCK PULLED into the Holiday Inn parking lot and came to a halt in front of Room 133. Lyons exited the passenger's seat as Mingo's Town Car and the other Black Charge vehicles pulled into vacant spaces. He walked swiftly to the door, stuck the key in the lock and pushed inside, holding the door as Mingo, three of his gunmen and James, Schwarz, Blancanales, and Jonathan Shomari filed into the room.

Mingo walked directly to the bed and took a seat. Lifting the phone, he got an overseas operator, then turned toward the wall and whispered the number. The man's bodyguards clustered around him as he spoke into the phone in some tribal dialect Lyons couldn't even identify, let alone understand. The men from Stony Man Farm dropped into chairs around the table next to the sliding glass door. Lyons hooked the leg of a chair with his foot, spun it around to face the South Africans and sat.

A few minutes later Mingo hung up, and he and James began to discuss future gun deals. The Phoenix Force warrior had limited experience working undercover, but so far he had played his part admirably. Lyons had done his share of undercover work, both in vice and narcotics, and he knew the traps that faced the clandestine operator at every turn.

In many ways it was like acting, and the LAPD even contracted with some of the acting coaches in Hollywood to help train their officers. But Lyons knew there was at least one major difference between undercover work and acting: if you messed up on stage, the audience might throw tomatoes. If you messed up undercover, the audience threw bullets.

"I will take four thousand more M-16s," Mingo said. "But the price must come down for that many."

James shook his head. "Can't do it, my friend. Like I told you before, you had my rock-bottom deal on this first one."

Mingo didn't answer.

The Phoenix Force warrior stood and walked to the door, his eyebrows lowered in thought. To Mingo, it would look as if he were trying to think of another approach to the bargaining. But Lyons knew what was really going on in the man's head. James was about to get into the real purpose for their dealings with Black Charge.

"Let's leave price alone for a little while," James said. "We'll work it out somehow. What I need to know first, is where do you want the weapons delivered?"

Mingo raised a huge hand and scratched his double chin. "This shipment must go directly to South Africa."

James turned to face the wall. Silence fell over the room as the men waited. Finally Mingo said, "Is there a problem with that?"

The ex-Navy SEAL pivoted back and dropped into a seat near the television. "Mingo," he said, "four thousand M-16s isn't a big order for me, but it isn't small, either. But what it damn sure is, is enough to land me behind bars for a good twenty years." He folded his hands on his lap and looked directly into the big African's eyes. "What it amounts to is, you've checked me out. You know Edmond Nxumalo is on the level. But for all I know, you could be South Africa's Dirty Harry."

Mingo frowned.

"A cop," one of his men said.

The big man's face broke into a grin. "If I were the police, why would I not have arrested you during the gun deal this evening?"

"Because ten dozen shooters are peanuts," James replied. "You could have been setting me up for the kill." He leaned forward as he continued to stare at the giant on the bed. "I'll level with you. What's really bothering me is that I don't think there are one thousand men in the whole Black Charge outfit. So why do you want that many guns?"

Lyons watched Mingo continue to scratch the fat under his chin. The big man closed his eyes as if trying to decide just how much he should reveal. Finally the eyes opened, and Mingo said, "You are correct. We do not have that many men. But weapons wear out, malfunction and must be replaced."

James sat back in his chair and smiled. "That's a crock of shit and you know it," he said. "I figure with four thousand 16s, and the number of Black Chargers you've really got, each man would have about ten apiece."

Mingo's face tightened. Lyons held his breath, his hand moving casually toward the Colt Python beneath his jacket.

The big man stood up, pacing to the door in thought. After a long silence he turned around and said, "We are going to arm the tribes. Weapons and ammunition is being provided to the Boers, and we must do the same so our people can protect themselves."

"That's a little hard to buy, too," James said. "Who is it arming the Boers?"

Again Lyons felt his breathing halt. The moment of truth had arrived. Everything James and Able Team had done so far, all the effort they had put into climbing the Black Charge ladder to Mingo and then gaining his confidence, had led to this one simple question.

"I don't know."

James didn't give up. "You've got to have some idea."

Mingo studied the Phoenix Force warrior. "Why are you so interested?"

"Because I'm trying to find out if you're on the level. Or with the FBI or BATF or CIA or some South African agency, that's why."

Mingo walked back to the bed and sat down. "We suspect it is some European business interest. Rumors are all we have."

Lyons sighed. All that effort and Mingo couldn't give them more than they already knew.

James glanced at Lyons, then turned back to Mingo. "What price are you willing to pay for the M-16s?" he asked.

"One hundred dollars per weapon," Mingo said.

"Make it one-twenty and you've got a deal."

"One-ten."

"Sold," James said, and stood up again. "I'll make some phone calls tonight and contact you in the morning. You heading back to the Big Easy?"

Mingo nodded. He stood and walked out the door. He glanced at Shomari, then his men followed him out of the room.

James locked the door behind them, then turned to the men of Able Team. He blew air through his tight lips in disgust.

Lyons started to speak, but as he opened his mouth, an explosion sounded in the parking lot. Automatic submachine-gun fire followed the blast, and screams of agony drifted eerily into the motel room.

The former cop raced across the room, his right hand jerking the Python from leather as his left ripped open the door. Pressing his back against the wall, he stuck his head around the corner.

The Lincoln was a crackling inferno of fire, flames dancing from under the hood and through the shattered windows and windshield. As Lyons watched, one of the back doors opened, and a giant, shrieking shape emerged, engulfed in flame.

Mingo twirled through the parking lot like a comet entering the atmosphere.

The autofire resumed, and Lyons turned his eyes to the street where four men wearing khaki uniforms stood behind a Pontiac Grand Prix. Submachine guns danced in their hands, the bullets streaking from the barrels into the bodies of the Black Charge men who had jumped out of the other cars.

Still howling in torment, Mingo continued to spin through the parking lot. Then a burst of autofire pounded his flaming form, and the giant whirled one final time before falling to the asphalt.

The men in the street continued to fire, downing the Black Charge men in a barrage of bullets as Lyons, followed by the other men from Stony Man Farm and Jonathan Shomari, raced out of the room. A burst of fire flew past the ex-cop's head and he heard a dull grunt.

Turning, he saw Jonathan Shomari stare wild-eyed at the night sky, then collapse to the ground.

The men in the khaki uniforms ducked into the Pontiac and took off as Lyons raised the .357 Magnum to eye level and pumped off two rounds at a front tire. The car swerved, and the bullets drilled harmlessly through the front fender.

"The panel truck!" the Able Team leader shouted. He raced to the passenger's door as James and Blancanales jumped into the back and Schwarz slid behind the wheel.

Lyons kept his eyes on the Pontiac as he opened the door. A khaki arm wearing a red band shot through the back window as it raced under a streetlight. A voice screamed out something in the night.

The Able Team leader jumped into the panel truck as Schwarz backed it away from the door. He had seen the insignia on the armband and the stiff-armed salute. And while the man's words had been impossible to understand, Lyons knew what they had to have been.

Sieg Heil!

Mingo hadn't lied about the problems with the American Nazi Party.

The red armband had sported a bold black swastika.

CHAPTER SEVEN

The key turning in the lock drew everyone's attention to the door. A moment later it opened, and David McCarter walked into the room. "The back's covered," he said. "Three men in the alley are posing as winos."

"You sure they aren't for real?" Bolan asked.

The Briton nodded. "One of them forgot to wash off his after-shave."

"Did it seem like they knew we were here, or more like a routine surveillance?"

"Hard to tell. But my guess is routine. Like maybe they've got men stationed at hotels all over the city just in case Dingaan shows up."

The Executioner frowned. That meant one hell of a lot of men. Were there really that many Recces who'd gone over to the other side?

McCarter read his mind. "I don't think they were GI. Just a feeling. Something about the way they moved, maybe. My guess is Boer Resistance."

Jameson stood up and paced to the wall. Turning back, he said, "Maybe both. The BRM and traitors are working together, is my guess."

The Executioner nodded, then his mind returned to the plan he'd been formulating when he sent McCarter to scout out the hotel. If the Briton was right, and the men watching the hotel were there only as a precaution, it would make things easier. The Recces, or Boers, or whoever they were wouldn't be quite as alert as if they had a positive make on the hotel.

The warrior knew it still wouldn't be a cakewalk getting Dingaan out of the building. If the alley door was covered, that meant all the exits would be. And that in turn meant that he and Phoenix Force might as well get Dingaan out of the hotel by going straight through the lion's mouth.

Bolan glanced at Rafael Encizo and Yakov Katzenelenbogen as they adjusted their short brown wigs. They looked like something out of a bad female-impersonation act, and the Executioner's frown deepened. Both men had shaved closely, and Peggy Pendergrast had applied a thick layer of makeup over the shadows. But that did little to erase the clearly masculine lines of their features.

Gary Manning coughed from his seat on the bed, and Bolan turned his way. The big Canadian shook his head. "They aren't going to fool anybody who looks very close."

"Manning's right," Bolan said, standing up.

"Herb," he said as Pendergrast exited the bathroom, "what we need is a diversion. Think you might be up to it?"

Pendergrast's eyes gleamed as he tossed the towel back in the bathroom. "Peggy and I were in lots of little theater productions back home in Fort Smith," he said. "That's where we met, matter a fact. Why, I even played—"

Bolan raised a hand. "You've convinced me. Something simple. A loud argument with someone." He turned back to the rest of the men in the room.

"Okay. David, you and Gary take point. If anything seems suspicious, turn around and stop us before we hit the lobby door. You got it?"

The Briton and Canadian both nodded.

Bolan turned to Katz, Encizo and Peggy. "Peggy," he said to the woman, "are you sure you want to go through with this?"

Peggy Pendergrast glanced nervously at her husband, then a new determination entered her eyes. "Yes. Herb and I both want to help."

"Then you, Katz and Rafael will take Dingaan next. Peggy, you've done some acting. I want you to speak in a soft voice from the time you enter the lobby until you hit the front door. Just simple conversation with your girlfriends is what I want it to look like."

Peggy nodded her understanding.

The Executioner's gaze fell on Dingaan, who had taken a seat at the table after changing into the dress. "Stay in the middle of the group," he ordered. "Let the others block the view. And keep quiet. Your voice isn't only recognizable as male, it's been heard on news broadcasts enough to be just recognizable."

Dingaan smiled, then nodded.

"Jameson and I'll bring up the rear. Remember, if it looks bad before Dingaan hits the lobby, we abort and come back here. But once he's through the door, there's no turning back." He paused and drew in a breath. "What are you guys driving?"

"Chevy Nova we picked up at the Boer farm," Katz said over his shoulder as Peggy finished with his wig. "Parked in a lot across the street. Front."

"Good. David, stay in the lobby until we've left, then bring up the rear. Gary, go on out and get the

Chevy over to the Saturn. I'll take Dingaan, Rafael and Katz in the Saturn. Jameson and the others will slip in with you."

"How about Peggy and me?" Herb Pendergrast asked.

"If everything goes smoothly," he said, "you just come back into the hotel. If not, we'll take you with us." He paused. "Ready?"

Everyone stood up.

McCarter opened the door. "Looks clear," he whispered. He, Manning, and Pendergrast proceeded to the lobby while the others waited.

The Executioner counted off thirty seconds in his head, then nodded to Katz. The Israeli led the way down the steps with Peggy on his arm. Lindall Dingaan walked a half step behind the duo with Encizo almost crushing into his back.

Bolan counted another thirty, then he and Jameson descended the stairs. They pushed through the door to the lobby in time to hear a loud Southern accent say "This is what you people call *room service?*"

Herb stood in front of the front desk banging his fist down on the tabletop. "Goddammit, I called down over an hour ago. All I asked for was one damn grilled cheese sandwich! Is that so hard?"

The Executioner's eyes scanned the room. McCarter stood near the front entrance holding a newspaper. Manning was watching the tropical fish in the lobby's huge aquarium, and in turn watching the lobby in the reflection. Two men and a woman sat on a couch next to the fireplace. Two more men stood midway in the lobby. A lone hunter wearing a light raincoat over his khakis leaned against one of the columns supporting the ceiling.

All of their heads had turned toward Herb.

Any, or all, could be the enemy.

Peggy's hands moved animatedly in front of her as she and Katz led Dingaan and Encizo toward the door. Bolan and Jameson followed ten paces behind as Herb Pendergrast continued his tirade at the confused desk clerk.

"And another thing, goddammit—"

Peggy, Katz, Dingaan and Encizo drifted across the lobby as if invisible.

They were two steps from the door when it happened.

A tour of elderly people, cameras swaying around their necks, their arms laden with packages, hit the entrance like a herd of water buffalo. A man wearing an orange jumpsuit and a pukka-shell choker necklace led the way into the lobby. "Come on, Pat, hurry!" he said around a thin cigar in his mouth. He stopped suddenly and turned, grasping the arm of a woman behind him. "We've got to change and—"

The woman stopped, trying to jerk her arm free. "Bill!" she said. Then another couple crashed into her back and knocked her forward. She flew headfirst into Peggy Pendergrast, who in turn fell backward, taking Lindall Dingaan with her to the floor.

Bolan's hand shot under his coat as Dingaan's wig went skittering across the lobby floor.

"Pat! Look!" the man in the orange jumpsuit yelled as he fumbled for the camera around his neck. "Look! Why, it's Lindall Din—"

The words were cut off by the roar of a semiautomatic pistol. A large jagged hole appeared in the tile next to Dingaan's head.

Bolan jerked the .50 Desert Eagle free of leather as his eyes turned toward the fireplace. The two men and the woman seated on the couch had risen to their feet. One of the men held a SIG-Sauer P-220 in both fists, fighting the recoil and preparing to fire again. The woman had drawn a Glock 17L from her purse and was racking the slide. The third man had a Heckler & Koch P-7 M-13 halfway out of his pants.

The Executioner fired before the man with the P-220 could trigger his follow-up shot. The lone boom of the big .50 sent the gun tumbling from the man's fingers as the body flew back against the fireplace. Out of the corner of his eye, Bolan saw Jameson's Z-88 buck twice. Both rounds drilled through the woman's chest and drove her to the floor. A pair of 9 mm rounds fired from the aquarium area entered the third gunner's chest. The man staggered back, squeezing the trigger once.

The round flew toward Manning, shattering the aquarium, spilling water and fish across the big Canadian's feet.

High-pitched screams erupted from the terrified people in the tour group. The Executioner turned his gun toward the man in hunting clothes, standing against the column in the center of the room.

The man threw up his hands, his face a mask of fear, surprise and confusion.

Katz and Encizo had already pulled Peggy and Dingaan to their feet and were fighting their way through the elderly tour group toward the door. A flash of dull steel caught the Executioner's eye, and his head swiveled toward the front desk.

Two men in suits had appeared from a side entrance. One pulled a subgun from an open briefcase as the other dropped the sights of a Z-88 on Dingaan.

The Executioner squeezed the trigger twice, the first round catching the subgunner in the shoulder and spinning him into Herb Pendergrast against the desk. The man from Arkansas fell to the ground as Bolan fired again, this round boring through the killer's forehead and dropping him like a stone. The warrior turned back to his initial target and took him out of play with a shot that sprawled the gunner across the desk.

Bolan scanned the floor and saw Herb Pendergrast crouching at the end of the desk, safe from the line of fire. He turned toward the front entrance, where McCarter, Encizo, Peggy and Dingaan had already disappeared.

"Let's go!" he shouted to Jameson and Manning as he sprinted toward the front steps of the hotel.

A silhouette in pants, and four more in skirts, could be seen hurrying down the sidewalk to Bolan's right as he bounded down the concrete steps in front of the hotel. To his left he heard more running feet and turned in time to see a pair of men wearing Recce fatigues raise Armscor submachine guns.

The Executioner squeezed the trigger twice, sending a round into each man. Just to his rear, he heard Manning's Beretta and Jameson's Z-88 join the attack.

Bolan and Jameson cut across the grass as Manning took off across the street toward the Chevrolet.

The Executioner heard more gunfire from the parking lot, then the sound of the Chevy's revving engine. He and Jameson caught up to the others a block later as they rounded the corner in front of the Saturn.

Manning screeched the Chevy to a halt next to the Saturn as Bolan slipped behind the wheel. With Dingaan on the back floorboards and Encizo and Katz piled on top of him, he threw the car into Drive, then turned to McCarter as the Briton opened the Chevy's passenger door.

"Take Peggy with you," Bolan ordered. "We'll meet at the zoological gardens. Half an hour. We'll make arrangements for her to get back then, after the heat's died down."

McCarter nodded and shoved the woman into the car.

The tires of the Saturn squealed as the Executioner pulled away from the hotel and started down the street. He glanced into the rearview mirror.

Except for the Chevy making a U-turn, the street was clear. For the moment they were safe.

But for how long? Bolan wondered. Every step he took proved to him that the South African government was riddled with spies and traitors. While he knew the majority of the Recces had to be loyal, they had been so heavily infiltrated that prudence dictated that he treat each man as a potential Benedict Arnold.

The Executioner turned the corner and checked the mirror again, then slowed the Saturn to the speed limit. He had to get Dingaan to safety, to a place where he would be surrounded by people who could be trusted. And in the entire country of South Africa, the warrior could think of only one place remaining that might fit that bill.

The Zulus themselves. If he could get Lindall Dingaan to his Zulu people, they could hide him for weeks if necessary.

Again Bolan glanced into the mirror. Yes, once there, Dingaan would be safe.

The trick would be getting him there.

CARL LYONS PULLED the panel truck out of the Holiday Inn parking lot and into the street. Two blocks ahead he saw the Pontiac slow as it neared the access ramp leading to the South Dixie Highway.

The big ex-LAPD cop trod the accelerator, doing his best to coax some torque out of the sluggish vehicle. Like guns, or knives or clothes for that matter, no one auto could meet every challenge that came up during a mission, and he had chosen the truck in order to transport the M-16s, little knowing it might eventually be needed for a high-speed chase.

The Nazis' Pontiac hit the ramp and started upward, northbound toward Miami. Lyons slowed the truck. So far, he didn't think the enemy gunners knew they were being followed. There had been many vehicles in the parking lot during the attack, so the truck didn't stand out.

But the moment the driver spotted the panel truck, the Pontiac would race away from the slower vehicle.

Lyons came to the top of the ramp and saw the Pontiac a quarter of a mile ahead, in the slow lane. He stood on the gas again, and the panel truck chugged forward.

"We'll never catch them in this thing, Ironman," Schwarz said, voicing the Able Team leader's thoughts. He reached for the window handle. "Want me to try a shot?"

Lyons considered it. He had pulled within ten car-lengths now, an easy shot on the ground, but damn tricky with a moving target. If he could inch closer without getting spotted . . . maybe.

A Toyota Celica suddenly cut in front of the truck, forcing Lyons to hit the brakes and swerve. No, the traffic weaving in and out of the lanes would prevent shooting. A blown tire in the Nazi car could easily result in a multicar pileup that took the lives of innocent people.

Unless they were fired upon, making it imperative that they protect the other cars with return fire, Able Team would keep a low profile.

Lyons drove on, creeping up on the Pontiac. He pulled around a slow-moving Volkswagen Rabbit convertible full of teenage girls, then cut back into the slow lane behind an electric blue Chevy Corvette directly to the rear of the Pontiac.

The Nazi vehicle tooled steadily down the highway at sixty-five miles per hour.

"So far, so good," Blancanales said from the rear of the truck.

A moment later the Corvette pulled out of the slow lane and skirted around the Pontiac. Lyons jerked his foot off the accelerator. Too late. He saw the eyes of the man driving the Nazi car turn toward the side mirror. The Pontiac suddenly sped up.

"They've made us," Lyons growled as a gun barrel extended out the rear window of the Pontiac. A hardman leaned his torso out, twisting toward the oncoming panel truck. He fired a quick burst of 9 mm rounds that sailed harmlessly to the side of the truck as Lyons swerved onto the shoulder, then floored the accelerator and moved back to the middle of the highway.

Schwarz hung out the passenger's-side window. He leveled his Beretta on the hood and returned fire, popping a steady sequence of semiauto parabellums after the Pontiac. The gunner in the Pontiac fired one more quick burst, then the car rushed forward out of range.

Blancanales and James had leaned forward between the seats. "Wish we had that," James said, pointing toward the Corvette as it raced down the exit ramp toward a Ramada Inn.

Lyons made his decision in a heartbeat. He hit the brakes, swerving across two lanes amid a symphony of honking horns and screeching tires. He caught the Corvette as it crossed the frontage road in front of the motel, then followed it up the drive.

Schwarz turned to Blancanales. "Ask, and ye shall receive."

The Able Team leader turned back to the highway. The Pontiac had disappeared in the distance. "There isn't room for all of us," he said as they neared the brick archway in front of the office. "Gadgets, you and James. Pol and I will catch up to you as soon as we can."

Schwarz and James piled out of the panel truck as the Corvette rolled to a stop in front of the Ramada office. Schwarz raced around the trunk of the bright blue sports car as the driver, a young man in his early twenties, opened the door and swung his legs out.

Lyons backed up and waited, not wanting to block Gadgets's way to the access ramp. He watched Schwarz transfer his briefcase to the hand holding his equipment bag and pull the Corvette's door the rest of the way open. "Welcome to the Ramada Inn," he heard Gadgets say through his open window. As the driver rose to his feet, Able Team's electronics specialist reached out and tore the keys from his hand. "We'll park it for you."

On the other side of the vehicle, Calvin James gripped his own gear bag with one hand and pulled a slim young woman wearing a ribbed tank top and short floral skirt to her feet with the other. She looked confused. "I'll just wait in the car if it's all—"

"Sorry, ma'am," James said. "Violation of motel policy." He nudged her aside and jumped in as Gadgets threw his baggage into the back seat and slid behind the wheel.

A moment later the Corvette's tires screamed in agony as Schwarz pulled out of the parking lot onto the ramp.

The man and the woman stood and watched, their mouths hanging open.

Lyons pulled the panel truck around the gaping couple and followed.

SCHWARZ KEPT the Corvette's transmission in second as he darted up the ramp. The mighty engine howled for relief, then quieted as he shoved the stick into third. They passed the Yield sign and crossed onto the South Dixie Highway.

A moment later the Able Team electronics wizard shifted into fourth and brought the speeding sports car close to ninety miles per hour. By the time he hit fifth, the vehicle was doing a neat one hundred twenty toward Coconut Grove.

"Remind me to pick up one of these babies next payday," James said, grinning.

"Dream on, public servant."

They whizzed past a sign announcing University Drive and the University of Miami. Then suddenly the rearview mirror lit up in blue-and-red light. "Oh-oh," James said.

Schwarz nodded. "We can outrun him, no problem," he said. "But—"

"—We can't outrun his radar," James finished for him.

"Right. Grab the briefcase."

James twisted over the back seat and snatched the attaché from the tiny seat. He flipped the clasps, opened the lid and saw a portable programmable police radio. He ripped the cigarette lighter from the dash, plugged in the adapter and heard the buzz and whir of airwaves.

The police siren wailed.

"There's a book," Schwarz said, keeping one eye on the road ahead, the other on the flashing lights in the rearview mirror. "Look in the pocket in the lid."

James's hand shot inside the elastic fabric and came out holding a small pamphlet.

"Find Florida, then, uh, Dade County, I guess. Yeah. They'll have radio access to whatever department this guy's from."

The Phoenix Force warrior thumbed through the pamphlet. He found the Dade County police as another cop car passed in the southbound lane, flipped its lights and began cutting a U-turn across the median.

"Now," Gadgets instructed, "just punch in the frequency number."

James did. A variety of garbled cop-speak sounded through the receiver as the scanner skimmed across the frequencies. James zeroed the scanner in on Dade County, pulled the receiver from the clip inside the briefcase and held it to his lips as a third police car raced up a side ramp to join the chase.

Who should he be? By now half of the cops in Dade County would be headed their way. He needed a department and a story. Quick.

"DEA nine-eleven, Dade County police," the Phoenix Force man said into the radio. "DEA, Dade County."

"Come in DEA," a female voice came back.

"Dade County, be advised. Blue Corvette traveling at a high rate of speed on South Dixie Highway is one of ours. It's a ten-six in pursuit. Request you pull all units off."

There was a pause on the other end of the line, then a gruff man's voice replaced the woman's. "DEA, ten-nine identification."

James took a deep breath. They weren't buying it. They intended to check out his story through channels before giving up the chase. "DEA nine-eleven, Dade County."

"Stand by." The radio scratched again.

Schwarz continued to monitor the rearview mirror. "We're outrunning them," he said, "but they aren't backing off. It won't be long until they set up a roadblock."

James took another deep breath, then keyed the mike again. "DEA nine-eleven, Dade County."

The same sullen voice came back. "Stand by, nine-eleven."

"All right, listen to this," James said into the mike, suddenly making the surly voice on the other end sound like Mary Poppins. "This is DEA nine-eleven, we're in undercover pursuit of a vehicle loaded with coke, and your lights and sirens are screwing things up. Is that clear enough?"

The radio didn't answer.

James thumbed the mike again. "Let me put it to you another way, Dade County. Get your men off our tail or we'll launch an investigation to find out just who's responsible for screwing this deal up. You got that?"

There was another long silence, then the gruff voice came back. "All units northbound on South Dixie Highway, ten-twenty-two. Repeat, ten-twenty-two all units."

The flashing red-and-blue lights behind them suddenly disappeared.

James replaced the microphone but kept the briefcase open in his lap, just in case. They crossed the line into Coconut Grove, and he saw Schwarz grinning behind the wheel. "Spectacular," the Able Team man said.

"Hey. I'm good, but it wasn't that good."

"I didn't mean you," Schwarz replied. He nodded toward the windshield as he slowed the Corvette.

James looked ahead to see the taillights of the Pontiac.

The vehicle left the highway and started down the ramp toward Leon Boulevard.

"YES, SIR, the president has returned to the office," the secretary said. "May I tell him who is calling?"

"Pollock," Bolan said.

"Please hold."

The warrior heard a click, then the pleasant strains of a Strauss waltz filled his ears.

The Executioner looked out through the glass of the telephone booth. The lines of Johannesburg's famed zoological gardens could barely be seen in the early-morning darkness. He turned toward the street. The Saturn and Phoenix Force's appropriated Chevy Nova were parked on the street. He could see the movements inside the Saturn as Encizo, Katz and Dingaan changed clothes.

A moment later Van Peebles was on the line. "Colonel Pollock. I have just received word of the assassination attempts at the safehouse and hotel. There is a traitor in our—"

"Midst," the Executioner interrupted. "I hate to be the one to break the news, Mr. President, but there's more than one. Outside of a handful of men, most of them with me right now, I don't know who I can trust."

There was a long pause on the other end, then Van Peebles said, "Yes, I understand. Just tell me where you are. I will send a detachment of officers to you immediately."

"With all due respect," Bolan said, "I haven't fared well with your commandos so far. I don't want more of your soldiers. What I want is a plane and pilot. I'll handle things from there.''

Van Peebles cleared his throat. ''Surely you realize I can't allow you to just—''

Bolan broke in again. ''Fine. Then I'll just drop Dingaan off on your doorstep and catch the next flight back to the states.'' His voice grew lower. ''Look, it's my way or no way. That was the agreement from the beginning.''

Van Peebles paused for a moment. ''All right,'' the South African president finally said. ''There is a small airport on the east side of the city. Mal Adriaan. Do you know it?''

''No.''

''Dingaan will. It is civilian, but the military uses it, as well. I will have a plane ready when you arrive.''

''Okay. I want a pilot, too.''

''You'll have one. What is your destination?''

Bolan hung up. The South African government had more leaks than a net, and what Van Peebles didn't know he couldn't inadvertently let out. Lifting the receiver again, the Executioner tapped in the number for Stony Man Farm and waited while the complex system to prevent tracing went into effect. He glanced toward the cars again, and saw Katz get out of the Nova, lean against the door and light a cigarette. A minute later, Barbara Price picked up the line.

''Barb, it's Striker.'' Quickly the Executioner ran down what he had in mind in order to ensure Dingaan's safety.

''You say Katz is with you now?'' Price asked.

''That's affirmative.''

"Put him on. Aaron's almost one hundred percent sure he's located the money source. Ijsselmeer, Inc. A gold-and-diamond cartel out of Amsterdam. The CEO's a man named Direk Brouer. Ring a bell?"

"Uh-uh."

"He doesn't have a record, but a secret Interpol file is interesting. They know he's been involved in several scams that involved corporate use of mercenaries."

Bolan looked back at the Chevy and saw Katz watching him. He motioned the Israeli forward.

The warrior stepped outside and handed the Israeli the receiver. "Price," he said simply, and moved on to the cars.

Bolan leaned down and rested an arm on the window. He stuck the other inside the car and took the woman's hand. "Peggy, we can't thank you enough. Tell Herb for us."

Peggy nodded excitedly. "My pleasure. I'll be the belle of the bridge club when we get back to Fort Smith."

Bolan turned as footsteps padded up the sidewalk behind him. "We're off to the Netherlands," Katz told him.

"So I heard."

"Want us to follow you out to the airport first?"

Bolan hesitated. The airport was also used by the military, Van Peebles had said. So far, the only assassination attempts had gone down in places isolated from the South African government. The airport should be safe. There'd be too many witnesses. "No. Go on. If there's another attempt, it won't be at the airport."

Katz nodded, circled the Saturn and got into the Chevy. Encizo got out and followed. Bolan got behind the wheel of the Saturn with Jameson and Dingaan still in the back seat. He pulled the car away from the curb and started down the street.

The skyline of Johannesburg reminded Bolan of the skyscrapers of New York City as he followed Dingaan's directions toward Mal Adriaan Airport. They drove first to the east edge of town, then the black South African leader pointed him north.

Darkness had given way to morning light when the sign announcing Mal Adriaan caused Bolan to turn again. He glided through the unguarded entrance gate and drove slowly toward the lone runway past the terminal.

The Executioner's hand moved automatically to the .50 Desert Eagle on his hip when he saw the contingent of Recces surrounding the Beechcraft Baron. Drawing the weapon, he rested it on his lap as the Saturn slowed to a crawl. "Get ready," he told Jameson.

"I think we're safe. See the lieutenant in charge?"

Bolan's gaze locked on to the only soldier with bars on his shoulders. He frowned. The man looked familiar.

"He's my brother," Jameson explained.

The Executioner returned the Desert Eagle to its holster, but his hand stayed on the grips as he came to a halt.

"Colonel Pollock," Lieutenant Jameson said as he hurried up to the window. "My brother was at the safehouse. Have you any idea if..." His voice trailed off as his eyes moved to the back seat. The Executioner saw relief wash over the man's face.

"Want to kiss me, *sir?*" the sergeant asked his brother.

"Not in a million years," the grinning lieutenant said as he opened Bolan's door.

The warrior stepped out of the Saturn. He could hear the Beechcraft's engines warming up as he opened the back door for Dingaan. He helped the black leader to his feet and turned to Lieutenant Jameson. "You got a pilot ready?"

"Behind the controls. But I didn't know who you were bringing with you when I gave out the assignment, Colonel. My brother can fly this bird, too. If you'd rather—"

"I would," Bolan said without hesitation. The Recce sergeant had proved his loyalty over and over in the past twelve hours. Having him fly the Baron would mean one less uncertainty the Executioner would have to put up with.

Bolan took Dingaan's arm and ushered him toward the plane. They boarded with Jameson as the sergeant's brother explained the change to the pilot. The man nodded and stepped down.

Less than a minute later the Beechcraft Baron left the runway and climbed into the air.

Jameson dipped a wing, and they headed south toward Swaziland, the lights of the skyscrapers gradually fading into the distance. Below they saw the thick, dark jungle for which Africa was famous.

The aircraft continued to gain altitude, then leveled off. Bolan watched the snowy white clouds drift peacefully across the sky, then turned to Dingaan in the seat behind him. "Better see if you can catch forty winks, Mr. Dingaan," he said. "Who knows when we'll get another chance."

"Thank you, I will. *If* you will call me Lindall."

"You got it, Lindall." Bolan turned back to face the sky, settled into his seat and closed his eyes.

The Executioner was just drifting off when Jameson's voice roused him back to consciousness. "We've got a problem...."

Bolan opened his eyes. Ahead he saw a tiny speck coming their way in the sky. As it grew larger, the lines of a Saab 37 Viggen became clear.

"He's coming right down our throat," Jameson said. He lifted the microphone to his mouth, but before he could speak the Saab's KCA 30 mm gun erupted.

Jameson froze in shock as a round struck the plane. The Beechcraft jerked forward, throwing Bolan back against the seat. Then the windshield in front of him shattered, sending a storm of fragmented glass flying through the plane like razor-edged hail.

Bolan looked at Jameson as the plane leveled off.

The Recce sergeant's eyes stared ahead, wild and covered with the dull film of death. A crater the size of a softball had opened in his chest, and blood spurted onto the control panel.

Bolan dived for the stick.

Then another round struck the Beechcraft. The Executioner fought for control as the plane started down. Through the windshield, he saw the blue sky mixed with white clouds twirl out of control. Then the blue gave way to the overpowering color of green.

Then all went black.

CHAPTER EIGHT

Schwarz slowed the Corvette, letting the Pontiac get all the way down the ramp before stomping the foot feed and leaving the highway. He and James reached Ponce de Leon Boulevard just in time to see the Nazi car turn left.

The electronics man grabbed the portable radio, programmed in Able Team's intraunit frequency and lifted the mike to his lips. "Able Three to One," he said. "Got your ears on, Ironman?"

"One to Three," Lyons came back. "Ten-four."

"We've caught up to them in Coconut Grove. Take the Leon Boulevard exit, then a left." He paused, looking into the rearview mirror even though he knew the sluggish panel truck would still be miles behind. "How far back are you?"

There was another pause, and Schwarz could almost see the Able Team leader squinting through the darkness, trying to read a road sign, a mile marker, anything that would give him a fix on his position. "Four to five miles, best I can make out," Lyons replied. "Keep them in sight, Gadgets. But don't engage until we get there."

"Affirmative. We'll keep you updated." He handed the mike to James and turned left after the Pontiac.

The Nazis had slowed to the speed limit, and now drove causally past Douglas Park, crossed Twenty-second Street and Tanami Trail, then turned right on Flagler. Schwarz kept the Corvette two blocks behind, gunning the big engine and racing through the intersection when a yellow light threatened to cut them off at Seventeenth Avenue.

James kept Lyons and Blancanales updated, and by the time they passed the Orange Bowl the lethargic panel truck was less than a mile behind. But when they reached the eastern entrance to Miami Stadium, the Pontiac suddenly sped forward, running a red light and racing toward Thirty-sixth.

"They've made us again," James said into the microphone as Schwarz squealed the Corvette's tires through the light and around the honking motorists.

"Drop back," Lyons said. "Don't—"

James cut him off with the button. "No way, Ironman. We'll lose them in all this traffic. There's more side streets here than ants at a picnic." He dropped the microphone back into the briefcase, set it on the console and twisted over the back seat, opening his equipment bag. Pulling out a leather pistol case, he unzipped it and removed a blue steel handgun with a fourteen-inch octagonal vented barrel.

Schwarz followed the speeding Pontiac onto Thirty-sixth Street. "What the hell is that?" he asked as they raced past the Jai-Alai Fronton.

"Thompson," James said. "Center Contender."

"Oh, hell," Schwarz said. "Wish I'd brought my ear protectors."

James grinned as he rolled down the window. He braced his left foot against the floorboard, kneeling on the seat with his other knee and strapping his calf down under the seat belt. Then, leaning out the window to the waist, he dropped the sights on the Pontiac's right rear tire.

No, a blowout there would send the Nazi car fishtailing into the oncoming traffic. He glanced to his right. They were passing a row of small businesses. Pedestrians lined the street.

Two submachine guns extended from the rear of the Pontiac, and for the first time they were close enough for James to ID under the streetlights—9 mm Erma-Werke MP-40s/IIs. Vintage, late 1943.

Nazis were taking their heritage seriously.

The two subguns fired simultaneously, sending sprays of 9 mm parabellums toward the Corvette. Schwarz twisted the wheel to the right, and James felt the seat belt tear into the back of his calf.

They breezed under a sign, announcing Miami International Airport in half a mile. James looked to the right. Ahead he saw two vacant lots. If he could time it right, so the big round hit the tire just before they reached the fields, and if he didn't miss...

The 9 mm volleys continued to fly at the Corvette. A round struck the roof of the car a foot from James's chest. Another whizzed past his head. On the programmable radio inside, the Phoenix Force warrior heard Carl Lyons's frantic voice. "Dammit, Gadgets! James! Answer!"

The vacant lots loomed on the right. Ignoring the bullets flying past his head, James stretched farther and dropped the Thompson's front sight on the left rear tire of the Pontiac. He started to squeeze, but a bump in the road threw the barrel high and wide.

James took a deep breath and struggled to get the Center Contender back on target. A swerve by

Schwarz ruined his sighting again. The hot burn of lactic acid buildup started in his arms and shoulders as he continued to hold the heavy weapon at arm's length.

Then, just as they reached the first vacant lot, the Thompson's front sight fell on the rubber. James jerked the trigger before the barrel could move again and felt the mighty rifle round drive his arms back and up.

Rubber exploded through the air. A flopping piece of treaded white wall flew up and over the roof of the Corvette. The Pontiac jerked to the right, jumped the curb and began spinning 360-degree circles through the loose dirt and grass.

Schwarz hit the brakes, squealing around a car in front of the Pontiac, then cut a sharp turn into the driveway that led into the lot.

James dropped the Thompson on the seat. He drew his Beretta 92 with one hand and grabbed the microphone with the other. "Thirty-sixth Street past the Fronton," he said into the radio. "Just before the airport." He dropped the mike and charged out of the car into a cloud of dust as Schwarz skidded to a halt.

A khaki-clad man stumbled out of the Pontiac, choking for air in the dust storm. He saw James and raised the MP-40 in his arms.

The Phoenix Force warrior popped off two rounds, hitting the Nazi first in the face, then the throat as his head flew back to expose the neck. The man jerked back against the car, then slithered to the ground.

Two more of the Nazis burst from the vehicle, MP-40s blazing in their hands. In his peripheral vision, James saw Schwarz jump from the Corvette, level his own Beretta on a tall blonde and stroke the trigger in two quick double taps. The first duo of rounds caught the Aryan supremacist in the left shoulder, spinning him around. Schwarz's second assault took off the back of the man's head.

James swung his weapon toward a chubby man with his tie tucked into the front of his uniform as Schwarz zeroed in on the Nazi's companion. Both enemy gunners were punched to the ground by tribursts of 9 mm parabellums.

The Stony Man warriors advanced cautiously toward the Pontiac. The driver sat in his seat, head resting on the steering wheel, turned away.

Excited screams reached them from up the street, and the two men glanced up to see several people moving cautiously toward the lots.

Tires screeched as James and Schwarz reached the Pontiac. The ex-SEAL looked over to see the panel truck jump the curb. He waved Lyons to stop, then reached down to grasp the driver by the hair and raise his face.

Blood streamed from the man's forehead onto the collar of his khaki shirt. James jabbed a finger into his neck.

The pulse was fast and weak, but there.

James grabbed the unconscious Nazi under the armpits and hauled him out of the car. Schwarz picked up the man's ankles, and they carried him to the truck.

Blancanales had the side door open by the time they got there. Tossing the man through the hole, they raced back to the Corvette, retrieved the radio and other gear, then hurried back to the truck as a police siren sounded a few blocks away.

The man in the Nazi uniform began to regain consciousness as Lyons pulled the panel truck away from the curb. "Cuff him," the ex-cop said. "We'll find some nice quiet place and see what he has to say." He turned around briefly, looking at Calvin James. "Cal, you've done a hell of a job. But with Shomari dead, I'm afraid Katz would skin me alive if I kept you any longer. But if you ever want to change units..."

"Thanks. I guess I better get over to Amsterdam and give them a hand. No telling what might happen to those boys without me looking after them."

The men of Able Team laughed. Schwarz pulled a plastic Flex-Cuff from his pocket, rolled the Nazi to his side and wrapped the strip around the man's wrists. "You know, James," he said as they started away from the oncoming sirens. "You and I work pretty well together. Maybe we ought to just dump all the rest of these bozos and form our own unit."

"Yeah, but what would we call ourselves? 'Force' and 'Team' are already taken."

Blancanales turned around in the shotgun seat. "How about the Dynamic Duo?"

Flashing police lights appeared behind them. Lyons cut down a side street.

"I like it," Schwarz said. "But I get to be Batman."

"Uh-uh," James replied. "It'll never wash. You got to be Robin. Black Man and Robin."

"Just what I need. Another joker. You know that job offer I just gave you, Cal?" Lyons said.

"Yeah?"

"Forget it."

THE EXECUTIONER OPENED his eyes and wiped the blood from his face. His fingers moved to the laceration in his brow as his brain struggled to remember what had happened, where he was.

Somewhere close by, a bird chirped. Then the cackling laughter of a monkey mocked his confusion. The Executioner frowned, staring through the shattered glass in front of him—a windshield? Through the windshield, a tangled web of torn vines and leaves mixed with the contorted nose of an airplane.

The Beechcraft. It all came back.

Bolan twisted in his seat to where Jameson's dead body gaped wide-eyed in the pilot's seat. Blood still pumped from the Recce's open chest wound, meaning the Executioner couldn't have been unconscious long. Unsnapping his seat belt, he turned and knelt in the seat.

Lindall Dingaan sat slumped in the chair behind him, his eyes closed. Bolan reached over the seat and pressed a finger into the black leader's carotid artery. He felt nothing.

The Executioner was over the seat in a heartbeat. He pushed the release button on Dingaan's belt and jerked the strap. The belt held firm, and it was then that he saw the mangled, deformed metal catch. Reaching under his right arm beneath the Beretta's offside magazine caddies, he drew his combat knife and positioned the blade with the serrated edge against the seat belt. He watched Dingaan's face as he sliced through the heavy canvas.

Heart attack? He didn't know. He wasn't a doctor. What he did know was that Dingaan was half a step away from death.

Bolan slid the knife back into its sheath and dragged Dingaan out of the Beechcraft, positioning the unconscious man on his back on the soft jungle floor. He dug the palm of his right hand into the South African's sternum, placed his left on top and leaned forward several times.

Dingaan didn't stir.

The Executioner tilted Dingaan's head back and began CPR.

The warrior broke into a sweat, stinging the gash on his forehead as he continued to fight for the life he saw ebbing away in front of him. Finally Bolan's efforts paid off.

Lindall Dingaan coughed softly.

Bolan checked the pulse again. Weak. Feeble. But there.

A moment later the ACA leader opened his eyes briefly.

The Executioner fished through the man's pockets until he found the bottle of nitro tablets. Prying Dingaan's lips apart, he placed one of the tiny white tablets beneath the man's tongue.

The hum of an aircraft overhead sent Bolan's eyes skyward. Yes, they'd be coming to check out their work, make sure he and Dingaan were dead.

And finish them off if they weren't.

Dingaan stirred again. Bolan reached down, gently shaking him. The deep brown eyes opened again.

"We've got to get out of here," the Executioner said. "They're coming to check it out. We've got to go."

Slowly the black leader shook his head. "I...can't. Please. Go on. I am as good as—"

"You ever were," Bolan finished for him. He heard the plane pass over again and rose to his knees. His hand found the Victorinox SwissChamp pouch on his belt and pulled the ruler from the side pocket next to the knife. A compass was attached to the ruler's end, and he sighted southeast, then returned the instrument to its holder.

Sliding both arms under Dingaan, Bolan cradled the man like a baby, then rose to his feet.

"Please . . ."

Bolan set him feet first on the ground and turned around, hoisting the little man onto his back. Dingaan clasped his arms around the Executioner's neck, and they took off. Through the thick treetops, the warrior finally saw the plane—not the air force fighter that had downed them, but a slower-flying bush plane with South African markings.

What the hell was going on? he wondered as he bulldogged his way through the thick foliage. The air force was trying to kill one of its nation's leaders? Well, why not? The Recces had tried.

There were a number of possible explanations, the most likely being that whoever had piloted the fighter had been given false info as to who, or what, it contained. He would, after all, never get close enough to see Lindall Dingaan's famous face.

Bolan ducked under a low branch and saw a boa constrictor curl tighter around the tree. Mosquitos and other insects attacked his face, arms and chest as the plane buzzed again, trying to locate the exact site of the crash before dropping in the search-and-destroy party.

More traitorous Recces? Probably.

As they started across a clearing, Bolan heard the plane. It had risen higher, and he knew what that meant.

The enemy had spotted the crash site. Now they had gained altitude to give the search party room to jump.

The Executioner watched as four tiny figures fell from the plane. A second later the parachutes opened, looking like minuscule black triangles against the sky.

Bolan moved farther from the clearing and placed Dingaan on the ground, his back against a tree. There was no way he could outrun the well-trained, well-conditioned soldiers who were about to touch down. Not with Lindall Dingaan on his back. They would go first to the crash site, quickly ascertain that he and Dingaan had survived and hurry down the trail of broken branches and vines the Executioner had been forced to leave in his haste.

The warrior looked down at Dingaan. Determination covered the man's face, but every pore in his body seemed to emanate exhaustion.

The mind was willing, but the body had quit listening to its commands.

The Executioner knew there was only one course of action. Pulling the .44 Desert Eagle from its hip holster, he extended the weapon butt first to the ACA leader. "You know how it works, Lindall?"

Dingaan took the pistol as if it were a snake. "I have fired guns, but I have never enjoyed doing so."

Bolan nodded. "Neither have I, but I've found it a necessary evil." He knelt and began piling loose vines, sticks and leaves on top of Dingaan's feet and legs. "I'm covering you up for a little while. I can't carry you and fight at the same time."

"You are going back to the plane?"

The warrior nodded. "It's our only chance. I've got to ambush them before they realize we've left the plane."

Bolan rose to his feet and frowned down at the pile of vegetation. Dingaan was hidden, but the heap was conspicuous—obviously man-made in the otherwise natural jungle surroundings. It wouldn't fool anyone who took more than a casual glance in the direction of the tree.

Well, if things went well, the enemy soldiers would never reach this spot. And though it might sound cold when put into words, if the upcoming confrontation at the crash site went poorly, it wouldn't matter. Lindall Dingaan would die anyway.

Even if the Recces didn't find him, if the Executioner fell to the rounds of the enemy, the ACA leader wouldn't have the strength to survive the perils of the jungle on his own.

"Keep still," Bolan said as he pulled the sound-suppressed Beretta from his shoulder harness. "I'll be back as quick as I can."

THE FIRST THING Katz noticed about the Ijsselmeer Building was the height. At ninety-nine stories, it made other buildings that would normally have been called skyscrapers look like saplings growing next to a giant redwood.

Katz pushed his plate away and lit a cigarette. He had chosen the unpretentious little café across the street from the Ijsselmeer for two reasons. First, through the window he could see the front entrance to the building. Men and women in business attire came and went. But they seemed outnumbered three to one by the uniformed security guards that Stony Man Intel confirmed were nothing more than mercenaries and assorted other thugs.

The Israeli had watched David McCarter enter the building under the pretense of business. Now they would see just how far the Briton could get before he was turned away for not having an appointment with Direk Brouer.

But there was another reason Katz had chosen the café, and it was far more personal.

He had eaten there several years earlier, and the food had been excellent.

The former Israeli Mossad operative inhaled a lungful of smoke and let it trickle out his nose. Lunch had been what the Dutch called *Hollandsche Koffie-tafel,* or roughly translated, the "Dutch coffee table." It featured several types of bread, and slices of various meats and cheeses. It differed from the typical Netherlander's breakfast only in that it was always supplemented by a hot dish. This day's serving had been a meat croquette, and it had been delicious. At least the Phoenix Force leader assumed it had been.

Since it was the first decent meal he'd had in days that hadn't come out of a can, he couldn't be sure. A Hostess Twinkie on white bread with ketchup might have tasted good at this point.

The Phoenix Force leader sighed and gazed at his empty plate. It was almost like not seeing a woman for a month. When you finally did, she appeared to be the most beautiful creature you had ever seen. No matter what she looked like.

Katz looked out the window and continued to smoke. He didn't mind the hardships leading Phoenix Force brought on. They were a small price to pay for the feeling of accomplishment he felt each time he led his men on a mission that resulted in good triumphing over evil. Corny, but that was what it boiled down to. Good versus evil. Right versus wrong. Old Testament justice, with the good guys in the white hats fighting the bad guys in black.

A grin lifted the corners of his lips as he realized the irony of his last analogy. No, the black-and-white metaphor didn't apply to this mission. The entire battle they were fighting was to prove that black and white were *equal*.

The smile on the Israeli's lips faded as McCarter appeared in the revolving door across the street. A second later the Briton was crossing to the café, a briefcase dangling at his side.

Katz sighed, then took another drag off his cigarette. McCarter hadn't had time to get into the offices on the top floor. His reconnaissance Intel of the building would be limited. The Israeli stubbed out his cigarette as the Briton pushed through the door. McCarter had gone undercover as a Liverpool gemstone broker looking to hook up with Ijsselmeer. The story had been thin. It had had little chance of success from the beginning, but had been worth a try since it couldn't hurt anything.

The former SAS officer walked to the window table and dropped his briefcase into a chair across from Katz. He shrugged, then crossed the room to the buffet table, filled a plate and returned. "I got as far as the hallway on the top floor," he said as he sat down.

"Then I was stopped by a pair of chaps who looked like they'd just stepped out of a WWF wrestling ring." He stopped speaking, unfolded his napkin and placed it in his lap. "They had the audacity to call on, and learned that not only did Mr. Trevor Hickle-Smith not have an appointment, but Mr. Brouer had never even heard of poor old Trev."

"The bloody cheek of them."

McCarter's eyebrows rose again in mock surprise. "Exactly as *I* would have phrased it, Mr. Katzenelenbogen. We'll make an English gentleman out of you yet." He slapped a thin slice of Swiss cheese between two pieces of rye bread and took a large bite.

A young woman wearing a crisp white pinafore appeared at the table, poured more coffee for Katz and promised to return with a can of Coke for McCarter. As soon as she'd left again, the Israeli said, "So, what *can* you tell me?"

McCarter held up a hand and swallowed before answering. "Lots of security, Katz. Both uniforms and rough trade in plain clothes such as I mentioned earlier. The guard might lighten up somewhat after business hours. Maybe. In any case I have a feeling we're in for an interesting evening."

Katz turned his eyes toward the door as Gary Manning walked in, grabbed a plate and loaded it down with food. The big Canadian took the seat next to McCarter.

"What's the police situation look like?" Katz asked.

Manning pulled a Dutch police uniform shoulder patch from the hip pocket of his slacks. "As a vacationing Canadian Mountie I got the royal treatment.

Tour of the facilities. Even had coffee with the commandant in his office." He broke off as the waitress walked up, then said, "Just water." He turned back to Katz. "I told him I was doing a master's thesis in criminology and was interested in patrol concentrations. To boil it down, they've got a light crew working this area. As you'd imagine, they concentrate more on the red-light area." He took another bite.

"Any specifics?" Katz asked.

"Only one car cruises this sector between 3:00 a.m. and 7:00. That's the good news. The bad is, the reason they go light is that most of the businesses down here have a private security force roughly the size of the Red Chinese Army. Guess who he mentioned as an example."

"Ijsselmeer, Inc.?"

"Ijsselmeer, Inc."

"Like I said," McCarter cut in. "This is going to be interesting."

The three men looked through the window as Rafael Encizo came around the corner and entered the café. The little Cuban's face was unusually pale as he walked directly to the table and sat down next to Katz.

The Phoenix Force leader nodded toward the buffet. "Better eat while you've got the chance, Rafe."

Encizo shook his head. "I grabbed something on the street at one of the sandwich shops."

"God, not that raw stuff?" McCarter asked.

"I was so hungry I was halfway through the thing before it dawned on me it was raw. Anyway, I've lost my appetite. But I'll tell you what I found out." The waitress returned with McCarter's Coke and Manning's water. Encizo shook his head, and she left again.

"I don't think there's a chance in hell of breaking into that place without setting off an alarm. I only had a few minutes in the alley. That's where the alarms and wires are centered. They've got cross-trips like you've never seen. Backup systems out the wazoo. The whole thing can be neutralized—all alarms can—but it could take a lot of time to figure it all out. And they had four guards patrolling the alley. Guards who were quick to give me directions when they saw I was lost and escort me back to the street themselves."

Encizo sat back in his chair and said, "There's got to be an easier way in. You heard from James yet?"

Katz glanced across the street as a commercial van pulled up in front of the Ijsselmeer Building. Two men in green coveralls carrying toolboxes got out. Each wore an equipment belt around his hips, which made them look like gunfighters in a Western movie. "Yeah," he said. "He's in Miami. Able Team's through with him, and they'll put him on the shuttle to D.C. He should show up sometime tonight."

"They find out anything on their end about the government guys on the Ijsselmeer payroll?" Manning asked.

Katz shook his head. "The Black Charge deal ran into a dead end. But they've hooked into the American Nazi Party and think there might be some connection."

Across the street, one of the men in coveralls set his toolbox on the sidewalk, pulled something from his wallet and showed it to the Ijsselmeer doorman.

"There it is," Katz said, standing up.

The rest of the team looked up. "There what is?" McCarter asked.

"Our ticket in. The easier way. Wait here."

Without another word the Phoenix Force leader was through the door and hurrying across the street.

CARL LYONS PULLED the panel truck to a halt in front of Miami International Airport. "This is as far as we go," he said to James. "Sorry, but we're all allergic to metal detectors."

James grinned and handed his weapons over the seat to Blancanales, who put them on the floor at his feet.

The Phoenix Force warrior slid open the door. "Well, I hate long goodbyes," he said. "See ya." A moment later he was walking through the glass doors toward the Miami-Washington shuttle.

Lyons pulled away from the terminal. Blancanales turned around in his seat to where Schwarz sat on the floor next to the Nazi. Gadgets had kept up an almost nonstop, low-key verbal assault on the man since they'd captured him, and Blancanales had to admire his comrade.

He might be the one who was officially trained in psychological warfare, but Schwarz was a natural. The electronics genius certainly had his own style. Crude but efficient.

"...so you see, Rolf," Schwarz said, calling the Nazi by the nickname he'd given him when the man refused to identify himself. "It's real simple. We trade favors. You tell us what we want to know, and we don't cut you up into little pieces to use for chum when we go marlin fishing in the morning."

Rolf's frightened face twisted into a forced snarl. "You are soft. You will not do it, and even if you do, I will not care. I am prepared to die for the Fourth Reich."

"Oh, how nice." Schwarz patted the man on the arm. "You going to give us a speech now? Something about Hitler maybe? A speech where you gradually slip into a phony German accent even though you were probably born and raised in Butte, Montana, by folks who were a mixture of Swedish, Irish and Czech?"

"My parents came from Dusseldorf after the war," Rolf said. "And Hitler, whom you mock, will some day be regarded as the most important man of the twentieth century. Time will prove him out." The fright seemed to leave his voice, and his face took on the mad glow of the true believer as he spoke.

"Good God," Schwarz said. "The accent's *already* started."

The panel truck drove on through the streets of Miami as the banter between Rolf and Schwarz continued. When they reached the South Dixie Highway again, Lyons pulled up onto the southbound ramp, driving back in the direction they'd come.

Blancanales settled into his seat. He knew what the Able Team leader was doing: taking his time finding a suitable place to hide out and interrogate their prisoner, giving Schwarz time to adequately soften the subject up.

"The people of America are fed up with the problems they must deal with in regard to the mongrel minorities," Rolf went on. His confidence was growing. He had said enough to offend anyone but a pureblood Aryan with no moral conscience.

"Our strength grows daily," Rolf continued, his voice rising like that of a drug-crazed zealot. "By the turn of the century we will have rid the country of the niggers and hebes who contaminate it."

"Boy, this is getting good," Schwarz said. "I can almost see your brown eyes turn blue when you talk, Rolf." He looked up toward the front. "Wish our buddy Katz was here to listen to this."

Blancanales shook his head. "We'd never keep this guy alive long enough to interrogate."

The same hotel and motel road signs they'd passed earlier began popping up along the highway. They passed the Ramada Inn where they'd procured the Corvette as Rolf went on another tirade about the Jews.

"The gold exchange, for example. If the Jews were not running it, you would pay less than fifty percent of what you pay now to buy your wife a wedding ring. Have you ever stopped to think about that?"

Schwarz chuckled. But underneath the laugh, Blancanales could see Gadgets's anger growing like a bubbling volcano. "I think maybe you asked the wrong guy."

Rolf took him literally. He looked at Blancanales. "How about you? Do you realize what the Jews have done to business ethics in this country?"

"No, I don't. But even if they'd ruined business altogether, I don't call that a very good reason to exterminate a whole race."

Rolf spit again. Suddenly Lyons stepped on the brake. "I've heard all I'm going to listen to," he growled.

A motel sign became visible at the side of the road— Grandma's Cabin Kitchenettes, it read. Refrigerators. Stoves. HBO. Roomy And Clean. Come Stay With Us! There was a cartoon sketch of a motherly-looking woman with old-fashioned spectacles and an apron with a steaming bowl in her hands next to the words.

Blancanales grabbed Lyons by the arm. "No way, man. Let's do it right." He pointed to the sign.

Lyons glowered for a moment, then threw the truck in gear and turned down a blacktop road toward Grandma's. Twenty minutes later they pulled onto a gravel drive. Tiny cabins the size of large outhouses speckled the landscape. Lyons pulled to a halt in front of a hand-painted sign that read Office.

Blancanales got out and walked in. The office smelled of garbage, urine and chewing tobacco. A threadbare couch stood against the wall across from the registration counter. A multicolored dog of mixed parentage lay in the corner, its eyes closed.

Grandma turned out to be a man.

The old-timer who stuck his head up over the counter hadn't shaved in a week or so. Body odor flowed from a sweat-soaked undershirt that had started out white but now was brown. He shoved a registration card in front of Blancanales, then went back to the half-empty fifth of Jack Daniel's on the desk and the pornographic movie on the TV.

Blancanales signed in, dropped a twenty-dollar bill on the counter and took the key to Cabin 6 from the man. "It does have a kitchen, right?" he asked.

"Sign says so, don't it?"

The Able Team warrior was tempted to mention that the sign also said something about "big and clean" but decided against it.

Rolf was still spouting his Nazi propaganda as Lyons pulled the panel truck down the row of cabins to number 6. Blancanales got out, made sure there were no curious eyes and slid open the door.

Schwarz had the muzzle of his Beretta against the side of Rolf's head. "One word," he said, "just one word. And I almost hope you do."

Lyons came around the side of the truck, jerked Rolf's arm behind the man's back and pushed him toward the door. Blancanales inserted the key, and a moment later they were inside. Lyons shoved the Nazi into a tattered armchair next to the bed and turned to Blancanales. "You got five minutes," he said. "Then I get *my* turn."

Blancanales took a seat on the bed and stared at Rolf.

A smirk covered the Nazi's face.

"I'm going to tell you a story," Blancanales said.

"This ought to be good."

"It is. I'm an Italian Jew."

Rolf spit on the floor.

"When I was a young man in my home village near Naples," Blancanales went on, pulling the story out of the air as he went, "there still remained a fascist element. They terrorized our community by night. Houses were burned. Men were killed. Women were raped...the same women the fascists said were unclean. They said that hair from a Jew carried infection, but they still raped the women. Does that make sense to you?" He narrowed his eyes in the icy stare he had learned so many years ago during training. Cold. Angry. But controlled.

The smirk began to fade from Rolf's face. For the first time the Nazi seemed to fully comprehend that he was at the mercy of his captors.

"Yes," Blancanales said. "I see you have guessed the rest of the story. My mother was raped. Not only raped, but tortured before they killed her." Slowly, a little bit at a time, he let his voice rise in both sound and tone. Carefully Rosario Blancanales let the same extremism he had heard in Rolf's voice creep into his own.

"Do you know how they killed her?" he asked.

"No, God no." Rolf's eyes flitted around the room as if he might find help. "How should I know? I wasn't even alive then, and I sure wasn't in Italy."

"No, but you may have done the same thing yourself here. Because from what you have told me, it is a form of execution that you'd approve of." He paused. With each sentence he had said, he had let a tiny bit more Italian accent sneak into his words, as if his English had been learned and faded when he became excited.

"They gassed her!" Blancanales shouted. "The same way your führer did millions of others."

He was on his feet in a flash. Grabbing the bound man by the front of the shirt, he jerked him out of the chair and dragged him into the kitchen. Rolf went flying against the wall as Blancanales reached down and opened the door to the large stove. He turned on the oven, then bent down and extinguished the pilot light. The faint smell of gas filled the air.

"No!" the Nazi screamed.

Blancanales drove a fist into his belly to silence him. The man doubled over, opened his mouth, and the contents of his stomach emptied over the dirty tile.

A second later Lyons and Schwarz were bending him down, folding him like a piece of dirty laundry and cramming him headfirst into the oven.

"For the first time in your life, you'll know how it feels to be a victim!"

The Nazi's body flopped around as he tried to back out of the oven, but Lyons and Schwarz maintained pressure on the oven door. Screams, then whimpers came from the inside of the oven. "No... Please, no..."

Blancanales waited until Rolf had quieted, then twisted the dial on the oven to high. The old equipment generated a loud click, and a steady hissing filled the air from the escaping gas. "It's real easy," Blancanales said. "Just breathe in deep."

The screams died down again. Silence followed as Rolf struggled, then his panicky voice choked out of the opening in the door, "Please! Turn that thing off!"

"Do you want to talk?" Blancanales asked.

"Yes! I'll tell you what you want to know. Just turn off the gas!"

With an audible click, Blancanales obliged. "But you stay there until you answer the questions. I can turn this thing on at any time if I think you are stalling."

As it turned out, the man Schwarz had called Rolf was really named Bob Burns. And while he wasn't from Butte, Montana, as Schwarz had predicted, he had grown up in Gary, Indiana, and had only a small strain of German running through his veins on his mother's side. He knew very little about what was happening on the planet Earth outside of the tiny, hate-fueled world in which he himself lived.

But he did know one thing of interest to the men of Able Team.

He knew that David Moler, *the führer* of the American Nazi Party, had cut some kind of deal with a corporation in Amsterdam. And that Moler had something in his safe that belonged to the Dutch conglomerate.

Bob "Rolf" Burns was ashen-faced and trembling in a very un-Aryan-warriorlike way when Blancanales hauled his head out of the oven five minutes later. The Able Team psychological-warfare expert's voice had returned to normal as he leaned the man against the wall. "I'm not Italian. Or Jewish. But now you know what an ignoble way it would be to die like this."

CHAPTER NINE

Barry Lanzerac's home, as well as the training camp and stronghold for the Boer Resistance Movement, lay hidden in a small patch of tropical forest in the Transvaal, north of Pretoria, near the tiny village of Lydenburg.

Lanzerac was proud of the spacious ranch-style home. He had built it with his own hands, from foundation to roof, taking extra pains to do it right, and had put in the extra effort that the Boers had once used to settle the Transvaal.

That, of course, had been before the government had grown soft and allowed the kaffirs to begin taking over the Afrikaner way of life.

From his seat under the straw gazebo to the side of the parade ground, Lanzerac watched two squadrons of BRM troops practicing hand-to-hand combat. Although farmers, rather than professional soldiers, by trade, they were good men. They were willing to risk their lives for what they had worked all their lives to obtain.

Lanzerac watched now as Lyl Van Der Meir wrested a ten-inch fighting knife from the hand of one of the instructors. Even though blood covered his hand as he pulled it away, he held on to the knife. A year ago the most dangerous weapon Van Der Meir had ever held had been the blade of a plow. He had known nothing of combat and had never dreamed he would learn.

Then a band of seven Seshoeshoe tribal outcasts, on the run from the law, had taken refuge in his barn one night. The next morning when his wife had gone to milk the cows...

Lanzerac let the thought fade. What the kaffir bastards had done to Van Der Meir's daughter was too hard to think of. Besides, it made him think about his own wife, or ex-wife now.

A white-hot hatred suddenly filled Lanzerac like boiling lava. The bitch. The whore. She had done it just to spite him. She could never have fallen in love with the kaffir.

Both the memories of Van Der Mier's wife and his own combined to turn Lanzerac's hatred to a nausea that threatened to make him vomit. He forced his mind to more pleasant things.

At least Helen Van Der Mier had been revenged when Lyl came knocking on Lanzerac's door the very afternoon of her rape and murder. The Boer Resistance Movement had gone into action immediately, doing what the South African government couldn't, or wouldn't, do.

They had tracked the Seshoeshoe high into the Transvaal and caught them on the banks of the Groot Letaba as they tried to make their escape into Zimbabwe. Four of the seven had died during the gun battle. The other three had thrown down their weapons and walked out of the bush, their hands held high above their heads. As far as Lanzerac was concerned, this had proved not only that kaffirs were cowards, but that they were inferior in intelligence to the white race.

Because their surrender hadn't gotten them the leniency they had assumed it would. What it got them was their raping penises sliced off as they lay staked out in the grass.

Lanzerac took a sip of the beer on the table in front of him as two flatbed trucks suddenly rounded the curve on the jungle road and stopped at the gate. Two guards stepped down from the fence, opened the gate and waved them through. As the trucks kicked up dust on their way toward the gazebo, Lanzerac saw David Yancy's straw cowboy hat bobbing up and down in the passenger seat of the lead vehicle.

Behind the wheel sat a black man in faded fatigues. In the rear of both trucks, Lanzerac could see both black and white faces. The white men in back wore BDUs similar to his own. The blacks clinging to the side rails wore traditional Zulu war feathers and other garb.

Lanzerac took another sip of beer to wash the taste of the sight out of his mouth. He hated the subhuman kaffirs, and he hated working with them. As far as he was concerned, the black mercenaries they had hired were no different than the bastards they would soon help destroy.

And he vowed that when it was over, he would see to it that they were dead, as well.

The trucks pulled to a halt, and Yancy's boa constrictor cowboy boots dropped down to the ground. The black man on the other side joined him as they walked to the gazebo. Lanzerac watched Yancy. It didn't seem to bother him to work with the kaffirs. Perhaps he had spent so much time with them in Vietnam that he had grown used to their ways.

The beer mug traveled back to the BRM man's mouth. But then, Yancy was a fool, a boob who might have been a good soldier in Southeast Asia and later in Rhodesia, but who had now grown older and was as soft as the government in Pretoria. He was in this only for the money Direk Brouer paid him. And a man who fought for nothing more than money soon lost heart.

"What say, Bar?" Yancy grinned as he took a seat under the gazebo and tossed his sweaty hat onto the table. The black man took a seat next to him, and Lanzerac glared at him.

Under other circumstances, he would have killed a kaffir who dared join him at table.

"Bar, this is Robert Kitwana, the guy I told you about. I worked with him years ago in the Rhod. Bob's going to drive the guns on into the chief in the next village after we hit the Xhosa. I'll go with him, but he'll do the talking—he's Swahili, but he speaks Bantu. They'll believe him."

The big Swahili reached a hand across the table toward Lanzerac.

The BRM leader just stared at it.

Kitwana drew back.

Yancy gave an embarrassed cough. "Anyway, we're all go. We'll take a couple of bodies from the first village into the next one. A little more proof for the chief that the Zulus sold out to you bloodthirsty Boers." He laughed and slapped his knee.

"And the Zulu village?" Lanzerac asked.

"Buck Templeton's leading that party. They'll do the same thing there, just reverse the blame. Buck's got a black with him who speaks Bantu as well as Kitwana, and when they're done, they'll move on into the next village same as us. Tell the chief it was Xhosa who've teamed up with you guys, then offer them the guns at a price they can't refuse.'' He paused, pulled a handkerchief from his back pocket, wiped his face, then grinned. ''By this time tomorrow, we'll not only have the two tribes looking for each other, they'll be looking for any Boer farm they can burn along the way.''

Lanzerac sat silently. He didn't like that part, but it was necessary. As Brouer had said, sacrifices had to be made in order to rile the fence-sitting whites who still might not vote to repeal the referendum. And if it got too out of hand, or the government troops didn't come in and provide protection, it would give him an excuse to move his own men in and finish off the two tribes altogether, which would show the country, and the world, that the Boer Resistance Movement had saved the whites of the nation from destruction.

And place him in a stronger position when things began to reorganize.

Lanzerac lifted his mug and drained what remained. He might even find himself in a stronger position than Direk Brouer, which was where he needed to be if he intended to take the country over instead of it turning into one big subsidiary of Ijsselmeer, Inc.

He set his mug down and stood, heading toward the trucks. Lanzerac ran his eyes quickly over the black mercenaries disguised as tribesmen, then moved to the second truck. Throwing back the tarp, he saw a dozen cases of Belgian-made Fabrique Nationale FAL assault rifles, and smiled.

A lot of kaffirs would be killing one another in the next few days.

Lanzerac grasped the whistle on the lanyard around his neck and stuck it in his mouth. He blew shrilly, and the combat drills in the parade ground came to a halt. He waved the men forward, and they double-timed it to the trucks.

"Climb up," he said as the men piled in next to the phony Zulus. "We're about to make some changes around here."

THROUGH THE TOPS of the trees, Bolan watched the parachutes descend as he retraced his steps toward the clearing the Beechcraft had carved out of the thick jungle. As the falling chutes neared the earth, the men dangling beneath them came into focus—four men, OD and khaki fatigues, Lyttleton R-5 5.56 mm assault rifles, Z-88 9 mm pistols in tanker holsters across their chests.

They were Recces, all right.

The bright white fuselage of the wrecked aircraft began to show through the greenery surrounding the Executioner, and a moment later he stepped into the clearing. As he did, he saw one of the four paratroopers dip a shoulder and fly out of formation, disappearing over the trees. The other three fell out of sight, triangulating the plane.

Bolan paused a moment, formulating his plan. Where had the fourth man gone? Had he simply caught a last-minute gust of wind and been blown away from the others, or did he have his own agenda?

Or had he seen some sign of the trail the Executioner and Dingaan had made as they fled the wreckage and headed in that direction?

Bolan didn't know. But at the moment, he had three other Recces to worry about. He had used part of his shirt for a bandage for his head, and his bare chest was hardly covered with camouflage. With the three men approaching from three sides, the best he could hope for was to conceal himself in the foliage until they reached the plane, then pick them off with the silenced Beretta.

But the plan had flaws, one of which was that no matter where he hid, at least one of the men would have to pass close by. And without proper cammies, he stood a good chance of being spotted.

The Executioner shrugged out of his shoulder holster. The next best plan would be to *let* himself be spotted, but on his terms.

He sprinted to the cockpit, climbed in next to Jameson and pulled his carryon from under the seat. Quickly he donned a clean shirt, buttoned the front to the throat and tucked in the tails. The shoulder rig. went back into the bag before he ripped the bloodsoaked shirtsleeve from around his head and hid it under the seat.

The bleeding started again as soon as he removed the makeshift bandage. It oozed down over his forehead, then dripped onto the clean shirt as the Executioner tucked the Beretta between the seat cushion and his left thigh.

A twig snapped from the six-o'clock position. He heard footsteps moving quietly at three o'clock. He waited but heard no other sounds.

Now he had two missing Recces.

Bolan leaned back against the seat, letting his head fall lifelessly at an angle away from Jameson. He opened his eyes, staring inanimately into space as the dead man next to him did.

The Executioner felt the heat and humidity in his eyes immediately. The trick now would be to keep them open. One reflexive blink at the wrong moment would mean his death.

He stared ahead, his eyes glossing over as two sets of footsteps reached the clearing. They started toward his side of the plane, and in his peripheral vision he saw a tall lanky man wearing a camouflage bandanna tied around his head. His shorter partner wore an OD boonie hat. Both carried Lyttletons in the assault position, aimed toward the plane.

The Executioner held his breath, cognizant that the smallest move of his chest would bring a burst of 5.56 mm slugs streaking into it. His eyes began to tear over as the two men continued to approach.

The man in the boonie hat reached Bolan's side and jammed the barrel of his assault rifle into his ribs. Pain shot through his side as he let the momentum of the poke shift his weight. His eyes threatened to close of their own accord as the man in the bandanna took up position at his partner's side. He looked down at the shorter man, who nodded.

The tall man in the bandanna stuck two fingers in his mouth. A loud whistle echoed through the jungle. Then the Executioner heard footsteps approach the plane on the pilot's side.

Bolan continued to hold his breath, almost blind now from the air on his irises. He had to wait until the third man, who'd been holding back to cover the other two, showed himself and Bolan could fix his position.

The man in the boonie hat climbed up and leaned into the plane. His chest pressed against Bolan's face, hiding it from view as he checked the rear of the Beechcraft. The Executioner took advantage of the moment to close his eyes, feeling the warm relief rush through them. He opened them again as the man leaned away and excitedly said, "The kaffir isn't here."

As he spoke, another face appeared through the window, just past Jameson. "What?"

Bolan's left hand came to life, streaking beneath his leg for the grips of the Beretta. He raised the weapon and thrust it into the chest of the man in front of him. The short trigger pull sent a 3-round burst of 9 mm parabellums into the man's sternum and sprayed blood, skin and flesh back onto the Executioner. The Recce fell forward, trapping his gun against his body.

The warrior pushed the man back and swung the Beretta across his body as the man in the bandanna brought his Lyttleton into play. Another burst from the Beretta sent blood and flesh flying from the wet barrel. But another trio of 9 mm hollowpoints preceded the mess, catching the tall Recce in the throat and face.

A volley of rounds erupted from the other side of the plane, and the Executioner ducked lower beneath the corpse on his chest. Out of the corner of his eye, he saw Jameson's body dance as it caught the first wave of the attack, then the man in the boonie hat jerked as the penetrating 5.56 mm NATO rounds passed through Jameson and into him. Using the bodies as shields, the Executioner transferred the Beretta to his right hand and fired through the window, his third burst of fire narrowly missing the last Recce as the man dived out of sight beneath the Beechcraft.

Bolan heard the rustle of tangled undergrowth beneath his seat as the Recce assassin squirmed under the plane. He dropped the near-empty Beretta, pried the Lyttleton from the hands of the dead man on his chest, then shoved the body out of the plane to fall on top of the Recce's dead partner.

A pistol round drilled into the cockpit from below, streaking between the Executioner and Jameson before exiting the roof of the plane. Bolan dived to the open door and grasped the top of the window as another round shot up through the seat where he'd sat a moment before.

Unable to maneuver the assault rifle in the narrow confines beneath the Beechcraft, the Recce had switched to his Z-88. More 9 mm rounds flew into the cockpit as Bolan swung himself out and onto the roof. He saw the jagged, gray-edged holes on the top of the plane's white roof as he reached up and grabbed the nearest branch. He pulled himself up into the tree as bullets continued to fly through the cockpit.

There was a pause in the action as the enemy gunner changed magazines, then the blind assault started again. The man was taking no chances. He intended to saturate the cockpit with enough lead to be sure his enemy was dead.

Bolan pulled himself higher into the tree, climbing from branch to branch until he towered twenty feet above the wreckage. Although the man wasn't yet aware of it, the third Recce was trapped. It was only a matter of time before he crawled from beneath the plane.

From his vantage point the Executioner scanned the clearing below, hoping to see some sign of the paratrooper who had sailed away from the others early on. He saw nothing, and as he took a seat on a sturdy limb the certainty of where the man had gone suddenly sank in.

The fourth Recce *had* seen something that had caused him to break away from the others. And that something had to have been a sign that would lead him to Dingaan.

Well, he'd have to deal with this first, then hope like hell he could get back to Dingaan before the assassin located him.

Bolan's trigger finger tightened on the Lyttleton as the man beneath the plane emptied three more magazines into the cockpit. Then silence fell over the jungle once more.

Finally a khaki-clad arm moved from under the front of the Beechcraft. The arm dragged out a torso, then the face of the final traitorous Recce appeared, and Bolan got his first good look at the man.

He wore aviator sunglasses beneath his brown BDU cap.

And he never knew what hit him.

The Lyttleton cut a swath of death ending the Recce's life on the ground next to the plane.

But by the time the man had drawn his final breath, Bolan was sprinting through the jungle toward where he'd left Dingaan.

YAKOV KATZENELENBOGEN crossed the street to the Ijsselmeer Building and strode to the front door. He nodded to the doorman and walked into the lobby in time to see the two workmen step onto an elevator.

The doors closed behind them.

Katz slowed. Okay, he'd already found out one of the things he needed to know. It wasn't hard to get into the Ijsselmeer Building during working hours. McCarter had done it, and he'd proved it just now. So why had the guard at the door checked the electricians' identification?

Katz smiled. Because the electricians were going to be working after hours.

The former Mossad agent strolled toward the elevators as he watched the lights above the car. He watched each progressive floor number light up, then fade, as the elevator climbed the shaft. Finally the number 39 appeared. He heard a distant ding, then the sound of the doors opening drifted faintly down the shaft. He waited as the car traveled back to the lobby, then stepped through the doors and punched 39.

The two men stood facing an open fuse box at the bend in the L-shaped hall as the Phoenix Force leader stepped onto the thirty-ninth floor. They had placed their toolboxes next to their feet and spoke quietly as he paused to pull a piece of scrap paper from his pocket. Then, his eyes frowning at the paper, the Israeli started down the hall.

Katz felt the pain shoot through his ankle as it struck the edge of the toolbox in the middle of the hall. He let a small yelp escape his lips as he fell forward, striking the back of the man who had shown the ID to the doorman.

The two men crashed into the fuse box, rebounded and went sprawling to the floor.

The ex-Mossad agent rolled to his back on the cold tile, grunting in pain. He grasped his knee first, then let his hand fall to his ankle before returning to his knee.

The man next to him jumped to his feet, cursing in Dutch. He looked down at Katz, his eyes full of anger, and continued in the unfamiliar language.

Katz spoke in French, knowing that a good many Dutch spoke that language, as well as German.

"You are a clumsy old man," the workman replied, switching to French. "You—"

Before he could go on, the man next to him reached out and grabbed his arm. The conversation returned to Dutch as he pointed to the toolbox in the middle of the hall and whispered in a frightened voice.

The Israeli didn't have to speak Dutch to know what the man was worried about. In English it would have been the words "negligence," and "law suits." The demeanor of the man who had fallen suddenly changed. "Are you all right, old man?" he asked in French.

Katz continued to hold his knee and moan.

Both men reached down and helped him to his feet. "Can you stand?" the second workman asked.

"I...I think so," Katz whispered hoarsely.

"I am sorry," the second man said. "I should never have left the toolbox—"

A glare from the second man stopped him in mid-sentence, and Katz could translate the look as well as the Dutch. *Don't give him any ideas as to culpability.*

"Can you walk?" the second man asked. "We will help you to your appointment."

"No," Katz groaned. "Take me to the elevator. I just want to go home."

The men exchanged another glance, then each took an arm and helped the Israeli down the hall.

Katz limped on board as soon as the elevator doors opened, bracing himself on the rail against the wall.

"Can we help you out of the—" the man he had fallen into asked.

"No!" Katz said. "You have done enough already. I don't want to see you again. Just let me go."

The two men looked worried as the doors closed in front of them.

Katz smiled as soon as the car started down. He reached into his back pocket, pulled out the workman's billfold, and opened it. He sorted through a variety of credit cards, family pictures and other paraphernalia, finally finding a plastic card that bore the same logo as the truck parked outside.

The elevator stopped again at the lobby. Pocketing the ID, Katz stepped through the doors and walked past the desk. A large box caught his eye, and once again, although he neither spoke nor read Dutch, he had seen similar boxes on registration desks the world over.

The Israeli walked to the lost-and-found box, dropped the electrician's billfold through the slot and left the Ijsselmeer Building. The limp had vanished as he hurried back across the street to join the other three men of Phoenix Force. He glanced at his watch as he pushed through the door.

They'd have to hurry. Business hours would be over soon in Amsterdam, and Phoenix Force had some shopping to do.

THE UNSUSPECTING XHOSA village southeast of the city of Ladysmith in Zululand never stood a chance.

The trucks came rolling out of the jungle and drove casually toward the rows of grass huts. Women toting clay pots full of drinking water from the nearby stream glanced up, then went on about their business. The children, many of whom were engaged in a game similar to baseball, paused to turn toward the vehicles, then went back to their stick and ball.

At peace with the nearby Zulu, Tswana, Sepedi and Sheshoeshoe tribes, the younger men, the warrior-hunters, had felt safe in leaving the village early that morning to replenish the dwindling supply of meat. The few men who remained were elderly—far too old to fight.

But one of the old men, a slender, wrinkled, gray-haired elder of the tribe known as Nonsizi, squinted through the bright sunlight toward the oncoming vehicles, and sensed trouble.

Before the interracial disease of rheumatoid arthritis had struck Nonsizi, he had been a mighty warrior within the proud ranks of the Xhosa, and though his hands were now twisted into painful disfigured knots, his faculties were still as alert as they had been thirty years before.

Nonsizi continued to watch the trucks. Something was wrong. He didn't know what it was, or even why he knew. But he knew.

As the trucks drew nearer, Nonsizi felt the same surge of adrenaline rise up in his throat that he had once felt as he approached a grazing wildebeest with his bow. "Run!" he cried in the Xhosa dialect of the Bantu language.

Now both women and children stopped to stare at the old man. "Has he never seen a truck?" one of the children quipped, and this brought laughter from the others. The mothers quickly hushed the display of disrespect, but then one of the other children whispered, "Be careful, Nonsizi, they are angry rhinoceroses in disguise!" And this time even the women were forced to cover their smiles as the children broke out in mirth.

Nonsizi watched as the trucks neared. He saw the glimmer of sunlight off several metal objects in the beds, and realized that was what had alerted him earlier. The men, Zulus and Boers together, carried rifles.

He experienced a moment of confusion. Although he had never learned to read or write, the history of his people had been passed down to him through word of mouth. The Zulu and Xhosa had once been one people. They had become divided in the late nineteenth century, when the great chief Dingaswayo had set up an autocratic military organization. The tribe had divided, but the two factions had lived in peace, with the Boers and Englishmen their only enemies.

So why were Zulus now advancing on the village adorned in battle dress, and in the company of the white man? Had they come to warn the Xhosa of some danger of which they were unaware?

The Zulu alone, perhaps. But the Boers? Never.

The rush of adrenaline leveled off, and deep depression filled Nonsizi's soul as he experienced a premonition of death. His own, and that of many others.

The trucks were still a hundred yards away when Nonsizi limped back to his hut. He wrapped his gnarled hands painfully around the same bow he had once used to feed the tribe and protect it from its enemies during periods of war. The weapon had become almost a religious icon in his heart, and as he tenderly lifted the quiver that held his arrows, his eyes fell on the new feathers he had carefully glued just below the heads only the day before.

The sight of the old man and his weapon brought more hilarity from the children as Nonsizi hobbled out of his hut. "Look!" one of the older boys who had recently returned from school in Pretoria cried. "Nonsizi will shoot his arrows through the engine blocks, then dance a war dance around the dead trucks!"

A woman holding a baby in her arms shifted the child and placed a hand on the old man's forearm. "Don't be foolish, Nonsizi," she whispered. "It is just the government trucks bringing supplies."

Nonsizi wrenched his gaunt arm away and stumbled toward the center of the village as the trucks suddenly sped up. Every muscle and joint in his body screamed in protest as he drew an arrow from behind his back and nocked it into the bowstring. He heard the laughter rise again as his shaking hands drew back the shaft and brought it to his cheek.

"Run!" he screamed once more.

Had the people of the village taken the old man's advice, many more than the four who escaped would have lived. But they continued to laugh, many of the women now giving up all effort to hide their delight at the old man's folly and joining in with the children.

The trucks slid to a halt in the center of the village amid clouds of dust. The men, both black and white, raised their rifles, and only then did the rest of the Xhosa people realize they were in danger.

The first shot struck Nonsizi in the thigh, and drove him to the ground. The bow fell from his warped hands. The arrows scattered from the quiver as the people around him finally heeded his advice. Their laughter had become terrified screams as they scattered in all directions, much like the old man's arrows.

Nonsizi dragged his twisted body across the dirt to his bow. As the Zulu and Boers dropped to the ground and sprayed the village with rifle fire, his hand found an arrow and slipped it into the string. He rose to a sitting position, and as the pain raced through his joints like the flames of a campfire, he drew the arrow back to his cheek once more and let it fly.

The shaft flew true, and Nonsizi felt a moment of satisfaction as the razor-edged rock tip pierced the belly of a black man in Zulu war regalia. The Zulu cried out in a language unknown to Nonsizi, and the strange sound brought a confused frown to the wrinkled face. The man looked Zulu. He fought with Zulu weapons, and was adorned with the same feathers, skins and paint Nonsizi remembered during the war years.

Then Nonsizi saw a white man wearing boots made from the skin of a boa constrictor swing a rifle his way.

He saw the rifle jump in the man's hands, but heard nothing.

Suddenly, for the first time in years, the fire in the old warrior's joints disappeared. He felt a warm, relaxing rush flow through his body. A smile replaced the frown on his lips, and the curiosity he had felt only moments before at the Zulu's odd words vanished.

Nonsizi realized suddenly that he was dying. But instead of grief, the smile that had formed on his lips grew to laughter. He had feared he would eventually die of the disease that had already maimed him, but he saw now that he would leave this earth as he had always hoped, in the only way fitting for a man who had spent his life as a Xhosa warrior.

He would die as a warrior.

Nonsizi closed his eyes. For a brief moment he wondered if any of the tribe would survive to alert the other villages that the Zulu and Boers had joined forces to destroy them. Then, unbeknownst to him, another burst of fire from the white man's rifle ended all thought.

FIFTY MILES FARTHER southeast, just north of the Tulega River, a Swahili woman dipped a shirt into the Indian Ocean and began scrubbing it with a brush made from the hair of a water buffalo. She thought briefly of the washing machine her mother and father at home in Kenya used without thought, and her gaze drifted to the other women doing their wash this day.

Four of the Zulu women stood in a row next to her, at work on the mixture of modern manufactured garments and traditional skins that belonged to their families. Their bare breasts jiggled as they scrubbed.

Sanura turned back to the task at hand, a hot flush warming her cheeks. She had been with the Tonga Zulu here at Amatikulu in Zululand for nearly two months now, and still their casual attitude toward nudity embarrassed her. Enough so that she wore an American-made tube top over her own ample breasts, and ignored the whispers and giggles that she knew went on behind her back.

The transplanted Swahili stood straight for a moment, stretching her back and wiping the perspiration from her brow with the back of her hand. She gazed out over the blue waters, watching the peaceful tide roll in. The tranquility—no, the *romance* of the setting—reminded her of why she had chosen to give up the modern conveniences of a life in Nairobi and move to a Zulu village that the South African government made sure advanced little past the Stone Age.

Romance.

Sanura threw the wet shirt over her left shoulder on top of several other already washed items and pulled another soiled garment from her right. She bent again, soaking the cloth in the water, squirted it with soap from a squeeze bottle—another habit she knew brought laughter from the native women—and began scrubbing again.

A tiny smile trickled across the face of the Kenyan. She had met her husband at university in Nairobi, and to call their relationship love at first sight would qualify for the understatement of the year. Chaka, named after the mighty Zulu chief who had succeeded Dingaswayo, had stirred a passion in her heart beyond what she had thought possible. Backward and unskilled in the ways of the world, he had nevertheless exuded a machismo that had charmed the most sophisticated black women from all over Africa. But it had been Sanura who won his heart, and during the next four years, while Chaka mastered the skills that would eventually bring him back to lead his people into the twentieth century, they had married.

Sanura finished the final shirt, turned and waded back through the water to shore. She spread the garments carefully across the flat rocks to dry in the sun, then lay down next to them and closed her eyes. Another smile danced at her lips as she compared this beach to the one at Mombasa where she and Chaka had often gone during their college years. No ice cream and snow-cone vendors *here.* No rum punches or frozen daiquiris with little paper umbrellas floating atop the glass to drink under the shade of a thatched-roof gazebo bar constructed from a building kit manufactured in London.

Behind her Sanura heard noise. She opened her eyes, twisted on the rocks and saw an ox-drawn sled halt in front of the huts. Several of the women still washing clothes hurried up through the surf. They disappeared into their grass homes, returning a moment later with bowls and buckets and began shovelling corn into the receptacles.

The Swahili woman pulled herself lazily from the rocks and walked to her own hut. She found a large clay bowl and followed several others to the cart.

Corn had been scarce during the past few months, the drought bringing on the worst crop failure the country had experienced in years. It was best to ''get while the getting was good.''

Sanura filled her bowl, stowed it on the small wooden table in the hut and returned to the beach. The clothing was almost dry, and she threw it over her shoulders, giggling softly as her mind pictured her mother ironing and starching her father's stiff white oxford cloth shirts.

The only starch the women of Amatikulu were familiar with was in the corn. And if they had ever seen an iron, they would think it was some new weapon the Boers had invented to further torment them.

A sudden flush of shame washed over Sanura. She wondered first what had caused it, and then, in one of those brief dramatic twinklings in which one's soul is opened to the mind, she realized it was her own scorn of the backward Zulu women that had brought on her guilt.

Sanura stopped midway up the beach to her hut. So she was Swahili and came from a tribe that boasted twenty centuries of contact with the outside world. So what? The Swahili, the Zulu, the Xhosa—all the tribes of Africa had the same skin. They were members of the same race, and more importantly than that, they were members of the human race.

Chaka had chosen to return to his people to become a leader of the Tonga Zulu. Perhaps some day he would even follow in the footsteps of his uncle and become a great leader of all of South Africa. If that happened, she would return to a more modern way of life.

But in the meantime she had chosen to support her husband, which meant she had chosen the Zulu as her new people. And while she had done everything in her power to assist her husband in modernizing both their practices and attitudes, it was time to put an end to the arrogance that had accompanied her help.

If she was to be a Zulu, it was time she threw her prejudices aside and began acting like one.

Sanura let the clothing on her shoulders fall to the ground. Later she could wash them again if necessary. Right now she had something far more important to do.

Slowly the Swahili woman slipped the tube top over her head and let her breasts swing free. And with the freedom of her nudity, she suddenly experienced a spiritual freedom she had never before known.

An elderly woman who had not acknowledged her existence since the first day Chaka had brought her home suddenly appeared at Sanura's side. She smiled, nodded approval and had started to speak when the sound of truck engines moving toward the village suddenly filled the air.

Sanura glanced curiously toward the path leading into the trees. A moment later two truckloads of men appeared. Some were white, the rest black. The happiness in her heart rose to new heights. Blacks and whites riding together in the same truck? In South Africa? Perhaps she wasn't the only one who had experienced an awakening from prejudice today. Perhaps South Africa was finally taking a step forward from the bigotry in which it had existed since the Dutch had first settled here.

Sanura turned to the woman still clutching her arm. "The whites are Boers," she said excitedly. "Are the black men Zulus from another village?"

The old Zulu woman's fingernails dug into her arm. She shook her head. "They are Xhosa," she whispered.

"Let's go greet them," Sanura said cheerfully, her heart nearly bursting with love.

But for some reason, the old woman held back.

CHAPTER TEN

Carl Lyons watched Charlie Mott drop the small jet through the air. The wheels hit the tarmac, the brakes hissed like an angry cobra, and a moment later they were gliding to a halt at the end of runway four at Los Angeles International Airport.

"Signed, sealed and delivered," Mott said from behind his mirrored sunglasses. He tipped the visor of his green-and-yellow Athletics baseball cap.

The men of Able Team popped open the aircraft's bubble top and dropped to the ground. As they began unloading their equipment bags, two vehicles cut across the runways toward them. Lyons squinted through the sunlight to see a maroon Dodge with enough antennae sticking up out of the hood and trunk to make it look like a harpooned whale. The second vehicle was a cream-colored Ford sedan.

The vehicles came to a halt next to the jet, and the drivers got out. Both wore identical navy blue pin-striped suits, black wing-tipped shoes and black sunglasses.

They might as well have had Justice Department tattooed on their foreheads.

The taller of the men, still not quite six feet, walked forward and extended his hand. "Special Agent Pete Cornwalis," he said. "Call me Pete."

Lyons grabbed the hand as Schwarz and Blancanales continued to unload the plane. Cornwalis turned to the man who'd driven the Ford. The shorter agent still held the car keys in his left hand. He would have done well to hit five foot eight in cowboy boots and couldn't have tipped the scale at more than a hundred and forty. "Special Agent Rick Loving," Cornwalis said.

Loving shook hands with Lyons, then the two Justice men waited for the big ex-cop to introduce himself and his team. When that didn't happen, Cornwalis cleared his throat uncomfortably.

"Is the tan sedan for us?" Lyons asked as he took a canvas assault rifle bag from Blancanales.

"That's affirmative," Loving said.

Lyons carried the rifle to the car, took the keys from Loving and opened the trunk. "Thanks," he said simply.

The two agents followed him back to the plane, where he grabbed a suitcase in each hand. "Sir," Loving said. "Could we ask..."

Schwarz took a briefcase Mott handed him from the plane and looked up. "Sure you can ask," he said. "And the answer is yes. We could use some help. Grab an armload, boys."

Cornwalis and Loving looked at each other, shrugged and began to help transfer the luggage from the plane to the Ford.

When the job was complete, Lyons slid behind the wheel. Schwarz got in next to him, and Blancanales jumped into the back. The Able Team leader started the engine.

Cornwalis tapped nervously on the window.

Lyons rolled it down. "Yeah?"

"Uh, we don't want to be nosy," the Justice agent said, "but we're really kind of curious as to who you guys are. Uh, Treasury? Justice?"

"No."

Cornwalis laced his fingers together and popped them. "Well, my guess, with all the secrecy, is DEA."

"No again."

The taller agent turned to his partner as Lyons jammed the stick into Drive. "Well, uh, we got orders from Mr. Brognola to rent a vehicle and meet you here. But he didn't tell us who you were. And when the Big Man calls personally and gives an order, we've learned it's best just to do it and not ask questions."

Lyons nodded. "A damn fine policy." He tapped the button, rolled the window back up and drove away.

Schwarz opened a briefcase, pulled out the cellular phone and tapped in the number for Stony Man Farm. He switched the instrument to speakerphone so Lyons and Blancanales could hear, then said, "Hi, Barb. Kurtzman get us the address for America's number-one goose-stepper yet?"

"Stand by."

A series of clicks echoed over the speaker, then Kurtzman's voice came on. "It's 1410 Suggett Avenue," the Bear said as Lyons pulled away from the airport onto the highway. "Beverly Hills, as you might expect. Housing addition called Sleepy Hollow. Everything's unlisted, as you also might expect. I had to get into the IRS to find it. The house, utilities, everything's listed under the name of Terrence Jenkins.

Moler keeps a low profile when he's not on a platform screaming about white supremacy."

"I believe I'd do the same in his shoes," Schwarz said. "There must be about two billion people the world over who'd like to toss a frag grenade down his throat."

"You can count me in," Kurtzman said as Lyons turned up the access ramp to the freeway. "You guys familiar with Moler's background, or you want me to fill you in?"

"Got a general bio on him, Bear," Lyons said. "But go over it for us." He hit the horn, cut in front of a slow-moving tractor-trailer and headed toward Beverly Hills.

Kurtzman cleared his throat. "Born and raised near Pine Bluff, Arkansas. Grew up poor. Left school after the eleventh grade to work the oil fields in Texas and Oklahoma. Evidently the guy's always had the gift of gab, because during the boom he talked someone into lending—I didn't say renting or leasing—lending him a drilling rig. Hit big on a deep well, and the money started flowing in faster than he could count it." The Stony Man computer genius paused.

Lyons heard a match strike, and realized Kurtzman was taking advantage of the opportunity away from his sensitive computers for a quick smoke of his pipe. When he spoke again, it was around the stem. "He was in the Klan as a teenager, but switched over to the American Nazi Party after he struck it rich. Probably bought his way into the top echelons."

"So why the move to L.A.?" Lyons asked.

"Your guess is as good as mine. He's dabbled in the film industry. Produced a few pro-Nazi documentaries. But my guess is that what we've got here is just a backwoods farm boy who got lucky and decided Los Angeles was a better place to live like a king than Pine Bluff.''

Schwarz laughed out loud. ''So what you're telling us, Bear, is that this hillbilly discovered oil. So he packed up his clothes and moved to Beverly. Hills, that is. Swimmin' pools and movie stars—''

''I knew that was coming,'' Blancanales groaned.

Kurtzman chuckled. ''That's basically right, Gadgets. But don't underestimate the man. He might be uneducated, but he's not stupid. The American Nazi Party membership roll has doubled since he took over three years ago.''

''Anything else?'' Lyons asked as an exit sign announcing Rodeo Drive in half a mile appeared.

''Negative,'' Kurtzman said. ''I can keep digging—''

''Do that,'' Lyons said. ''Able One, out.'' He nodded to Schwarz, who hung up.

Lyons slowed at the exit as Schwarz traded the briefcase for a gray metal suitcase. He flipped the latch, opened it and began punching numbers into the computer keyboard on the underside of the lid.

A map of Beverly Hills lit up in yellow on the screen.

Schwarz typed in ''Sleepy Hollow housing addition'' and an area a quarter-mile north of Rodeo Drive turned green. The electronics man added ''Suggett Avenue,'' and a short street near the rear of the green turned red. He typed again, and the designated area enlarged, forcing the surrounding portions off the edge of the screen. He turned the briefcase in his lap so Lyons could see the screen.

Ten minutes later they turned off Weston Boulevard and passed a deliberately aged wooden sign announcing Sleepy Hollow. Lyons slowed the Ford as they drove through a tunnel of towering royal palms, then came to the first street.

Schwarz whistled, staring at the three-story yellow brick mansion that was half-hidden behind a high hedge just beyond the wrought-iron fence.

Lyons glanced toward the map on the screen, turned onto Philbert and drove four blocks past more palatial homes with carefully tended gardens, tennis courts and swimming pools. He turned again at Suggett, and suddenly they were motoring past 1410.

"Oh, this ought to be a piece of cake," Schwarz said.

Lyons kept his eyes ahead on the road as they passed the entrance to Moler's mansion. A half-dozen uniformed men wearing swastika armbands over their khaki shirts stood guard just behind the gate in the eight-foot, razor-wire-topped chain-link fence. More of the Erma-Werke MP-40 submachine guns Able Team had encountered in Miami hung from slings over the guards' shoulders.

Just behind the men stood a brick guardhouse. Half-hidden by the hedge that appeared to surround the property, through the corner of the picture window that was visible, several more khaki uniforms could be seen. As they drove on past the entrance, the men of Able Team caught a glimpse of a rambling, two-story Colonial-style manor. A thin ledge separated the floors, running the circumference of the house.

Blancanales whistled through his teeth. "The place looks like a cross between Graceland and a POW camp."

Lyons drove on, circling the estate, which sat like an island in the middle of Sleepy Hollow. They passed a break in the trees and caught another view of the house across a vast open area. An Olympic-size swimming pool, tennis courts and several outbuildings completed the picture.

They also saw the towering light posts that would illuminate the grounds come nightfall, and at least three dozen more armed men patrolling the grounds.

A smaller gate stood at the northeast corner of the property, equally guarded. Lyons passed it, circled on, then left the housing addition and turned back onto Philbert. Pulling into a convenience store, he threw the Ford into Park, sat back against the seat and closed his eyes.

Okay, even if they blasted their way through the gate, someone in the guard shack would notify the house. There'd be a welcoming party of who knew how many goose-steppers with MP-40s waiting for them before they were halfway up the drive. And Moler himself would have plenty of time to dispose of whatever he was keeping for Ijsselmeer.

No, the way he saw it, there were two avenues of approach. They could climb or cut through the fence that night, hoping they didn't overlook any alarms. But a place like Moler's was going to have backup alarms, and probably backups for the backups. The chances were ten to one that even Gadgets couldn't

spot them all. Even if he did, they'd have to cross the
open area under the lights. And even if they made it,
they'd face the same problem with alarms again once
they reached the house.

The former L.A. detective reached up and pinched
the bridge of his nose with his thumb and index finger. Plan B would be to infiltrate undercover. According to Stony Man, that's what Katz and the men
of Phoenix Force were about to attempt at the Ijsselmeer Building in Amsterdam. But that was a different ball of wax. As large as Moler's estate might be, it
wasn't a hundred stories with thousands of people
coming and going amid whom you could get lost. No,
Moler's castle centered around one man, and anyone
allowed through the gate would be there to see him.

He would know if they didn't have an appointment
and be as curious as hell as to who they were.

Lyons turned off the ignition, got out and entered
the convenience store. He pulled a can of caffeine-free
Diet Coke from a refrigerated rack at the rear of the
room and walked to the counter. A man wearing a red-
checked shirt stood whispering into the telephone.

"Come on, Larry," the man said. "Cover for me.
I been tryin' to get this chick to go out with me for
over a month." There was a pause, then he said,
"Okay, okay, I know it's against policy to take another guy's shift. But who's gonna find out? One
checked shirt's the same as another."

Lyons felt his heart jump.

"Well, fuck you, too!" the man behind the counter
said into the phone. He slammed down the receiver
and turned to Lyons. "That all?"

Lyons nodded, gave him a dollar and took the change.

Gadgets and Pol were waiting when he got back to the car. "Get Stony Man on the phone again," he ordered as he slid behind the wheel.

Schwarz smiled as he punched the buttons on the cellular again. "You've obviously thought of something, Ironman. So how do we get in?"

The big blonde backed the car away from the convenience store, turned back onto Weston and headed toward Sleepy Hollow again. "Right straight through the front door, Gadgets. Right through the front door."

A SOLITARY SHOT—an earsplitting roar—boomed through the jungle. A short burst of autofire followed.

The first blast had been the .44 Desert Eagle he'd left with Dingaan. Easy to identify, as the only combat handgun louder was the pistol the Executioner now carried in his fist—the .50 Desert Eagle. The order of progression had been Dingaan firing first, then the Lyttleton R-5 of the Recce who'd left the other three while still in the air.

Which probably meant the inexperienced leader of the African Civil Assembly had missed and been mowed down with return fire.

The gunfire halted as abruptly as it had begun. Bolan slowed as he neared the site. Whatever had happened was over, and there was no sense bounding into range and letting the Recce take off his head with what rounds remained in the Lyttleton.

But a surprise awaited the Executioner as he paused near the last stand of bushes before reaching Dingaan. Kneeling, he drew back a limb.

The Recce paratrooper lay on his back on the ground, blood pumping from a hole the size of a golf ball in the center of his chest.

Dingaan had emerged from hiding and stood over the body. He held the big .44 Magnum in both hands, the barrel shaking as he trained it on the man's head.

Bolan stepped out from behind the tree. "Mr. Dingaan," he said.

Dingaan swung the big Magnum his way, then lowered it. His head fell to his chest, and he let the gun slip from his hand to the ground. "I was trained as a Zulu warrior since birth," he said. "But this is the first time I have ever killed a man."

"You've never had to before," the Executioner answered, walking forward to pick up the weapon.

Dingaan's hands still shook at his sides as Bolan rose back to full height. He looked up at the Executioner. "You have killed many?"

Bolan nodded.

"Does it become easier?"

"Yes. But you never get to like it. What happened?"

Dingaan shook his head. "I heard someone approaching. He stopped right in front of me. At first I thought it was you."

Bolan frowned. The cover of vines and leaves he had left over Dingaan had been too thick to see through. "What made you decide it wasn't me?"

He nodded at the corpse on the ground. "He called out to me."

Bolan nodded. "And it wasn't my voice."

"No, and I could hear him chopping through the trees with a machete. You did not have one when you left."

"I could have picked one up from one of the other Recces."

"Yes," Dingaan admitted. "I thought of that. But there was another thing that convinced me it was not you."

The Executioner waited as Dingaan's grin widened.

"When he called out to me, he called me 'Lindall,'" the black man said, smiling. "You usually do not. I fired through the leaves at his voice. I was lucky, I guess. The bullet hit him in the chest, I think."

Bolan stooped over, grabbing the Recce's machete from the ground and glancing again to the crater in the man's chest. The heart had stopped pumping, the blood had cleared, and the hole now stared back at him like some giant deadeye. "I'd think so, too." He turned back to Dingaan. "Can you walk now?"

"I think so. I had the opportunity to rest and take another pill while I waited."

"Good. How far to your people?" Bolan asked.

"I do not know," Dingaan replied. "We are in Xhosa country."

"Are the Zulus and Xhosa on good terms these days?"

"Always. Occasionally a minor dispute arises, but nothing serious. If we can find an Xhosa village, they will help us get to my people."

Bolan nodded. He pulled the ruler-compass from the SwissChamp pouch, charted a course southeast and raised the machete. He led the way, chopping through the thick vegetation with the eighteen-inch blade. They moved slowly, a step at a time, stopping so Dingaan could rest every half hour or so.

Two hours later Bolan heard footsteps behind them. He paused, cocking an ear. Several men. Barefoot. Xhosa?

A second later more footsteps sounded to the left and right. They, whoever "they" were, were surrounding him and Dingaan. Closing in.

Not usually the way friends greet one another.

The Executioner handed the machete to Dingaan and drew both Desert Eagles. He used the big autopistols to brush the foliage away and continued forward. They came to a small clearing and started across.

Suddenly a dozen men in Xhosa tribal war colors stepped out of the clearing across from them. Feathers, paint and small tattoolike scars covered their bodies. A few of the men carried bows and spears.

The rest aimed Belgian FAL automatic assault rifles toward the Executioner and Lindall Dingaan.

Bolan halted, motioning for Dingaan to do the same. He dropped the Magnums to his sides as two dozen more men entered the clearing on both sides.

The Executioner heard the leaves rustle behind him. He didn't bother to turn. He knew what he'd see.

One of the men in front of them stepped forward. Tall and muscular, he wore tight necklaces carved from animal bones around his neck. Matching bracelets adorned his arms to the biceps, and his face had been painted with orange and black tiger stripes. He dropped the FAL to the end of the sling over his shoulder and reached behind him.

Another man handed him a spear.

The leader shouted something in Bantu and raised the spear to his shoulder. He continued speaking, his voice gradually rising in both sound and pitch.

Although he didn't understand the man's words, Bolan knew by the tone that the speech was accusatory. "Can you understand what he's saying?" he whispered to Dingaan.

"Some of it," the black leader said. "It is a different dialect, but something to the effect..." He paused, cocking an ear. A puzzled look suddenly covered the black leader's face, and when he spoke again, his voice held an air of astonishment. "That we slaughtered an entire Xhosa village! Murdered women and—"

The leader of the African Civil Assembly halted in midsentence as the spear suddenly flew through the air toward the Executioner.

STONY MAN FARM WASN'T a place where you relaxed during dull moments, particularly during a mission. The fact was, Barbara Price realized as her fingers tapped the keyboard of her computer, there were no dull moments during an operation. And there were damn few in between campaigns.

Price hit the Return key and waited. At the moment she had little to do in her role as mission controller. All three "field arms" of Stony Man Farm— Able Team, Phoenix Force and Mack Bolan—were temporarily out of pocket. But that didn't mean she'd be filing and polishing her nails for the next few minutes. Barbara Price wasn't the type to lie low and be thankful for the rest while others did the work.

She had buzzed into Kurtzman and volunteered to help in the vast computer investigation that he and his team were involved in. And she'd drawn the biographical information on the Ijsselmeer board of directors to fill her spare time.

Price leaned forward as a picture appeared on the screen. Beneath the face of a graying man with a Vandyke beard was the name Hans Redink. She had begun to read the bio below the picture when the phone to her side suddenly buzzed.

The Stony Man mission controller answered before the first ring had ended. She recognized Gadgets Schwarz's voice immediately. In the background she could hear the purr of a car engine and the sounds of more traffic outside the vehicle.

"Afternoon, Barb," Able Team's electronics expert said. "Got a hard-ass ex-cop here who wants to talk to you."

Price heard a click, then Lyons's voice came over the speakerphone. "We've reconned the house," he said. "Here's what we need. You prepared to copy?"

In the background Schwarz whispered, "He still talks like a cop, Barb. You can take the boy out of police work, but you can't take the police work out of the—"

Lyons's voice overrode the rest of the comment as he read off a list of items.

Price whistled. "You want fries with that?"

"No, but send me twenty blacksuits," Lyons replied.

Price's mind went immediately to work, doing its own inventory from memory. Stony Man Farm kept everything imaginable on hand. Everything that might be used during a mission. The problem was that nobody's imagination was big enough to predict the course of each op, and some of the stuff Lyons wanted would take some creativity.

"Give me an hour, plus flying time, Ironman," Price said. "Where do you want it delivered?"

There was a pause on the other end. "Make it the airport again, and use the same Justice Department agents as the go-betweens. Hal's got them scared to death, and they'll do what they're told without asking questions."

"Affirmative." Price hung up, then pressed the intercom button for Leo Turrin in the training office. Turrin, formerly a deep-cover agent with high-level Mob connections, had recently added supervision of Stony Man's training department to his duties.

"Yo," he said as he picked up the phone.

"Leo, I need twenty blacksuits ready to go within the hour. Any problem?"

"Nope. I got most of them shooting up Hogan's Alley at the moment. No hassle pulling them off. Full battle dress?"

"No," Price said, fully aware that what she was about to add would make anyone unfamiliar with Stony Man Farm think she'd lost her mind. "They'll be wearing Nazi uniforms."

Turrin didn't bat an eye. "I'll round them up and get them over to the airstrip," he said. "But the uniforms? Sorry, Barb, can't help you there."

"I know. Just get the men ready."

Turrin hung up.

Price disconnected and pressed Cowboy John Kissinger's number in the armory.

"Yeah, Barb?"

"Cowboy, how many MP-40s do you have on hand?"

Kissinger laughed. "Three or four, I think. Have to check for sure. Not a big demand for them these days."

"No good," Price said. "I need twenty-three."

"That's no sweat," Kissinger came back. "Give me a day or two and I'll—"

"That's no good, either. We've got less than an hour."

"Can't do it. But if it's just pre-1945 German submachine guns you're looking for, I can make up the difference with Gerot Potsdams or Bergmanns. I got the Bergmanns in either MP34/1 or 35/1. Both 9 mm parabellums."

Price hesitated. Lyons had been specific on the 40s, and the way he planned for things to go down, appearance during the first few seconds would be crucial. But the simple skinny on the deal was they didn't have enough MP-40s and couldn't get them within the time frame Able Team needed. Well, this was no different than any other op she'd ever worked on. No matter how well you planned and thought things out, something always came up. So you worked around shortages and unforeseen circumstances.

"Do it." It wouldn't hurt to send the other subguns. If Lyons decided they were better off without them, all he had to do was leave them on the plane. "And I'll need twenty-three pistols from the same era."

"Now here, there's no problem," Kissinger told her. "You want Lugers or Walther P-38s?"

"Ironman didn't say. Send twenty-three of both, and let's make it two thousand rounds for each subgun. Drop to a grand on the pistols."

"You got it," Cowboy came back. "How soon you—"

"Ten minutes ago," Price said, and pressed the flash button. She dialed Kurtzman and waited as the intercom buzzed again.

The easy part was over. What came next would be a little trickier. But she'd had an idea while talking to Kissinger, and it might not be as hard as she'd thought when Lyons first read her the list.

"Bear," Price said as soon as Kurtzman answered, "pull off the Ijsselmeer hunt long enough to find me twenty-three Nazi uniforms. Able Team's already in the L.A. area. Try the Hollywood studios' inventories. Someone's wardrobe department should have them."

"Hang on."

Price twirled in her chair and watched Kurtzman through the glass wall. He had the receiver scrunched between his cheek and shoulder as he pounded the keyboard.

A moment later the computer ace said, "Oh, my God, I can't believe it."

"What?" Price asked.

"I tapped into MGM. They're about to shoot a remake of *Casablanca.*"

"You can't be serious. They'll never top the original. But there weren't that many Nazi parts in that show, were there? There was that obnoxious colonel and his flunkies with the French cop, but—"

"You're forgetting Bogart's flashbacks to Paris," Kurtzman said. "When the Nazis came marching in and he and Ingrid Bergman had to skip town. Plenty of swastikas in those scenes."

"You're right. Has MGM got the costumes together yet?"

She waited as the sound of computer keys tapping lightly in the background returned. "That's a big ten-four," he said a moment later. "They start filming next week. First scenes they've got scheduled are on set right there in the studio."

"That's terrific. Now, how do we get our hands on those uniforms?"

"No problem. I just enter a few MGM interoffice memos. Like, maybe twenty-three of the uniforms need to go out for last-minute alterations, dry cleaning, that sort of thing." He paused. "You sending any other stuff out by air?"

"Uh-huh."

"Good. I'll be finished long before the plane gets there. I'll arrange it so Lyons and the boys can pick the uniforms up at the studio themselves."

"Bear, you're a genius. Buzz me when everything's in place."

"You got it."

LESS THAN TEN MINUTES remained in the work day, and the electricians' truck was still parked in front of the Ijsselmeer Building as Katz led McCarter, Manning and Encizo up the walk to the front doors. They had left a nearby uniform shop only moments earlier, and all of the men wore green coveralls identical to those they had seen on the real electricians. They carried toolboxes, as well.

But the tools inside Phoenix Force's steel boxes weren't screwdrivers, wrenches or pliers.

The doorman stepped outside as Katz came to a halt. He was resplendent in the gold braid covering his shoulders and the bill of his cap, but the bulge under his left arm wasn't lost on the Israeli. The man stood at attention and muttered something in Dutch.

Katz pulled the electrician's ID out of the front pocket of his coveralls and handed it to the man.

The doorman squinted down at the card, then looked up frowning. He spoke again in Dutch.

Katz shrugged. "Do you speak French?" he asked in that language.

"Yes," the doorman answered, switching languages. "You are French?"

"Indeed," Katz said. "Born and bred in Paris."

The doorman's eyebrows lowered. "What I said was, this picture doesn't look like you."

Katz had been ready for that. He chuckled. "I was younger when the picture was taken. You will have to excuse the vanity of an old man, I'm afraid."

"Ah. Then you have been with the company a long time?"

"Longer than I care to remember." The Phoenix Force leader reached for the card, but the doorman drew it back.

"Then how is it that you have never learned to speak Dutch?"

Katz mentally kicked himself. In the hustle and bustle of getting the coveralls and other equipment necessary before the Ijsselmeer Building closed for the night, this discrepancy had never occurred to him. If he'd had time, he could have worked a story around the problem. As it was, he would be forced to gamble, take a shot in the dark.

The Israeli snatched the card away from the doorman and looked at his watch. "Do you think Amsterdam is the only city in which our company does business?" he asked irritably. "I myself have worked in Marseilles, Munich and Brussels, to name only three." He stuffed the ID card back in his pocket. "And do you think that we were sent here to discuss all this with you?"

The doorman's face flushed red. He started to answer, but Katz cut him off. "The answer is no. We were sent here because the electrical problems you are experiencing in this building are far more complex than was believed at first. Mr. Brouer would like the problem taken care of before morning, but if we must stay here much longer and endure your thinly veiled accusations, that will not be possible." He paused again, letting it sink in. "And *you* will get to explain all that to Mr. Brouer."

The doorman opened the door and ushered them in.

Katz led the men of Phoenix Force across the lobby to the elevators, spotting three more uniformed security guards and another in plain clothes. He punched the Up button, then waited as the car chugged its way down. A moment later the men from Stony Man Farm were heading up to the thirty-ninth floor.

The former Mossad operative knew that the next few minutes were crucial. Although the doorman had cowered at the thought that he might have to face Brouer, he would soon get over it. And when he did, he'd realize that Katz's story had a hole or two in it. When that happened, one of three things would follow.

If he decided to ride it out, hoping for the best, Phoenix Force would be home free. The worst-case scenario would be his calling the company to verify that they'd sent additional help. If that happened, there was little Phoenix Force could do. All missions had weak links, and this was the one for the infiltration of the Ijsselmeer Building.

In between the best and the worst of what might happen was the possibility that the doorman would contact the original electricians directly. That was an area over which the men from Stony Man Farm did have some control, and Katz intended to make sure the men in the green coveralls where out of the way in case that happened.

The elevator doors slid back, and Katz stepped out, peering down the hall. The fuse box where the men had stood earlier was open, but the hall was empty. He pulled a set of earphones out of his toolbox, wrapped them around his head and plugged the attached cord into what appeared to be a Sony Walkman.

The other members of the team did the same.

"Fan out," Katz said. "Radio in as soon as you spot them."

McCarter, Manning and Encizo nodded and took off down side halls.

Katz walked to the fuse box, then turned down the "L" at which he'd done his pratfall earlier in the day. He turned two more corners in what was proving to be a confusing labyrinth of walkways, and ran head on into a uniformed guard as he made the last turn.

The guard's hand went automatically to the SIG P-210 on his belt as he stepped back, eyeing the man before him. Like the doorman, he spoke angrily in Dutch.

Katz shook his head.

"English?"

"Yes," the Israeli said.

"If you would get the music out of your ears," the guard said, pointing to Katz's earphones, "you could hear people coming."

"I am sorry. I was sent to join the other electricians. Have you seen them?"

The guard's hand relaxed and fell to his side. "Yes. Take a right at the next hall. Two doors down. The vacant office." He straightened his gun belt and hitched up his pants. "The door was open when I passed a few moments ago."

Just then Manning's voice whispered into his ear over the air waves. "I've found them," he said, then gave directions similar to the ones the guard had given.

"Thank you." The guard nodded, and they walked away toward opposite ends of the hall.

McCarter and Encizo had joined Manning in the hallway outside the vacant office by the time Katz arrived. All three men stood with their backs against the wall, out of sight of the electricians working through the open door. Through the hole Katz could see the signs of remodeling. Wallboard had been stripped from the walls, and sawdust covered the floors.

The two electricians faced away from the door. The one Katz had bumped into earlier held a red plastic current tester. The other was busy splicing a line that hung between the studs in the exposed wall.

Katz motioned for Encizo and McCarter to stay where they were and waved Manning inside with him as he crossed the threshold.

The electricians turned as the Phoenix Force warriors entered the room. They frowned, then looked at each other.

Katz didn't bother to speak. He stopped a step in front of the man he'd collided with, pulled the Beretta from under his coveralls and slammed the barrel against the electrician's temple.

The other man started to scream, but Manning's big right fist closed both his mouth and his eyes.

McCarter and Encizo hurried in and locked the door behind them. Katz and Manning bound the electricians hand and foot with their own wire and fashioned gags from a pile of rags they found in the corner.

Katz glanced up at the acoustical ceiling as his teammates opened their toolboxes, producing pistols, knives and mini-Uzi submachine guns. There was still the chance that the doorman had called the electrical company's offices, and if he had, the security guards would mount a door-to-door search. They had to get the electricians out of sight. Themselves, too.

The Israeli spotted a painter's ladder against the wall. He pulled the legs apart, climbed to the ceiling and pushed up the nearest section.

Two-by-eight joists, three feet apart, ran the breadth of the room. Katz pulled himself up through the opening and stood tentatively on one, bouncing lightly up and down.

The beam gave a cracking sound but held firm.

The men below didn't need to be told. McCarter and Encizo hurried up the ladder to join him. Manning grabbed one of the unconscious electricians, then the other, passing them upward. The other three men from Phoenix Force pulled the bodies into the ceiling and balanced them on the joists. Manning pulled the ladder up out of sight after him.

Katz replaced the ceiling section, and suddenly they were cast into darkness.

"What do we do now?" Encizo asked.

"Try to keep these chaps from falling through the ceiling," McCarter said dryly.

"And wait," Katz added.

CHAPTER ELEVEN

This time DEA Special Agent Charlie Johnston knew where he was. At least which city, anyway. The City of Angels, L.A., Los Angeles. He had been stationed there during his probation year with the Drug Enforcement Administration and recognized the airport runways the minute he and the other nineteen men chosen for this mission had transferred from the Farm's windowless transport plane to the bus.

What he didn't know was why they were now in a concrete building, dressing in World War II Nazi uniforms. Or why they had traded their SIG-Sauer P-220s for Lugers, and their Colt 9 mm carbines for the ancient German MP-40s that a BATF agent had corrected him for calling "Schmeissers."

The door in the plain concrete wall opened, and a big, tough-looking man in a Nazi colonel's uniform walked inside. He wore a 9 mm Luger, the same weapon they'd been issued, in a tanker holster across his chest.

Johnston didn't know the man from Adam, but something written across the colonel's face spelled *cop.*

Two shorter but equally rugged-looking men followed him in the door. Both seemed to carry themselves like career soldiers.

The tall man walked to the front of the room. He rolled down a screen and picked up a wooden pointer. The other two walked to the back of the room and set up the projector that they'd brought with them.

The cop cleared his throat. "All right. Everybody up."

Twenty heads stopped what they were doing and turned to the front of the room. Someone cut the overhead light, the projector beam flashed on, and a moment later they were staring at the diagram of a house and large estate. The layout showed a house just off-center within the tract. To the northeast Johnston saw another large building. Someone had printed "guard barracks" within the rectangular box. Just south of the barracks was a large swimming pool and bathhouse. Tennis courts, a skeet shooting range and a driving range circled the property on the other side of the house.

"It's not important that you know who owns this place," the cop said, "but you're all good men, you're smart, and there's enough clues—what you're wearing, for one—that some of you will figure it out before the mission is complete. I'll have to ask...no, I'll have to *order* you to consider this part of the contract you signed earlier to reveal nothing about the Farm that you inadvertently discover." He paused. "Is that clear?"

Twenty heads nodded silently.

"Good." The man in the colonel's uniform pointed toward a gate in the southwest corner. "Half of you— B Team—will enter the main gate here, right behind my men—A Team. I think you'll recognize the face of your leader." He pointed the stick across the room to the man who had been in charge of training at the Farm, then went on. "C Team will cover the other gate." The pointer moved up and to the right. "The director has picked one of you to take command. The mission of both teams is the same. Simple, but crucial to the overall plan." He tapped two small buildings just inside the gates. "Take control of the guard shacks, and do it before word can reach the house. The guards will have telephones, of course, and there's a shortwave antenna on top of each building, so we have to assume they have radio contact, as well."

Johnston's roommate at the Farm, a Treasury agent named Craig Clarke, raised his hand.

"Yeah?" the man with the pointer said.

"Sir," Clark said. "Am I out of line asking what you're looking for in the house?"

The cop frowned. "We don't know for sure. It may be just the owner...a chance to find out what he knows. But on the other hand, we have reason to believe he's hiding something that we need. And if that's the case, we don't want it destroyed before we get our hands on it."

"But, sir," Clarke said hesitantly, "if you're not searching for anything specific, how in the world did you get a judge to sign the search warrant?"

Johnston watched a tiny smile start to form on the face of the man in the colonel's uniform. At the rear of the room he heard a chuckle from one of the other two. Then the colonel's face tightened again, and he said, "Any other questions?"

The twenty blacksuits shook their heads.

"Okay. I'll lead my team—" the pointer traced the winding drive that looped around the skeet range and swimming pool "—into the house." He turned from the diagram again to face the men. "B and C teams will take over at the guard shack, replacing the real guards. Maintain that position until you receive further orders." He paused, drew in a breath and let it out. "Any questions?"

The hand of a man Johnston hadn't met shot up. "Sir," he said, "what do we do if someone attempts to enter the grounds while you're in the house?"

"Turn them away," the cop said. "With whatever force you find necessary."

Clarke had another question. "Has local law enforcement been notified?"

"No."

The man cleared his throat nervously. "Uh, suppose they—"

"Get a phone call about gunshots, show up and want in?" The man with the pointer shrugged. "I can't answer that. But you men were chosen because you're supposed to be good. You're supposed to be intelligent and creative. So prove it to me if you have to. But remember this—we're on the same side as the cops. The first rule is no cops get hurt."

Johnston grinned. He'd been right about the colonel. If he wasn't a cop now, he had been one.

The man at the front of the room paused once more and slapped the pointer against his open palm. "Anything else?"

The men remained quiet.

"All right, then. Listen for your name while you finish dressing." He pulled a sheet of paper from his pocket. "B Team—Buxton, Camp, Outhier, McGinley, Roberts..." He went on to read the rest of the

names for B Team, then followed with a list for
C Team.

Johnston listened closely. He never heard his name.

"All right, get ready to roll out," the man at the
front of the room said, dropping the pointer. "Any
final questions?"

Johnston raised his hand. "Sir, you never read my
name."

The cop dropped his eyes back to the list. "You
Johnston, Charles?"

"Yes, sir."

The man in the colonel's uniform nodded. "You're
commanding C Team," he said simply, then he and
the other two men who'd come in with him walked out
of the room.

THE HAND HOLDING the big .50 Magnum Desert Eagle flew instinctively upward as the Executioner took
a half step to the side. The leaf-shaped spear head
scraped across the metal of the gun and deflected the
shaft away.

The spear sailed into the brush behind Bolan and
Dingaan.

Bolan dropped the sights of his weapon on the
forehead of the man with the tiger-striped face. His
finger moved back on the trigger, and during the split
second it took before the trigger engaged the hammer, a thousand questions raced through the Executioner's mind. Among them, two stood out as
prominent.

First, why had the peaceful Xhosa decided to attack two lone men in the jungle?

And second, where had the men standing before him now obtained the Belgian Fabrique Nationale FALs? The weapons were brand-new. They hadn't a scratch on them yet, and in fact still gleamed with packing grease.

Bolan's trigger finger suddenly stopped as he saw the Xhosa warriors fumble with the safeties on their unfamiliar weapons. These men didn't know what they were doing. Someone, somehow, had put them up to this.

Dingaan threw his hands in the air, palms out toward the warriors. "Wait!"

The Xhosa froze in their tracks.

Bolan moved slowly, dropping the Desert Eagles to waist level, then sliding the barrels back down into his hip holsters. "Tell them we didn't come to harm them," he whispered out of the side of his mouth to Dingaan. "Tell them I could have killed them before they got the safeties off their weapons. And make sure they know that we know they don't know how to use the rifles."

Dingaan nodded. "I will get those points across. But I hope you don't mind if I am a little more diplomatic. Embarrassing Bantu warriors about their lack of knowledge seems like a bad idea right now."

"Diplomacy's your department. Just do it before the shock wears off, one of them figures out his rifle, and I have to blow him away."

Dingaan took a tentative step forward, his hands still raised in peace. The men, still fumbling to find the safeties on their weapons, raised the rifles toward him. Dingaan looked the chief in the eye and said something in Bantu.

The chief's eyes opened wide in hatred as he replied.

"I asked him if he knew who I was."

"And?" Bolan prompted.

"Oh, he recognizes me, all right. That's the problem." Before Bolan could speak, he went on. "I'm Zulu, and according to him, the Zulus and a band of Boers massacred a Xhosa village not far from here while these men were out hunting."

"Boers and Zulu?" the Executioner said. "That doesn't make sense. That's like getting oil and water to mix."

"I agree." Dingaan turned back to the chief and began to speak in the same soft, even voice that had calmed Herb and Peggy Pendergrast at the Hotel President.

Bolan watched as the Xhosa tribesmen began to relax. Dingaan was a master statesman, and what he said seemed to have an almost intoxicating effect on people. He made the Executioner think of other great charismatic orators. Franklin and Jefferson. Winston Churchill. John F. Kennedy.

The Executioner watched the barrels of the rifles lower. With his powers of verbal persuasion, it was a good thing Lindall Dingaan was on the right side. And it was easy to see why the enemy wanted him dead.

Dingaan finally stopped speaking. The man with the tiger-striped face answered. His voice was now less emotional, but in the eyes above the stripes, Bolan could see that none of the anger over the carnage at the village had left him.

When he had finished, Dingaan turned back to Bolan. "He's not completely convinced that we didn't have anything to do with it, but he's willing to let us live long enough to prove that we didn't."

"Tell him about the plane crash," Bolan said. "Give him directions and suggest he send a couple of men to check it out. Explain about the Recces who attacked us after the crash."

Dingaan did.

The Xhosa chief frowned. He stood thinking for a good two minutes, then turned back to his tribesmen. He waved his hands back in the direction from which Bolan and Dingaan had come, and two of the men took off through the trees.

As the runners left, an idea suddenly struck the Executioner. "Ask him how they know it was the Zulu and Boers if they were away from the village during the attack."

Dingaan nodded. He turned back to the chief and spoke again in the soft, soothing voice. A moment later he told Bolan, "Four children escaped, and these men found Zulu arrows, as well as empty cartridge casings. One of the Zulu was killed by an old warrior who was still in the village. His body is still there."

"The body was left there?" Bolan asked. "Isn't it the Zulu custom to take their dead back home?"

Dingaan nodded. "Yes, particularly in a situation like this where it would not jeopardize any more lives."

Bolan knew that something was wrong here. He didn't care what they found at the scene of the massacre; the thought of the Boers teaming up with the Zulu was inconceivable. "Ask him if we can see the body—the Zulu who was killed."

Dingaan spoke again.

The chief gave it another moment's thought, then agreed. He motioned to his men. They surrounded Bolan and Dingaan, and then the party started off through the trees again.

Fifteen minutes later they reached the ravaged village. The chief led them to the center of the butchery, then stopped and waved his hands excitedly. Tears poured forth from his eyes as he rambled on in words the Executioner couldn't understand.

Bolan surveyed the destruction. Tendrils of black smoke still curled toward the sky from the torched huts. What little livestock the Xhosa had owned—a few emaciated cattle—lay dead, their throats slit.

As the chief had said, spears, arrows and brass casings littered the ground. Dingaan lifted a spear from the dirt and held it close to his eyes for inspection. "It is Zulu," he said, nodding. "But this makes no sense, either. It is newly made. It was not damaged in the battle. It does not even look as if it was used. So why discard it?"

Bolan remained silent as he continued to study the scene. It was looking more and more as though the Zulu, if it had been the Zulu, wanted to make sure they got credit for what had happened. "Where are the bodies of the villagers?" he asked Dingaan.

"They would have tended to their loved ones first," the black leader said. "It is the custom of all Bantu peoples."

The chief raised a hand, motioning them forward. They followed the man with the striped face to the edge of the camp, and Bolan saw a pair of bare brown feet sticking out from behind a smoldering hut. The chief jabbed his finger at the body, then leaned forward and spit.

Bolan studied the corpse. The man had worn tattered Levi's. Although it was hardly an uncommon practice for the tribesmen of Africa to mix Western clothing with native dress, the jeans looked strangely out of place when combined with war feathers, bracelets and necklaces, and the white spots of war paint that covered the man's face and neck like flat pearly measles.

"Now I am convinced," Dingaan said.

"About what?" Bolan asked.

"This man is not Zulu," Dingaan said simply. "Battle is a religious undertaking to my people. The correct clothing is as important as the correct weapons. Denim trousers? Perhaps to work, or to a dance at the kraal. But not into battle."

The Executioner's frown intensified. He knelt next to the body and saw the tiny diamond-stud earring in the left ear. He waved Dingaan down, and the black leader knelt next to him.

Dingaan squinted, looking at the man's ear. "Earrings? Yes, but not that kind."

Bolan noticed a lump in each of the dead man's front pockets. He reached forward, but the Xhosa chief suddenly stepped in front of him.

Dingaan held up his hand. Slowly the chief stepped back.

The Executioner reached into the man's right pocket and pulled out a set of keys. Several looked like either house or office keys. One had the Ford emblem on the side, and another evidently belonged to a safe-deposit box. "Are many Zulu driving Fords through the jungle these days?" he asked Dingaan.

The ACA man smiled. "Of course not. We are a Chevy tribe, for the most part."

Bolan reached into the other pocket, and his fingers struck the lump. He knew what it was before he pulled it out.

The Executioner rose to his feet and held a large roll of hundred-dollar bills in the air. "U.S. currency. Now it's me who's convinced."

"Of what?" Dingaan asked.

"This man not only isn't Zulu, he's American," the Executioner said. "It was the Boer Resistance Movement that massacred this village all right, but it wasn't Zulus with them. The BRM has hired black American mercenaries to pose as warriors from your tribe."

"Mercenaries, yes," Dingaan said. "But how can you be certain they are American? They could have been paid in any currency."

The Executioner held the keys in the air and let them sparkle under the hot African sun. Hanging from the ring in the center, slightly lower than the keys, was a round, black key bob. The side view of a white football helmet was imprinted in the middle.

Los Angeles Raiders, read the tiny words beneath the helmet.

MUSCLE CRAMPS SENT FIRE screaming through Yakov Katzenelenbogen's thighs, and the sharp edges of the two-by-eights that made up the ceiling joists sliced into his knees. The air in the ceiling above the room was hot, thin and smelled like paint and the carcasses of dead rats, and in general the Phoenix Force leader wasn't having a very good time.

Katz glanced at the luminous hands of his watch. Twenty minutes had passed since he and the other members of Phoenix Force had hauled the electricians into hiding above the office. They were still unconscious, safely out of the way where they couldn't tell security that they had no idea the company had sent more help. The plan of the men from Stony Man Farm still had only two defects.

The doorman could have called the electrical office to confirm the arrival of more workmen. Or the guards might make routine searches of the building to check on night workers. If either possibility turned out to be true, it could be hours before the search party got around to this office.

Katz shifted his knees and felt the pain shoot through his thighs again. Phoenix Force would just have to wait. They had to get a fix on the status quo before they made their way toward the penthouse offices of Direk Brouer, CEO of Ijsselmeer, Inc.

Gary Manning put the Israeli's thoughts into words as they balanced precariously between the sections of ceiling. "Are we having fun yet?" the big Canadian whispered.

Katz smiled in the darkness. The smile disappeared as he heard the sound of footsteps outside in the hall. Then a key scraped into the lock.

The former Mossad operative reached down, slipping a corner of the ceiling section up over a joist as the door opened. Below, the light flicked on. A sharp beam shot up through the half inch of space that Katz had uncovered, casting an eerie glow over the faces of

McCarter, Manning and Encizo. Katz looked down and saw the heads and shoulders of a dozen men, some in uniform, others wearing suits and ties, file into the room.

A man wearing sergeant's stripes on the sleeves of his security uniform stopped just below the opening and spoke in Dutch. It was unfortunate that no one on the team spoke the language.

The man who had spoken pointed to one of the toolboxes on the floor. Screwdrivers, hammers and short scraps of plastic covered copper wire fell over the sides of the open lid. He spoke again to a man in plain clothes, who nodded.

Katz leaned closer at an uncomfortable angle, trying to read the man's body language. He could only speculate and hope. He speculated that the sergeant of the guards was saying that the electricians had probably taken a break.

And he hoped that none of the men below would decide to look inside Phoenix Force's toolboxes. Although their weapons and ammo were now in the ceiling, not many electricians Katz had ever known carried around empty toolboxes. That in itself would draw suspicion.

A soft rustling to the Israeli's side caused his head to jerk. He saw the man McCarter was balancing regaining consciousness. If the electrician made a noise or fell through the ceiling, it would mean a firefight. And that in turn would mean Phoenix Force would have to vacate the premises before they had a chance to make their way to the penthouse office.

In the weird half-light McCarter drew his Browning Hi-Power and rested the barrel on the electrician's forehead. Leaning close to the man's face, he raised his index finger to his lips.

The electrician understood. His body stiffened.

Katz looked back down into the hole in time to see the man in the suit shrug. The sergeant led the way back out into the hall and locked the door. The former Mossad man waited, mentally summing up what he had seen and formulating a conclusion as the men's footsteps clicked away down the hall.

The Ijsselmeer security men hadn't entered the room with their weapons drawn, and their attitude had been too cavalier for them to have been hunting anything specific. His guess was that this had been a routine night inspection of all offices.

But a dozen men patrolling the halls of a closed building? Nobody hired that many guards unless they had something to hide. It was time to find out what that something was.

Katz pulled the section of ceiling the rest of the way back, grabbed a beam and lowered himself back into the room. His rubber-soled boots made a light squishing sound as he dropped to the tile, then he reached up and helped Encizo down through the hole. Manning and McCarter lowered the two electricians, then followed as Katz and Encizo stretched the bound and gagged men out on the floor.

Katz nodded to Manning. The big Canadian unzipped the black belt pack around his waist and pulled out a small leather case that looked as if it might contain a pen-and-pencil set. He flipped the lid and produced a hypodermic needle and small vial of colorless liquid. Kneeling next to the closer man, he filled the syringe as Katz rolled up the man's sleeve.

The electrician stared up in terror.

"It is only Pentothal," Katz whispered into the man's ear in French. The electrician's eyes relaxed, then closed as Manning plunged the needle into his arm.

As soon as the other man was asleep, Katz moved to the door. Through the translucent glass, he saw the distorted hallway. Inching the door open, he poked his head into the hall. Clear.

The Israeli led the way to the elevator, then stopped. There were enough security men on the premises that if one noticed the car going up to the penthouse, he should figure it was just a fellow officer. On the other hand, the guards very likely had prescribed duties that were performed the same way every night. If the elevator violated those preordained assignments, it would raise some eyebrows. And a little voice in Katz's head told him that Direk Brouer wouldn't want the guards snooping around his private office under any circumstances.

Katz moved on to a red exit sign and pushed the door open to the stairs. He heard Manning grunt behind him, then ushered the men through to the steps. He knew what was bothering the Canadian, and it wasn't the exercise involved in the sixty-floor climb they were about to undertake.

It was the time element. They had no idea how long it would take to find the list of double agents in the South African government.

The Israeli waited until the last of his team had started up the steps, then swung the door silently closed and started after them into the darkness.

LYONS FELT THE COLLAR of the wool uniform scour his neck as he twisted the wheel of the big Cadillac. He'd worn a lot of different types of undercover clothes during his lifetime, both as an L.A. cop and during his stint with the Farm. But he'd never worn anything that irritated him this much.

No, the scratchy wool definitely rubbed his neck the wrong way. Not to mention his soul.

The Able Team leader adjusted the headset mike in front of his face as the gate to David Moler's estate appeared up the street. "A Team to B," he said. "You ready, Puss?"

"Affirmative, Ironman," Leo Turrin came back. "Just give us the word."

"Stand by," Lyons replied, slowing the Caddie to a crawl. "A Team to C. Come in C Team. Answer me, Charlie."

Charlie Johnston, the bright young DEA agent who had impressed both Turrin and Hal Brognola during his brief stay at Stony Man, came on. "C Team in place, sir. We're ready to rock and roll."

"Stand by."

Lyons pulled into the drive and slowed to a halt in front of the gate. Next to him Blancanales opened the shotgun door and stuck a leg out, rising above the car to make sure his uniform could be seen by the guards. He motioned them forward, then got the rest of the way out and slammed the door.

Two men carrying MP-40s started toward the gate. One wore a dirty-blond mustache that completely hid his upper lip. The other carried a large round key ring. Both had looks of puzzlement on their faces.

Lyons waited as Blancanales walked forward to meet them. The plan was simple. Rosario "Politician" Blancanales hadn't gotten his nickname by accident, and if he could talk his way through the gate, great. It would make things easier. But if that didn't work, they had a backup plan in place.

But under no circumstances were the two guards who now met Pol on the other side of the gate going to make it back to the shack to radio the house for further orders.

Lyons's foot rested just above the accelerator as he watched Blancanales talking to the two guards. The one with the mustache glanced over his shoulder toward the brick building behind him. When he turned back, he shook his head.

"They aren't buying it," Schwarz said from the back seat.

Blancanales said something else and got another shake of the head. The man with the mustache held up a hand, then started toward the guardhouse.

Rosario Blancanales opened the flap on his holster and jerked a sound-suppressed Luger 9 mm from the pouch. Through the closed windows of the Cadillac, Lyons heard a soft *pffffft* and watched the archaic toggle bolt on top of the pistol blow back and up, jacking another round into the chamber. A moment later the Nazi with the mustache lay on the driveway.

The man holding the key ring looked from his partner to Blancanales, his eyes opening wide in surprise as he went for his side arm.

A second round from the Able Team warrior's weapon sent the Nazi sprawling to the pavement. The key ring clattered from his hand and rolled along the gate.

Blancanales knelt, stretching his arm through the gate toward the key. Lyons watched his fingers brush the ring—just out of reach. The ex-cop glanced toward the windows along the front of the guardhouse and saw several strange faces peering through the glass, trying to figure out what was going on.

Pol tried again for the key ring, then jumped to his feet. He pressed the muzzle of the Luger against the gold padlock securing the gate and pulled the trigger. The screech of lead against metal was louder than the quiet 9 mm, and before it died down, he was swinging the gate inward.

"Move in!" Lyons shouted into the headset. He gunned the accelerator, and the Cadillac darted through the space. A shrill shriek accompanied by a metallic crunch met his ears as the front bumper collided with the opening gate and drove it on in.

Lyons hit the brakes, screeching the big car to a halt as the iron entryway rebounded off the fence and came swinging back.

Schwarz leaned over the seat and opened the passenger's door as the gate struck the bumper once more.

A split second later the men of Able Team were tearing up the drive past the swimming pool toward the house. In the rearview mirror Lyons saw the white Chevy van carrying B Team roar through the gate. Turrin popped from the front seat as the side door swung open. The little Fed turned and sprinted toward the guard shack, ten Stony Man blacksuits at his heels.

Lyons swerved the Cadillac to a halt in front of Moler's mansion and jumped out. He raced up the steps and vaulted to the porch.

The Able Team leader's last thought as his boot struck the door was that he hoped Turrin and Johnston had secured the guard shacks in time.

CHARLIE JOHNSTON HEARD the colonel shout "Move in!" and nodded toward Craig Clarke behind the wheel of the Chevy van.

Clarke threw the gearshift into Drive, and the vehicle rounded the final corner toward the northeast gate of the estate.

A trio of Nazi guards stood smoking just behind the iron gate. MP-40s hung from their shoulders. They held their cigarettes in that irritating, baroque, palm-up method that had always made Johnston want to slap the smokes out of the actors' hands when he'd seen it in old movies.

Through the window on the other side of the fence, men in Nazi uniforms were seated behind desks. None of the guards, either in or out of the guard shack, appeared to be the least bit worried.

Johnston breathed a silent sigh of relief. Moler's estate was big—big enough that the Nazis at this gate hadn't heard the gunfire he'd heard over the headset.

The three men at the gate looked up as the black van came up the drive. Johnston smiled through the windshield and waved, as if he'd just spotted a long-lost comrade.

The three guards squinted into the van, trying to figure out which one of them he recognized.

"Now," Johnston said simply.

Clarke floored the accelerator, and the van shot forward. The reinforced steel bumper slammed the gate doors where they merged, popping the chain as the guards dived out of the way. A moment later the Chevy screeched to a halt next to the brick guard station, and the rear and side doors slid open.

Eight Farm hardmen clad in Nazi regalia piled out of the van as Johnston and Clarke shot from the front seat.

The surprised guards rolled to their feet, fumbling for their MP-40s. Johnston and his men raced forward, the torpid 9 mm autofire from their own primitive MP-40s filling the air.

A guard with a shaved skull caught the DEA agent's first burst of fire, his khaki uniform turning dark with blood as the deadly rounds pierced his thighs and chest.

Out of the corner of his eye Johnston saw Clarke mow down a man wearing a neatly trimmed red beard. The Nazi danced like a marionette on the end of a string as the sluggish rounds jerked him back and forth. One of the other men behind Johnston finished the job, taking out the final outside guard with a steady stream of parabellums.

Johnston's foot hit the entrance to the guard shack as it had done to countless crack-house doors over the years. He felt a thrill of exhilaration as the wood splintered around the lock. The door swung inward, and as had also happened so many times during drug raids, Johnston heard the "bees" buzz over his head.

He hit the ground as a round ripped through the edge of the swastika armband on his shoulder. Just as well, he thought, as he rolled to one knee and brought the MP-40 to waist level. The emblem of murder and mayhem had caused a knot in his stomach ever since he'd slipped it up his arm.

The DEA agent held the trigger back, sending two short bursts into the belly of a man wearing a major's uniform. The Luger that had destroyed Johnston's armband dropped from the man's limp fingers as he fell facedown on the floor. More gunfire exploded around the DEA man as Farm blacksuits poured through the door behind him.

Johnston heard a voice in the far corner of the room. "Main gate to house," the voice whispered. "Come in, house! Main gate to—"

The DEA man swung his weapon toward the noise. Another Nazi was crouched behind a green metal desk. The wires to a console shortwave mike ran from the top of the desk out of sight. Johnston dropped the sights on the desk and cut loose with a long burst of 9 mm rounds. Black holes appeared in the green metal, their edges ringed in gray as the hot rounds burned away the paint. The man behind the desk stopped talking and leaned forward into sight, the console mike still gripped in his hands. He opened his mouth to speak, but blood poured forth instead.

Six more men fell to the blacksuits' onslaught, then Clarke ended the foray with a final volley of rounds into a Nazi corporal who had dived for the telephone on his desk.

Suddenly the guard shack became silent. Then the silence was broken by the radio.

"House to main gate. House to main gate. You have traffic?"

Johnston bent over the major and pried the mike from his dead fingers. He felt his chest heave for oxygen. Okay. Inventive and creative, the colonel had said. He tried desperately to remember what the man's voice had sounded like as he'd squatted behind the desk. He couldn't. Lowering his own voice to a whisper, he said, "Main gate to house. Negative, house. False alarm."

There was a pause on the other end. Then the voice said, "House to main gate. Guard on radio duty, identify."

Johnston rolled the major to his side and stared briefly at the name tag on his uniform. "Major Brisdon," he whispered again, then coughed and cleared his throat."

"You don't sound like yourself, Major."

"Flu bug," Johnston croaked. He knew how weak the cover was, and almost crossed his fingers as he waited for the next response.

"Major Brisdon," the voice said, "report immediately to—"

Then Johnston heard three simultaneous hisses over the radio. The voice stopped talking, and a moment later the A Team colonel came on. "A Team to C. Your gate secure?"

"Affirmative," Johnston replied. Those three guys—whoever the hell they were—were good. They were already in the house.

"Maintain status," the colonel said, and clicked off.

Johnston hurried to the front of the room. He pointed to three blacksuits to his right, then stuck his finger through the open door and pointed to the Nazis on the ground. "Get those men inside!" he ordered.

The DEA agent glanced at a door in the wall. "Clarke, you and Burelli drag those bodies into that rest room, if that's what it is. Get them out of sight, anyway." He turned to another man. "Find a mop, Koffman. There should be a utility room here somewhere. And get this blood off the floor." He paused for breath, then went on. "I want this place as spick-and-span as your mama's kitchen in case the cops—" the screech of approaching sirens suddenly cut him off "—*when* the cops show up. Move it!"

Koffman was already mopping up the blood on the floor as Johnston hurried to the door. He stepped aside as the three blacksuits dragged the bodies of the gate guards inside and deposited them in the rest room. Moving on to the gate, he remembered the torn swastika armband and ripped it away. He stuffed the red rag into his pocket as the first of four squad cars turned into the drive, red lights flashing and sirens blaring. The DEA agent closed the gate and wrapped the broken chair through the bars, then stood back and shot his arm up in a Nazi salute.

Two police officers got out of the lead vehicle, broke the thumb snaps on their holsters and drew automatic pistols. They walked cautiously forward as three more pairs of officers exited their cars and fanned out, covering the front.

An older cop with gray around the temples stopped just the other side of the gate. He nodded in disgust as Johnston walked forward. "You the head Kraut in charge here?"

Johnston nodded.

Disgust covered the police officer's face as he eyed Johnston's uniform. "Okay, Hitler, what happened?"

"Nothing happened, Officer," Johnston replied.

The younger cop, a kid who looked to Johnston as if he might have to start shaving soon, shoved his face into the bars. His jaw tightened in a fierce grimace that almost made Johnston burst into laughter. It made him think of the tough-guy persona he'd tried to effect when he'd been a rookie himself. "Look," the kid said, "we got a call that there were shots fired. Don't tell me nothing happened. Something happened, and we intend to find out what."

"Shots fired?" Johnston said. He smiled. "The neighbors are exaggerating again, I'm afraid. They're Communists." He nodded over his shoulder. "Some of the men were watching a cop show on television with the door open." He knew the officers wouldn't buy it. But he also knew that at this point, they had no probable cause to come on the property without being invited.

The older cop looked down at the snapped chain and broken lock. "How'd that happen?"

Johnston shrugged. He pointed to the black Chevy van still parked next to the guard house. "Brakes went out. Lucky it was on private property, huh? Some innocent citizens might have gotten hurt otherwise."

The young cop's face had turned red, and Johnston knew he was fighting the urge to take a poke at him through the bars. Well, let him. If he did, the older man would be more worried about lawsuits and police-brutality charges.

"You mind if we come in and take a look around?" the older cops asked.

What Johnston said next surprised the hell out of him. Because he'd heard it himself so many times as a cop, he couldn't believe he'd actually say it himself. "You got a warrant?"

Neither cop answered.

"I didn't think so. Since you got no warrant and nothing happened here, it's time for you to go. Go on. Get the hell out of here. We know our rights."

The young cop gripped the bars until his knuckles turned white. Finally the older man pried them away from the gate, and they started back toward the cars. "Ten-twenty-two!" the man in blue yelled to the other officers.

Johnston waited until the four cars had left, then walked back to the guard shack. His duty wasn't over. He and the other men on loan to the Farm had to take care of anything else that came up while A Team was still in the house. He opened the door, stepped inside and sat down at a desk.

It was a hell of a world, Charlie Johnston thought suddenly. Sure, everybody did have rights. Should have rights. But those rights had been distorted to the point where criminals and hate mongers seemed to have free rein these days.

Johnston smiled, though. He'd never seen it happen before, and he didn't expect to ever see it happen again. But for once that distortion had worked out for the best.

CHAPTER TWELVE

The white football helmet on the black L.A. Raiders key chain sparkled like snow under the hot Zululand sun. Bolan let it dangle in front of him as he watched the lined face of Lindall Dingaan wrinkle further in thought. The man seemed to age ten years as the truth and magnitude of what was happening sank in.

"Then the Boer Resistance Movement is attempting to start a war between the Zulus and Xhosa?"

Bolan nodded. "It appears that way. And if they massacred the village here, there's a good chance they did the same thing to your own Zulu people. And made it look like the Xhosa and Boers were responsible."

"My God..." Dingaan breathed. He reached under his robe, produced the bottle of nitroglycerin tablets and slipped one under his tongue. "My people will not only come here looking for revenge, but they will lay waste to every innocent Boer family they encounter on the way." His eyes closed in thought. When he opened them a moment later, he started to continue. "We must—"

A sudden thrashing in the jungle just beyond the village caused Dingaan to halt. He, Bolan and the Xhosa chief turned toward the noise and saw a slender young black man dressed in Xhosa war regalia come stumbling out of the foliage in exhaustion.

The man staggered to the chief, then fell to his knees panting. When he'd caught his breath a moment later, he looked up and began to speak in Bantu.

Bolan watched Dingaan's eyebrows rise. The grim expression of hatred returned to the chief's face. "Lord help us all," Dingaan breathed softly.

"What?" Bolan demanded.

"There is a Zulu war party less than three miles from the village. They are headed this way."

The Executioner shook the key chain. "Tell the chief what's going on."

Dingaan reached out, trying to take the chief by the shoulder, but the man turned quickly, barking orders to his fellow tribesmen. Low, muffled war chants issued from the lips of the Xhosa warriors as they lifted spears, bows and the newly acquired automatic rifles over their heads. The chief shouted again, and another slim scout raced up. He stood briefly next to the panting man on the ground as the chief spoke, then sprinted off into the trees, down a path Bolan assumed led to the next village.

Dingaan moved forward again, this time successfully grabbing the chief by the shoulders and spinning the man to face him.

Fire burned in the Xhosa's eyes. His hand shot automatically to the dagger suspended around his waist. Dingaan dropped his arms, stepped back and spoke in a soft voice, pointing to the key chain in Bolan's hand.

The chief hesitated, then shook his head.

Dingaan turned to Bolan. "He does not believe me."

Bolan hurried toward the chief, stopping momentarily as a tribesman carrying a case of rifle ammo raced toward the center of the village where the warriors had gathered. The Executioner shoved the roll of American money into the chief's face. "Keep trying," he ordered Dingaan.

The black leader spoke again. The chief frowned, then answered.

"He is still skeptical, to say the least," Dingaan told the Executioner.

Bolan turned around, reached down and hauled the still-panting Xhosa scout to his feet. "Ask him what weapons the Zulu carried."

Dingaan turned to the young man and spoke again in Bantu. The scout pointed excitedly to the men with the rifles as he answered.

The Executioner didn't need a translation. He turned toward the chief. "That's what I figured," he said directly to the man. "FALs. Exactly like the ones you were provided. Does that tell you anything about where they came from?"

Dingaan started to interpret, but the chief held up his hand. He had figured it out for himself. He spoke rapidly in the strange language, waving his arms wildly as he spoke.

"He understands," Dingaan said. "But he says that if the Zulu attack, his warriors will have no choice but to defend themselves and the village."

The African Civil Assembly leader glanced around. "At least what remains of it."

The Executioner looked off into the jungle, in the direction from which the runner had come. He could almost hear the pounding of feet as the misinformed Zulus raced toward the Xhosa village, their hearts lusting for the blood. For retribution. For justice.

Bolan understood that feeling. Their families had been killed, and although no amount of revenge could ever bring their loved ones back, the Zulu knew that justice demanded that the guilty pay for their crimes.

A momentary sadness crept over the Executioner. Brief glimpses of his mother, father and sister flashed out of his memory bank. In some ways what had happened to the Xhosa and Zulu wasn't so different than the events that had led him into his one-man war against murder and mayhem so many years ago.

Bolan pushed the painful visions from his mind. There was one big difference, though. And that was the fact that while there was a guilty party involved in the massacres, a guilty party that should, and would, pay for its crimes if the Executioner had anything to say about it, the culpable group wasn't the warriors of the two tribes who were about to annihilate one another.

Reaching out with both hands, Bolan grabbed Dingaan by the shoulders. "You've got to make him understand that if he goes to war with the Zulu, he'll be playing right into the hands of the Boer Resistance men."

Dingaan nodded. "I have already made that point. He will not advance on the Zulus, as he would otherwise. But he says he will not run, either. Unless the Zulus leave Xhosa country, they will be killed."

The Executioner looked at the chief, who nodded as if he'd understood. Turning back to Dingaan, Bolan studied the man. The stress of the past few days had taken its toll. As he watched, Dingaan coughed, and even that effort seemed to leave him breathless.

The situation was simple yet complex. The Zulu had to be convinced of the truth concerning the BRM's plot before they reached the Xhosa village. The Executioner had no doubt that the skilled statesman he saw before him now could pull it off. But by the looks of him, there was no way Lindall Dingaan could run through the jungle to meet his fellow tribesmen without dropping dead after the first ten yards. And Bolan himself didn't even speak the language.

The Executioner stared into the weary eyes in front of him. "Take another pill."

"What?" Dingaan answered.

"Take another nitro pill."

Dingaan frowned in confusion, then lifted his robe again and slipped another of the tiny white tablets into his mouth.

Bolan looked down at the scout who still squatted on the ground. "Tell him to show us where he saw the Zulus," he told Dingaan.

The black leader spoke to the man in Bantu.

The scout looked hurriedly to the chief, who nodded.

In one smooth motion Bolan stooped and hoisted Lindall Dingaan onto his back.

"What—"

Bolan had no time to explain. He and the scout broke into a jog toward the trees.

YAKOV KATZENELENBOGEN knew that even if Stony Man Farm had not demanded it, Phoenix Force would have stayed in top physical condition. Each of the warriors he commanded was different in terms of skill, size and strength—differences that made each and every one of them invaluable to the team.

Rafael Encizo could near a four-minute mile on a good day, and while Gary Manning might still be a half lap behind when the little Cuban crossed the finish line, the big Canadian neared world-class power-lifting status in the bench press. All five of the men were skilled martial artists, but David McCarter and Calvin James took the discipline one step further.

Either one of them could have given Chuck Norris or Steven Seagal a run for his money.

Yes, Katz thought as he puffed his way up the final set of stairs to Direk Brouer's penthouse, Phoenix Force was in great shape. But there were sixty floors between the thirty-ninth and the ninety-ninth. Each floor consisted of two stairwells having ten steps each. That made twelve hundred steps they had raced up as quietly as possible, carrying weapons and gear that probably averaged out to about fifty pounds per man.

And that physical exertion would take its toll on anyone. Maybe even Superman.

Katz twisted the front of his miniflashlight and shot the light up at the gray steel door. He traced a rectangle around the cracks between the door and frame. There appeared to be no wires; no alarms. Direk Brouer evidently figured he had so much security below that the digital lock just above the shining brass knob was enough.

Katz glanced over his shoulder at the men standing on the steps just below him, and his gaze rested on Manning. The big Canadian was Phoenix Force's explosives expert. He could blow the door. He might even be able to rip it from its hinges with the mighty shoulders that threatened to burst through his electrician's coveralls. But that wasn't what Katz needed right now.

As the men from Stony Man Farm continued to catch their breath, Katz trained the beam of his flash on McCarter. The Briton had picked up all kinds of skills at both Sandhurst Academy and in the Special Air Service. He could probably get through the lock as well as Katz himself, with his Mossad training.

The Israeli shifted the light to Encizo.

The little Cuban grinned. Without being told, he stepped up to the lock.

Katz stepped back, holding the light just to the side of the doorknob. Yes, Encizo was the man for this job. The CIA had trained him for anti-Castro attacks in his homeland, and the ability to get clandestinely in and out of locked doors had been only one of the ex-patriot's fortes.

Encizo pulled a small notebook and pen from the pouch on his belt. Katz guided the light to the page and watched while the little Cuban numbered the lines one through nine. Then Encizo pressed his ear against the lock and slowly punched the number 1.

Raising his head, he drew a line through the number in his notebook. The Cuban systematically went through the numbers, striking out all but the 3, 5, 7 and 9. When he'd finished, he pressed those numbers again, holding his ear against the door once more.

Katz held the light for him while he changed the order in his notebook to 5, 7, 3 then 9.

Taking a step back, Encizo punched the digits in that order. A faint buzz sounded from the door.

The Israeli twisted the knob. It opened.

The men from Stony Man Farm stepped into the reception area and closed the door behind them. Katz waved the flashlight across the room, quickly taking in the receptionist's area, several small filing cabinets and the large picture windows that looked out over the bright lights and channels of Amsterdam.

"David," the Israeli whispered, then nodded toward the receptionist's area.

The Briton slid into the chair behind the computer and tapped the On button. A low hum started as the machine programmed itself. The former SAS officer opened a plastic file box containing three-and-a-half-inch disks as Encizo moved to the door in the far wall.

The new digital lock took less time than the first. Thirty seconds after he'd started, Encizo led the way into Brouer's private office. Again Katz used the flash to recon the room—a large oak desk with another PC, a wet bar against the wall and another breathtaking view of the city through the window.

"Take the computer, Rafael," Katz ordered. "See what you can call up. Gary, start on the filing cabinets. You know what we're looking for. Anything that looks like it might be a list of the double agents on Brouer's payroll."

The two men nodded. Encizo dropped into Brouer's thickly padded leather armchair as Manning slid open the top drawer of the nearest cabinet.

Katz walked to the window, staring out over the intertwined canals that made up Amsterdam. Mechanically searching the files, both hard and soft copy, was only one aspect of the hunt. Brouer's secrets might be found filed away on page or disk like any other information. If they were, Phoenix Force would find them.

None of them—McCarter, Manning, Encizo, or Katz himself was any Aaron Kurtzman when it came to computers. But they knew how to work the machines and what to look for.

Katz moved to the corner next to the windows, shining his light on a framed print of Vincent van Gogh's *The Potato Eaters*. The haggard, impoverished faces seated around a wooden crate looked back at him.

The Israeli had a different plan of attack. He might be wrong, but if he had been in Direk Brouer's shoes, he'd have kept the list of double agents in one of two places. Either on his person at all times or hidden so well that anyone who chanced to make it through the tight security still wouldn't find it.

Katz reached forward and lifted the van Gogh off the wall. He found a bare wall, rather than the safe he'd hoped for. He replaced the painting and moved along the wall, lifting prints and original canvases. Each time the blankness behind the frames seemed to laugh at him. He moved across the room, checking quickly behind a small bookshelf, then sliding the light along the wall to the wet bar. He transferred the bottles of spirits and mixers from the shelf behind the bar to the cabinet and pried at the corners of the mirror. It was bolted fast to the wall.

Katz started to turn, the flashlight's beam moving in an arc as he twisted. Then suddenly he stopped.

Something had caught his eye. Something was out of place, or maybe just . . . different.

But what?

Slowly the former Mossad agent turned back toward the bar. The flashlight beam drifted across a light switch, then a small candelabrum fastened to the wall. His arm slowed as his pulse quickened.

The light stopped on an electrical outlet in the wood paneling next to the sink.

Katz squinted at the two triple-pronged plug-ins within the white plastic rectangle. The three holes in each stared back at him, looking like a pair of cartoon faces. That was what had caught his eye. This outlet was what had made him uneasy. But why?

The Israeli leaned in, aiming the light straight onto the electrical outlet. It looked no different than any other. Except...

Katz turned and looked along the bar, seeing an electric blender at the other end. He hurried toward the appliance, unwrapping the cord around the base as he retraced his steps back to the outlet. Grasping the rubber end, he shoved it at the wall.

The prongs hit the plastic inside the holes.

Katz transferred the cord to his prosthetic hand, using his other to bend the prongs slightly outward. This time the plug scratched awkwardly into the socket. The Israeli pushed the blender's On switch.

Nothing happened.

Katz ripped the cord out of the wall and pulled his Swiss Army knife from his pocket. Flipping out the small screwdriver blade, he went to work on the screw between the prong holes.

That was what had tipped him off. The size of the outlet. It wasn't much bigger than the normal unit, just enough to have caught his subconscious eye.

And enough to hold one of the three-and-a-half-inch floppy diskettes that both of the computers in the penthouse worked off.

A moment later the plastic cover fell off in Katz's hand. But instead of electrical wiring in the hole, he saw another piece of flat white plastic. A small handle extended toward him, and the Israeli pinched it between his thumb and forefinger.

When he pulled forward, the wall safe swung out like a lazy Susan cabinet.

Katz reached into the tiny vault and pulled out the disk. He turned and hurried toward the desk where Encizo had pulled up the files on another disk. "Anything promising?" the Israeli whispered.

Encizo shook his head. "Not so far."

The Israeli opened the disk door, pulled out the disk and inserted the one he'd just found. "What program are they using?" he asked.

"WordPerfect," Encizo answered. "Take your choice—5.2, 5.1 or 4.2."

Katz punched in the numbers for 4.2 and hit the gray F5 key. The file menu for the hard disk appeared on the screen. He hit the appropriate keys, and the menu changed to the floppy disk.

The disk contained only one file. It was innocuously entitled A. The Israeli moved the cursor to A, then hit the key to retrieve the file.

A column on the left listed dates; the center column, amounts of money.

But the column on the left looked like a mangled mass of nonsense.

An uneasy feeling, not unlike the one he'd gotten when he'd seen the electrical outlet, settled in Katz's heart. The Israeli couldn't read Dutch, but he was fluent in German, and there were certain similarities between the two languages. At least enough similarities that he could see that the document was in some type of coded gibberish.

Looking back to the left-hand column, Katz heard a bell go off in his head. The first date corresponded with the assassination of Robert De Arnhem.

And someone had been paid one hundred thousand dollars on that date.

He looked down the list. The next date had been the day after the assassination—the day that Phoenix Force had arrived in South Africa and battled the black invaders at the Boer farm.

The same coded name on the right had picked up another hundred grand that day.

Skipping down the list, Katz saw that the same coded name appeared several more times. He moved to the last entry and drew a deep breath. This was not only a list of the traitors—it was a timetable of destruction.

The last date was still three days off, the same day as the election to repeal the referendum. But the amount had already been entered.

The same man who appeared at the top of the list would make a cool million that day.

Katz rubbed the stubble of beard on his chin. There were at least twenty different traitors on Brouer's payroll. But one man seemed to lead all the rest.

Encizo had been looking over his shoulder. The little Cuban now flipped a switch on the laser printer next to the computer, and the machine hummed on. Katz programmed the computer, and a copy of the list shot out of the printer.

He moved to the fax machine on a table next to Brouer's desk. A few moments later the coded page was heading over the wires to Stony Man Farm.

Katz wiped sweat from his brow. Maybe Kurtzman could make sense of the mess. He erased the evidence of the fax transmission, then stuffed the hard copy into his coveralls and looked up. "We've got all we're going to get," he whispered to Encizo. "Go tell Gary and David to get ready. We leave in two minutes."

Encizo nodded and tiptoed out into the reception area.

Katz killed the printer and computer and hurried back to electrical-outlet–wall-safe. He had started to replace the disk when he heard the footsteps in the hall.

A moment later glass broke, then gunshots exploded in the reception area.

Katz raced to the door in time to see an army of Direk Brouer's security mercs charging into the room.

LYONS'S FIRST KICK rocked the solid oak door on its hinges, the brass knocker clattering back and forth as if he'd knocked.

The Able Team leader brought his leather storm trooper boot back up to his knee, then lashed forward again, the force of the blow sending the barrier swinging inward.

Lyons went in low, his MP-40 gripped in his fists and aimed at gut level. The door rebounded off the wall, and he shouldered it back as Gadgets and Pol raced in behind him.

The ex-cop had lost count of the doors he'd broken down during his long career. But he hadn't lost track of the technique or the list of priorities.

The first objective was always to get in. However you could. Once inside, your eyes swept the room, the weapon in your hands following. Lyons had been well trained, and followed procedure.

The former L.A. cop caught a brief glimpse of the empty dining room off the hall to his left. A multicolored crystal chandelier hung over the long formal dining table. His line of sight moved on to the marble-trimmed spiral staircase directly in front of him. Also empty.

By the time he turned to his right, the man in the Nazi corporal's uniform was halfway into the hall from the living room. He'd been trained, too, but the expression of terror on his face told Lyons his education had never been tested by combat.

The Able Team leader made sure it never would. He shoved the barrel of his subgun into the Nazi's belly as the man ground to a halt. The corporal never got a chance to pull the trigger of the weapon in his hand. Nine-millimeter rounds exploded from the MP-40, staining the carefully pressed khaki blouse with powder burns and blood. They exited the Nazi's back, pulling more blood, flesh and fragments of spinal column in their wake.

As he pulled back the bloody subgun, Lyons heard 9 mm explosions go off next to him. The weapons in both Schwarz's and Blancanales's hands jumped with recoil. Turning, the ex-cop saw a Nazi with sergeant's stripes tumble over the railing of the staircase.

Lyons glanced again to both sides of the hall. Through the living and dining rooms he could see more doors opening into various areas of the mansion. He motioned Gadgets right, Pol left, then raised the MP-40 and started up the coiled stairs.

A head wearing a black SS cap appeared over the second story railing as he hit the first step.

Lyons blew it off.

He moved on as quickly as caution would allow, twisting up the steps, pulling the trigger here and there to create his own cover fire. He heard the sound of muffled boot steps as he reached the landing and dropped to one knee.

A second later a young Nazi with a bad complexion stepped out of a hall that led toward the rear of the house. A volley of parabellums sailed over Lyons's head.

A return volley from the Able Team leader's MP-40 caught his attacker in the thighs, belly and chest. The enemy jerked in death as his weapon fell from under his arm and tumbled down the steps.

Lyons heard the click of an empty magazine and dropped the German subgun. He pulled both the Colt Python .357 and sound-suppressed Government Model .45 from hiding underneath his uniform blouse. With the revolver in his right hand, the auto in his left, he stepped over the body in front of him and looked down the hall from which the Nazi had come.

A closed door waited at the end. It had been painted a dull flat black, and the famous German Iron Cross had been emblazoned in red in the center.

Four other doors lined the side of the hall. He would have to pass them first.

His back against the wall, Lyons shuffled quietly along the carpet. Downstairs, from the directions in which Schwarz and Blancanales had gone, he heard more gunfire—MP-40s mixed with other explosions from a variety of weapons. He pushed on, silently hoping that the 9 mm weapons of Able Team were winning out over the other calibers.

A whisper came from one of the side doors. Then suddenly two men jumped out into the hall. Dropping to his belly this time, the ex-cop avoided a volley of 9 mm slugs from the enemy gunners. He double-actioned the Python twice, simultaneously thumbing the safety on the Government Model and pulling the trigger.

The man to his left went down with a .45 in the throat.

The man to his right caught both .357 Magnums in the face.

The Able Team leader was on his feet again in a heartbeat, fully aware of the narrow line he was walking. Beyond the black door at the end of the hall, Moler might even now be attempting to destroy evidence that could be the key to the entire Stony Man operation. He had to move fast.

But there were two more doors to pass, both of them open. Unless he missed his guess, men were inside waiting—men who had heard what had just happened in the hall and wouldn't make the same fatal mistake as their fellow fascists. So if he got too anxious now, and died before he reached Moler, the head goose-stepper would not only destroy the missing links Able Team needed, but he might destroy the rest of Able Team, as well.

Lyons used a boot to push a corpse out of the doorway and stepped into the bedroom where the man had hidden. His gaze swept the room, determined it empty, and he moved to the window.

The window opened with a tiny squeak. Lyons stopped, listening, trying to pick up any hint that the sound had been heard down the hall.

Nothing.

Moving quickly now, the ex-cop pulled himself through the second-floor window to the thin ledge that ran the circumference of the mansion. He glanced out over the carefully tended backyard, then moved cautiously toward the next window, stopping just to one side.

Through a crack in the curtain he saw another bedroom. Three men stood close to the hall door, their backs to him. One held an Erma MPE, but this close to their racist master, the other two had foregone the lure of vintage Nazi weapons and entered the last decade of the twentieth century.

A fat Nazi with a receding hairline gripped a 9 mm H&K MP-5 subgun in his chubby fists. The third man held an MP-53, virtually the same weapon, but chambered for 5.56 mm assault rifle cartridges.

Lyons took a deep breath. He had to figure there were perhaps the same number of men across the hall. And time was running out. He glanced overhead and saw a small gargoyle sculpture built into the brick. The tiny monster's ugly face looked like a bad effort to imitate Notre Dame—a curious parallel from Lyons's point of view. Most white supremacists lumped Catholics into the same scorned pile as Jews, blacks and other minorities. But he didn't have time to question the Nazis' philosophy. And for what he needed at the moment, the gargoyle would work quite well.

The Able Team leader leaned into the window for balance and shoved the Python and .45 into his waistband. Carefully he unthreaded his Garrison belt from its loops, then rebuckled it. Looping the strap over the gargoyle's snarling head, he leaned back, testing the strength.

It would hold. At least long enough for what he intended.

The big ex-LAPD detective took another deep breath, then threw himself backward, swinging three feet out over the lawn, then back. He kicked with both legs as his feet hit the glass, and a split second later he was crashing through the window into the bedroom.

Lyons jerked the pistols from his waistband as he landed on his knees.

The three Nazis at the door had whirled in surprise, momentary shock preventing them from firing at the intruder.

Pain shot up through Lyons's thighs and down his calves as he squeezed a double tap from the Python into an imaginary X-ring on the chest of the man holding the Erma. The Government Model bucked in his other hand as the man tumbled to the floor, and three big .45s popped from the barrel to take the Nazi with the MP-5 in the face and neck.

The man with the carbine raised his weapon and cut loose with a wild burst. The bullets sprayed harmlessly over the Able Team leader's head as he brought up both pistols and squeezed the triggers.

The bullets crossed in midair, the .45 burrowing a hole through the Nazi's right cheek, just below the eye. The booming .357 drilled through the left cheek, slightly higher and taking that eye with it.

Lyons leaped to his feet. It was time to move on.

The ex-cop shoved the empty revolver into his waistband and drew the 9 mm Luger from the tanker holster across his chest. He covered the distance to the door in two long strides and fired both weapons as he sped into the hall.

The .45 struck the doorjamb next to the face of an older man with gray hair. The 9 mm from the toggle slide of the Luger caught the Nazi in the shoulder, spinning him around. A second round finished him off.

The ex-cop didn't wait. He drove a shoulder into the falling corpse and, using the man as a shield, propelled him back into the room. A volley of gunfire exploded, and Lyons felt the tremors as the rounds struck the body in front of him. One round penetrated the gray-haired man's arm, continuing on to graze Lyons's shoulder. The flesh burned under his torn Nazi blouse as he dropped his shield and raised the Luger.

Lyons squeezed three times, feeling the weird recoil drive his hand up and to the right as the toggle bolt jacked new rounds into the chamber. His first parabellum took out a Nazi with red hair. The second ended a life of bigotry for a tall, muscular fascist who was trying to clear a jam in his Mauser HSC. The third drilled into the lung of a Nazi wearing a colonel's uniform identical to his own.

Suddenly the second floor of Moler's Nazi playhouse was silent. The Able Team leader shoved a fresh magazine into the butt of his .45, filled the Python with a speedloader of .357 Magnums and let the Luger fall to the floor.

He ripped the swastika from his arm, dropped it next to the pistol and strode purposefully back out into the hall.

Carl Lyons could hear Schwarz and Blancanales coming up the staircase as he raised his guns again and moved toward the door with the Iron Cross.

CHAPTER THIRTEEN

With Dingaan on his back, Bolan followed the Xhosa scout through the thick jungle foliage. The leader of the African Civil Assembly couldn't have weighed over one-twenty, and the Executioner felt little more fatigue than he would have toting a full rucksack through the bush.

The scout stopped suddenly and held up his hand as a rocky overhang appeared through the trees in the distance. He glanced over his shoulder, his face a mask of perplexed fear. He whispered something in Bantu, then moved forward at a snail's pace.

Dingaan tightened his grip around the Executioner's neck and leaned forward. "He is confused," the black leader said in a soft voice. "We should have encountered the war party by now."

The scout stopped at the edge of the clearing. Bolan set Dingaan on his feet and moved to the younger man's side. Through the branches he saw the rock formation above and below the overhang they'd already spotted. Flowers and shrubs of every color, shade and hue grew wild around the bubbling brook that passed under the rocks. Birds sang in the trees overhead, and the entire setting looked like a postcard promoting the serenity of Africa's pristine wilderness.

The scout spoke again. Dingaan translated. "This is where he saw them. They stopped for water."

Bolan pivoted on the balls of his feet, looking back into the jungle toward the Xhosa village. The fact that they'd missed the Zulu could mean only one thing. The war party had taken an alternate route, maybe even splitting into factions to attack the village from all sides.

If he didn't get Dingaan back to them in time to explain what had happened, more needless killing would be the result. The Executioner lifted Dingaan again. "Tell the scout—"

"He has figured it out."

The scout took off again, racing double time down the path from which they'd come. Bolan sprinted after him, ducking under low-hanging branches and dodging stones and tree trunks as he encountered them. Here and there, birds, chimpanzees and other animals broke the silence, but for the most part Bolan's and the scout's running footsteps and steady breathing were the only sounds.

The Executioner remembered the route, and when they passed the trunk of a forked tree, he realized that the village lay just on the other side of the low rise ahead. He quickened his pace, passing the Xhosa scout and moving toward the final row of trees that guarded the camp.

Suddenly a shot rang out from the village. A volley of automatic-rifle fire followed, then the high-pitched war hoops of both Xhosa and Zulu met his ears. Bolan burst through the trees into the village as Tonga Zulus in skins, bracelets, necklaces and war paint did the same to both his sides. Across the village, on the other side of the row of grass huts, more Zulus leaped from the trees carrying spears, bows and Belgian FALs.

Dingaan released the Executioner's neck and dropped to the ground. He darted out from behind Bolan and ran toward the center of the clearing. The black leader held his hands high above his head as he screamed at the top of his lungs.

"No! No! No!"

Both the Xhosa and Zulu froze in their tracks. A synchronous gasp issued forth from the Zulus as they recognized the great leader who had come from their own tribe.

Dingaan moved forward, his hands still raised in peace. The Zulus kept their rifles trained on the Xhosa. The Xhosa aimed steadily at the Zulu. Then a young man wearing animal bones in his hair stepped out of formation and hurried to meet Dingaan. The men embraced.

Dingaan turned, waving the Executioner forward to join them.

Bolan walked forward. He was surprised when the younger man stuck out his hand. "I am Chaka," he said as Bolan grasped it. His English was clear, clean and clipped, the type of speech learned at an African university that had retained the British influence.

"My nephew," Dingaan added.

Chaka turned back to Dingaan and spoke in Bantu. The older man held up his hand again. "Please, Chaka. My friend does not understand."

The younger man switched back to English. "Dead," he said, his voice growing cold. "All of them. All of them . . . dead."

A lone tear formed in Lindall Dingaan's eye. It trickled down his cheek as he spoke in a choked voice. "Sanura?"

Chaka's gaze fell to the ground. For a moment the hardness and hate left his face and only sorrow remained. "My wife is dead."

Dingaan leaned forward and embraced his nephew again as sobs of anguish racked the young man's body. Then Chaka jerked away. "And *they* are responsible!" he screamed, pointing toward the Xhosa.

Dozens of rifle bolts clanged in the stillness as they slid home.

"No," Dingaan said in the soft, persuasive tone Bolan had already seen at work. But now the voice had weakened. "You were made to think so, Chaka. You were supposed to think so. But it is not true."

Chaka looked back, the anger returning to his eyes. "I saw it, Uncle."

"You saw Xhosa enter your village and kill your women and children?" Dingaan asked in the same quiet voice.

"I saw their spears and their bows that were left behind," Chaka replied through gritted teeth. "And I saw the bullet casings left by the Boers with whom they are in league."

Dingaan shook his head. "Would it surprise you to know that a band of Boers and *Zulu* attacked this village only hours ago?"

The expression of anger on Chaka's face metamorphosed into shock.

"Yes, Chaka," Dingaan went on. "And Zulu weapons, even a dead Zulu warrior was left here."

Chaka clasped his hands together and wrung them in agony. "No," he whispered. "No, that is impossible."

"I will show you," Dingaan said. Taking his nephew by the hand, he turned to the Xhosa chief. The chief nodded his approval, and the black leader led the younger man through a tunnel of still-raised weapons toward the hut where the black mercenary's body still lay. Bolan followed.

"But...he is no Zulu," Chaka said as he stared down at the body.

"No," Dingaan agreed. "Of course he isn't. And the men who attacked your camp were not Xhosa."

"Then who were they, Uncle?"

"Mercenaries hired to play the part. And Boers," Dingaan said. "But not all Boers, Chaka," he added quickly. "The members of the Boer Resistance Movement were behind this disgrace. But do not take your revenge out on innocent farmers."

"We won't, Uncle. Then the BRM set this up in the hopes that we would kill one another?"

Dingaan nodded. "They hope to create an uproar that will convince the whites once and for all that we stupid, bloodthirsty kaffirs cannot be trusted with the power to vote." He paused, holding out a hand to indicate that they should leave the hut. As soon as they were outside, he smiled. "Now, Chaka," he said in the ever-weakening voice, "please order your men to lower their weapons. They make me nervous."

Chaka returned a smile that was tainted with the grief in his heart. He shouted in Bantu, and the Zulus lowered their weapons. The Xhosa chief spoke, and his warriors did the same.

"Thank you," Dingaan said. "Now, we...must..." The black leader's voice trailed off, his face becoming a sudden mask of pain.

Then, clasping his chest, he fell to the grass.

DIREK BROUER'S reception area sounded like one giant explosion as both Phoenix Force and the Ijsselmeer security men opened fire.

Katz ducked behind a couch as a burst was directed his way. He lifted the mini-Uzi over the back of his cover and pulled the trigger, catching a glimpse of McCarter, Manning and Encizo behind other furniture around the room.

One round from the Israeli's first volley drilled into the silver badge on the chest of a security man and sent the guy spinning through the air. The former Mossad agent swung his weapon to the side, cutting a figure eight through the air and taking out two more uniformed men.

More men, uniformed and plainclothes, tried to jam through the door carrying pistols and submachine guns. Brass casings from the weapons of McCarter, Manning and Encizo flew through the air as the men hosed the doorway.

The bodies began to pile up.

"Move up!" Katz shouted, crawling from behind the couch to the door. McCarter appeared from behind the receptionist's area, joined seconds later by Manning and Encizo.

Using the stacked bodies as cover, Phoenix Force fired blindly through the door, immersing the hallway in a baptism of lead. Katz changed magazines twice in his weapon, then held up a hand.

His men let up on their triggers.

The Israeli risked a look, rising over the wall of dead flesh before him. The hall looked like a poorly tended morgue. A half-dozen uniformed bodies lay on the tile. One man in a blue suit had fallen into a sitting position against the wall and stared blankly off into space.

"Let's go!" Katz shouted. "There'll be more coming!" He vaulted over the dead men in the doorway and raced down the hall. A walkie-talkie still gripped in the fingers of the man in the blue suit squawked madly. Katz raced by it. Under other circumstances, the Israeli would have confiscated the radio in order to fix the enemy's position, but that would do Phoenix Force little good under the present circumstances, considering the language problem.

Katz heard the rest of the team behind him as he slowed at the stairs. No, he decided in a heartbeat. There was no time to descend on foot. They would have to risk the death-trap elevator and hope any of Brouer's men watching the lights above the car would think they were security.

The Israeli punched the Down button as the other men joined him, stepping back and fanning out around the door without having to be told. They knew what they were likely to face as soon as the car stopped.

A bell sounded as the elevator reached the penthouse floor. Then the door slid open, and four Ijsselmeer security men raised MAC-10 machine pistols.

Phoenix Force cut loose with their mini-Uzis as if they were all linked into one brain. The explosions threatened to deafen them in the narrow hallway, and the smell of cordite filled their nostrils as Brouer's men fell to the floor of the car.

Katz jumped inside, pushing the button for the lobby as McCarter, Manning and Encizo scooted the bodies to the wall and climbed aboard. A moment later the bell sounded again. The car began its descent.

The men of Phoenix Force waited silently, reloading their weapons as the elevator made its way to the lobby with excruciating slowness. Again they knew what might happen as soon as the doors opened. But this time it would be them cooped up in the small elevator. It would be Phoenix Force on display as if in a shooting gallery.

The light indicating the lobby lit up, and the car stopped. The doors rolled back.

And revealed an empty lobby.

"God looks after drunks and fools," Manning whispered as Katz led them quickly off the elevator. They passed the vacant information desk and had started toward the glass doors to the street when a sudden scuffling sounded behind them.

Katz, Manning and McCarter spun in unison, their fingers slipping inside the Uzis' trigger guards. Then each man let up on the trigger as alarm bells went off in their brains.

A tall bulky man wearing an Ijsselmeer security lieutenant's uniform stood against the wall just to the side of the elevator. He had waited out of sight until the last member of Phoenix Force had exited the car—Rafael Encizo. Then he'd looped an arm around the Cuban's neck and shoved the barrel of a Browning BDA into his ear.

The lieutenant spoke first in Dutch. Getting no response, he switched to English. "Drop your weapons!"

Katz hesitated, mentally kicking himself for not checking left and right as he'd stepped off.

"Drop them!" the security man screamed at the top of his lungs.

"No!" Encizo shouted. "Shoot him."

The lieutenant dug the pistol deeper into his ear.

"You'll die if you pull the trigger," Katz said calmly, his Uzi still pointed at both men.

"I am prepared to die," the lieutenant said. He nodded at Encizo. "Is he?"

Encizo stared ahead, his face deadpan. "Yes. Shoot the son of a bitch."

Katz stood frozen. He could see Manning and McCarter watching him, waiting to follow his lead. He ground his teeth together. Perhaps if they lowered their weapons, the man would relax his grip on Encizo. The moment he did, the Israeli knew the little Cuban would be out of the headlock and out of the line of fire.

"I will not tell you again!" the lieutenant shouted, cocking the Browning's hammer.

Katz listened to the hollow sound echo through the empty lobby, then slowly he let the mini-Uzi fall to the end of its sling. He held his hands up in the air as he saw McCarter and Manning lower their weapons.

The Israeli took a tentative step forward. If he could get within pointing distance, the .22 Magnum hidden in his prosthetic arm...

"Don't move!" the security man ordered.

Katz stopped in his tracks.

"You are fools, all of you," the lieutenant said. "Now, I will kill you all!"

The Phoenix Force leader watched the tendons in the man's hand tighten around the grip of the Browning and knew he'd made a mistake. His hands fell back to the Uzi suspended in front of him, knowing all too well that he'd never get a shot off in time, and even if he did, he stood as much chance of killing Encizo as he did the enemy.

Then a lone shot rang out. Katz saw blood shoot from the side of the lieutenant's head. A second later Encizo had squirmed out of the headlock, and the security man lay dead on the lobby floor.

Katz, McCarter, Manning and Encizo turned in the direction from which the shot had come. The Israeli squinted into the darkness behind the information desk, seeing the shadowy outline of a pair of arms bracing what looked to be a Beretta 92 over the desktop.

Then a familiar face appeared as the man behind the desk rose, walked around the side and shoved the Beretta into his waistband.

"Sorry I'm late, guys," Calvin James said. "Kind of rude to start the party without me, don't you think?"

FROM WHAT HE COULD SEE of the man behind the desk, Carl Lyons couldn't decide whether David Moler looked more like a frog or a pig. The man's tiny shoatlike eyes were barely visible within the fleshy folds of the skin dangling loosely over the sockets. But the jowls drooping beneath his invisible jawline were definitely frog. They made him look like he might burp out a massive croak any second now, then spring from behind the desk on his hind legs and plop into the fifty-gallon aquarium behind his desk.

"Not exactly what the führer had in mind for a master race, I wouldn't think," said Gadgets Schwarz at Lyons's side.

Schwarz and Blancanales had joined Lyons inside the head Nazi's office a moment after the Able Team leader had kicked the door off its hinges. The three men from Stony Man Farm now stood in front of Moler's redwood desk, their weapons aimed at the fat face behind it.

Moler's office was spacious; half office, half den. A small personal computer sat on the table to one side of the desk, a fax machine next to it. Besides books with both German and English titles, the bookshelves held Nazi helmets, caps, medals and a variety of World War II pistols and swords in glass cases. Nazi flags and banners covered the walls, and in the spaces they left vacant hung black-and-white photographs of Hitler, Goebbels, and other monsters from the Third Reich. A German march played softly from a built-in stereo CD player in the wall.

Lyons wasn't sure which was stronger, the nausea the spectacle brought to his belly or the spiderlike prickling that made his skin crawl.

Moler had sat silently since Able Team had entered the room. Now he settled back in his chair, laced his pudgy fingers together across his immense stomach and said, "You men are good. I never thought the police would get through my defenses."

"Hate to disappoint you," Blancanales said, "but we aren't the police."

"And thanks for the compliment." Schwarz smiled. "But don't flatter yourself. Your defenses weren't all that great."

Moler forced a return smile. "So if you aren't the police, who are you?"

"Let's just say we're interested in doing what the police can't seem to do," Lyons said. "Putting you out of business."

Moler unlaced his fingers, then redid them behind his head. Large half-moons of sweat appeared under the arms on his khaki general's blouse. "Come now, gentlemen," he chided. "There's no need to be rude. Tell me, what has become of my men?"

"The ones I met are dead," Lyons said simply. He turned to Gadgets and Pol.

"Us, too," Schwarz said. "They had nasty dispositions."

A glimmer of surprise entered Moler's eyes, then he smiled again. "Pity. But they can be replaced. All right, tell me what it is you want. Money, perhaps? You will get it. In exchange for my life, of course."

"Money," Lyons told him, "isn't the sixty-thousand-dollar word."

"Then tell what is."

Lyons stepped forward and leaned on the desk. "There's a connection somewhere between you, a Dutch gold-and-diamond cartel called Ijsselmeer, Inc. and the Boer Resistance Movement in South Africa. What is it?"

The slit eyes opened wide for a moment, then a rumble started deep within Moler. It turned into a laugh that shook his jowls and belly, making him look like some evil twin of Santa Claus.

"Is that all you want?" he asked. "No problem. I have no loyalties to either of those organizations, only to my own people."

"Yeah, your touching reaction when we told you your men were dead showed tremendous loyalty, Davie," Schwarz commented.

Moler ignored him. "I'll tell you exactly what happened. If you know as much as you've already told me, it means the relationship is over anyway. Do I have your word you won't kill me?"

Lyons uttered the hardest yes of his life.

"The connection is simple. I was contacted some time ago by a man named Direk Brouer, Ijsselmeer's CEO. He explained that his company stood to lose hundreds of millions of dollars if the kaffirs, I think he called them, received the vote and then nationalized South Africa's mining industry. Together we concocted a plan that would help both of our causes."

Moler lifted a small bottle of nasal decongestant from his desk, unscrewed the cap and jammed it first into his right nostril, then his left. Two boorish snorts echoed through the room, causing the jowls and belly to dance another jig. Replacing the bottle, he went on. "The referendum passed because the average white fence sitter was persuaded that the blacks were ready to play a part in South African politics. Brouer wanted to stir up enough trouble to convince them otherwise. So I agreed to recruit black mercenaries from the local street gangs to pose as kaffirs."

Lyons frowned. "You said you and Brouer came to an agreement that helped both Ijsselmeer and you Nazis. I see what Brouer got out of the deal, but how did it help you?"

Moler looked at him incredulously. "Most of the mercenaries from the street gangs are bound to die in South Africa."

"This guy's unbelievable," Schwarz said. "Tell me something. How on God's green earth did you get the black gangs to go for killing their own race?"

"The L.A. street gangs are only racially conscious when it serves their purposes," Moler said cheerfully. "The bottom line is that they will do anything for money. Watermelon ain't free, you know."

Lyons resisted the urge to shove the Python into the jowls and pull the trigger.

"Who do the gangsters hook up with in South Africa?" Lyons demanded.

"Guy by the name of Yancy," Moler said. "Darrel...no, David Yancy. He's an American in Brouer's employ. Brouer's liaison to Barry Lanzerac."

"Lanzerac. Top dog of the BRM," Lyons said.

Moler nodded, confirming it. He stood up for the first time, struggling to his feet with both arms and legs. "I've told you what you wanted to know," the Nazi leader said. "Now get out."

Lyons jammed the barrel of the Python into Moler's gut. The front sight and half the barrel disappeared, engulfed by flab. "There's just one problem," he growled. "We've got no proof."

Moler turned and waddled around the side of the desk to the wall. The guns in the hands of the men from Stony Man Farm followed him. He stopped in front of a flag bearing a swastika, then reached up and pulled it down.

The round face of a wall safe appeared.

Lyons cocked the Python. "Easy now," he warned as Moler spun the dial.

Moler opened the safe, reached in slowly and withdrew a brown nine-by-twelve envelope. He turned and handed it to Lyons.

The Able Team warrior opened the envelope and inside found a sheet of paper. Letters, numbers and other symbols were scrambled from top to bottom.

Blancanales looked over his shoulder. "What is it?"

"Bullshit, as far as I can tell," Lyons answered. He turned to Moler and cocked the Python. "What is it?"

Moler shrugged. "I don't know. Brouer gave it to me for safekeeping."

Lyons handed the page to Schwarz and nodded toward the fax machine. "You know who to get this to."

The men in the room waited silently while Schwarz sent the list to Stony Man Farm. When he finished, he nodded to Lyons.

"All right," Moler said. "You've got what you wanted, and you've got your proof. Now get out of here."

Lyons moved in. Again the Python disappeared almost up to the cylinder in Moler's gut. "We're leaving, all right, but you're coming with us."

"Then you're a liar. You gave me your word if I cooperated you'd let me go."

"That's right," Lyons said, grabbing the man's arm and steering him toward the door. "But I didn't say when."

"DAMN," Aron Kurtzman muttered as he stared at the scrambled letters and symbols on the monitor. Ever since the fax from Phoenix Force had come in an hour ago, he had struggled to make sense out of the garbled mess that had to be the list of traitorous South Africans on Brouer's payroll. It had taken half of that hour to realize he had only half of the list. That had put an entirely different slant on the thing, and he'd spent the rest of the time trying to decode what he had.

Kurtzman punched the Escape key and watched the screen go black. It was futile. With only half of the information, there was simply no way to turn the thing into logic. It left too many possibilities, too many interpretations, wide open.

The intercom buzzed sharply. Lifting the phone, Kurtzman glanced through the glass dividing wall to mission control and saw Barbara Price at her desk, the receiver pressed to her ear. "Yeah, Barb?"

Price swiveled her chair to face him. "Any luck?" she asked.

Kurtzman shook his head. "Half of something is nothing. It's like being a little bit pregnant. Or part drunk. You either are or you aren't." He paused. "And I aren't."

"You'll get it."

"I don't know. It's making me crazy. Katz didn't have any idea where the other half of these babies might be, did he?"

"Negative. In fact, he didn't even know it was only half when Phoenix faxed it in. Hal told them a few minutes ago when Katz called."

Kurtzman sighed. "They still in Amsterdam?"

"No. They're on their way to South Africa. They're going back to look for Striker. He hasn't touched base since yesterday."

The computer wizard sat quietly, trying to think of something to say. It was common knowledge around Stony Man that Barbara Price and Mack Bolan had a special sort of friendship. No one knew exactly how special, and everyone respected the two enough to keep from trying to find out. But Kurtzman knew that Price took on a special concern when Bolan appeared to be in harm's way.

He grinned through the glass. "Quit worrying, mission controller. He's a big boy. At least the biggest I've ever met. He'll be all right."

"I know, Aaron. But I—"

Kurtzman heard a click in the background.

"Wait a minute. There's something else coming in.

He watched her stand and cross the room to the fax machine. Price's eyebrows furrowed, then her eyes opened wide. She ripped a hard copy from the machine and hurried back to the phone.

"It's from L.A. Able Team. Another list, and it's got the same weird symbols and signs as the one Phoenix Force sent in."

"Well, get it in here!" Kurtzman bellowed, but Price didn't hear. By then she was already sprinting through the door and up the ramp to his console.

Kurtzman tore the paper out of her hand and set it on the console next to the screen. His fingers flew across the keyboard as he typed the new information, punched Enter and sat back. He could feel Barbara Price's warm breath on his neck as he waited for the computer to digest what he'd given it and spit out a list of double agents that made sense.

That didn't happen. Instead, "insufficient data" lit up on the screen.

"Dammit to hell!" Kurtzman roared.

Price gripped his shoulders. "What is it?"

"I don't know for sure. Something's still missing." He tapped more keys, pulling up his probability program and entering it into the computer's temporary memory.

The machine clicked and hummed, then the screen lit up again in orange letters: "One-word access code required."

Kurtzman pulled a handkerchief from his lab coat and mopped his brow. "Great," he said. "One word. So close and yet so far away." He turned in his chair to face Price. "How many words do you think there are in the dictionary?" he asked her. "Or forget that. It could be a Dutch word, or Afrikaans, or—"

"Settle down, Aaron. Somewhere there's a clue. You'll find it."

"Yeah, I'll find it. But how many people are going to die in South Africa between now and the time I do? How many—"

"I don't know," Price cut in. "But the longer you feel sorry for yourself and keep bitching, the longer it'll take."

Kurtzman's angry face turned into a grin. He slapped himself across the cheek and said, "Thanks. I needed that." Without another word he turned back to the screen.

Price patted him on the shoulder, then walked back down the ramp.

Aaron Kurtzman gave himself three more self-indulgent seconds, then cleared the screen and began tapping back into the Ijsselmeer computer five thousand miles away. "Thank God for Barb," he whispered. He usually didn't let himself get carried away like that, but on the rare occasions when he did, she was always there to get him straight again.

The link complete, Kurtzman began his new hunt. Somewhere in the files of the giant gold-and-diamond cartel, there had to be at least a clue as to what the access word would be.

CHAPTER FOURTEEN

Lindall Dingaan clutched his chest as tightly as if rigor mortis had already set in. He closed his eyes as Bolan dropped to his knees. The Executioner pressed a forefinger into the man's neck, searching for the carotid artery. He found the pulse, quick and weak.

Bolan cupped both hands over the man's sternum and threw his weight forward. For the second time in the past few hours, he performed CPR on the leader of the African Civil Assembly.

Dingaan finally opened his eyes. The Executioner lifted the man's robe, found the bottle of nitroglycerin tablets and slipped one under Dingaan's tongue. As the pill dissolved, he lifted him into his arms, cradling him like a baby. He turned to Chaka and the Xhosa chief, who stood with their mouths gaping open. "We've got to get a doctor. Is there one within a reasonable distance?"

Chaka translated the words into Bantu. The Xhosa chief replied, then turned to his warriors and shouted orders. Dingaan's nephew closed his own eyes a moment, and a disheartened expression twisted onto his face. He turned back to Bolan. "He says yes, but what he means is a shaman. A witch doctor, so to speak."

"Great," Bolan said, starting toward the nearest hut. "Is there any transportation?"

Before Dingaan could answer, a sudden volley of automatic-rifle fire blasted from the trees next to them. A Xhosa warrior dressed in lion skins twirled a full circle, then fell to the ground. Another volley took the man next to him, then a flatbed truck burst from the jungle path into the village.

The Executioner looked up to see two white men in the cab. One wearing a straw cowboy hat loomed over the steering wheel. The other, in the passenger's seat, wore a khaki safari jacket and leaned out of the window, firing an FAL.

The bed of the truck was filled with a mixture of men in camouflage fatigues and native war dress.

More autofire poured from the back of the truck as Bolan ducked into the hut. He lay Dingaan down and heard more rounds on the other side of the village as he drew the .50 Desert Eagle. By the time he had sprinted back outside, the truck driven by the cowboy had pulled to a halt twenty yards away. The attackers had dropped to the ground, taken cover behind it and now fired into the surprised tribesmen.

At least ten more of the Xhosa and Zulu lay dead on the ground.

Bolan fired a double tap of Magnum rounds toward the truck, then turned to the other side of the camp where a similar vehicle had parked. More tribesmen had fallen to the rounds of the BRM men and black mercenaries. Chaka himself lay on his belly, returning fire from his M-16 as blood streamed from his side.

The Executioner dropped to a knee, the Desert Eagle stretched in front of him in a two-handed battle grip. He sighted along the barrel, then squeezed the trigger. The big autopistol exploded, sending a Magnum round spiraling through the grooves, then the air, then finally the windshield of the truck before it embedded itself in the chest of a large black man behind the wheel, who slumped forward.

A 3-round burst whipped past the Executioner as he squeezed the trigger again. His next shot zipped over the bed of the truck and into a BRM man in a floppy boonie hat. The bullet struck the man between the eyes, and his skull seemed to fold in toward the nose as the Boer tumbled out of sight behind the vehicle.

A Zulu, impotently trying to clear a jammed slide on his weapon, fell to Bolan's side. The Executioner shoved the Desert Eagle back into his holster, dropped to the ground, rolled to the man and snatched the rifle from his dead hands.

Stretched on the ground, Bolan pulled back the bolt with his right hand, using the palm of his left to sweep the jammed cartridge out of the chamber. The mangled casing fell to the earth as he worked the bolt again to chamber a fresh load. Rolling onto his stomach, he steadied the weapon and sighted on the heads still above the truck.

A full-auto blast from the FAL took the top off two of the heads, one white, the other black, then the assault rifle jammed again. The Executioner dropped the weapon, realizing as he drew the .44 Desert Eagle that the BRM had tampered with the Belgian-made rifles before supplying them to the tribesmen.

Their purpose was the elimination of both tribes. If some of the weapons malfunctioned on both sides, so much the better.

The .44 spit twice, both rounds striking the face of a BRM gunman as he attempted to replace the empty magazine in his rifle. The impacts threw his head back, then his body jerked in reflex, throwing it forward again. He slumped facedown over the rail around the flatbed, blood streaming from what remained of his head.

Around him Bolan heard the war cries of the Zulu and Xhosa as they continued to return fire. Several more of the Boers and phony tribesmen fell, but the Xhosa and Zulu continued to die, as well, their FALs jamming, freezing and sometimes quitting altogether.

The truck engine behind him suddenly roared, and the Executioner looked over his shoulder to see the man in the cowboy hat backing the vehicle around. The Boers and black mercs had hopped back onto the bed, but still fired down at the tribesmen on the ground. The man in the safari jacket continued to send a steady stream of lead through the passenger window.

Bolan twisted, snapping off a shot as the cowboy threw the truck into gear and pulled away. The big Magnum round hit the man in the safari jacket just above the wrist, and the warrior heard him scream in pain. The assault rifle dropped to the ground. As the tires threw up dust and grass, Bolan fired twice more, his first round knocking a fake Zulu off the bed of the truck to do somersaults through the air before his face struck the grass. The second .44 crushed the chest of a Boer wearing a camouflage headband, and sent him crashing into the rear of the cab.

Then the truck disappeared down the jungle path.

Bolan turned back to the second truck as the roar of gunfire ceased. One of the phony Zulus had thrown the driver from the cab and taken his place behind the wheel. As he tried to turn, the Executioner squinted down the barrel and lined the Desert Eagle's sights on the left front tire.

The big Magnum exploded.

So did the tire.

The Executioner swung his weapon to the rear of the truck. The Desert Eagle screamed again, and the rear tire flattened. The driver downshifted, trying vainly to limp the lopsided vehicle over the rugged jungle path on the rims. The truck sputtered, then ground to a halt.

Chaka saw what the Executioner had done and fired a full-auto blast into the other rear tire.

"No!" Bolan yelled.

But by then, the third tire had flattened.

The Executioner leaped to his feet, sprinting toward the truck and the surprised Boers and mercs. He fired the big .44 dry, dropping two more BRMers, then traded it for the Beretta. The lighter weapon jumped in his hand, sending sound-suppressed 9 mm slugs hissing into three of the remaining invaders.

The Zulu and Xhosa teamed up on the last two men in the rear of the truck, riddling their bodies with arrows, spears and bullets.

"Hold your fire!" Bolan shouted as he neared the cab. He wanted some answers, and that meant keeping the black driver alive. But even as he spoke, he knew how impotent his words would be. As far as he knew, Chaka was the only man from either tribe with a command of English.

Chaka's frantic voice sounded above the gunfire as he attempted to translate the Executioner's orders. His words went unheeded.

Bolan was four steps from the cab when the 3-round burst shattered the windshield and ripped through the chest and throat of the man behind the wheel.

The Executioner ground to a halt as the explosions died down. An eerie silence crept over the village. He walked to the man in the cab, looked at the severed artery in his neck, then shook his head.

He could hardly blame the tribesmen. They hadn't understood his words and hadn't heard Chaka's. Inexperienced warriors didn't listen well to orders once the battle had started, and even though the Zulu and Xhosa weren't inexperienced, they might as well have been. The introduction of the FAL autorifles had given combat an entirely new meaning for them.

The Executioner turned around and saw the tribesmen who'd survived creeping tentatively forward. One man was helping Chaka to his feet, and Bolan saw that the wound in Dingaan's nephew's side wasn't deep. A tight bandage and a little direct pressure would stop the bleeding.

Bolan turned back to the truck, opened the door and hauled the body behind the wheel onto the ground. He dropped to his knees and saw the two spare tires mounted under the bed.

Two. Most vehicles that traveled terrain like that in South Africa carried two spares instead of one, which was the reason he had risked shooting out the second tire to ensure stopping the truck.

But Chaka had taken out the third tire, as well, which meant the flatbed might as well have carried no spares at all.

Bolan holstered the Beretta and walked around the truck, opening the other door. His eyes scanned the front seat. A shortwave radio mounted under the dash now hung from one screw. Both the receiver and microphone were scattered in bits and pieces over the floor. He opened the glove compartment.

And struck a gold more valuable at that moment than all that had been mined in South Africa since the dawn of creation.

The Executioner pulled the cellular phone from the glove compartment, held it to the sun and inspected it. Silently he thanked the universe that the instrument had escaped the cavalcade of bullets that had saturated the rest of the cab.

He had to get Dingaan not only to safety, but to medical attention. The Executioner's mind traveled back to the men in the cowboy hat and the safari jacket.

That place of safety for Dingaan was no longer with his Zulu people. Another attack from the BRM might come at any moment. No, the place he had in mind was far from Zululand. It would take some doing to get there, but might well be the safest place on Earth— for Dingaan, or anyone else.

And leaving the black leader there would also free the Executioner to return to South Africa, hunt down the cowboy and the man in the safari jacket and end the outrages of the Boer Resistance Movement once and for all.

Chaka limped forward, breaking into Bolan's thoughts. The Zulu held his side.

"Is there a flat area near here big enough to land a plane?" Bolan asked.

Chaka nodded. "A mile or so."

The Executioner nodded, as he began tapping the number of Stony Man Farm into the cellular phone.

"YOU KNOW, POL," Lyons heard Schwarz say from the back of the van, "there're certain drawbacks to being the good guys." The Able Team leader glanced into the rearview mirror. Behind him he saw David Moler jammed between Schwarz and Blancanales on the back seat. Gadgets's Beretta 92 was jammed into the Nazi's neck. Pol's pistol was pushed into the man's massive belly.

"Okay, I'll bite," Blancanales said. "Such as?"

"Such as always having to keep your promises. In this instance, letting this bigot keep breathing."

Lyons turned off the interstate and entered a low-income residential district in East Los Angeles. The apartment houses, duplexes, and single-family dwellings got progressively seedier as he drove along. Gang graffiti was prevalent, and he learned that this was the home of the Oak Avenue Sepulchers, that Cool Hand Willie Lives, and that the Sepulchers wanted to Kill Crips.

The Able Team leader turned again and drove four blocks past a series of single-story frame houses in dire need of repair and lawn work. Moler had given them the location of the Sepulcher crack house where the merc recruiting went on, but he hadn't known the number. Glancing over his shoulder, Lyons growled, "Point it out, pal."

Moler leaned toward the window. "There it is. Second from the corner. The one with the Chevy and Fiat in the drive."

Lyons stared out the window as they passed. Both cars showed primer through their ancient paint jobs. Except for the stone porch and concrete columns on each side, the house didn't look different than the others on the block. Both of the front window screens hung at angles from the frame, their tattered mesh blowing in the light evening breeze.

A pair of men wearing Raiders football caps and Dodgers baseball shirts sat on the front steps, their eyes bulging blindly in a drugged-out stupor. But though they seemingly paid the van no heed, the ex-cop knew the crack-house sentries had taken due note of the unfamiliar vehicle.

"Who's your contact with the Sepulchers?" the Able Team leader asked Moler.

"Negro by the name of Hambone," Moler replied.

Gadgets gave the man a hard smile. "I'm happy that our little talk about those kinds of names was heeded." Gadgets shrugged. Addressing no one in particular, he added, "We can't expect miracles, but it's a start."

The ex-cop drove on two blocks, then turned the corner and headed down the alley between the houses. He cut the lights before they reached the crack-house block, then scooted the van across the intersecting street and onto the gravel between the trash cans.

The backyard of the house was dark, but lights showed through a crack in the closed shades. Silhouettes moved back and forth.

Lyons cut the engine and said, "Let's go." Blancanales handed the Atchisson automatic shotgun to him. The big ex-cop checked the magazine while Gadgets and Pol did the same with their Heckler & Koch MP-5 submachine guns.

"You, uh, you going to give me a gun?" Moler asked quietly.

"Dream on," Gadgets told him.

"But I can't go in there unarmed, for God's sake."

Lyons twisted in his seat. "Then walk home," he said simply.

Moler glanced at the swastikas on his arm and the rest of his Nazi general's uniform. "You can't do this to me," he whined. "I wouldn't get ten feet."

"Then lock the doors and wait here," Lyons said as he opened the door and swung down from the van.

He crossed the alley to the gate, pushed quickly through and started toward the back door. Behind him he heard Pol's and Gadgets's boots sliding softly across the grass. When he reached the one-step porch, he twisted the doorknob. Locked.

Lyons stepped back. Might as well make a grand entry, he thought as he racked the slide of the Atchisson, aimed at the lock and pulled the trigger.

The wood around the bolt exploded in a rainstorm of splinters.

The former LAPD detective kicked the door and rushed through the opening. He found himself in a darkened hall. To his right he saw part of the kitchen.

To his left, in a bedroom, two figures sat huddled under the covers.

Lyons cut to the left, hearing Pol and Gadgets take the kitchen behind him. He found the light switch next to the door and switched it on as a thin man jumped to his feet and turned to face him. "What the fuck you think—" Then his eyes fell on the bore in the end of the shotgun, and his hands shot up in the air in surrender.

The Able Team leader stepped forward and swung the stock of the shotgun in a wide arc. It struck the man in the jaw with a crack almost as loud as the shell that had opened the back door, and he fell to the floor unconscious.

The ex-cop turned the barrel toward the bed. The woman clasped both hands over her eyes. "Stay exactly where you are and don't move a muscle." He heard 9 mm autofire open up in the kitchen as he sprinted out of the room and down the hall to the living room.

A man sitting on a couch dropped a glass crack pipe and made a grab for a nickel-plated revolver on the coffee table in front of him. Lyons aimed down, tapping the Atchisson's trigger and making the wheel gun jump off the table onto the floor. His second shot caught the doper in the chest. The man screamed and sat back abruptly.

Two Sepulchers who'd been sitting on the floor against the wall tried to rise, bringing up their MAC-10 machine pistols with them.

Lyons turned the Atchisson their way. The shotgun blasted a full-auto burst of triple-aught buck into the men, keeping them on the floor.

A bullet tore past the big ex-cop's cheek as he swung the Atchisson toward the front of the room where a gang member wearing a green bandanna on his head was firing a Colt Commando.

The Atchisson burped out a lone load of buck that caught the man in the thigh, sending him to his side on the ragged carpet. Still clutching the snub-nosed revolver, he rolled to his belly and brought the gun up again.

Lyons's next shot took off the top of his head.

The living room quieted. Two final bursts from the H&Ks erupted, then the house fell silent.

The Atchisson leading the way, Lyons crossed the living room and entered a dining area. He found Schwarz and Blancanales making their way toward him, their own weapons at the ready.

"All clear?" the Able Team leader asked.

"Yeah," Schwarz said. "But nobody we met had time to say much."

Lyons snorted. "There's a woman in the bedroom," he said. "Go check on her."

He stepped over several bodies in the dining room and entered the kitchen. Two more men lay on the tile, submachine pistols resting near their dead hands. Crack pipes, rocks, syringes and other drug paraphernalia littered the cabinets and sink.

Lyons cut back down the hall where he'd come in and entered the bedroom. Pol and Gadgets stood in the center of the room.

The woman's hands were still clasped tightly over her eyes.

"We told her she could drop her arms." Pol shrugged. "But she said she was waiting for you."

"Drop 'em," Lyons growled, and the woman lowered her hands to her sides.

"God, he's got a way with women." Schwarz chuckled.

Lyons walked forward. The woman looked to be in her early twenties. Her eyes were frightened but clear. He squinted at her arms. No needle tracks. Lifting her dress from the floor, he tossed it to her. "Put it on, then get up."

The woman complied, shrugging into the loose garment and then stuffing it down over her legs under the covers. She got out of bed and stood.

"Now, sit back down and show me your toes," Lyons ordered.

The woman knew why, and how. She sat on the edge of the bed, lifted one foot, then the other, and spread her toes with her fingers.

They were clear of tracks, as well.

Lyons sat on the bed next to her. "You're clean. So what in hell are you doing hanging out with a bunch of maggots like this?"

The tears started slowly, then suddenly flowed like a waterfall. "I...don't know," the woman said. "I just—"

The man on the floor started to stir, and Lyons stood up. He handed Blancanales the Atchisson, then reached down, grabbed him and hauled him to his feet. As soon as the man could stand on his own, he drew the Colt Python and placed the barrel under his chin. "Come with me."

Lyons led the man into the living room. "Which one of these dudes is Hambone?" he demanded.

The man was shivering when he spoke. "Ain't none of them the Bone, man. The Bone ain't here."

The Able Team leader walked him on into the dining room, then the kitchen. "I told you," the man said. "Hambone ain't here tonight."

"Then where is he?"

The man shrugged. "Don't know. Maybe back at his digs."

"So where are his 'digs'?"

"Downtown."

"Think you might be able to be a little more specific?"

The man shook his head.

The Able Team leader cocked the Colt.

The man gave him an address.

Lyons raised the big .357 and rapped on top of his prisoner's skull. The man had returned to dreamland before he hit the kitchen tile.

Moving back into the bedroom, the ex-cop took the woman by the hand and led her to the back door. "Get out of here. Don't come back. And stay away from places like this."

The woman nodded and ran out into the night.

Lyons, Schwarz and Blancanales returned to the van and climbed inside. Moler was nowhere to be found.

"Looks as if he changed his mind and took you up on your offer to walk home, Ironman," Pol said.

"Looks as if."

The Able Team leader pulled down the alley and started back toward the interstate. The next thing he needed to do was to touch base with Stony Man; see if Kurtzman or any of the other teams had come up with anything new.

Then he and the men of Able Team would go after Hambone and put an end to the recruiting of mercenaries to South Africa once and for all.

Two blocks before the highway, Lyons saw his second naked man of the evening. The body lay facedown, half in, half out of the gutter. He slowed, then pulled to a halt next to the curb, the van's headlights illuminating the pasty white flesh.

Gadgets jumped out of the back, ran to the still form and rolled it over.

The leader of the American Nazi Party, David Moler, stared at the stars in a dead trance. Only a trickle of blood oozed from his slashed throat.

Gadgets returned, jumped inside and slid the door shut. "Forget what I told you earlier, Pol," he said. "Being the good guys really does have its rewards."

THE JET DROPPED QUICKLY through the sky over the Blue Ridge Mountains of Virginia. Bolan watched McCarter manipulate the controls and bring the bird to a flawless landing on the runway at Stony Man Farm.

The Executioner looked over his shoulder, through the open door to the rear of the plane. Phoenix Force sat in the unusual configuration of seats. Spread out among the Stony Man warriors were three blind-folded men, two in white uniforms and one wearing hospital greens.

Two medics and a doctor.

Bolan barely suppressed a grin. Katz and his team could be a resourceful lot when the situation demanded it. They had already returned to Johannesburg when he'd called Stony Man from the Xhosa village. Upon learning of Bolan's location and predicament from Barbara Price, they had wasted no time kidnapping the doctor, the crew and equipment from the nearest ambulance, and then hijacking the aircraft.

As McCarter had piloted the jet through the sky toward the coordinates Price had passed on, two rows of seats had been ripped out and tossed from the plane to accommodate the gurney on which Lindall Dingaan now rested. The doctor and medics had tended to him, administering oxygen and determining that the coronary he'd suffered was minor.

The Briton guided the plane to a halt as the other men of Phoenix Force removed the blindfolds. Bolan looked through the glass and saw a personnel vehicle and ambulance streaking from the main house to the runway.

A few minutes later Dingaan had been loaded into the ambulance. Bolan, Katz and the doctor climbed in with him as the rest of Phoenix Force escorted the medics to the other vehicle.

Both the medics and the jet would be returned to South Africa as soon as possible. In the meantime they'd be housed along with the trainees in the barracks.

Bolan squatted next to the gurney as the ambulance started back to the house. Dingaan had been sleeping, but now his eyes opened.

"How are you feeling, Mr. Dingaan?" the Executioner asked.

The black leader smiled weakly. "I'd feel better if you'd do what I asked you to do."

Bolan frowned, then smiled. "How are you feeling, Lindall?"

The doctor answered for him. "He's still weak, and he needs rest. But the prognosis is good."

Dingaan nodded. "I couldn't have said it better myself." His eyes flickered back to Bolan. "Colonel Pollock," he said, "please tell me again what we are doing."

Bolan cleared his throat. "There was no place in South Africa where you were safe anymore. There are just too many leaks in the government. And even if the Boers didn't already know you were among your own people, it was only a matter if time until—"

"No, no, I understand all that. The part about the code word or something?"

Bolan nodded. Barbara Price had contacted them during the flight, advising that Kurtzman had discovered a clue to the access code he needed.

"Two of the teams I work with discovered a list of traitors in your government. The documents are in code, and there's a one-word access code needed to break the cryptogram. The chief of our computer department has discovered that code word has something to do with you."

Dingaan's brow furrowed, but he didn't reply.

A moment later the ambulance pulled to a halt at the front doors to the house. Bolan and Katz unloaded the gurney and wheeled it to the entrance. The Executioner punched the numbers into the lock, and the steel door swung open.

The doctor followed them through the entryway, through another locked door and into the computer room. Bolan saw Barbara Price stand and hurry toward them on the other side of the glass partition. She joined them as they wheeled Dingaan up the ramp to Kurtzman's terminal.

The Bear twirled his chair toward them. Dingaan sat up on the gurney, and the doctor started to object. The black leader held up his hand, then used it to shake Kurtzman's. "Lindall Dingaan," he said.

Kurtzman grinned. "So I assumed."

Bolan took a place to one side of Dingaan and felt Price move in behind him. The mission controller reached for his hand, squeezed it, then let it drop again.

Kurtzman glanced at Bolan. "You've told him what's going on?"

The Executioner nodded.

"What we need," Kurtzman said to Dingaan, "is anything you might know about Ijsselmeer, Inc. Anything you can think of that has a connection to you. With the help of the computer's probability program, I've learned this much—the CEO of Ijsselmeer has a sense of humor. The word he's used to access the code has something to do with you, Mr. Dingaan."

"Lindall," Dingaan said, frowning. "I know very little about the company, really. Just that they have millions of dollars of holdings in my country. They pay slave labor to the blacks who work the mines, reap enormous profits, then take those profits *out* of our country and back to Europe."

"You're proposing to nationalize the mines?" Kurtzman asked.

"It has been discussed. No one wants to do so, but it may be the only way to salvage the economy."

Kurtzman whirled to his keyboard. He typed "nationalize" onto the bottom right-hand corner of the screen, then hit Enter.

The garbled mess of letters and symbols remained the same, and he turned back to Dingaan. "Okay, let's try another tack. Do you know anyone who works for Ijsselmeer, maybe? A friend? Enemy? Anyone?"

Dingaan shook his weary head. "Not to my knowledge."

"Okay, then," Kurtzman said. "With Ijsselmeer, Inc., as the topic of discussion, why don't you just start talking. Say anything that comes into your head. Maybe we'll pick up on something." He glanced to Bolan and shrugged. "It's all I can think of to do."

Bolan nodded.

Dingaan sighed. "Ijsselmeer has been a problem for South Africa for as long as I remember. Like I said, they take advantage of the poverty, treat their employees like slaves—"

"Just about what you'd expect out of Brouer, though," Kurtzman interjected. "Go on."

"No, wait," Dingaan said. "What did you say?"

"I said it's what you'd expect out of Direk Brouer. To treat his employees poorly."

"Direk Brouer? What does he have to do with all this?"

"Well," Kurtzman replied, "he's the CEO of Ijsselmeer. I thought you knew that."

"No, I did not," Dingaan said. "But I do know a Direk Brouer. From Amsterdam. We attended Oxford together."

Bolan watched Kurtzman's face light up. Behind the forehead shining with sweat, he could almost see the wheels rolling. The computer ace turned to the keyboard and typed "Oxford" onto the screen.

Nothing.

Kurtzman turned back around, his face still glowing with excitement. "Tell me more about you and Brouer at Oxford," he said.

"Well, we weren't close, by any means. I was a political science major and I believe he was in the business school. If memory serves me, though, we did have one class together as undergraduates."

"What was that?"

"Economics."

Kurtzman entered "economics," but the computer didn't respond. He tried "England," "college" and "university" with the same results. When he turned back to Dingaan, some of his enthusiasm had faded. "What else? Tell me anything that pops into your head."

Now it was Dingaan's turn to get excited. "I just remembered," he said. "I beat him out for a position on the rowing team. I made the team, he didn't."

His zeal was infectious, and Kurtzman brightened again. He whirled back to his computer and in a flash of motion, "team" appeared on the screen. When that didn't work, he typed in "row."

The computer suddenly began to hum. Then, before their very eyes, the meaningless letters and symbols on the screen began to change into words.

Fifteen seconds later a list of names appeared on the screen, and the warriors of Stony Man Farm knew who the traitors in the South African government were.

Bolan read the name at the top of the list out loud. "Colonel Roland Van Boskirk. That explains the fighter that shot us down, Mr. Dingaan." He turned to the man, who nodded.

His gaze glued to the screen, Dingaan lifted a shaking finger and pointed. "Look at the last name."

Bolan turned back to the screen, and suddenly the mystery of how the Recces and Boers had known his every move before he made it became clear. And it explained why that had stopped after the crash, when he'd lost contact with the government.

The Executioner read the name out loud, his lips barely moving. "Norman Van Peebles."

CHAPTER FIFTEEN

Bolan hit the brake, and the Jeep Cherokee ground to a halt at the end of the Stony Man Farm landing strip. He threw the transmission into neutral, then waited as Jack Grimaldi landed the Learjet and taxied to a stop less than ten feet away.

Grimaldi and Hal Brognola got out and started toward the Cherokee. The Stony Man flyboy wore a brown suede Alaskan bush pilot's cap and fighter pilot's jacket. Brognola carried a briefcase and wore a navy blue pin-striped suit that made him look as if he'd just come from Madison Avenue instead of the Justice Department. But the stub of the masticated cigar in his mouth was all cop.

The Executioner leaned across the seat, opening the door as Brognola approached. The big Fed slid into the front seat. Grimaldi piled into the back.

Bolan turned the Cherokee toward the main house.

"Is the link to Able Team set up yet?" Brognola asked as he positioned the briefcase in his lap and opened it.

"They're standing by at your Justice offices in L.A. Lyons is chomping at the bit to go after this guy Hambone."

Brognola nodded as he lifted a page from the case and studied it. "Hambone's real name is Roger Jefferson. He's got a record a mile long."

"No surprise there," Bolan said as he pulled to a halt in front of the house and killed the engine.

The three men exited the vehicle, passed through the security checks and locks and soon found themselves tapping the combination on the steel door to the War Room.

Brognola walked directly to the head of the table, lifted the telephone receiver and pressed a series of numbers. He placed the receiver facedown into a speakerphone, and the warriors around the table heard it ring.

A moment later a voice said, "Justice Department, Cornelius."

"This is Brognola. Put my men on."

"One moment, sir."

A second later Lyons's voice said, "Yeah, Hal."

"You ready to begin?"

"Yeah. Just a minute. Let me clear the room."

The Stony Man crew heard muffled conversation in the background, then Lyons came back on. "Okay, Hal. Just the three of us now. Shoot."

Brognola opened his briefcase, removed a file and opened it. He sat down, and crossed his legs. "Okay. The way I see it, this monster had six heads. Brouer, Van Peebles, Yancy, Lanzerac and Able Team's new buddy, Roger Jefferson, a.k.a. Hambone. Brouer pays Lanzerac to stir up trouble in South Africa, Yancy to be the go-between to Amsterdam, Van Peebles and other government and military personnel to snitch, and Moler and Hambone to provide the black merc force. Well, Moler's dead." He paused again. "But if South Africa's ever going to get on the right track, we've got to cut those other five heads right off."

Brognola looked down at the speakerphone. "Ironman, you guys already have Hambone's address, and it checks out. He's all yours." He turned to Bolan. "Striker, I know that after seeing what Lanzerac and Yancy did to the tribes, you want them. And Van Peebles was almost responsible for Dingaan's and your deaths. But I've got a problem sending you back to South Africa right now."

Bolan waited.

"You're needed more for the Amsterdam leg of this thing," the big Fed went on. "Security around the Ijsselmeer Building was tight before Phoenix Force hit the offices. Now, it's unbelievable. They aren't going to fall for any 'workmen' ruses again, and it would take a full battalion of men to rush the building, not to mention the complications that would cause with Dutch authorities. I've had our two Charlies at work. Mott flew a quick recon over the building earlier today. He says they've even posted guards on the roof. And a blacksuit from the DEA who worked with Able Team—Charlie Johnston—he's staked out in a little apartment above the café across the street from the building. He says Brouer hasn't left the building since he came in after Phoenix Force's infiltration.

"So I've come up with an idea on how to take Mr. Brouer out," Brognola went on. "But it's a one-man job, and that means you, Striker."

"I'm listening."

"I've asked an old buddy to help out on this one. Bill Humphrey flew glides during World War II, and we need his expertise now. Striker, the roof guards will hear a conventional aircraft miles away. What I want you to do is jump from a glider. If you do it at night, my guess is you can take out the men on the roof before they even know what's hit them."

Bolan nodded, then turned to Yakov Katzenelenbogen. "Fine. Just as long as somebody gets Yancy, Lanzerac and Van Peebles."

"We will," Katz said simply.

Brognola nodded. "But we don't want Van Peebles dead. If he dies, it leaves the door wide open for all kinds of BRM propaganda. Van Peebles could come out of this a martyr." Pulling the cigar stump from his mouth, he held it in his hand. "A big show trial that's covered the world over will do a lot more good than Van Peebles's death."

The men around the table stood as if on cue.

"One more thing," Brognola added. "Able Team, you still listening?"

"We're here," Lyons voice came back.

"We've got to assume that Brouer is still in close communication with Lanzerac and Yancy. And while I think Moler and his Nazis were a buffer between Hambone and Amsterdam, I don't want to take it for granted. A phone call from one party to the next could ruin one or more of the strikes. All three ops have to go down simultaneously."

A breath of impatience came over the speakerphone, and Bolan fought a smile. Carl Lyons wasn't long on patience. Once he'd identified his target, he liked to pull the trigger immediately.

"We'll be waiting," Lyons finally growled. "Get the rest of the boys in the air."

Gary Manning opened the door, and the men from Stony Man Farm filed through.

LYONS STARED at the luminous hands of his watch: 1927 hours in L.A. That meant it would be 0527 in South Africa and 0427 in the Netherlands.

The men from Stony Man Farm had three minutes.

The ex-cop stared through the window of the van. Above the front entrance of the high rise apartment building across the street, just above the crest over the door, he saw the sign. Bradford Arms. Next to the door a window-booth protruded from the face of the building, making it look like the ticket window in front of a movie theater. A man in a light blue Pinkerton Security uniform sat behind a counter. He wore glasses secured to his neck by a thin chain. A few strands of the thin hair on top of his head had fallen over his forehead. His eyes were buried in a paperback book.

Lyons wondered briefly what the apartments inside rented for. A couple grand a month, maybe? More, most likely, with the security.

Roger "Hambone" Jefferson might have started out a poor street kid, but he'd used the profits he and the Sepulchers made off drugs and mercs to rise up in the world.

All the way to the nineteenth floor of the Bradford Arms.

Barbara Price's voice came over the headset in Lyons's ears, emanating from Stony Man Farm to the communications satellite orbiting Earth before being relayed down to the streets of Los Angeles. "Base to Phoenix One," the Stony Man mission controller said. "Come in, Phoenix One. Over."

A quarter of the way across the globe, Lyons heard Katz reply. "Phoenix Force in position, Base. Over."

"Affirmative, Phoenix," Price said. "Maintain position. Out. Base to Striker. Affirm, Striker. Over."

A tiny click sounded. A whish of wind came over the airwaves, and then Mack Bolan's voice said, "Striker here. Approximately thirty seconds to jump time. Over."

"Roger, Striker. Base to Able Team One. Come in, Ironman. Over."

Lyons spoke into the microphone in front of his face. "Able Team in position. We're all set. Over and out."

"Striker," Price said, "you're the one with the rigid timetable. You do the honors. Base out."

The radio traffic went dead for a few seconds, then Lyons heard one of the mikes click open again. The same swoosh of air he'd heard before met his ears, and then Bolan said, "Able Team...Phoenix Force... move in. Striker out. Literally."

Able Team exited the van and crossed the street to the guard window.

Lyons rapped on the glass, and the Pinkerton guard looked up from his book, startled. The man in blue tapped a button, and said, "Yes, sir?" over the intercom.

The Able Team leader pulled a badge case from the inside pocket of his sport coat and held it to the glass. "U.S. Department of Justice," he growled. "We need in."

The security guard's mouth fell open. "What is the nature of your business, sir?"

"It's Justice Department business, Officer," Lyons said. "And it's confidential."

The guard wiped the hair out of his eyes, then tapped a cloth book on the counter. "Sir," he said, "I have to have something to put in the log book."

Lyons glanced at Schwarz. The electronics man shrugged. Turning back to the guard, the big ex-cop lowered his voice to a whisper. "Come around to the door, Officer. I don't care to share our business with the whole neighborhood."

The guard nodded knowingly, his face taking on the expression of a man who never guessed he'd be privy to behind-the-scenes info pertaining to *real* police work. He pulled a key ring from the peg board behind him, climbed down off his stool and hurried out of his window-booth.

Lyons, Schwarz and Blancanales moved to the glass door next to the booth and waited. A moment later the guard appeared, fumbling with the key ring. Finally finding the right key, he shoved it into the lock and the door swung open. "Could I see your ID one more time please, sir?" he asked timidly.

"Why don't you show him yours this time," Lyons said to Blancanales.

The Able Team warrior smiled, reached inside his jacket, pulled out a long pistol that looked like a pellet gun and squeezed the trigger.

The tranquilizer dart hit the Pinkerton man in the neck. Lyons stepped up, catching the guard in his arms as the man fell forward, while Schwarz grabbed the door before it could swing shut again.

The Able Team leader dragged the guard into the deserted lobby. His eyes swept the room, then he nodded to a love seat against one of the walls. Gadgets and Pol pulled it out and pushed the sleeping guard between it and the wall. Then they crossed the lobby to the elevators. Lyons pushed the button to summon the car.

"What if he wakes up before we're through?" Schwarz whispered.

"He won't." Blancanales smiled. "There's enough Pentothal in him right now to give the old boy the best night's rest he's had in years."

The doors opened and Able Team stepped inside. As the elevator ascended the shaft toward the nineteenth floor, Lyons, Schwarz and Blancanales swung their MAC-10 machine pistols forward on the shoulder slings beneath their sport coats. Each man rechecked the magazine, then worked the bolt, chambering a round.

The elevator stopped, the door swung back, and they stepped into the hall. A pale blue runner carpet, the same shade as the Pinkerton guard's uniform, ran right and left. The highly waxed slats of a dark wood floor could be seen on both sides. Lyons led the way past potted plants and settee tables hosting elaborately shaded lamps. They came to apartment 1908 and stopped.

Schwarz pulled a set of picks from his pocket and knelt next to the door. Twenty seconds later the tumblers fell into sync, and the electronics ace inched the door quietly open.

As the door swung back, it revealed a living room decorated by someone with more money than taste. A zebra-striped divan stood in the middle of the room, facing a large forty-two-inch TV screen. Other jungle animals were represented in the furniture—a tiger skin armchair and another couch sporting the spots of a leopard, to name only two. Paintings of nude women were on several walls, and the smell of stale alcohol and marijuana smoke filled the air.

A voice from the rear of the apartment called out. "Jive Bug? That you, baby?"

Lyons walked swiftly across the living room toward the sound, the rest of the team at his heels. He stopped in front of a closed door, took a step back and kicked.

The door crackled like twisted cellophane as it flew back.

The ex-cop walked into the bedroom, his machine pistol pointing the way. Low, hushed rap music filled his ears as he groped for the light switch, then bathed the dark room in light.

The bedroom was as vulgar as the living room. Bras, panties and dresses were scattered across the floor. Mirrors covered the ceiling, and a circular bed stood near the far wall. A black face sporting a long wispy goatee lay half-hidden beneath the red satin sheets. The eyes in the face were glazed, dreamy and bloodshot. A crack pipe lay on the small table next to the bed.

Two moving lumps were visible under the covers. Then the bedclothes fell back to reveal the faces of two women, one white, the other black. They stared at Able Team with the same drugged-out gaze as Hambone.

"Get up, get dressed and get out," Lyons ordered.

All three started to move, and the Able Team leader raised the MAC-10 over his head. A 3-round burst of automatic rounds blasted into the ceiling, and chunks of shining mirror rained down like ice.

The women screamed. Hambone froze, his bare legs over the side of the bed.

"Not *you,* Hambone," Lyons said. "You just stay put."

The women darted from the bed, grabbed their clothes and wiggled into them.

"See that they get out all right, Gadgets."

Schwarz led the women from the room.

Hambone settled back on the bed and crossed his arms. "Okay," he said, his eyes now in focus. "What you motherfuckers want? Money?"

"Ever notice how many people ask us that right off the bat?" Blancanales said.

Lyons nodded. "Yeah. Okay, sure. That's a good start. Give us your money. The money you got from the crack that's killed who-knows-how-many kids."

A grin spread across Hambone's face. "I'll have to get up."

"Then get up. Slow."

The black man threw the covers back and stood, facing them as Schwarz reentered the room. The electronics man took a quick look, chuckled, then said, "Well, there goes that myth."

Hambone scowled and knelt next to the bed. He started to reach under it, and Lyons fired another burst into the ceiling.

The man's hands jerked back to his sides.

"Be *real* careful what you pull out from under there," Lyons warned.

The Sepulcher leader moved slowly this time, sliding a gray steel fire box from under the bed. He twirled the dial of the combination lock on the top, and as he did, the men of Able Team moved closer, training their weapons on him.

A speck of brown and blue caught Lyons eye as he stopped. Just beyond Hambone he saw a tan leather holster screwed into the bed frame. The grips of a dark automatic pistol extended from the top.

Lyons glanced to both his sides. Schwarz barely nodded. The expression in Blancanales's eyes told the ex-cop he'd seen the gun, too.

Hambone opened the lid of the fire box, then scooted back, still on his knees.

"There," the black man said indicating the wrapped packets of hundred-dollar bills inside. "Take it. There's a quarter million in there. I don't need it. There's plenty more where that came from."

"You think so?" Lyons asked. "Would it surprise you to know that your playmate David Moler's dead? So your pipeline for mercs to South Africa has been shut down."

Hambone shrugged. "There's always the crack."

"No, not always."

Hambone's eyes narrowed on Lyons, and for the first time since Able Team had entered the room, it appeared that the merc-running crack dealer realized it wasn't just a matter of paying the men off. Then the dark eyes relaxed, and the mustache above the goatee curled in a friendly smile.

The dealer twisted slightly, shielding the pistol attached to the bed from Lyons's view. He scooted backward slightly and placed a hand on the edge of the bed as if he were about to pull himself back to his feet. "Okay if I stand up now?" he asked.

"Sure," Lyons said.

Hambone turned his back to them and pulled himself up. When he turned back around, he held a blue steel Llama Large Frame .45.

The full-auto burst from Lyons's MAC-10 put an end to Jefferson's sideline of recruiting mercs, and to a large portion of the crack trade in East L.A.

YAKOV KATZENELENBOGEN peered through the thick foliage at the Boer Resistance Movement camp, studying the sprawling ranch house beyond the parade ground. Most of the lights were out, but a lone glow shone from one curtained window at the far south end of the dwelling.

A bedroom? Living room? Den?

Were Yancy, Lanzerac and whatever guards they had stationed inside, still awake at nearly 4:40 a.m.? Or had the light been left on either by mistake or as a precaution?

The Phoenix Force leader's headset crackled, and Barbara Price began her last-minute synchronization between the teams. Katz whispered into the face mike, then turned his eyes toward the barracks to his right as Striker and Able Team answered.

The BRM sentry rounded the corner of the building and started toward the house. The lone man seemed to be in charge of the entire installation. Ever since Phoenix Force had set up around the perimeter an hour earlier, he had paced continuously between the house and barracks, circled both buildings, then repeated the process in a never-changing routine.

But it was that very routine that had enabled Calvin James to sneak onto the premises for a quick recon and radio back that most of the men inside the barracks were still awake. James said they were playing poker. The Phoenix Force warrior had been unable to spot anything inside the house.

Katz heard Bolan tell them to move in, then the Israeli began his own last-minute radio checks.

"Phoenix One to Two," he whispered into the darkness. "How many men in the barracks?"

"Approximately thirty," James whispered back.

"Affirmative," Katz said. "Everyone copy that?"

The rest of Phoenix Force radioed confirmation.

"Then you heard the man," Katz said. "Move in."

The Israeli rose from his kneeling position and stepped from the trees, crouching as he sprinted across the parade ground toward the open front entrance to the barracks. Under the faint light of the quarter moon, he saw four other shadows emerge from around the clearing and circle the building.

As he neared the open door, Katz caught a quick glimpse of a dozen men seated around two tables in the center of the room. The ends of bunks extended into his line of vision from both sides of the one-room structure. Some of the beds held sleeping Boers.

Assault rifles and submachine guns of every make, model and size were disseminated about the room.

Katz leaped soundlessly onto the porch and pressed his back against the wall to one side of the door. He made a final check of the mini-Uzi in his fist, then glanced around the corner.

The poker games were still going on. Nothing had changed.

The Phoenix Force leader let his weapon fall to the end of its sling and jerked a fragmentation grenade from the clip on his battle harness. He hooked the pin over the thumb of his prosthetic hand, pulled, then tossed the frag through the doorway. It rolled under the nearest table.

One man managed to yell "Oh shit!" before it exploded.

Katz was through the door before the concussion had died down. Playing cards floated through the air, and he saw bodies and pieces of bodies scattered over the tables, bunks and floor.

But more men had survived the blast than died from it. And now they dived for their weapons.

Katz saw James enter the back door and cut a swath through the barracks with his M-16. The Israeli fell to his knees, firing a burst into a Boer spattered with a comrade's blood. The enemy clutched his chest, his FAL assault rifle clattering to the floor.

Fusillades erupted from all sides of the building now as McCarter, Manning and Encizo opened up through the windows. Katz swung his weapon toward a man stretched out on one of the top bunks. The Boer twisted away, lunging for a Lyttleton R-4 assault rifle on the wall above his head. The Israeli cut loose with a steady stream of parabellums that stitched up the man's spine.

A volley of rounds splintered the doorframe next to Katz's head, and he jerked back. A tall hardman with a beard adjusted his aim.

Before the Phoenix Force leader could respond, Manning swung around his M-16 and dropped the gunner.

Katz dived behind the nearest bunk and transferred the Uzi to his prosthetic limb. He dumped the magazine and rammed home a full one. He worked the slide as he rose to his feet, but when he looked around the room again, there were no more targets.

The Israeli walked forward, stepping over the corpses that littered the room. James met him halfway. "Let's go," Katz said. "The house is bound to have figured out this wasn't exactly an impromptu training exercise."

Katz led James out the door double-time. Manning, McCarter and Encizo were already halfway to the house. The Israeli motioned them to circle the structure as he and James headed for the front door.

The door opened as Katz's boot hit the porch. A man wielding an FAL stepped out and raised the weapon.

The Phoenix Force leader pulled the Uzi's trigger, sending a 3-round burst into the hardman's gut. Katz then shouldered him aside and burst through the door. Two more men, obviously hastily awakened, attempted to bring another pair of Belgian rifles into play. Katz held the trigger back against the guard, running another magazine dry as he cut a figure eight back and forth between the gunners.

Hurdling the bodies, Katz directed James down the hall toward the light that had glowed behind the curtains. They passed several empty rooms, then came to a closed door. The Israeli stepped to one side of the door and motioned James toward the other wall. He twisted the knob.

A blast of fire penetrated the door and roared into the hallway.

Katz trained his mini-Uzi at the knob and fired six rounds. The brass flew off the frame, and the door inched open. A roundhouse kick from Calvin James sent it crashing into an inside wall, and Katz leaped from cover to fire blindly into the room.

Return fire forced him back to the wall, but he had caught a glimpse of the two men in the room. Although the Israeli had never met either David Yancy or Barry Lanzerac, he had seen the safari jacket and straw cowboy hat just before the two men ducked behind the thick legs of an oak billiard table.

Katz leaned around the corner again, emptying the rest of his magazine into the room. He fell back again to reload, and James took his place, sending a volley into the heavy pool table.

"It's no good," the black Phoenix Force warrior said, falling back to reload himself. "The table's too thick. It's stopping the rounds."

Katz nodded. He lowered his face just above the floor, peering into the room. Just beyond one of the table legs, he saw what looked like a snake. He thumbed the mini-Uzi to semiauto and eased it around the corner. Lowering his eyes to the sights, he squeezed the trigger.

The 95-grain jacketed soft-point shot from the barrel at 1355 feet per second. It couldn't have slowed much by the time it streaked through David Yancy's snakeskin cowboy boots and sliced off three of his toes.

Yancy screamed and rolled to the side of the billiard table leg, both hands groping his foot.

James leaned into the doorway and finished off Brouer's head mercenary with a full-auto blast from his M-16.

Then the room exploded with the sound of shattering glass. Katz looked up to see a shiny metal trash can hit the top of the billiard table and roll across the felt, scattering the balls as it went. The can rolled off the edge closest to the door, then fell to the floor with a clank.

Above the table, the barrels of three M-16s poked through the splintered glass. Fire shot from their muzzles, and a second later a bloody safari jacket thumped to the floor on the other side of the billiard table.

Katz and James rose to their feet and walked into the billiard room as Enciso, Manning and McCarter stuck their heads inside the window.

"What was it you told Striker back at the Hotel President, Katz?" McCarter asked. "Just happened to be in the neighborhood and thought we'd drop in?"

BILL HUMPHREY FELT the cold wind bite his neck and press the goggles tight against his face. He wrapped the white silk Army Air Corps scarf tighter, then glanced at his controls—thirty thousand feet. Well, he could have told the crew at Stony Man Farm that without the altimeter. Fifty years of flying had left him with what he called his "eardrum" altimeter—he could damn near tell by the pops in his ears just how high they were.

Ahead, on the other end of the towline, Humphrey could see the lights of the B-52 bomber that Jack Grimaldi was flying. Grimaldi—now there was a pilot. They'd gone up together so the Stony Man flyer could judge whether the old man still had what it took. Brognola had nearly convinced Grimaldi that he did, but the kid wanted to see for himself. Well, he'd chased Grimaldi all over the Eastern Seaboard before Jack finally lost him.

Yep, Jack Grimaldi could fly, all right.

As the bomber continued to tow the glider through the night, Humphrey dropped a hand out of the insulated cockpit and ran it across the smoothly polished plywood of the streamlined craft. He didn't know where Hal Brognola had come up with this thing—just that they'd picked it up with the B-52 at an isolated runway outside of Stuttgart—but the bird was a piece of work. Old. He wouldn't be surprised if it had been one of the gliders the German pilots trained on before the war, back when they'd been restricted to nonmotorized flight by the Treaty of Versailles.

Grimaldi's voice came over the radio. "You still awake back there, Hump?"

Humphrey jerked the oxygen mask from his face and grabbed the mike. "I'll still be working long after you kids have had enough," he said. He stuck the mask back to his face and took a breath as Grimaldi chuckled.

"I'm showing thirty thousand feet," Stony Man Farm's chief pilot said. "You ready?"

"Let's cut her lose, Ace. I'll show you that the old saying's right—age and treachery will always win out over youth and vigor."

A moment later the towline fell away. Humphrey watched the bomber shoot on ahead as the glider slowed. He knew Grimaldi's work for the night wasn't over yet. In fact, it was just beginning.

Now the wind bit even harder into his face and neck as the sailplane glided silently under the stars. Humphrey looked down and saw the lights of what had to be Dusseldorf. He felt the grin return to his face as goose bumps broke out on his shoulders under the weathered, fifty-year-old, brown leather pilot's jacket he'd brought out of retirement for the occasion.

The man in the bright orange jumpsuit had flown bombers and fighters in Korea and added choppers in Nam. But motorized craft had never brought on the thrill, the exhilaration, the freedom that he'd felt carrying troops, field pieces, and even light tanks across the English Channel during World War II.

No, Bill Humphrey suddenly realized, he hadn't had this much fun in the past fifty years.

The sailplane glided over Dusseldorf and crossed into the Netherlands. Humphrey checked the altimeter, seeing that they had dropped a few hundred feet since cutting loose from Grimaldi. But that had to be expected in a sailplane. The ratio of forward glide to drop was thirty-five to one, and the German woody was performing admirably.

The World War II vet played the slope currents off a series of hills just north of Rotterdam, returning the glider to thirty thousand feet. Then Barbara Price came on the radio. "Base to Phoenix One."

As Price talked to Katz, Humphrey felt a big hand on his shoulder. "How long, Hump?" Bolan said behind him.

Humphrey saw the lights of Amsterdam appear ahead. He glanced at the control panel in front of him, then half turned in the cockpit, pulling the oxygen mask from his face again and talking out of the side of his mouth. "Two minutes," he shouted into the wind.

Price spoke briefly to Carl Lyons, ascertaining that Able Team was in position, then told Bolan he had the honor of putting things in motion.

The old pilot could hear Bolan maneuvering out of his seat. They hit the edge of the city, passed over an industrial area, and the rising thermals caused the glider to climb. Humphrey hit the spoilers on the wings and dropped the sailplane down through the sky again. Striker wanted a quick jump? He'd have one.

Ahead and below, black under the quarter moon, Bill Humphrey saw the famous canals of Amsterdam. Then the Ijsselmeer Building, all ninety-nine stories of it, stuck up like a sore thumb around the shorter buildings along the water. He glanced at the controls and began counting. "ten, nine, eight . . ."

Behind him Striker said, "Move in" over the radio. Humphrey felt the big hand on his shoulder again. "This one's for you, Hump."

Then Bolan dived from the plane.

THE COLD AIR gradually warmed as the Executioner fell through the sky. He ripped the oxygen mask from his face, jerked the rip cord, and the black chute and lines flowered up, disappearing into the dark.

The Executioner watched the lights below in Amsterdam, Europe's answer to New York—the city that never slept. As he drifted down, he checked his equipment.

His sound-suppressed Beretta 93-R 9 mm pistol hung under his arm in shoulder leather. The .44 Magnum Desert Eagle rode on his right hip, the big .50 on his left.

Slung over his shoulder and gripped in both hands was a Heckler & Koch MP-5 SD. A variation of the famous MP-5, it boasted an integral silencer. The system worked on two gas-bleeding chambers that made the SD the most quiet "off the shelf" weapon currently on the market. And after Cowboy John Kissinger's modifications, the H&K had been further suppressed to the decibels put out by a BB rifle.

The black Harris assault vest that hung from Bolan's shoulders carried eight extra 30-round magazines for the SD in the four slanted front pockets. Two smaller side pockets bore extra mags for the Beretta. Utility pouches scattered around the Cordura nylon held a variety of other equipment.

The warrior worked the slide of the subgun as he neared the roof. Below he could see at least six of Brouer's mercs in Ijsselmeer security uniforms. They watched the ground, having evidently been warned that an attack might be coming. Four spotlights were trained at the ground, covering all sides of the building.

"Just keep watching," Bolan whispered. "You'll never know what hit you." He raised the MP-5 and pressed the retractable stock to his shoulder.

A sudden squawk broke the silence. Bolan gazed overhead at a confused sea gull who'd flown in off the river and lost his way. The Executioner looked back to the roof in time to catch the glare of one of the spotlights full in the face.

One of the men on the roof shouted orders.

Bolan was still a hundred feet in the air as he squinted, looked to one side of the light and pulled the trigger. The H&K coughed quietly, and the light below shattered. But another spot took its place, and then the roar of automatic-rifle fire rose to meet him.

The Executioner squeezed the trigger again, this time sending a 3-round burst into the light. Glass shattered and the bulb blew as he released the snaps on his chute and fell the last twenty feet to the roof.

The black chute flew off into the night as the warrior's boots hit the asphalt. Firing from the hip, he cut a swath between two of the guards like a sickle harvesting wheat, then turned his weapon toward another of the spotlights as it swung his way. A steady burst of eight rounds broke the light and took out the guard manning it.

A hardman with a flashlight in one hand and an Uzi in the other shone his beam the Executioner's way. Bolan fired to the side of the light, catching the hired merc square in the chest with four hushed 9 mm slugs and punching him to the roof.

The Executioner pivoted to one side, holding the trigger back and spraying a guard wearing sergeant's stripes with the remainder of the 30-round clip. With no time to reload, he dropped the H&K to the end of the sling and drew the Beretta.

The 93-R was as quiet as the MP-5 as it spit controlled 3-round bursts into two guards who had fallen to their bellies on the roof. The pistols in their hands slapped the asphalt, the final sound before silence fell over the rooftop again.

The Executioner didn't deceive himself. While the H&K and Beretta were quiet, anyone on the penthouse floor below would have heard the gunfire from the guards' weapons. They'd be readying themselves for combat right now.

Shoving the Beretta back into his shoulder rig, Bolan slammed a full mag into the MP-5 as he raced across the roof to the steel door. He twisted the knob. It held firm.

With no time to search the guards for a key, the Executioner unsnapped a vest pocket and pulled out a small box. He removed a lump of C-4 plastique, added a blasting cap as he applied it to the door, then raced to the edge of the roof.

Turning again, the Executioner lined up the front and rear sights. A single semiauto round did the trick, detonating the bomb.

The door stood halfway open when the warrior sprinted through and found himself on a landing. The concrete steps led down to a glass door that opened into the penthouse. He started to descend, but as he did, an Ijsselmeer plainclothes security man burst from the doorway.

The hardman fired at Bolan with a subgun, the .45-caliber bullets striking the step in front of the Executioner and ricocheting back. Chips of concrete flew into the air, one striking the enemy gunner in the eye, making him scream.

A split second later Bolan ended the man's agony with a steady stream of 9 mm shredders.

The Executioner bounded down the stairs, pushed the corpse aside, and burst through the opening, coming face-to-face with four more Ijsselmeer hardmen.

The first gunner, in his early twenties, hadn't figured out what was happening yet, and he died before he did.

The second merc-guard was older and more experienced, but not experienced enough. His side arm was only halfway out of his holster when the Executioner's 3-round burst took off the top of his head.

The last two men were seasoned veterans. Their rounds blew past the Executioner before he could turn their way. Bolan caught a quick glimpse of a woman behind the desk as he dived to the floor and rolled. His back struck something hard, and he glanced up to see a pair of nylon-clad calves in red high-heeled shoes.

Twisting back, the Executioner fired from under the desk. The second-to-last guard had a bulbous nose, swollen, red and road-mapped with the veins of alcoholism. Bolan used it as his target. A lone round slapped into it, and the man's hopes for another drink vanished with his life.

The last man scrabbled behind a couch as the Executioner fired. The 3-round burst flew high over his head as the H&K ran dry again. Bolan jerked the Desert Eagle .50 from his hip and aimed at the man's cover, drilling three of the mammoth Magnums through the cloth and wood.

The scream testified that the guard had learned the difference between "cover" and "concealment" the hard way.

The Executioner rolled from under the desk, stood and turned to see a pretty young blond woman frozen in horror.

"Relax," Bolan told her. "I didn't come here for you."

In three long strides the warrior crossed the room to the door of Brouer's office and burst through.

The CEO sat behind his desk as frozen in fear as his secretary. He opened his mouth to speak, but nothing came out.

"Don't bother with the questions," Bolan said, the big .50-caliber Magnum trained on a spot halfway between Brouer's nose and hairline. "I know what they are. You want to know who I am, and what I want."

Brouer nodded curtly.

"I'll answer the second question first. I want an end to what's going on in South Africa. Not just the assassinations and genocide of the tribespeople, but an equal deal for everybody in the country, regardless of race."

Slowly the fear on Brouer's face turned to contempt. "You'd have pigs fly, as well, I suppose. The kaffirs are animals. They'll never vote or hold office."

Bolan stared at the CEO. Some men were beyond redemption. He'd met more than his share of bigots during the many years of his one-man war and some had been just as bad as Brouer.

But none had been worse.

Brouer's contempt became hatred. He stood up behind his desk. "So you want what you cannot have," he said. "So you must make a second choice, and I have a suggestion. I'll give you one million dollars right now. All you have to do is leave. No questions asked." He bent over and opened his desk drawer.

Bolan cocked the Desert Eagle.

"Don't worry," Brouer said, his hand moving slowly inside the desk and coming out with a checkbook. He opened it and pulled a pen from a holder on top of his desk. "You still haven't told me who you are," he said, his voice now steady, confident that enough money would solve anything. "To whom should I make it out?"

"How about the wife of President De Arnhem?" Bolan suggested. "Or the wives of the Zulus and Xhosa who died so you could go on living like this?" The Desert Eagle swept the office, pointing to the expensive furnishings. "Why don't you make it out to a black man named Chaka? His wife was killed by Lanzerac's men."

As slowly as the confidence had come, it began to fade. Panic started to spread over Brouer's face as he realized he had met a man who couldn't be bought. "Two million?" he said desperately. "Three?"

"Put your checkbook away. And I don't take American Express."

The color had faded from the CEO's face as he slipped the checkbook back into the drawer. His hand lingered a moment too long, and the Executioner could see the indecision in the man's eyes.

Bolan tightened his grip in the Desert Eagle, the barrel aimed at the CEO's chest. He knew what the man was trying to decide, and he knew what that decision would be.

The color suddenly returned to Brouer's face. With a blood-curdling scream he jerked his hand from the drawer, and Bolan saw the tiny nickel-plated Beretta Jetfire.

The warrior pulled the trigger once. The big .50-Magnum round exploded from the pistol, drilling through Brouer's chest and slamming him against the wall.

Bolan rounded the desk, stepped over the man and ripped the phony electrical outlet off the wall. He swung out the plastic safe, dropped it into a pocket in his blacksuit and turned around.

Brouer lay on his back on the floor. He was still breathing, his chest heaving as he struggled to hold on to his miserable life. Blood poured from the quarter-size wound in his front and the fist-size crater in his back. He whispered something.

The Executioner stopped next to him.

"You . . . told me what you wanted," the Ijsselmeer CEO sputtered, a frothy red foam flying from his lips. "But . . . I never found out . . . who you . . . are."

"You never will," the Executioner said, as the life faded from Brouer's eyes.

Above, Bolan heard the *whup-whup* of helicopter blades as Jack Grimaldi landed the chopper on the roof. Holstering the Desert Eagle, he strode out of the office and up the steps.

EPILOGUE

The den in the main house was the least used area of Stony Man Farm. Mack Bolan sometimes wondered why they'd even bothered to include it when the blueprints had been drawn up.

Today was an exception, though, and as Hal Brognola switched on the television at the front of the room, the Executioner glanced at the battle-hardened faces of the Stony Man warriors reflected off the screen.

The screen warmed up, and a woman wearing a light raincoat and matching hat held a microphone to her lips. A light drizzle fell on her shoulders. In the background Bolan could see a small building with a sign that read Voting Place. Men and women—all white—passed back and forth behind the news reporter. Farther in the distance the Executioner saw a sea of black faces behind wooden barricades. Signs he couldn't read extended from the crowd.

"This is Gale Denslow, reporting from Pretoria," the woman in the raincoat said into her mike. "South African police and military personnel have patrolled the voting precincts all day. So far, no incidents have been reported..."

"That's because no one's getting paid anymore," Gadgets Schwarz said.

"But officials are keeping their fingers crossed." Denslow paused as a man walked by behind her. The man wore a floppy, wide-brimmed hat, and long-sleeved work shirt under his vest. Obviously he was a Boer, and the reporter grabbed him by the arm. "Could I ask your name, sir?"

The man looked self-consciously into the camera, then finally said, "Vanwyngaarden."

"Mr. Vanwyngaarden, do you believe the referendum will be overturned?"

The man stared into the camera, more confident this time. He grasped the lapels of his vest and said, "No ma'am. I had my reservations last week, with all the trouble and all. But we see now who was behind it all. Not the kaffirs—"

"*Kaffirs,*" Gary Manning said, shaking his head. "I guess change takes time."

"Sticks and stones," Calvin James interjected. "At his point I don't care what he calls me. I care what's in his heart."

Everyone in the room nodded agreement.

The Boer on-screen paused and coughed. "What I meant to say was that it wasn't the blacks of this nation responsible for all the killing. It was a group of bloody bigots who don't have anyone's best interests in mind but their own."

Denslow nodded. "Thank you, Mr. Vanwyngaarden," she said and turned back to the camera as he walked away. She started to speak, then suddenly bowed her head, frowning. Her free hand shot to the tiny earplug in her ear. "This just in," she said, looking back up at the camera. "It appears something is happening at the presidential palace. We go now to Mike Shepherd."

The scene switched to the front of the presidential palace, where a dignified man in a raincoat similar to Denslow's stood in front of the iron gate surrounding the grounds. "Thank you, Gale," he said. "We have just received a report—you won't believe this—we have a report that President Van Peebles and several dozen government officials and military personnel have been arrested. Nothing has been confirmed yet, and we'll return as soon as we learn more. But let me repeat. We have an unconfirmed report that President Norman Van Peebles was arrested earlier this afternoon and might be charged with treason. Back to you, Gale."

The screen switched back to the men and women trailing in and out of the voting site behind Gale Denslow.

"So what's next for Van Peebles?" Encizo asked. "Impeachment proceedings?"

Brognola nodded.

"Yeah, well, what the hell happens if they don't find him guilty?" Lyons demanded. "I've seen stranger things than that happen in a court of law."

Bolan stood and stretched his arms over his head. "He's guilty, and we know it. Van Peebles will be leaving office, one way or another." The Executioner crossed the room and held a coffee cup under the spout on the dispenser.

Then the news camera zeroed in on a familiar face outside the voting site. Gale Denslow stood next to a small black man in flowing Zulu robes. Brognola turned up the volume.

"Well, Mr. Dingaan," the woman said, "you've had quite a week. But from all indications, you stand to come out the winner. No one expects the referendum to be overturned in light of what the public has learned concerning the connection between Ijsselmeer, Inc., and the Boer Resistance Movement. Is there anything you'd like to say?"

Lindall Dingaan smiled into the camera, and Bolan could feel the black leader's charisma reach out to him.

Dingaan had spent three days recovering at Stony Man Farm, then been flown back to his homeland in time for the election. He didn't look as though he was quite ready to pose for the cover of *Muscle & Fitness*, but he looked ten times better than he had on the trip over.

"Yes," Dingaan said. "I would like to thank everyone in this country who has voted to install equality, and I appeal to all those who did not to please rethink your position. We must all live together in harmony in South Africa, black *and* white."

It was a simple statement, yet the future of a country hung in the balance. Many had died so that equality could take a step forward. And the warrior could only hope that more blood wouldn't be spilled before all men and women could live in peaceful coexistence.

The hunters become the hunted as Omega Force clashes
with a former Iraqi military officer in the next episode of

by PATRICK F. ROGERS

In Book 3: TARGET ZONE, Omega Force blazes a trail deep
into the heart of Sudan. Trapped and surrounded by hostile forces, they must break out at any cost to launch a
search-locate-annihilate mission.

With capabilities unmatched by any other paramilitary
organization in the world, Omega Force is a special ready-
reaction antiterrorist strike force composed of the best
commandos and equipment the military has to offer.

Available in October at you favorite retail outlet. To order you copy now of Book 3: **TARGET
ZONE**, Book 2: **ZERO HOUR** or Book 1: **WAR MACHINE**, please send your name, address,
zip or postal code, along with a check or money order (please do not send cash) for $3.50
for each book ordered, plus 75¢ postage and handling ($1.00 in Canada), payable to Gold
Eagle Books, to:

In the U.S.	In Canada
Gold Eagle Books	Gold Eagle Books
3010 Walden Avenue	P.O. Box 609
P.O. Box 1325	Fort Erie, Ontario
Buffalo, NY 14269-1325	L2A 5X3

Please specify book title(s) with your order.
Canadian residents add applicable federal and provincial taxes.

OM3

Inner-city hell just found a new savior—

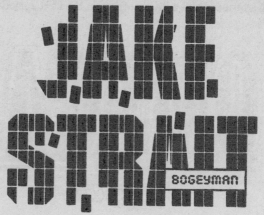

JAKE STRAIT

BOGEYMAN

by FRANK RICH

Jake Strait is hired to infiltrate a religious sect in Book 3: **DAY OF JUDGMENT.** Hired to turn the sect's team of bumbling soldiers into a hit squad, he plans to lead the attack against the city's criminal subculture.

Jake Strait is a licensed enforcer in a future world gone mad—a world where suburbs are guarded and farmlands are garrisoned around a city of evil.

The Peacekeepers are dispatched
to shut down the fighting
with brute force in . . .

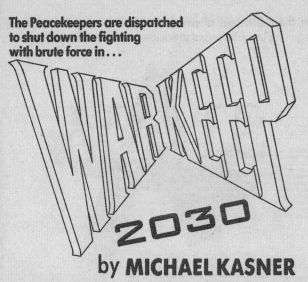

WARKEEP

2030

by MICHAEL KASNER

In Book 3: **FINGER OF GOD**, the Peacekeepers are up
against a ruthless and bloodthirsty enemy, with the specter
of nuclear holocaust looming on the horizon.

Armed with all the tactical advantages of modern technol-
ogy, battle hard and ready when the free world is threatened—the Peacekeepers are the baddest grunts on the
planet.

In the battlefield of covert warfare America's toughest
agents play with lethal precision in the third installment of

SLAM

by DAN MATTHEWS

In Book 3: **SHADOW WARRIORS**, hostile Middle East leaders
are using the drug pipeline to raise cash for a devastating nuclear arsenal and the SLAM commando unit is ordered to dis-
mantle the pipeline, piece by piece.

In the aftermath of a
brutal apocalypse,
a perilous quest for survival.

EARTH BLOOD

by **JAMES AXLER**

The popular author of DEATHLANDS® brings you an action-packed new postapocalyptic survival series. Earth is laid to waste by a devastating blight that destroys the world's food supply. Returning from a deep-space mission, the crew of the Aquila crash-land in the Nevada desert to find that the world they knew no longer exists. Now they must set out on an odyssey to find surviving family members and the key to future survival.

In this ravaged new world, no one knows who is friend or foe . . . and their quest will test the limits of endurance and the will to live.

Available in November at your favorite retail outlet.

GOLD
EAGLE ®

EB1

Don't miss out on the action in these titles featuring
THE EXECUTIONER, ABLE TEAM and PHOENIX FORCE!

The Freedom Trilogy

The Executioner #61174	BATTLE PLAN	$3.50	☐
The Executioner #61175	BATTLE GROUND	$3.50	☐
SuperBolan #61432	BATTLE FORCE	$4.99	☐

The Executioner®

#61176	RANSOM RUN	$3.50	☐
#61177	EVIL CODE	$3.50	☐

SuperBolan

#61430	DEADFALL	$4.99	☐
#61431	ONSLAUGHT	$4.99	☐

Stony Man™

#61889	STONY MAN V	$4.99	☐
#61890	STONY MAN VI	$4.99	☐
#61891	STONY MAN VII	$4.99	☐

TOTAL AMOUNT	$
POSTAGE & HANDLING	$
($1.00 for one book, 50¢ for each additional)	
APPLICABLE TAXES*	$ _____
TOTAL PAYABLE	$ _____
(check or money order—please do not send cash)	